SHADOWED WATERS

Coral Leend

MENTOR

This Edition first published 2000 by

Mentor Books
43 Furze Road
Sandyford Industrial Estate, Dublin 18
Ireland
Tel. (00353 1) 295 2112/3   Fax. (00353 1) 295 2114
e-mail: admin@mentorbooks.ie
www.mentorbooks.ie

ISBN: 1-84210-012-2

A catalogue record for this book is available from
the British Library

Editing and Layout by Mentor Books
Cover Design: Slatter-Anderson
Printed in Ireland by ColourBooks Ltd.

1 3 5 7 9 10 8 6 4 2

SHADOWED WATERS

ABOUT THE AUTHOR

Coral Leend has written many short stories and articles for women's magazines and publications for the last twenty years. She recently won an award in a Romantic Novel Competition for the first part of her novel, *Shadowed Waters*, held by *Women's Weekly*. She also won a bursary awarded by Iris Gower, the best-selling Welsh novelist.

Coral lives in a house overlooking the sea in picturesque Gower, South Wales. She is happily married with three daughters and six grandchildren.

*I dedicate this book to
my husband, Austin.*

*His love and faith in me
have never wavered.*

And coming events cast their shadows before.

Thomas Campbell
1777-1844

Contents

One

Miranda crouched low over Star's neck, urging him on recklessly, galloping as though chased by a thousand demons. The bitter tears washing her cheeks were dried by the wind, and her hair, torn from its ribbons, streamed behind her as she raced to escape the scene seared into her mind: the picture of her father so still and pale, so remote in his coffin.

The funeral would take place tomorrow; but with four days already passed, she still found it impossible to accept his death. But nothing she did could alter the reality that she would never see him smile at her again, never feel his loving arms around her, hugging her closely against his chest. At last, horse and rider completely exhausted, Miranda allowed the sweating animal to slow to a halt and slid from the saddle.

Flinging herself to the ground, she buried her head in her arms, surrendering to her grief.

'Papa,' she sobbed aloud. 'I love you. I want you. Why did you leave me on my own?'

Since she had been a tiny girl, as long as she could remember, Papa had taken her riding. In the beginning she'd sat in front of him on his own horse, his strong arms wrapped tightly around her as she leaned back against him, secure in his arms, secure in his love. 'Go on Papa! Jump over the hedge,' she remembered screaming, exhilarated, as they had cantered across the heath.

She had been but four years old when he began teaching her to ride – even younger the first time he placed her in a saddle, leading the docile pony around the yard himself, her face beaming as she basked in his approval. Papa was always so proud of her competence as a rider that sometimes he boasted a little to his friends. She loved him so much, even to imagine a life forever empty of that love caused a true, physical ache.

When Mama had died, four years ago, they had both been devastated, and turning to one another for comfort, had grown even closer. Papa, in turn, began relying on her for companionship, discussing problems of the estate with her, as he had previously done with Mama. When she was fourteen years old, she began acting as his hostess at the many dinner parties, always aware of his approving eyes on her.

'And now he's gone,' she wailed. 'And his love.'

At last, worn out, she drew a shuddering breath, struggling to compose herself as she remounted, then made her way home.

Turning into the curving drive leading to the house, she was dismayed to see a horse and carriage drawn up in front of the wide, sweeping steps. She groaned as, defying convention, she was riding astride, attired in a youth's shirt and tight, white breeches, tucked into short half-boots, covered by a skirted coat: her favourite riding clothes.

Hastily she cantered around to the rear courtyard, hauled on the reins, pulling Star to a halt. As she flung the reins over Star's head, a groom scuttled over to take the blowing gelding's halter. Jumping down, Miranda patted Star's heaving side.

'Give him a good rub down before his feed, Judd. He deserves it.'

'Yes'm. There's company, Miss Miranda,' he replied.

'Yes,' she said shortly, not inviting conversation.

Miranda was in a far from amiable mood. Wanting only to be left in peace and solitude, she would have liked nothing better than to sneak up the back stairs away from any well-intentioned visitors. She knew this was not possible.

She walked out of the pale, wintry sunlight and through the house into the dark panelled hall, its deep shadows broken by a kaleidoscope of jewelled colours, where the sun pierced the leaded lights of the long landing window. Her elderly manservant approached, his glance, taking in her untidy appearance, speaking volumes.

'Miss Miranda, you have a visitor. Mr William Langdon.' Thomas hesitated. 'You'll wish to change, Miss Miranda?'

She gestured impatiently. 'Why should I? It's only Mr Langdon.'

'He is here as your lawyer, Miss Miranda.'

She heard the reproach in his voice. 'He told you so?' Her words were clipped and apprehensive.

'Yes, Miss Miranda.'

She nodded. She would need to take a skimped toilet and make herself presentable before facing her visitor. She was forestalled when the drawing-room door opened and William Langdon came into the hall.

'Ahh! There you are, Mirry. I thought I heard your voice.' He took her cold hand in his. If he noted her dishevelled state, he hid it successfully. 'May I offer my condolences, Miranda. I know how much your father meant to you.' His usually twinkling eyes were serious and he squeezed her hand involuntarily.

'Thank you,' she whispered, catching her bottom lip in her teeth. Tears burned her eyes as she looked up at her father's oldest friend. 'You wish to see him?'

He nodded solemnly and she led him towards the library. The curtains were drawn and in the gloom the heavy oak coffin, ornately carved, stood on silver legs, the light from the flickering candles on top of it reflecting off the metal. A heavy, sweet smell pervaded the air, as William Langdon walked over and bowed his head over the coffin.

Miranda gave a muffled sob, and turning, William Langdon put his arms around her, gathering her to him in a great bear hug. 'Let it out, Mirry, don't hold back.' Miranda felt the words resound in his barrel chest as he held her tightly, rocking her gently from side to side. Her tears streamed down unchecked, wetting his brocaded waistcoat, as she buried her face against him.

When she eventually controlled herself he released her, giving her an enormous linen handkerchief smelling faintly of spice and tobacco. This brought further tears to her eyes, recalling the times her father had so often done the same when she was a little girl.

'I'm sorry I . . .'

'Enough said,' he boomed. 'Grief is better expressed, Miranda. Come along,' he said, ushering her back to the hall. Standing aside, he gestured Miranda into the drawing-room.

'Will you take tea, Mr Langdon?' she asked, recalling her manners.

'That would be very acceptable. You know why I have come?'

'To . . . to sort out Papa's affairs . . .?'

William nodded. 'Precisely.'

He began taking papers from his leather bag, spreading them over the table as Miranda summoned Thomas and ordered tea.

'There are quite a number of points to go over with you, Miranda.' His deep-set eyes examined her from under thick, bushy eyebrows. 'Perhaps you should sit here . . .' He broke off as the housemaid tapped briefly on the door and entered. Placing the silver tray on a small table she bobbed a curtsy.

'Do you want me to pour, Miss Miranda?' The maid's eyes, round with curiosity, slid sideways, skimming the papers briefly.

'No thank you, Molly. That will be all.'

She bobbed another curtsy, giving a second regretful glance at the littered table.

Miranda's initial apprehension returned with a

vengeance and her hand shook as she poured, slopping tea into the saucer. At eighteen, too young to inherit, she realised she would be twenty-one before the Rushton family's fortune became hers. What provisions has Papa made for me? she wondered. Who will act as my guardian until I become of age?

'To continue,' he said pedantically. 'I have some . . . surprising news for you about Stanton . . . I mean your father. His marriage to your mother was not his first.' He paused, shooting her a perceptive glance, noting her shocked expression.

'Not his first . . .? I . . . can't believe . . . but Papa would have told me . . .?' The words caught on her tongue as she digested the information. Then her mind cleared, leaving her icy cold, forewarned of his next disclosure. 'Does . . . does that mean I have a sibling?'

William nodded, his face sympathetic.

She clapped a hand to her mouth, her eyes huge. 'Why was I never told?' She gnawed at her finger. 'You were aware of this?' she accused, her voice trembling. 'How could you have kept this from me?'

'My dear.' He came over and put a comforting hand on her shoulder, gripping it hard. 'Calm yourself. It is not the threat you might believe,' he added, realising her fears. 'There was a child of that marriage, a boy, but he does not, I emphasis not, inherit your father's estates.'

Miranda stared at him, with astonishment, shaking her head. How could an elder brother not inherit their father's estates? It was incredible!

'Why?' she whispered, unconvinced, still apprehensive. 'Why would Papa do such a thing?'

William Langdon nodded. 'You may well ask. But Stanton, I mean your father, was a law unto himself as we both know.' He broke off, reading her distress. 'Drink your tea, Mirry. Give yourself a minute to accept the idea.'

Obediently Miranda gulped her tea, the hot liquid scalding her mouth unheeded. I have a brother, she thought. I have a brother. Curiosity began to replace apprehension. What is he like? How old is he? Will I meet him?

'Does he know my . . . our father is dead? Does he know he has a sister?'

'We'll take it from the beginning, Miranda. Luke . . . your brother . . . was two when your father's first wife died giving birth to a second child . . .'

'Here? She . . . they . . . were living here?'

'Yes. They . . . '

'So everyone in the house knows about this?' she gasped. 'Everyone except me?' She dropped her head, staring at the floor, feeling betrayed.

William regarded her silently for a few minutes.

'Do you wish me to continue?' She nodded bleakly, and he carried on: 'After her death, I regret having to say this, but your father seemed to reject Luke, almost as if he resented him. They were never close and Stanton was strict with the boy, overly strict perhaps. Luke was eight when your father remarried.'

'My mother knew also?' Her voice was desolate.

'She did her best to befriend him, a lonely child, but with little success. Luke was uncommunicative and rebellious, both at home and in school, earning your father's disapproval.' He paused, taking another sip of his tea.

'Luke and your father had an appalling . . . eh . . . disagreement. Enraged, Stanton severely flogged the boy and he ran off . . .'

'How old was Luke then?' she interrupted.

'Twelve. He never returned home. Disinheriting him, your father forbade everyone to mention Luke or his mother. He threatened all the servants with instant dismissal should they break this instruction. That's the reason you've heard nothing all these years,' Mr Langdon said, almost plaintively.

Miranda digested this in silence. Although he'd always been indulgent with her mother and herself, she knew there was another side to her father. He could be a harsh disciplinarian to his servants and tenants, and now, Miranda realised, to his son, Luke.

'Have you contacted him? My brother?' The word sounded strangely unreal.

'That's the reason I didn't come here earlier.' He sounded relieved she was accepting his news calmly. 'I managed to locate Captain Llewelyn from . . .'

'Captain Llewelyn?'

'Didn't I say? Luke has taken his mother's maiden name.'

'Why has he rejected the Rushton name?' Miranda demanded.

'Something to do with his inheritance in Wales perhaps? He lives there with his mother's family. Luke was a sea captain with the East India Company, but resigned his commission when he inherited a small business, Llewelyn Shipping.'

'Does he receive nothing from my father?'

William pursed his lips thoughtfully. 'A small sum. It

seems your father felt Luke had proved his worth as a man. Rising to take command of an East Indiaman is no mean feat. Stanton, I mean your father, leaves him a . . . rather small bequest. However, all else is in trust for you, until you come of age.' He paused, before continuing reluctantly. 'But now we come to the last part of the will. Your father requests that your brother, Luke, be your trustee and guardian.'

Miranda stared numbly at him. Her unknown brother, who must resent her very being, was to be her guardian for almost three long years! Tears she was unwilling to shed, burned her eyes, as she stared straight ahead, stony-faced and rigid.

'Miranda!' The chair creaked as William Langdon leaned forward, hands on bulky thighs, peering into her face. 'You heard me?'

She nodded, turning her head away from his gaze.

'Have you nothing to say?'

She swallowed hard. 'When will he arrive?' she asked, struggling to prevent her voice trembling.

'Arrive? He doesn't . . . at least not to stay. You are to live in Wales, at his home, Bryncarog.'

He held Miranda's attention fully again now as she flashed angry eyes at him. Rage swelled up inside her, replacing her sorrow.

'I have to go to Wales, away from my home, to live with a stranger whom I have been told is my brother!' Miranda enunciated each word coldly and deliberately, furious also with William Langdon for being in collusion and imparting the news. 'That is ridiculous!'

He swallowed uncomfortably, his turn to nod

dumbly. Stretching his neck, he lifted his chin and scratched it self-consciously, then ran a finger inside his high, cravated collar.

'It is for your benefit, Miranda.' He sounded unconvinced. 'You can't live here alone.'

'Why not? Why can't I live in my own home?'

His face registered shock. 'You're a woman! It is an impossible situation.'

Miranda rose abruptly and began pacing the room with quick, angry strides, trying to gain control of her temper.

'Because I am a woman, I am forbidden my own home! Papa never asked me to follow the stupid rules of society, he ignored them himself. He employed a tutor for me, not a governess. I was taught such things as mathematics and Latin, and my father approved of these unwomanly subjects. He relied heavily on me as he got older, even asking my advice on certain aspects of his business. You know he did!' She spun round, appealing to William Langdon, her father's dearest friend and confidant. 'Why does he want me to go to some unearthly place to live? With people I don't know? Who will probably resent me?'

Lifting his shoulders, he shook his head, his puzzlement plain. 'Mirry, I don't know. I really can't say how he reached his decision. But I do know your father would do nothing contrary to your interests; he loved you far too much. You can be certain he gave the matter much thought before making his will, which incidentally was only rewritten six months ago.'

She pounced on this fact. 'Six months ago? How strange! Is it likely, by any chance, that this Luke took advantage of my father's illness to influence him?' she spat.

'Miranda. Your father understood fully what he was doing. You have to accept that.'

She rubbed a hand through her hair and took a deep, calming breath. Dropping down on a chair again, she clasped her hands tightly in her lap. 'Does the house have to be closed up while I am away?'

'Many of the servants will remain, caring for the manor, preventing decay . . .'

'Will the others be unemployed?' Her voice rose with concern.

'They will be taken care of,' he assured her. 'Most rooms will be closed and shrouded. The lands and tenants will be managed by the present estate agent, under the indirect supervision of your brother. Luke assured me he will pay regular visits to ensure everything is in order, "shipshape" as he expressed it.'

This mention of her brother suddenly made her begin to think of him as a person, living, thinking, speaking, like herself. 'What is he like . . . Luke?'

'I was impressed with him, Mirry. He is authoritative and self-assured, and struck me as being sincere in his concern for your welfare. I think you'll agree when you meet him.'

As William Langdon took his leave Miranda waited only for Thomas to close the door before wearily climbing the stairs, head down, shoulders drooping. She longed for the comfort of a hot bath, feeling lonely and ill-used, so alone.

'Ellen!' she called.

Her maid's rosy-cheeked face appeared over the top of the banister, her expression concerned.

'I've got your bath all ready, Miss Mirry, just you hurry and get those horsey smelling clothes off.' She wrinkled her nose with disgust.

Miranda dropped into the brocaded chair in her dressing room, leaning her head back as Ellen struggled to pull off her boots.

'Don't know why you get all togged out in boys' clothes when you've got such pretty clothes of your own. Come on! Mustn't let that water go cold after Silas bringing it up all ready for you.'

As Ellen continued her good-natured grumbling, Miranda breathed in the heady vapours perfuming the air, released from the aromatic essential oils Ellen had added to the water in the large wooden tub.

'Mmm, that's good!' Miranda lowered herself into the water, relaxing at last, as Ellen, sleeves rolled above sturdy forearms, scrubbed vigorously at her mistress' back with a rough cloth.

'Don't know how I'll get all those tangles from your hair.' She dipped a small, pewter jug into the bath, pouring water over Miranda's head before working soap into a lather, her fingers probing her scalp. Miranda began to revive as Ellen finally began rinsing her hair, using the pewter jugs of steaming water standing ready.

'Ellen, did you know my father was married before?'

Ellen paused in the act of pouring, jug still held in mid-air, eyes half closed, and regarded Miranda warily.

'Another wife?' Her voice held false surprise.

'And a son. Don't pretend, Ellen.' Miranda knew her too well. 'I want to know all about them. My father

24

is . . . is no longer here to forbid you to talk about them any more.'

'Suppose not.' Ellen continued pouring water over her mistress. 'But the truth is I've only heard talk from my own mother. She was the first Mrs Rushton's maid as well as your Mama's.'

Miranda pushed her hair away from her face to study Ellen more closely.

'What have you heard about her, and Luke, my brother?'

'She was different from your Mama, but she was very pretty too. Her hair was very dark, almost black, so Ma told me, and she had a creamy, pale skin, with pink cheeks. She had the bluest eyes she'd ever seen, it was the first thing you'd notice about her, Ma said, they were so lovely.' Her eyes were thoughtful as she recalled her mother's tale. 'There's a portrait of her upstairs in the lumber room. I've seen it. Just like Ma said she looked.'

'Upstairs? You must show me!' Miranda hurried to climb out of the bath, dripping water over the floor, to Ellen's scolding, as she wrapped Miranda in a fluffy towel from the wooden clothes-horse.

As soon as she was dry, Miranda pulled on her green velvet bed robe, fumbling to do up the buttons, anxious for a glimpse of the unknown first Mrs Rushton.

'What about her son? Have you heard about him?' she demanded, as they climbed the narrow stairs to the attic and the long forgotten lumber room.

Ellen nodded. 'Yes, he was like her in looks. But wild, my Ma said he was, always in trouble with your father. And reckless, he would ride any horse bare-backed, he wasn't afraid of anything or anybody. He spent a lot of time with the servants. I think most folks were sorry for him because . . . ' She broke off abruptly, reddening uncomfortably.

'Because my father was harsh with him,' Miranda bleakly finished her sentence. 'William Langdon as good as told me that.'

'I don't know much about it really, it was before I was born. '

They reached the small landing, where Miranda had hardly ever been before; its carpet was shabby and faded. The rusted handle was stiff and the door groaned reluctantly on its hinges as they pushed it open. The smell of dust hung thickly in the air, catching in their throats. There was one grimy window, high in the sloping roof, which let in very little light. Piles of vague shapes loomed around them, and Miranda was able to make out the huge rocking horse she had used as a child.

'We'll need a candle.'

Ellen returned to the small table on the landing, where a candlestick held a stump of burnt-down candle and a tinderbox. Ellen struck a spark and light flared, illuminating the room. Miranda held the candle high, as Ellen pulled at a pile of framed pictures leaning together in one corner.

'Here it is!' She tugged one free and placed it in front of the others, rubbing the dust off with her long, dark skirt.

The flickering light revealed an exceptionally

beautiful girl, not much older than Miranda herself, with delicate, regular features. Her enormous, violet blue eyes dominated her face even in the portrait. Her blue gown mirrored the colour, emphasising this feature, unusual with her raven locks. Her name 'Bronwen' was painted at the bottom.

'Why did Papa hide it here?' Miranda whispered, her voice trembling. She reached out a hand to the portrait, touching the girl's face. 'I don't understand, Ellen. Why didn't he tell me . . .?' Her voice ended on a sob and she buried her face in both hands.

'Come on, my lovely. I know, I know.' Ellen gathered Miranda's trembling body against her, hugging her tightly. 'You'll always have me, Miss Mirry.'

'I know that, Ellen.' Miranda leaned against her maid, hugging her back, and Ellen kissed her cheek.

'Come on, let's go back downstairs. It's no good upsetting yourself, it won't do any good.'

Back in her bedroom, Miranda sat at her dressing table as Ellen brushed her frizzy locks, which had been tangled into a red-gold mat by the wind. Miranda knew she resembled her mother – the most beautiful mother in the world, she had believed. Now she was having second thoughts.

'She was lovely, wasn't she? Luke's mother. Bronwen is an unusual name.'

'It's Welsh I'm told, and she was no more beautiful than you and your own mother,' Ellen said staunchly. 'I'd just love to have big green eyes like yours and that lovely curly hair.'

Curly was an understatement. Miranda's hair was a

riot of small waves, but when wet, it abandoned itself into corkscrew curls, tumbling about her face in a wanton, unladylike manner. Picking up her silver filigree hand-mirror, Miranda inspected her reflection more closely. My eyes look like a cat's eyes, she decided, studying them. Set far apart, with yellow and amber flecks, they slanted up at an angle in her heart shaped face. Yes, definitely cat's eyes. She was not sure whether that pleased her or not. And her skin? It had never worried her to see her fair skin lightly tanned after exposure to the sun on her daily rides, or marred by the slight sprinkling of freckles across her nose.

Miranda had never been displeased with her appearance but was never overly fond of it either. Sometimes she revelled in dressing in the softest silks and velvets, displaying her mother's jewels, playing the lady. This had often been from necessity, when she had acted as hostess at her father's frequent dinner parties.

At other times Miranda enjoyed being a tomboy, wearing boys' clothes and ignoring her femininity completely. She had discovered this latter act had the oddest effect of making her feel more capable and self-reliant. She'd often pondered over this fact, concluding it must be the male apparel which made her feel less vulnerable, as unfortunately, women always must be.

A violent resentment of her own sex suddenly overwhelmed her. It is definitely a man's world, Miranda decided, wishing desperately that she had been born a boy. In that situation, it would be unnecessary for her to leave home, to be at the tender mercy of an unknown brother.

Two

That afternoon, Mrs Langdon arrived to act as a chaperone until Miranda's departure. An enormous woman, tightly corseted, she overwhelmed Miranda as she descended the steps of the landau. She clasped Miranda to her, smothering her face against her well-endowed bosom as Miranda struggled to escape the overpowering smell of lavender, mingled with perspiration.

'My poor, poor child. You poor, motherless orphan. I am so sorry, Miranda my dear.'

Buried against her, unable to reply, Miranda wriggled to free herself from the firm grasp. She staggered back as Mrs Langdon released her to peer into her face.

'My poor Miranda. You have no need to worry, I am here. I'll look after you until you leave for Wales.' Her mouth turned down disapprovingly, obviously disagreeing with the decision. Fascinated, Miranda watched Mrs Langdon's multitude of chins wobble as she shook her head, tut-tutting. 'Most unsuitable. Yes, most unsuitable,' she repeated. She had a habit of repeating herself. 'You could have lived with William and me and our dear daughter Elizabeth. You would have been most welcome.'

'Thank you, Mrs Langdon. You're very kind.' But the idea of living with her filled Miranda with as much horror as her move to Wales.

'Take the luggage around to the back!' Mrs Langdon instructed the driver. 'And, Thomas, I expect you to make sure they go carefully with it!' she commanded. 'Carefully!'

With astonishment, Miranda regarded the pile of trunks weighing down the landau; enough luggage to last at least a year, not the six weeks left before Miranda's departure. Mrs Langdon handed her bonnet and cloak to the servant before sailing into the dining-room. Taking charge at once, she rang for service, ordered tea, then sank gratefully into a chair.

'Now my dear, have you no black clothing?' Her lip curled with distaste as she examined Miranda's deep-blue cashmere dress. She tutted, her chins wobbling as before. 'No black clothing for the funeral tomorrow?'

'None. I have never worn black; I know Papa would not wish me to. He always liked Mama and me to wear bright colours.' Tears shimmered in Miranda's eyes as she wistfully recalled his delighted inspection of her new dresses, the way his eyes lit up with pleasure and pride. 'Green and amber were his favourite for both of us.'

'Well, you will have to wear black now. Send a messenger for your dressmaker to come immediately. She must alter some black garment to fit you, for tomorrow. It is most unsuitable to go around like that. Most unsuitable.' She sailed over to pull the bell cord again. 'Then you will have to order appropriate mourning garments for home and to take with you.'

The funeral was a low-key affair in accordance with her father's wishes; Miranda was so numb with grief that she was hardly aware of what was going on. She received the sympathy and condolences of friends and acquaintances with gracious dignity, but later on would be hard pressed to remember who had spoken to her.

Over the following depressing weeks Miranda was to discover almost all her actions were most unsuitable as far as Mrs Langdon was concerned. Attempting to assuage her grief by riding, Miranda was forced to sneak out of the house, evading Mrs Langdon, because it was most unsuitable for her to ride when in mourning. Miranda became so weary of her voice, droning on and on, that she almost began to welcome leaving Rushton Hall just to escape.

It had been settled that Miranda's maid would accompany her to Luke's home, then remain with her. Not wanting to deprive Ellen of her family, Miranda had initially approached her cautiously about it, but Ellen had decided without hesitation. Devoted to Miranda, she enjoyed fussing over her; at those times she seemed much more than just a year older than Miranda. But on other occasions, Ellen could be girlish and giggly, a companion confiding all her secrets to

Miranda. She had been her personal maid since Miranda was fourteen, and Miranda regarded her as a friend as well as a maidservant. It was a great relief to know Ellen would be accompanying her in her exile.

'Are you still quite certain you want to come with me?' she asked Ellen again, as the departure date grew imminent.

Ellen stopped brushing Miranda's hair, putting her hands on her hips. 'Now you know I want to come, Miss Mirry,' she chuckled. 'It will be a real adventure, going to Wales.' Her face grew even more pink-cheeked than usual at the thought, her eyes sparkling. 'I've heard it's a very wild country with real smugglers around the coast.'

'Really? Where ever did you hear that?' Miranda asked.

Colouring slightly, Ellen shook her head, her eyes downcast.

'I think I know! Was it from Nezer?' Miranda knew Ellen still held romantic yearnings for the gypsy lad who had spent last summer on their land. Her father had always allowed the Romanies to camp unmolested at selected sites on the estate, believing they did little damage if their presence was accepted. In return they understood they should abide by his rules, or face the consequences of the local magistrates. It had worked well, even if it didn't meet with the approval of some local landlords. This was another example of her father's lack of convention.

Ellen nodded. 'They do travel to parts of Wales,' she admitted.

'What about leaving poor Judd?' Miranda asked

with a teasing grin, realising only too well how Ellen felt about the groom.

'Judd!' Ellen exclaimed. 'That horrible man.' She tossed her head dismissively. 'If he thinks I want to wed a man near old enough to be my father he's got another thing coming.'

Miranda giggled, enjoying her indignation. She was aware Judd had expressed an interest in Ellen, which was not returned.

Miranda's trunks were soon packed, filled with the hateful, new black clothing; even the petticoat lace was threaded with black ribbon. Miranda loathed the dreary, old-fashioned style of the garments, knowing her father would have hated to see her in these clothes. But she had been worn down with the weight of Mrs Langdon's disapproval. Having felt so unhappy and depressed, Miranda couldn't be bothered to put up any resistance.

Two half-mourning garments had also been made for her, but Miranda had managed to persuade Ellen to include a few of her favourite, most unsuitable, dresses and riding habits. These were carefully hidden from Mrs Langdon's eagle gaze, beneath the rest of the luggage, along with two sets of boys' riding clothes and boots.

Departure day dawned, relentlessly bright and sunny, not fitting Miranda's mood at all. Blinking back threatening tears, she gave a perfunctory glance in the mirror. In unrelieved black, the dress and covering perlise seemed to swamp her. Miranda thought black unbecoming to her complexion, draining away her natural colour, leaving her face wan. Her hair, tamed for once, was scraped back under a horrible black bonnet, adorned with ribbon of a similar hue. I look like a child, Miranda decided.

Tapping the door as she entered, Ellen bobbed a curtsy. Her chubby face was flushed and animated, her eyes expectant.

'Miss Mirry. It's Captain Llewelyn. Your brother, he's arrived!'

Miranda's heart gave a sickening lurch and she put both hands to her waxen cheeks. Apprehensively she glanced at Ellen, who read the question in her eyes.

'He's very handsome. Proper gentleman, but very stern looking.'

Stern looking, like Papa could be, the thought raced through her mind. She took a few deep breaths before leaving her room, trying to control the nausea she felt rising, determined not to disgrace herself.

She descended the stairs in a sedate, ladylike manner, hiding her panic. What will he make of me, the usurper? she wondered.

Voices came from the drawing room and, as she entered, she saw William and Mrs Langdon talking to a man who turned towards her. His outline towered before the window, his shoulders wide against the light, shadowing him from her view. As he took a few long strides towards her she received an impression of restrained strength, a lion ready to spring. He took her proffered hand firmly, held her cold fingers in a hand hard and calloused, unlike those of other gentlemen of her acquaintance.

'Miranda.' His voice was deep and resonant, but he spoke softly. His eyes, the deepest, most arresting blue she had ever seen, narrowed as his penetrating gaze studied her face intently. 'Allow me to express sorrow for your loss.'

She swallowed the lump in her throat and nodded. 'Thank you, Captain Llewelyn. But . . . it is your loss too.'

A shutter seemed to descend over his eyes. He was silent for a moment before he inclined his head in acknowledgement. 'My loss was many years before now.' His voice was distant.

For a few minutes they stood examining one another, each of them unaware of their actions. Then Miranda noticed Mrs Langdon watching proceedings with interest, obviously delighted to be witnessing this meeting between heir and disinherited heir.

Releasing her hand, he turned away, his eyes roving about the room. His gaze stopped on the portrait of her mother hanging over the fireplace, and he walked slowly over to it, studying it silently. Uncomfortably Miranda recalled that other portrait, banished to the attic.

'That is my mother,' she said hesitantly.

'It is just as I remember her.'

She bit her lip, embarrassment flooding through her. How could she have forgotten he lived here after their father's second marriage and had known her own mother. Neither of them spoke and Miranda was aware of the ancient grandfather clock ticking noisily.

'You will take some refreshment before the journey, Captain Llewelyn?' Mrs Langdon said. She shook her head, chins wobbling. 'It is most unsuitable to travel on an empty stomach. Most unsuitable.'

'Thank you for your concern, Mrs Langdon, but I have already eaten at the coach-house.'

William Langdon turned a sympathetic glance towards Miranda. 'Well my dear, you have a long journey ahead. Are you ready to make a start?'

Miranda nodded dumbly and pulled the bell cord. Thomas appeared silently, his eyes roaming with satisfaction over Luke's well tailored, tight-fitting coat, cut away at the front to reveal fashionably-straight trousers.

'The luggage is loaded, Captain Llewelyn.'

'Thank you, Thomas,' Miranda snapped, furious the servant had addressed Luke in preference to herself. 'We will attend when we are ready.'

She saw disapproval flash in Luke's eyes and she glared at him, her mouth tightening, showing him her annoyance. How dare this man infer criticism of her handling of the servants in her own house!

There was an uncomfortable pause, then William Langdon broke the silence. 'We understand your reluctance, my dear.'

Miranda flushed, then said in her most arrogant manner. 'I am ready to leave now, Captain Llewelyn.'

'Miranda. Under the circumstances I think we could forgo formality and address each other by our given names. Mine is Luke.'

Miranda held herself rigid and was silent, not willing to be brow-beaten; he was treating her like a child. Then she had a mental picture of her reflection in the bedroom mirror, of the childish garments, and realised he saw her as a child. This annoyed her still further as there was nothing she could do to alter her unfavourable appearance. She darted a glance at him, saw he was watching her, his face cold and stern. A shiver ran through her. This man was to have sole control over her life for the next three years and already he disliked her. She would never reveal her fear, never show him how she felt. Never!

It had been arranged for Rushton Hall's carriage to convey them to the nearest Post House where they would begin their journey to Wales.

Miranda lifted her head, her chin jutting determinedly. 'Well . . . Luke?' Her words were hard and clipped. 'My coach is waiting, shall we leave?'

He regarded her silently for a moment, his brow puckering slightly as though examining her for some sign of the misery he expected. This pleased her. Let him find me hard to understand, she decided, that is just how I want our relationship to be. This man will not intrude upon my feelings and emotions. I will not allow it!

'If you are quite ready,' he affirmed.

'I can see no point in prolonging our departure,' she said curtly.

She swept towards the door, her back ramrod stiff. Ellen was waiting in the hall, dressed for the journey. Her face was anxious and unhappy and her eyes red and downcast. Alongside her stood Eliza, Ellen's mother, who took Miranda in both arms, hugging her firmly.

'I'm so sorry, Miss Mirry, my dear. Your Papa was a good man,' she whispered in her ear. Miranda bit her lip as she added: 'My Ellen will care for you. She really loves you, as we all do.'

Miranda nodded wordlessly, returning her hug. Then she caught sight of the rest of the servants Thomas had lined up on the steps, and her eyes filled with unshed tears which threatened to brim over, as she embraced many of those so dear to her.

First was the stooped form of Miranda's elderly nursemaid, brought from her retirement for the farewell ceremony. 'God bless you, my child,' she croaked, catching her hand and kissing it. 'Take care.'

Next, Molly, the housemaid, unable to speak, bobbed a curtsy and gripped Miranda's hand.

Then their stout cook, Marjorie, dabbed at her eyes with the corner of her apron. 'Don't you fret, Miss Mirry, you'll be back home in no time. Just you see.' Then one by one came the others in turn, each one twisting the knot in Miranda's heart a little tighter as they took their leave.

Lastly Thomas bowed formally to her, his faded eyes sad. 'God go with you Mistress, we look forward to your return. Have a safe journey.'

Luke took Miranda's hand, assisting her into the carriage, but she studiously kept her face averted from him. She settled herself fussily into a corner, making a big show of spreading her skirts, wanting to gain time to compose her emotions. As Luke assisted Ellen into the coach, Miranda saw the tears streaming down her friend's face, and hastily looked away.

She gave a slight shudder and, head held high, she watched Rushton Hall disappear from view, flooded with an overwhelming foreboding that it was the last time she would ever see her home again.

They sat in silence, absorbed with their own thoughts. Very much aware of Luke's overwhelmingly masculine presence, which seemed to fill the coach, Miranda was able to examine him discreetly, as his reflection was plainly visible in the glass window of the coach. His face was brooding as he intently studied the passing landscape, now and then leaning forward to get a better glimpse of some long remembered landmark. Miranda wondered what his feelings were as he saw the scene flying past, the estates which he probably felt were his by right, and which now belonged to her. She knew how she would feel if the situation were reversed and for the first time felt a glimmer of sympathy for Luke, instead of resentment.

She examined his features, searching for some resemblance to dear Papa but could find none. Indeed he had the countenance of his beautiful mother, but in a completely male, rugged form. A small silver scar, tinged with blue, seared the skin across one cheekbone, disappearing into his dark, curling side-whiskers but, rather than detracting, it lent a daredevil appeal to his features. He was an exceptionally handsome man.

His eyes suddenly met Miranda's in the glass and she blushed a deep crimson, realising he knew she had been watching him. He gave a half smile and turned towards her. 'I thought I had forgotten all about Rushton, but I see I was wrong. It has changed remarkably little in the years I have been away.'

'It must be a strange return for you,' Miranda replied reluctantly. 'You were only a child when you went away, I believe? Have you ever returned since?'

'No!' He didn't elaborate on the statement and Miranda was determined to ask no more. His eyes were cold again now, his face assuming a grim expression, making Miranda wonder if harsh experiences at sea might have caused it.

She glanced away, to see Ellen staring open-mouthed at Luke, a dazed, adoring expression on her face. 'I hope you are enjoying the scenery, Ellen?' Miranda said pointedly.

Ellen started, and flushed, knowing only too well what her mistress meant. 'Yes, Miss Miranda, ' she said meekly, turning to the window.

Luke threw Miranda a questioning look and pursed his lips thoughtfully but said nothing.

Leaving the Rushton coach, they joined the first of the Post Coaches, which were to convey them on the rest of their passage to Wales. The journey towards Gloucester dragged, with seemingly endless changes of horses as Miranda sat locked in her misery, knowing she was going further and further from all she loved.

If only Mama were still here it might be bearable, she thought, but I am quite alone in the world now. Nobody really cares about me or what happens to me. Waves of self-pity washed over her as she allowed herself to wallow in her grief.

'Are you feeling unwell, Miranda?' Luke's words startled Miranda out of her introspection to find his eyes regarding her drawn face with concern.

'I am quite well, thank you,' she whispered. She sat up, twisting the string of her reticule tight around her fingers. Her mind groped for any subject of conversation and a thought, which had crossed her mind more than once, flew to her lips. 'Why did you adopt your mother's maiden name?' she blurted.

His eyes widened, startlingly blue against his tanned face, and his mouth opened slightly. He took a deep breath and, before answering, shot a swift glance at Ellen who was looking discreetly out of the window. 'Just as Stanton, our father, rejected me as a son, so I rejected him as a father. I no longer wished to retain the Rushton name.' The words were dismissive, clipped and matter-of-fact.

'I see.' Miranda clenched her teeth together, hot tears burning her eyes. Dear Papa, I loved you even if your son did not. She lifted her chin, fighting to prevent her voice trembling. 'Mr Langdon tells me you and Papa met in recent years?'

'We did.' His eyes had returned to her face.

'Didn't you alter your opinion then?'

He gestured impatiently. 'It had been too long, Miranda. Let us say we . . .' he paused reflectively.

'Then why did he decide to make you my guardian?' she spat, her face challenging.

'I was about to say we had reached a state of mutual respect . . .'

'And you persuaded him to . . .'

'Don't be ridiculous, Miranda,' he interrupted with exasperation. 'You're talking like a spoilt child . . .'

'Isn't that how you regard me?' She glared at him, clenching her fists tightly in her lap.

'I think we had better let this subject drop,' he said curtly. 'If you wish to discuss it further we will do so at Bryncarog.'

'Yes . . . Captain,' she said with heavy sarcasm.

Luke's mouth tightened but he didn't answer.

'This is where we are to spend the first night,' Luke said at last, as the horses turned under an archway leading into the courtyard of a brightly lit coach-house.

They peered out with relief as Luke leaned over to open the carriage door and, disregarding the steps, leapt down. He held out his hand and Miranda and Ellen climbed out stiffly, weary of long sitting, even though the seats were well cushioned and comfortable. Luke went ahead to make sure their rooms for the night were reserved and to order refreshments.

'I'll be glad of a nice soft bed to stretch out,' Miranda confided to Ellen.

Ellen didn't reply, but walked silently at her side, head down. Miranda turned towards her, wondering if she had heard. Then seeing the dumb misery on her maid's face she was filled with remorse for her unthinking selfishness. Ellen, just as much as I, she thought, is leaving behind all she knows and loves . . . and for my sake. How could I have been so selfish and thoughtless? She caught Ellen against her, hugging her and kissing her cheek and Ellen responded with a quick hug in return.

'Ellen, I am sorry. I haven't been concerned about you at all.' And wanting to say something to shake her out of her apathy added: 'I am a selfish trollop.'

Miranda received the response she had anticipated when both Ellen's mouth and eyes opened wide with dismay at the word she had deliberately used.

Ellen's reply was equally predictable. 'Oh, Miss Mirry! You should never use such words. It's very unladylike.'

'Yes, most unladylike,' Miranda said, mimicking Mrs Langdon's voice. 'And most unsuitable.' They both giggled, as they had done so often before at Mrs Langdon's expense, gaining a respite from their misery. Then feeling more light-hearted, the girls held hands as they entered the inn.

They made good time as far as Gloucester, as the roads they had travelled so far had all been Macadamised, providing a good, fast surface. But as they travelled further into Wales, the roads there had not received such benefit, becoming increasingly rough and pitted, making their journey far less comfortable. As well as being thrown around continuously, they kept bouncing and landing with bone-jarring bumps each time the coach jolted into a pothole. The two girls hung onto the straps, causing their arms and shoulders to ache. Luke seemed quite unaware of their discomfort, indifferent to their predicament, and Miranda's temper began to rise at his lack of concern.

'Surely you can ask the coachman to go more slowly,' she snapped, as she nearly lurched to the floor yet again.

As Luke raised his eyebrows in amazement, an elderly man, occupying the corner seat opposite Miranda, smothered a little smile.

'I am afraid the man has a tight schedule to observe, Miranda.' His tone was deceptively placating, as though talking to a child. 'This is one time when you will have to make the best of a little discomfort, my dear, unfamiliar as it may be for you.'

Miranda's face flamed, silenced by the scorn in his voice as she digested his insinuation that everything was made easy for her. But his harsh words struck home forcibly. What else lies in store for me with this arrogant young man in this wild country of his? she wondered bleakly.

At times the coach was forced to a walking pace, held up by ponderous wagons and farm carts, which toiled sluggishly along the road ahead of them. As soon as they were sighted, the coachman on the rear seat would sound his horn until the carts lumbered reluctantly to one side. But as often as not there was no place for the carts to pull over and the coach would be forced to slow down behind them until there was room to pass.

This heavy traffic made poor surface conditions even worse, any heavy shower immediately turning the unmade roads into sticky quagmires, the mud clinging to coach wheels and horses' feet. At other times they would bowl past rows of carts and private carriages lined up patiently on the side of the road.

'What on earth are they all waiting for?' Miranda asked as they flew past yet another row.

'They have to pay a toll before they can pass. We are more fortunate. The Post Coach is allowed through without stopping.'

'Do they have to wait long?' She felt sorry for the people waiting with such resignation.

'Sometimes it could be an hour. The toll gates cause hardship to many of the ordinary people. There is a lot of resentment about the tolls in Wales,' Luke said.

As the landscape grew bleaker, a damp grey mist seeped down, clinging around the windows, appearing to swallow the horses as they galloped ahead into it. To Miranda it produced an alien, surreal effect, as though they were driving into the mythical land of the underworld of Greek mythology.

Three

It was dusk when they finally pulled into the cobbled courtyard of the Mackworth Arms, in Swansea. Porters bustled about, unloading the luggage, ostlers rushed to attend to the horses, as Miranda and Ellen climbed stiffly from the coach to be ushered inside by Luke.

'Refreshments for the ladies, if you please,' he ordered, as the host hurried forward to welcome them. 'Have you seen any sign of the Bryncarog carriage?'

'No, Captain Llewelyn. I haven't set eyes on Wyn, though he's not exactly reliable is he?' he chuckled. 'You'd best set your mind on a long wait. Get yourselves a good meal inside you, I would.'

Luke's face tightened and his eyes blazed, blue melting to steel, but he nodded to the landlord. 'A good idea, but we'll take light refreshment only. There'll be a meal prepared for us. Some good, strong tea and some oatcakes should suit us well enough.'

Miranda was glad not to be on the receiving end of Luke's anger, wondering how hard a taskmaster he had been to his crew at sea. He obviously had more of her father in his nature than was revealed by his appearance.

As they unwound a little, Miranda began taking more notice of her surroundings. She was surprised to hear people talking in an unrecognisable language.

'Are they speaking Welsh?' she asked Luke, previously believing it was a dead language, rather like Latin.

He smiled at her. 'Yes. Welsh is the first language in much of Wales, though not in Swansea itself.'

'Do you speak Welsh?' she queried, correctly assuming he had never lived in Wales as a child.

He shook his head. 'Unfortunately not. I've only a minimum knowledge of the language, acquired since I came to live here.' He grinned. 'It serves me well enough.'

'Did you live in Wales when you were serving with the East India Company?'

He gave a wry laugh. 'Hardly, Miranda. I visited occasionally, but I spent most of my time at sea or in the Orient.'

'Your mother spoke Welsh?'

He stopped eating, hand poised in mid-air, glancing at her face. 'How would I know? She died when I was two,' he said caustically.

Miranda bit her lip, feeling foolish. How could she have forgotten? Hadn't their father disregarded Luke after her death? Luke probably thought she had asked deliberately. 'Forgive me,' she snapped, venting her discomfort on him. 'I had forgotten.'

His eyes held hers in a hard stare for a few condemning moments before he continued eating.

'Wyn has arrived with your coach, Captain Llewelyn,' the landlord called from the doorway.

Hastily, they scrambled to gather their belongings as Luke stalked out ahead.

'Where the hell have you been?' he roared at his manservant, quite unheeding of the presence of the ladies. 'And why aren't you wearing a bloody neckerchief?'

Ellen gasped, putting a hand to her lips. Quite unperturbed, the manservant, grubby, untidy and dishevelled, scowled belligerently. ''orse shed a shoe didn't 'e,' he grunted.

'Which one?' Luke demanded, with obvious disbelief.

''ow do I remember?' Wyn grunted, waving an arm at the horses.

Suddenly realising Miranda and Ellen were witnessing this exchange Luke inhaled a deep, calming breath through his nostrils, letting it out slowly. 'In future you will make sure David checks them before you leave. I want it done regularly to be certain they are secure,' he said, turning away impatiently.

Miranda stared at the ancient Bryncarog coach with disbelief. Badly in need of a coat of paint, with rusting, peeling patches, it had certainly seen better days. Assisted by Luke, they climbed the rickety steps to find the interior no better. Its threadbare cushions were losing their horsehair filling, their colours unrecognisable and parts of the tapestry wall-lining dangled in shreds. The springing left much to be desired, jolting them with shuddering discomfort as the coach bounced over the cobblestones.

Leaving Swansea, they followed a road running alongside miles of sandy beach to their left. Miranda peered out curiously, but by now it was too dark to see, and the clouded sky shadowed the moon most of the time, allowing it to emerge occasionally to silver the water. An invigorating ozone smell was very evident, as it blew straight in through a broken pane of the coach. Miranda became aware of the sibilant dash of the waves, endlessly thrusting and retreating along the beach.

'Is that the sea I can hear?' she exclaimed, gesturing towards the beach. 'I never realised it would be so loud.'

'But you must have been near the sea before?' Luke asked with surprise.

'Of course! I've been to Bristol, but it wasn't like this.' She leaned towards him, showing the first sign of interest in her new home. 'Is Bryncarog near the sea?'

'Very much so. It's built almost on the cliffs, between two bays. It actually overlooks the smaller one.' He nodded towards the sea side of the coach. 'You'll hear it a great deal louder than that at times.'

'That must suit you well? It must make you feel you are back on board ship?'

Luke half smiled without answering. The coach turned off the road into a smaller one and, clutching the strap, Miranda stared out into the darkness as the coach bumped its way towards Bryncarog. Eventually it pulled to a final halt, allowing them to descend the coach for the last time.

Wyn drove off at speed, almost before they were able to alight from the carriage. Miranda tried to get a glimpse of the poorly-lit house, which was to be her home for the next few years. Compared to Rushton Hall, it was small and gloomy, with few windows showing any welcoming glow. It appeared to loom dark and menacing before her as she approached, sending a shiver of apprehension running through her.

At the worn wooden portal, Luke turned a rusting, ring-handle and pushed at the door, which didn't move. Putting his shoulder against it, he shoved harder, but it remained firmly closed. Muttering inaudibly under his breath he lifted the dragon's-head knocker, rapping it firmly as it reverberated though the house.

A distinct impression that the house was unoccupied added to Miranda's unease. Who else lives in this manor? she wondered. Who am I to share my banishment with, other than Luke? She had scarcely spoken to Luke during the journey, and now regretted her omission. She decided she should have ignored his boorish aloofness, and discovered more about her new family when she had the chance.

Luke had just repeated hammering at the door, when they heard the squeak of bolts being withdrawn and a querulous voice calling: 'All right. Coming I am.'

The door was opened about a foot and a crack of light flooded the portal. A hunched, female figure peered out, a candle held aloft in one hand.

'Trying to knock the door down, are you? Who is it?' Her tone was sharp and suspicious.

'Captain Llewelyn,' Luke responded. 'Open the door please, Ceridwen.'

The door slowly swung back, creaking ominously, as though they were about to enter a dungeon. The interior did little to relieve Miranda's apprehension. The only light in the gloomy hall came from the candle in Ceridwen's hand, as her beady, unfriendly stare critically appraised them from a wizened face.

'One of these the heiress then, is it?' Ceridwen's quivering, toothless mouth seemed to snap shut, at the end of each sentence, her chin springing towards her hooked nose. The grumbling voice lacked respect, and Miranda wondered if she was the servant she had taken her for. 'I suppose you'll be wanting me to call Mrs Cain?' She started to hobble away as she was speaking, but Luke caught her arm, taking the candle from her hand.

'I'll take the light, if you please, Ceridwen. Is there a fire in the drawing room?'

Either not hearing or pretending not to, Ceridwen continued on her way, muttering something unintelligible in Welsh. Luke snorted with audible frustration and Miranda smothered a smile at his inability to control his own servants. It seemed Luke did not have it all his own way here.

'This way,' he said shortly. Throwing open a door on the right, he held the candle aloft and ushered them in. Although no other candles were lit, the room was illuminated by a bright coal fire burning in a wide grate which was carved from some sort of pale marble. Immediately Miranda felt more welcome. Luke walked over to a pewter candelabra to light candles, which flared into radiant life, and then lit more in a holder on the opposite wall.

'Thank you,' Miranda murmured as he helped her off with her cloak. She turned as a dumpy little woman came bouncing through the door towards her, to take her into her arms. Hugging Miranda warmly, she pressed her face against her cheek.

'Miranda. That is your name isn't it? So pretty. Lovely to have you. It will be nice to have another woman's company. I'm Charlotte, Luke's aunt.' She spoke breathlessly in short sentences. She stood back, head on one side, subjecting Miranda to an appraising look. 'You're such a pretty girl. But I thought you were older.'

'I . . . I am almost nineteen,' Miranda said, taken back. Then remembering her manners, returned the embrace, grateful that at least someone wanted her here. 'Thank you, Charlotte . . . thank you for having me.'

'Are you hungry, my dear? You'll be tired after that long journey. Welcome back, Luke. And who is this? Your servant?' She smiled at Ellen who had been standing, downcast and silent, throughout this exchange. 'What are you called, girl?'

'Ellen, Miss,' she replied, bobbing a curtsy.

Charlotte giggled, amazing Miranda when she said: 'Goodness, our servants never do that. They'll think you are the lady of the manor, Miranda.'

Every movement of Charlotte's was fussy, matching her voice. With quick, springy steps, she moved to snatch the bell cord with a sharp jerk. Miranda saw a woman in her fifties, a plump face lined with a washed-out prettiness. She had a colourless complexion, greying hair, cut in an unfashionable short style without sidecurls, her dress the high-waisted mode of the past. But when she returned to Miranda, her faded blue eyes were surprisingly shrewd in her worn face, seeming to miss nothing.

'That Ceridwen, I hope she has the food ready. She's a law unto herself. I ordered stew, my dear. Made from good Welsh lamb. You will enjoy that.'

Miranda smiled, warmed by her friendliness.

Without knocking, Ceridwen put her head in the door, looking resentfully at Charlotte. 'Well, what is it now?'

'Take Miss Miranda's maid up to her room. She will want to change.' Charlotte was not in the least perturbed by Ceridwen's manner. 'And make sure she has hot water.'

'Huh! I never! A maid that wants waiting on,' was the sharp reply. 'Wyn'll 'ave to see to that. I haven' no time.' She disappeared, shutting the door firmly.

'Excuse me, Charlotte, Miranda,' Luke nodded to both of them. 'I'll make sure Wyn brings hot water for you and your maid. Come along, Ellen.'

Ellen left, her uneasiness apparent by her rigid stance. Miranda felt a renewed pang of guilt for bringing Ellen here, away from her family, to what might prove to be a hostile environment. She made up her mind then, if Ellen was unhappy she would make sure that Luke returned her home. Miranda had been very much aware of his sympathy and understanding for Ellen throughout the journey, more perhaps than he had shown towards her, and recalled that as a child he'd been befriended by the Rushton servants.

'I expect you'll want to bathe before dinner. Poor Miranda, torn away from your home.' Charlotte's hands fluttered, encompassing the whole room. 'I know what it's like.'

'You haven't always lived here?' Miranda asked, looking about her curiously, noting the sturdy, unadorned walls where the firelight cast flashing shadows.

'No. I went to live in North Wales. When I was married, you know? But my husband was the younger son, he inherited little.' She shrugged eloquently and her eyes narrowed. 'I never managed such a good match as Bronwen.' Miranda thought she had detected a note of envy creep into her voice. Charlotte bobbed over to an armchair near the fire, gesturing Miranda to another.

'Bronwen was your sister?' Miranda queried, as she sank gratefully into the sagging armchair, exhausted after the long journey.

'That's right.' Charlotte stabbed at the fire with the poker.

'How did Bronwen meet my father?' she probed, as she still knew nothing about her father's first marriage.

'During a weekend at Bath. We did socialise well then.' Charlotte pulled a little *moue*. 'We were staying with friends of Papa's. Lord Mark, I believe it was.' She glanced at Miranda to gauge her reaction.

'And my father was there also?' Miranda asked, curious to hear a first-hand account of this event.

'Yes. It was the first time Bronwen and Stanton had ever met.' Seeming to lose interest in the conversation Charlotte picked up some embroidery from a small table, inadvertently drawing Miranda's attention to its scratched surface and lack of polish.

'They liked one another?' Miranda said, trying to draw her back to the conversation.

Charlotte looked up. 'Oh yes! He was quite besotted with her,' she said, slightly mockingly.

'And they met again? After that?'

She nodded. 'Stanton came here a few times.' Her glance flashed across Miranda's face. 'They got married not long afterwards. In Scotland.'

'In Scotland?' Miranda said with surprise.

'Indeed. Bronwen and Papa were staying there with relatives.' Charlotte lifted her shoulders, as though mystified. 'It seems Stanton couldn't wait for her to return home. He followed her there. They got married, toured around a bit, then went back to Rushton Hall. Bronwen always did get her own way.' She fluttered her head slightly, pursing her lips, and Miranda was certain Charlotte envied her sister.

Miranda rubbed her hand across the arm of her chair, picking absent-mindedly at the worn fabric. She frowned, her thoughts wandering to that portrait in the attic, understanding something of her father's bitterness at Bronwen's death, realising why he'd resented Luke. 'Her death was tragic,' she murmured. 'She was very young. You must all have been shocked.'

'We were. She was my only sister.'

'I've seen her portrait. She was beautiful.'

Charlotte patted her hair, preening slightly. 'We were very much alike. I was also a beauty then. Everyone said so.'

'I am sure that's true. You are still very lovely,' Miranda said politely. But an image of Bronwen's portrait was imprinted in Miranda's mind, and she wondered if a similar one hung anywhere in this house. Charlotte would have been hard pressed to equal that beauty.

'That's life.' Charlotte gave a brittle laugh, and sprang up from her chair. 'Come along. I'll take you to your room. You'll want to refresh yourself.' She picked up the pewter candelabra and Miranda followed her up the stairs, the worn, uncarpeted wood resounding hollowly beneath their feet. From what Miranda could see in the poor light, the walls were built of the same grey stone as the drawing room, with a sparseness of paintings and tapestries giving a bare, unlived-in atmosphere.

Shadows danced on the walls, as Charlotte bounced across the room to light the candle on the dressing table. Miranda crossed to the window, where she heard the sea murmuring beyond. As she pulled back the curtain, there was a loud thump on her door.

'Come in,' she called.

The door was flung open and Wyn stamped in unceremoniously. 'Food's ready,' he said tersely. 'You'd best come, if it's 'ot you're wanting it.' And he stamped back out, banging the door noisily behind him.

Charlotte pulled a face. 'We'd better go down. We don't want to upset them.' She beckoned conspiratorially, and it struck Miranda how childish she seemed. It gave an uncomfortable impression of an empty-headed girl disguised in an older woman's body.

Hurriedly, Miranda washed the grime from her face and hands, leaving further ablutions until later, and chased after Charlotte. As she followed her back along the dim corridor Miranda concluded that the household budget spent little on candles.

Miranda was surprised when a subdued Ellen appeared to wait at table as, being Miranda's personal maid, she had never done so at Rushton. Although Miranda hadn't thought she was hungry she managed to eat a reasonable meal. The food was tasty, good and substantial, with liberal chunks of meat and vegetables in the stew. At least I will not starve, she thought, even if I might find it rather gloomy.

Luke spoke little, seeming preoccupied.

'I wonder where young Huw can be?' Charlotte twittered.

'Who is Huw?' Miranda asked, dabbing her mouth with her napkin. 'I don't believe I've heard his name mentioned before.'

Charlotte shook her head, a bird ruffling its feathers. 'I don't expect you have,' she retorted. 'Luke wouldn't mention him. Huw is my son,'

Their meal finished, Miranda rose, ready to retire. The journey had exhausted her and she longed to wash and climb into bed. As they were leaving the dining-room, a tall figure approached from the region of the servants' quarters.

'Good evening Mother, Luke. Well, well, are you Miss Rushton?' The lanky frame towered above her. Two laughing hazel eyes scrutinised her, a lazy smile lurking around his lips. 'I thought you'd be older.'

The second time Miranda had been told that today,

57

she was not caught unaware this time. She lifted her head imperiously: 'I am not the child I appear in these ridiculous garments, sir. I am nearly nineteen,' she said frostily.

His smile widened, revealing beautifully even teeth, and he gave her a teasing, mock bow. 'I do beg your pardon, Mistress. Most ungallant of me, I hope you will forgive me.' The slight, subdued Welsh lilt, added an attractive softness to his voice, intriguing Miranda as much as his appearance. She opened her mouth to reply when Luke spoke.

'Miranda, allow me to present my cousin Huw Cain. Huw, Mistress Miranda Rushton.' Luke's voice was flat and expressionless.

'Mr Cain,' Miranda murmured, holding out her hand.

'You are very late, Huw,' Charlotte broke in, her smile indulgent. 'I was wondering where you were until this hour. Miranda is just off to her room. She is worn out, poor dear.'

'Good night, cousin. I look forward to seeing you tomorrow.' He lifted her hand and kissed it, and Miranda saw that smile twitching his lips again.

She snatched her hand away. 'I feel you mock me, sir. I need no false gallantry.'

His smile faded as he regarded her with surprise. 'I assure you I meant no disrespect, Miss Rushton . . .'

'Very well, Mr Cain,' Miranda nodded, her eyes holding his. Then she addressed everyone: 'I hope you will all excuse me? I am exhausted after the journey.' She turned towards the stairs. 'Good night. I think I can find my way alone.' Gathering up her skirts in one hand, clutching a candlestick in the other, she mounted the stairs. As she passed along the landing she heard Luke's voice and stopped to eavesdrop.

'I'll thank you to treat my sister with the respect she deserves,' he growled.

'What on earth do you mean?' Huw drawled. Miranda peeped over the rail to see Huw leaning back nonchalantly against the newel post, as Luke stood intimidatingly near, his body rigid. 'I meant no disrespect,' Huw repeated. 'I was trying to make her feel welcome . . .'

'Just remember what I said,' Luke hissed through his teeth.

'You really do appear an incorrigible puritan at times, Luke . . . on the surface at least . . .' Huw stopped as Luke gripped his arm, looking down impassively at his hand. 'Please remember, Luke, you are not on board your ship now; you cannot order me about.'

'Just heed my words, Huw. Don't cross me!'

Miranda dodged back out of sight as Luke spun around and stalked away. So that was another thing she had learned: there was no love lost between the two cousins.

Luke banged the library door shut behind him and grimaced with frustration, wishing Huw did not resent him so much. He reached for a tinderbox and struck a spark from the flint, the candle flame flaring up briefly, before settling, as he applied the taper. A paperweight on the desk,caught its light and he picked it up, turning it in his hand.

It was at times like this that he bitterly regretted his decision to resign his commission and take over the running of Llewelyn Shipping. But what else could he have done? How well he recalled his Uncle George's words that day, nearly four years earlier. He had been paying a visit to Bryncarog and was about to take his leave, when George said out of the blue:

'Luke, my boy, I want you to promise me you will take over the firm when I am gone.'

'Take it over? Me?' Luke exclaimed, with genuine astonishment. 'But you have Huw already in the firm with you. You don't need me.'

The old man shook his head regretfully. 'The lad has no flair for it, Luke, he has no idea at all . . .'

'He's young, sir, give him a chance. With time . . .'

George leaned forward and gripped Luke's arm. 'That is what I haven't got, my boy. Time!'

'You don't mean . . .?' Luke hesitated, frowning at his uncle. He had grown fond of the old man during his visits over the years, and didn't wish to hear what he was obviously trying to tell him.

'That's exactly what I do mean, Luke. I have suffered many years from a blood condition, which is rapidly getting worse. My strength is failing, I have no vitality and, I must admit, I've let the business slip. My physician can do nothing more to help me. He tells me I must put my affairs in order as my time is limited. I had hoped Huw would grow into the work . . .' He broke off with a shrug.

'But surely you could steer him in the right direction?'

George sighed. 'Don't you think I have tried? To

tell you the truth, Luke, Huw simply has not enough interest in the business.'

'He is probably depending on you too much, sir. What if you put him in charge immediately? Made him accountable? Wouldn't he then show more application?'

George shook his head. 'No, Luke. I hate to admit this about my own sister's boy, but he wants nothing more than to be provided with an easy living . . . '

'Then you must make him aware of the true circumstances. I am sure once he realises his responsibilities . . . '

'Given time . . . perhaps he would pull round,' George agreed. 'But as I said, I have not the time, nor in fact the energy, to try any longer. Luke, unless you come and manage the firm, Llewelyn Shipping will be driven to bankruptcy.' George fixed a solemn gaze on Luke. 'That is after more than eighty years of hard work, my boy. My father, your grandfather, started this firm as young man. Luke, I am depending . . . no, begging you to save it from ruin.'

'But . . . I'm a sailor, I know nothing of business.' Luke groped for an escape from the noose he felt drawing tight around his neck. 'I'm at sea most of the time. I'd have no means of governing Huw's . . .'

'I will make you managing director with full control.' He directed a hard look at him and, as Luke would have spoken, continued: 'If you can successfully run a large ship, and all its crew, at sea, you surely can run a small shipping business? I am confident your experience as a sea captain will give you the necessary command over Huw,' George added dryly.

Luke regarded him glumly. 'But . . . to run the firm successfully, I would need to resign my commission in the East India Company.'

George nodded. 'You would need to live here. At Bryncarog. I'd appreciate your sacrifice, Luke . . . and so would your mother if she were alive. You are very like her, you know? In spirit as well as looks. She was the apple of your grandfather's eye, they were very close. He never really recovered when she died so tragically. So young! She had a deep regard for her father . . . and this firm was his life.'

Luke observed him silently.

'I have your word?'

Reluctantly Luke had given his word, and lived to bitterly regret it. He realised Charlotte and Huw believed he had contrived to obtain his position in the firm, and could fully appreciate Huw's hostility at being usurped. That did not make his position any easier.

And now he was further burdened with Miranda. She was so spoiled and difficult, it was going to be no easy task to control her wilfulness. Already he was beginning to recognise that acting as her guardian was another promise he would probably regret. Sighing deeply, Luke flung himself into the leather chair behind the desk, running a hand through his hair as he pondered his self-inflicted problems.

Miranda quickly fell into a deep, exhausted sleep, not waking all night. The next morning she awoke to the sound of the sea, and the mournful shriek of gulls, loud in her ears. She leapt out of bed, and ran over to look out of the window, rubbing her hand over the grimy pane to clear a patch before she could see through it.

The view was inspiring. The manor was perched on a promontory which jutted out into the sea between two bays. Positioned on the west side of the promontory, it overlooked the smaller bay and, her room being on the west side of the house, Miranda had a view of the beach and across it, to its opposite bank.

Craning her head to peer further, she saw the mouth of a small tidal river, cutting its way across pale yellow sand, and the opposite side of the estuary mouth lined with a jagged mass of rocks. The tide was in, grey and angry-looking, frothing and surging against the rocks, with a stray wave exploding at intervals into a high column of spume. Miranda stood mesmerised by the restless, turbulent energy.

With a slight tap on the door Ellen came in, her appearance more cheerful than on the previous evening.

'Good Morning, Miss Mirry. I hope you had a good rest. I know I slept as if I was in the graveyard itself.' She carefully inspected the floral china-bowl on the washstand before pouring hot water into it, and placed clean towels on the rack.

'Thank you, Ellen,' Miranda said, delighted to see her maid's good-natured face, wondering how she would have fared without her. She squeezed Ellen's hand impulsively. 'I am so glad you are here with me, Ellen.'

'It is only what's expected. It's my duty, Miss Mirry,' Ellen said brusquely, but her face turned pink with pleasure. 'And it is just as well I am here to look after you. The servants have no idea how to look after gentry. No idea at all.' She tutted, shaking her head scornfully.

'Is that why you waited at the table last night?' Miranda asked, remembering her surprise. She patted the bed for Ellen to sit there.

'It certainly is, Miss.' She sank down, shaking her head again. 'They have no proper housemaid, no serving-maid, nothing! I'll have to teach them a few things. But Ceridwen the housekeeper, or whatever she's supposed to be, is a proper witch. Bad tempered old hag,' she said with feeling.

Miranda smiled at her description, having already formed a similar opinion. 'What servants are there?' She pulled up the feather pillow behind her back to be more comfortable.

'Not many! A mixed crowd I can tell you, Miss.' Her brow furrowed thoughtfully. 'There's Olwen, who is a sort of nursemaid to a child called Gwennie . . .'

'Gwennie? Is that Gwendoline? I seem to recall Charlotte spoke of her last night.' She leaned towards her maid. 'Who is she?'

'I don't really know Miss Mirry; a ward, I think. But Olwen, the girl looking after her, is not a proper governess or anything. I think she usually waits at the table, but last night she had been sent into the village on a message.'

'And that is all the staff?' She leaned back against her pillows.

'There is a skivvy, she's a bit soft in the head I think. She comes in from the village each day. Then there's a groom, and there's Wyn, you know him? The one driving the coach? He seems to be hanging around the kitchen all the time. I think he's Ceridwen's husband, they keep looking at me and gabbling away in that heathen tongue to each other. David looked uncomfortable, so I expect . . . '

'David?'

'He's the groom, he seems nice enough.' She gave a little nod, smiling.

'Well that's something. I hope you will not find it too hard, Ellen.' She sighed, adding firmly: 'But you are not to do other people's work! I forbid it!'

As Miranda attended to her toilet, she wondered if she would see her two male relatives this morning, but when she entered the dining-room she found they had already left. Charlotte was still sitting at the table, eating her breakfast. She was dressed in rather a shabby house-dress and wore old-fashioned glasses as she read a journal.

'Good morning, Miranda, my dear. Help yourself to breakfast.' She waved her arm towards the sideboard, which held an assortment of covered dishes in blue and white china. 'There are some kidneys and chops left. At least I think so,' she said, without concern.

Lifting a cover, Miranda wrinkled her nose at the congealing, greasy food, which had not been kept properly warm in chafing dishes. She selected a small portion of scrambled eggs with butter and toast.

'Did you sleep well?' Charlotte asked, putting down her journal.

'Excellently. I believe this sea air must suit me.' Miranda reached for the butter.

'Yes. I missed the sea when I left home,' Charlotte confided.

'You mean when you got married? Why did you return here?' Miranda asked, buttering her toast.

'My husband died in a riding accident. I was only thirty-three.' Charlotte heaved a huge sigh, raising her shoulders.

'How dreadful.' Miranda cut through her toast, scattering crumbs across the tablecloth.

Charlotte nodded. 'Yes. So I came back to Bryncarog to keep house for my brother, George. My Huw was still a little lad.'

'Is George the uncle that my lawyer said had left Llewelyn Shipping to Luke—?' Miranda stopped brushing the crumbs together when Charlotte broke in waspishly.

'But he didn't leave it to Luke.' Her neck seemed to stretch up and she glared at Miranda. 'It was left to both Huw and Luke.'

Uncomfortably aware of her faux pas, Miranda hastened to add: 'Of course, Mr Langdon didn't go into details . . . your brother was unmarried?'

'No. He was married, but his wife died childless. She was always sickly. He welcomed my return to keep house.'

'It must have been a great relief for him.'

'It's three years since George passed away.' She sniffed, dabbing her nose with her handkerchief. 'And I always believed he regarded Huw as a son. The son he never had.' She paused, the pale eyes contemplating Miranda, almost slyly. 'But when he died, we found Luke shared Huw's inheritance.'

Miranda detected a note of anger in her voice again, and realised Charlotte regarded Miranda's own inheritance over Luke in the same light. She obviously believed Huw should have been the sole heir and deeply resented Luke.

Light footsteps raced along the wooden boards of the hall and a child, about five years old, charged through the door, pulling up abruptly as she saw Miranda. Eyes huge and round, she stared inquisitively, chewing her finger.

Charlotte looked over her glasses at the child. 'There you are, Gwendoline. Take your finger out of your mouth and come and meet Miss Miranda. This is Gwennie, Luke's ward,' she explained.

Reluctantly Gwennnie removed the offending finger and took a few steps into the room, bobbing a curtsy.

'Cat got your tongue?' Charlotte snapped.

'Good morning, Mrs Cain and Miss Miranda,' she responded shyly.

'Hello, Gwennie.' Miranda smiled encouragingly. 'Are you coming over to talk to me?'

Gwennie crept over to stand alongside Miranda, eyes downcast. 'Are you very rich?' she whispered.

Miranda raised her eyebrows.

'Ceridwen said you're very rich,' she added with awe. She stood on one leg, rubbing the other foot against the back of her leg.

'It is very rude to pass remarks, Gwennie,' Miranda scolded gently. 'I expect you have been told that?'

The child blushed and nodded, her finger returning to her mouth.

Wanting to soften her words, Miranda asked: 'Have you had your breakfast yet?'

Gwennie's eyes flashed up to Miranda's face and with a shock she saw their sapphire blue colour, the exact colour of Luke's. His ward? More his child, surely? she thought.

'Yes, thank you,' she whispered.

'Would you like to take some tea with me? Perhaps we can get to know each other.'

Her face lit up. 'Yes please.' She beamed at Miranda, and noisily dragging one of the heavy, carved oak chairs closer, climbed up onto it, smoothing down her skirts self-consciously as Miranda poured the tea.

'Sugar?' Miranda's hand poised over the bowl.

The child nodded, her face going pink. She was enchanting. A tiny elfin figure, her hair tumbled in black curls past her shoulders and her sooty lashes, fluttering like butterflies against her cheeks, highlighted her creamy skin.

'She will enjoy that,' Charlotte said sharply. 'She loves being the centre of attention.' She flashed a disapproving glance at Gwennie, whose mouth trembled, and turned down at the corners when she added: 'Take care, little madam!'

Miranda regarded Charlotte in surprise. Her remarks seemed unnecessary since Gwennie had not misbehaved in any way. She found the child delightful, perhaps somewhat subdued, but decided she was probably shy. She obviously held Charlotte in some awe, as her head kept swivelling to observe her.

Finishing her meal, Miranda dabbed her mouth with her napkin. 'Will you show me around, Gwennie?' she asked.

Gwennie nodded eagerly, grasping Miranda's hand in her small one, and pulling her from the room. In daylight Miranda was able to study more of the house, which was a small manor, built about two centuries earlier. It was sturdy and well constructed of some grey stone, which she later found to be limestone; it must have been an impressive house in its time, but had been allowed to run down. The solid oak of the wide, turned staircase was splintered and worn, sadly deficient in polish, as were the rotting window frames. Similarly, the carpets were shabby and threadbare, their colour faded.

Gwennie's quick steps raced from room to room, where the good quality furniture, mostly heavily carved dark oak, showed similar neglect. Miranda wondered why Charlotte didn't take the servants in hand. A painting of two girls hung on one wall and she immediately recognised one as the alluring Bronwen; the other, a paler, less exotic mortal, must be Charlotte, she decided.

'Do you live here all the time?' Miranda asked Gwennie, intrigued by her position in the household.

Gwennie nodded, racing off across the room again, her feet echoing hollowly on the wooden boards. Miranda grabbed her as she flew back.

'Stop! You're making my head spin. Come and talk to me for a minute.'

Gwennie stopped, her finger going to her mouth again as she stared, wide-eyed, at Miranda.

'Why do you live here? Are you an orphan?'

The child shook her head. 'No.'

'Are your parents alive then?' Miranda asked, smoothing the child's thick curls off her face.

She shrugged, dropping her head. 'I don't know.' Gwennie shook her head, and Miranda raised her chin gently, to find her eyes shimmering with tears.

'What's troubling you, little one?'

'Why do I live here?' One tear escaped, trickling down her cheek.

'Don't be a little goose. You live here because . . . ' Miranda hesitated, her mind searching for an acceptable reason. 'So that you can wear pretty dresses and learn lots of things,' she continued. But inside, Miranda reacted angrily to this admission. How dare Luke deny the child her own mother. 'How old are you, Gwennie?'

'Five.'

'Are you learning your letters yet? Perhaps I can help you?' Miranda liked the idea, it would give her something to occupy her time.

'Mistress Kate comes for that.'

'A governess?' Miranda's face fell.

'Oh no! Kate's not a governess.' Gwennie gave a gurgling chuckle, hunching her shoulders. 'Her father's very rich. She's nice. I love Kate. She's very pretty,' she confided. 'Her hair's silvery, and she smells like . . . like flowers,' she added.

'I look forward to meeting her. Shall we go outside?'

'Yes.' Dropping Miranda's hand she skipped ahead through the hall and down the stone steps, skirts and petticoats flying in the April breeze, revealing white pantaloons beneath. She twirled around several times until forced to stop, staggering and giddy.

Miranda caught her as she would have fallen, and

her delighted laugh tinkled again. 'You can't catch me,' she shrieked, darting out of Miranda's arms and racing along the drive.

'Oh yes, I can!' Gathering up her skirts, Miranda raced after her, chasing her around the corner to bump headlong into a figure approaching from the opposite direction. She held onto the two strong arms which gripped her, and she was aware of the knotted iron-hard muscles beneath the cloth. She looked up into Luke's face.

'Very ladylike.' He grinned, for once his eyes dancing with amusement. 'I see you have found a suitable companion.'

Furiously Miranda yanked herself from his grip. 'Companion?' she spat. 'I am trying to entertain a little girl. How dare you patronise me and regard me as a child!'

His smile faded, his eyes cold. 'Yes, I agree. Children like to be noticed,' he said impassively. 'Though I believe it does no good for any child to receive too much attention. They sometimes become spoiled.'

'Spoiled? Do you mean me?' Miranda clenched her fists, her face pale as her temper rose. 'You are contemptible, speaking to me like . . . '

'Don't be silly, Miranda. You have an overblown image of your own importance. What makes you think every remark or thought has to refer to you?' His face was impatient.

Speechless Miranda stamped her foot with frustration . . . and he laughed, infuriating her even further.

'Do you realise when you are cross you resemble a spitting ginger cat?' he taunted and, turning his back on her, he walked away.

Tears rushed to her eyes, and she dashed them away roughly with the back of her hand. Realising she was panting, she took a few deep calming breaths. I hate him! she thought. He is an arrogant, stiff-necked, unfeeling brute . . . I know he meant me! Miranda was certain he was comparing her indulged upbringing with his own and was jealous of the closeness she had enjoyed with their father. He resents me as much as I resent him. He must wish I had never been born, she decided forlornly.

She dropped down onto a stone bench alongside the wall, pressing her hands together, trying to control their trembling.

Gwennie came running back. 'Come on, Miranda. You were 'posed to catch me!' She scrambled up alongside Miranda, huge blue eyes searching her face. She slipped a hand into Miranda's. 'What's the matter?'

Miranda bit her lip and swallowed hard and her smile never reached her eyes. 'Nothing is the matter, Gwennie.'

'Shall we play hide and seek?'

'That's a good idea. You go and hide and I'll count to one hundred.' She watched Gwennie race around the corner, her own emotions now under control. I'll get back at Luke, she vowed silently. I'll find a way to show him I'm not a child. I'll force him to admit I'm a person to be reckoned with, not patronised.

Four

That afternoon, Miranda wandered around to the rear of the house to look for the stables, wistfully thinking of Star back at her family home. He will be wondering what has happened to me, she thought. The gate, leading into the stable compound, lurched back drunkenly on one hinge as she pulled it towards her, as though it was about to fall off completely. Wyn, lounging against the carriage he was supposed to be cleaning, darted a surly glance at her as she entered the yard and continued to puff at a smelly pipe. Ignoring her greeting, he bent down to pick up a wooden bucket and shoved it under the pump, lethargically working the handle. The familiar, pungent odour of animals and manure was reassuring as she entered the stable, and a few of the horses pricked their ears forward with curiosity, looking back at her over their shoulders. Halfway along she stopped by a black stallion, his coat gleaming like silk, and spoke softly to him. He snickered back a greeting but as she entered his stall he lifted his head threateningly with eyes widening. Miranda showed no fear.

'Now, now! Behave yourself!' she scolded. 'You're not cross with me.' Ignoring his warning, she fondled his velvety nose admiringly. 'You're a beauty,' she whispered. 'I wonder what your name is?'

'Oh God!'

Miranda turned at the muffled exclamation, to see a young man staring at her with apprehension.

'Careful Mistress! Please come out! That horse is dangerous.' Dropping the tack he'd been holding, he sidled cautiously into the stall and gripped her arm as the horse's eyes opened wider, whites showing, its nostrils flared.

'There, there, my beauty. Calm down! What's wrong?' Miranda spoke softly and soothingly to the animal. She held her ground, continuing to stroke his soft nose. 'Why is he dangerous?' she asked, in the same even tone.

'Wild he is, Miss, not properly tamed,' the boy whispered, fear in his voice. 'Please come out, Mistress. If anything was to happen to you . . .'

'All right. You back out first, I'll follow.' Miranda spoke quietly but with authority, unconvinced by the boy's tale. She had been amongst horses all her life, understanding them too well to take fright easily.

Once they were out of the stall, the relief on the boy's plain freckled face was mixed with admiration as he explained deferentially: 'Only Captain Llewelyn can ride Satan, Miss. No-one else dares. Satan threw

Mr Huw once, and he thinks Satan needs more breaking in.'

'Rubbish!' Miranda retorted. 'I would easily ride Satan. Saddle him ready for me and I'll go and change.'

The boy's mouth dropped open with astonishment, his eyes wide again with amazement. 'I can't do that, Miss. More than my job's worth, it is.'

She hesitated, realising the boy's dilemma. He may not even know who she was. 'Are you David? The groom?' She smiled at the short, stocky young man trying to allay his fears.

'That's right, Miss.' He touched the carroty forelock which fell over his forehead, his good-natured face beaming. 'You . . . you're Mistress Miranda, the Captain's sister.' His voice held awe. 'The heiress.'

'My goodness! Why does everyone call me the heiress?' Miranda snapped with irritation. 'As if it is some sort of title. Is that all you've been told about me then?'

He blushed crimson, dropping his head and shuffling his feet in embarrassment. 'It is not much I've heard, Miss. Just talk at the house, with Ceridwen and Wyn like.'

She turned away impatiently. 'If only my Star were here,' she sighed. 'I miss him so much.' She saw David's eyes on her, full of understanding.

'Your horse, is he, Miss? I can understand you missing him.'

Miranda nodded. 'I've had him since he was a foal. As soon as he became big enough, I rode him every single day.'

'We've got some other nice horses, like,' he offered, adding belatedly, 'Miss.'

'Very well, saddle me . . . that one,' she said, selecting a large grey mare, which showed promise. 'What is her name?'

'Cariad, Miss.' He began backing her out of the stall.

'Cariad? The name is unfamiliar.'

'Welsh it is, Miss. It means darling, and she is too. She's my favourite,' he added, patting her rump.

Miranda was determined to ride Satan at some future date, but would allow David to become used to her first; he would soon learn to trust her riding abilities. Miranda also wanted Star brought here to Bryncarog, if possible. She must remember to bring the subject up with Luke when she saw him next.

So Luke is Satan's only rider? she mused. Our father was an exceptional horseman; so this accomplishment has obviously been in inherited by both of us. I wonder what Luke's reaction would be to finding his little sister riding Satan? she pondered. The idea gave her immense satisfaction. He will discover I have a will and determination to match his own. This is the way to show him I am not the helpless child he takes me for, she vowed.

Miranda raced back upstairs and burst into her room. She startled Ellen, who was surrounded by a sea of clothes, busily unpacking Miranda's trunks.

'Ellen, I want a riding costume. We did bring the brown one, I believe?'

'Yes, it's here, Miss Mirry. I hung it up this morning. But I've not had time to press the creases out yet,' she said doubtfully, taking it from the closet.

'That will do very well.' Miranda was more than relieved to see it, knowing the warm brown cashmere fabric flattered her pale complexion, rather than draining it, as did black. 'Have you unpacked my boots?'

'I think so . . . but I'm not sure about the habit.' Ellen shook out the jacket and held it up critically, brushing at it with her hand. 'You want to give a good impression, 'specially on your first day.'

'Impress whom? There is no-one here to impress, unless you mean poor Charlotte?' she giggled. 'Or Ceridwen,' she added, pulling a face.

'Her!' Ellen sniffed, her expression a perfect example of a servant's disdain for one considered her inferior. 'Who cares about her? She walks around in a ragged old skirt. It needs a good wash, it's disgraceful.' She stopped, darting her mistress a sideways glance. 'But what about Master Huw?'

'Master Huw?' Miranda said casually. 'What do you mean?'

Ellen pursed her lips, not taken in, as she knew Miranda too well. 'He's very handsome, Miss Mirry.' Her expression was disarmingly innocent as she examined the hem of the riding skirt.

'Perhaps. Though he lacks the polish of the men I have been acquainted with. But in this backwater I suppose I can hardly expect otherwise. He is quite attractive,' she conceded.

'Then, Miss Mirry, you'll wait for me to . . .'

'No, Ellen. It is quite satisfactory as it is,' she directed.

To Miranda's surprise as she approached the stables she found both the grey and Satan tethered outside, saddled ready to ride.

'Am I to have a choice after all then?' she laughed, but stopped abruptly as Luke came out of the stables.

'Hello, Miranda.' He gave a slight bow, his glance travelling swiftly over her riding attire, which she knew suited her much better than the ill-fitting garments she had been wearing.

'David tells me you wish to ride?' Picking up the colour of his silk cravat, his eyes flashed a startling blue. 'I'm sorry I am unable to accompany you but I have a call to make.'

'I have no wish for company,' she dismissed him. 'And you have no worry on my behalf, I am well used to riding alone,' Miranda added frostily, still unforgiving of his earlier, contemptuous comments. 'I would have chosen Satan but David tells me you are his only rider.' Her tone was deliberately mocking.

'That is so,' he said, his face impassive. 'But in any case, I would prefer you to take no risks whilst in my care. Cariad will give you a good ride, I am sure.' He bent his athletic form to cup his hands, ready to assist her onto the grey.

'Thank you!' For the second time, Miranda was very much aware of his restrained strength as she gripped his arm, the bunched muscles taut beneath his sleeve.

'David, accompany Mistress Miranda on her ride, please.' Luke called over his shoulder.

'But I've just told you I don't need—' Miranda began with exasperation.

'Miranda. You may well be a capable rider, though I have not yet witnessed your skills, but you are unused to the local terrain and its inherent dangers.' His eyes were steely now, his lips pulled tight. 'Please realise my only concern is for your safety, not to thwart your pleasure as you believe.' He vaulted into the saddle, touched his hat to her with his whip and cantered away.

David shuffled uncomfortably as Miranda glared after Luke, breathing hard. She twisted her own whip in her hands as though she wished she could bring it down on Luke's back. How could he humiliate her like this in front of the servants?

'I'm sorry Mistress, but I have to take the Captain's orders, don't I? I won't get in your way.'

'You'll have to catch me first,' she snapped and tapped Cariad on the rump, causing her to gallop away with David hastily leaping up on another unsaddled horse in order to follow her.

The road led away from the house, climbing a little before it divided into two. One continued inland and the other wound towards the cliffs, overlooking the bay to the west as it followed the headland. Miranda chose the latter road and picked her way along the unmade path. She found herself high above the sea, looking down on the restless water below.

Reining in her horse, she carefully walked Cariad a few paces nearer to the cliff's edge above the bay, drinking in the wild beauty of the scene below. The wind, blustery today, was damp against her face as it blew in from the southwest, here and there breaking the surface of the grey water into white, foaming patches. Looking back into the bay, Miranda could see up the little valley disappearing inland and the mouth of the river that bubbled through it, spilling across the beach. Where grassy turf took over from the sand, the valley climbed to a higher level and, near a small waterfall, nestled a little cluster of whitewashed cottages.

Tapping her heels against Cariad's side, she continued further onto the headland, thorns catching at her clothes as she cantered along paths worn between tangles of brambles and gorse, already full of buds bursting with golden bloom. Once on the headland, she could see the limestone rocks below, torn into a jagged coastline from endless pounding by the waves. From her viewing point, the second, larger bay on the eastern side of the dividing promontory, was visible.

This beach, dressed with corn-bright sand, stretched virgin and unmarked, although at the furthest extremity the beach was broken up by a layer of low rocks creeping down to the sea. These rocks swept up to join larger ones, which formed the furthest boundary of the bay. A number of small sailing boats bobbed around in that area of surrounding water.

On either side of her, beyond these bays, fingers of land probed into the sea, forming numerous inlets, receding behind one another into the distance in paling shades of green and pewter. 'It's beautiful,' she whispered.

Alongside her, David smiled, nodding. 'Yes, Miss. There's a fair sight, isn't it?'

Cariad snorted, tossing her head and Miranda dropped a hand to her neck. 'Can we get down onto the beach?' she asked.

'You mean Llanmor, the big one, Miss? There is a path leading to it, a way yonder it is. But the tide's coming in now, it'll soon be covering the hard sand.'

'But surely that is a long way off?' She pointed, shading her eyes with her other hand. 'It seems such a large expanse of uncovered sand.'

'Would be better not to risk it, Mistress. By the time we get the horses down there like . . .'

'Does the sea rise and fall the same time each day?'

David laughed. 'Why no, Miss. Full tide's roughly an hour later each time.' His lips still turned up slightly with amusement. Having lived near the sea all his life, he could not believe anyone was unaware of this simple fact. 'And there's two tides a day.'

'So we will probably be able to go down there tomorrow? But certainly the next?'

'That's right, Miss.'

'I shall look forward to riding on the beach.' She turned the horse's head away from the sea, making her way back up the path towards Bryncarog.

'Does Gwennie not take her meals with the family?' Miranda enquired, seeing only Charlotte waiting in the dining-room that evening.

'No. Just luncheon and not always then. Olwen sees to the child's welfare.' Her eyes darted at Miranda, then slid away. 'She shouldn't regard herself as one of the family.'

'Not unless she is one, of course?' Miranda replied, studying Charlotte's face.

But Charlotte ignored the remark. 'Will you take a sherry, my dear? The men seem to be missing as usual.'

'Thank you.' As she took the crystal glass from Charlotte's hand, she perceived a slight chip on its rim.

A big-boned awkward girl soon appeared to wait at the table, head drooping shyly, her threadbare, woollen dress covered by a crumpled white apron. Miranda noticed her large hands, red and chapped, as she shuffled the plates awkwardly onto the table. One slid sideways, almost landing in Miranda's lap.

'Take care, you foolish girl!' Charlotte snapped impatiently.

'Sorry, Mrs Cain,' Olwen whispered, her plain face turning blood red, behind the curtain of lank hair hanging untidily over her face.

Miranda felt sorry for the girl, realising she was very shy and unsure of herself and vowed to mention it to Ellen. Her capable maid would soon take her in hand.

Left to themselves, Charlotte began her chattering as before and Miranda seized this opportunity to learn more about the Llewelyn family background.

'I thought Olwen was Gwennie's nursemaid?'

Charlotte's eyebrows rose. 'Nursemaid? Well . . . I suppose you could call her that. It seems a very grand title. She see to the child's welfare.'

'What are her circumstances? Gwennie's, I mean?'

Charlotte threw a suspicious glance at Miranda. 'I know nothing about the matter,' she said primly. 'She is Luke's ward.'

'Is she Luke's child?' Miranda said bluntly.

Charlotte gasped, her face turning pink. 'Miranda!

I am shocked! Really shocked. Such talk is not for ladies.' Waggling her head, she began rattling her cutlery across her plate, as though engrossed in cutting her meat.

Realising she was not going to receive an answer and unwilling to further upset Charlotte, Miranda changed the subject. 'Where are Luke and Huw this evening?'

'I never question their whereabouts.' Charlotte reached for the salt-cellar, tipping a scoopful onto the side of her plate.

'Do they manage the firm between them?' Miranda took the salt handed to her by Charlotte.

Charlotte's mouth tightened. 'Yes. But Luke likes to call the tune.' She tossed her head. 'Huw succeeded very well before Luke arrived.'

'You mean Huw managed the firm before Luke arrived?' Miranda sipped a mouthful of soup.

Charlotte pursed her lips, her pale eyes hard and bright. 'Yes. Without Luke,' she snapped. 'My brother's health was failing for many years. Long before he died, he depended on Huw to manage everything.'

'I see. So at that time Huw ran the business for your brother single-handed?'

She nodded. 'Of course. No sea captain in charge then. No one to tell Huw what to do.' A note of bitterness had crept into her voice, and once again Miranda read her resentment at Luke's role in the family business.

'Then surely Huw is experienced enough to reach his own decisions without reference to Luke?'

'Huw is anxious not to cause disharmony. He's too easy-going.' She shrugged her shoulders dismissively. 'He lets Luke get away with it. Those high-handed ways of his. He always gets away with it!'

A surge of empathy with Huw swept through Miranda, and she nodded sympathetically. 'I can well understand your feelings. I have already been on the receiving end of Luke's arrogance.'

Charlotte smiled, nodding her approval at Miranda's words. 'Too good-natured, that's Huw's trouble. He was always a happy child. Never any problems with him. Now Luke—'

'Good evening, ladies. Forgive me for being late.' Huw sauntered towards them with long, lazy strides. Bending, he dropped a kiss on his mother's cheek, as she dimpled with pleasure. He pulled the cord for the servants to serve him food before pouring himself a sherry. Standing, glass in hand, he towered over Miranda. 'And how is my cousin today? Recovered from the horrors of your journey, I hope?' His tone was interested and friendly.

Miranda observed that, though his lanky frame was slighter than Luke's, his bearing was athletic, and his well-cut clothes hung immaculately on his frame. A suavely handsome man, with a smooth, boyish face, Miranda perceived an attractive dimple clefting his chin each time he smiled. His hair, straight and blonde, kept falling over his heavy-lidded hazel eyes, and he had an engaging habit of throwing it back with one hand.

He conversed easily during the meal and Miranda found herself falling under the spell of his winsome smile. She felt it embraced her, as it swept across his face, before terminating in that tantalising dimple. Unlike Luke, Huw seemed interested in what she had to say, hanging on her every word. By the end of the evening Miranda had to agree with Charlotte, Huw's easy-going charm must prove instantly attractive to all . . . especially the ladies.

Five

Miranda got into the habit of riding each day with David; it helped to take her mind off her misery about her father. She enjoyed exploring the surrounding area, but the more she went riding, the more determined she became to have Star brought to Bryncarog. Near the end of the second week, she was returning from her ride when a carriage turned smartly into the courtyard. A fine carriage, windows and paintwork sparkling, it was drawn by a well-matched pair of horses, their coats gleaming, harnesses bright with polish. The dark green livery of the driver matched the colour of the coach and its accoutrements, comparing favourably, in Miranda's eyes, with the coaches at Rushton Hall. Miranda wondered who could be visiting. She shielded her eyes from the sun, trying to catch sight of the occupants, but only got a glimpse of a lady's rose-coloured bonnet, be-ribboned in deeper pink, which effectively hid her face.

Miranda cantered behind the coach and dismounted onto the worn step, handing her reins to David as the coach driver jumped down to open the carriage door. He assisted a tall, graceful girl to emerge She was elegantly attired in a carriage-dress of fine wool which topped a sprigged muslin dress, the colours of its flowers matching her bonnet. Catching sight of Miranda on the step, she hesitated, frowning in surprise. Then her face cleared, her generous mouth widening into a smile. She took a few steps towards Miranda, holding out her hand.

'Mistress. Forgive my impertinence, but are you Miranda, Luke's sister?' Her voice, low and melodious, complemented her serene, oval features. She had a flawless, rose-petal complexion and pale-blonde hair which peeped from her bonnet.

'I am.' It was Miranda's turn to be surprised, and rather nonplussed, that this stranger should know her. 'But I must confess you have the advantage over me.'

The woman chuckled, and to Miranda's amazement, impulsively reached forward, and gripped her shoulders, kissing her cheek lightly. 'I am—' she began.

Before she could finish her sentence a dynamic bundle of flying skirts and pantaloons flung itself at her, two arms entwined tightly around her legs. 'Kate! Kate!' Gwennie shrieked.

'Gwennie, my sweet, you will have me over,' Kate laughingly protested. Stooping, she gathered the child in her arms and dropped a kiss in her hair. 'And you know it's very bad manners to interrupt your elders,' Kate admonished gently, putting a finger to her lips.

'But she's Miranda, the Captain's sister,' Gwennie said, tugging at her sleeve.

'So you're Kate?' Miranda examined her frankly, judging her to be about five years older than herself. 'I've been waiting to meet you. Gwennie has told me much about you. But in truth I expected a woman of mature years, Gwennie mentioned silver hair . . .' She broke off, silenced by Kate's low, throaty laugh.

'She always insists my hair is silver,' she chuckled. Then, her expression becoming serious, she murmured: 'Allow me to offer you my condolences, Miranda. It must be extremely hard for you, having lost your father, to also have to leave your home.' Over Gwennie's head, she appraised Miranda. 'I must admit you are not in the least as I expected either.'

Miranda frowned. 'Did you expect me to resemble Luke?'

Kate's laugh bubbled again, without false embarrassment. 'Yes. I suppose I did, foolish of me of course. I must have expected those smouldering blue eyes and thick black locks.' Her words drew Miranda's glance to those other tumbling, black curls beneath Kate's hand and as her glance followed Miranda's down, Kate removed her hand from Gwennie's head.

'Then I am sorry to disappoint you as I follow the looks of my own mother,' Miranda said shortly. She tapped her riding whip against her thigh.

'Disappoint me? When you are so lovely? But I confess I'd entirely forgotten you and Luke had different mothers.'

Miranda smiled, warmed by her honesty. 'It doesn't matter.'

'I've been looking forward to your arrival, ever since Luke told me you were coming to Bryncarog.' She smiled, catching Miranda's hand. 'As soon as I saw you I realised you could only be Miranda. I overheard my servants say you had arrived. Olwen called with a message, and you know how they gossip. She remarked how pretty you are.'

Kate pushed her arm companionably through Miranda's as they entered the house. 'I hope we can be friends . . . Miranda? I take it we can dispense with formality? There are few girls near my own age living near . . . though I realise I am older than you,' she hastened to add. She gave Miranda's arm a squeeze. 'I always wished for a younger sister.'

Miranda nodded, though she didn't agree. She had always thoroughly enjoyed being an only child, though it had since proved untrue. She had revelled in her doting father's indulgence – nothing had been too good for his little girl. Captivated by Kate's frankness, she found her openness and complete lack of pretence refreshingly different. A rebel herself, Miranda empathised with this facet of Kate's character, deciding they probably could become friends.

Charlotte came bouncing into the hall. Seeing Kate, both hands quivered into the air, before settling to pat her hair and flutter down her skirts. 'Why, Miss Kate! I had no idea you were here,' she chirped breathlessly. 'You've come to help little Gwennie with her reading? Or to meet Miranda?' she added, her eyes flying to Kate's arm linked with Miranda's.

'Both I hope, Mrs Cain,' Kate said, as she undid the ribbons on her bonnet.

'Where are those servants?' Charlotte darted round impatiently, almost bumping into Ellen who had appeared silently behind her.

Ellen dropped a small curtsy. 'Can I take your perlise and bonnet, Mistress?' she said quietly, addressing Kate.

Charlotte nodded with approval. 'We will take tea in the drawing-room, please, Ellen,' Charlotte instructed her regally.

Miranda smothered a smile, sure Charlotte was well pleased with her new servant, so attentive to the proprieties of correct behaviour. Had Thomas been here, he would have had everything at Bryncarog running like clockwork in under a week, Miranda thought bleakly. Unbidden, thoughts of Rushton Hall flooded through her, filling her with an overwhelming longing to be in her own home with all the people she loved. Dear Papa . . . Miranda allowed her mind to wander, paying no attention to the conversation.

'Miranda . . .?'

She gave a start, realising Charlotte and Kate were both looking at her, obviously expecting a reply. Miranda bit her lip, trying to swallow the lump which had suddenly formed in the back of her throat. 'I'm sorry?' she said, her voice croaky.

'We were sympathising with you being so far from home.' Kate's warm brown eyes seemed to read her feelings.

Miranda nodded, but distanced herself from the small talk which Charlotte loved. The more Miranda began to know Charlotte the more she reminded her of a pecking bird, head on one side, eyes darting everywhere, missing nothing.

By the time Charlotte retired for her afternoon nap, Gwennie had fallen asleep on the chair near the window.

Hearing Miranda's little sigh of relief, Kate gave a gurgling chuckle. 'You find her wearing?' she whispered.

'She is very sweet,' Miranda protested, not wishing to be disloyal. Aware she had neglected Kate, Miranda groped for a subject of conversation. 'Your father has a coal mine, I believe someone said? I know nothing of industry. It is all agriculture where I live.'

'Well, you probably know as much about coal as I do.' Kate pulled a face. 'It's not exactly exciting, and horribly hard and dirty labour for any man. I wish Papa was engaged in some other commerce.'

'There is a great deal of industry in these parts, I believe?' Miranda's knowledge of Wales was limited, though she had tried to learn more about the area before leaving home.

'Very much so. The port of Swansea is growing by the year. It will soon be challenging Bristol at this rate. Of course Luke spends much time away on business in Bristol, doesn't he?'

'Does he? He doesn't confide in me,' Miranda said shortly. 'He treats me like a child.'

'Surely not?' Kate's expression was thoughtful. 'I think you misjudge him. 'He is a man who conceals his true feelings, I believe . . .'

'Hides his feelings!' Miranda spat, jumping to her

feet. 'He has revealed them only too clearly to me. He dislikes me, finds me nothing but an unfortunate nuisance.'

Kate's brows wrinkled, her face crumpling with distress. 'I'm sorry to hear you say that, but I'm sure it's not true. I know he would be upset to hear you saying that.'

Miranda shrugged, unconvinced. It was obvious Kate liked Luke. The young woman studied Miranda reflectively. 'I hope you don't mind but do I understand the situation correctly? Charlotte mentioned that you and Luke met recently for only the first time?'

Miranda nodded. 'That's quite true. I wasn't even aware of his existence until after my father's death,' she said bitterly.

Kate was obviously shocked by this admission. 'But that's dreadful. How could it happen? You mean to say your father never told you that you had a brother?'

'He told me nothing of Luke or his mother.' Her voice trembled slightly as she added: 'I always believed my mother was Papa's first and only wife.'

'But . . . didn't your mother realise it was your father's second marriage? Surely the servants must have known? Would have said?'

'The servants said nothing, though it seems everyone, including Mama, did know,' Miranda replied, turning away from Kate. 'I was fourteen years old when Mama died, but she had never mentioned Luke or Papa's first wife to me. It seems it was Papa's wish. Apparently Luke was only two when his mother died.' Miranda sighed. 'I'm afraid Papa was remiss in this matter,' she admitted reluctantly. 'I know he could be harsh at times, though with others, never with me or Mama. You see, Luke's mother died in childbirth with their second child, and it seems Papa . . . ' She hesitated, reluctant to admit to her father's discrepancies.

'It seems what?' Kate prompted.

'It seems Papa was bitter when his wife and baby died and . . . well . . . he almost rejected Luke. It appears he and Luke were never close, never saw eye to eye and . . . and Luke eventually ran away from home. It was before I was born. Papa forbade everybody, including my Mama, to mention Luke or his mother. Luke never returned to Rushton Hall before Papa died.'

'Poor Luke,' Kate whispered, her eyes glistening with unshed tears. 'I've never heard this sad tale before.'

Miranda was silent and walked over to the window to stare out blindly. For the first time she was able to empathise with that lonely little boy, unwanted and unloved. Able to understand why Luke considered her self-centred and spoiled.

'It must indeed have been a great shock for you to discover this unknown sibling?' Kate flashed her a puzzled glance. 'And of course you would have believed yourself to be your father's heir. Forgive me for asking, but do you and Luke share the inheritance? I ask only because the servants keep referring to you as the heiress.'

Miranda turned back from the window, rolling her

eyes in despair. 'I know. In actual fact . . .' She hesitated, her heart racing uncomfortably as the injustice of her father's will finally hit home. Shrugging her shoulders she sidestepped the question. 'Papa's lawyer has all the details. He will sort everything out when I come of age.'

Unaware of Miranda's discomfort Kate continued: 'Luke must welcome his inheritance coming into the business; the firm is in dire straits, I hear. It may be long past, but my father says the war years were not kind to Llewelyn Shipping. Many local seamen were pressed into service . . .' She broke off as she caught sight of Gwennie, now awake, yawning and stretching sleepily. 'Did you have a nice nap, Gwennie?'

Miranda was glad of a diversion as Kate addressed the child. 'As soon as you're ready we'll go to the nursery,' Kate said, smiling.

'You'd like some cordial before you start?' Miranda asked. 'I'm thirsty myself and I'm sure Gwennie would appreciate a glass of milk.' She pulled the bellcord a few times, but there was no response from the servants. She gave an exasperated sigh, snapping crossly: 'There is absolutely no point in having a bell cord. I'll leave you both to your studies and send someone along with your refreshments.'

Miranda made her way to the kitchen and found Ceridwen's bent form, hunched over, cleaning vegetables at the scrubbed wooden table. She turned and scowled at Miranda.

'Didn't you hear the bell?' Miranda said sharply.

'Busy, aren't I?' Ceridwen whined. 'Only one pair of 'ands I've got.' Miranda was shocked at the malevolence in the woman's beady eyes.

'Are there no other servants to help you?'

'Help? Huhh! Just these!' She waved both gnarled hands in the air, spattering muddy water over Miranda. 'I does everything.' As she crossed to the fire, she wiped her hands in the checked flannel apron she wore over her red skirt, her wooden clogs clacking on the flagged floor.

'Not even a kitchen maid?'

Ceridwen ignored her, lifting the lid off the pan suspended over the fire, and dropping it to the floor with a noisy clatter.

'Well I would like some service now, please, Ceridwen,' Miranda said firmly, 'and I will see that you get some extra help in the house.' Disregarding Ceridwen's mutterings, Miranda gave her instructions and walked away. She intended to see that both a housemaid and kitchen maid were put into service at Bryncarog before the week was out.

The more Miranda considered Kate's words the more disturbed she became. Obviously if Llewelyn Shipping is in financial trouble, Luke is even more likely to begrudge me inheriting Papa's estates, she thought. Surely Papa should have realised this before he put me in Luke's keeping? She sighed deeply. Luke has every reason to hate me, she decided.

The sun was low in the sky by the time Miranda heard Gwennie's feet running up to the drawing-room where she sat playing the piano, which was badly out of tune. Gwennie tapped on the door and skipped over to Miranda, followed by Kate.

'No more lessons today, Miranda.' The child hung onto the scratched top of the piano, balancing on one leg, swinging the other, her thumb stuck in her mouth. 'I like that music.'

'I'm leaving now, Miranda,' Kate said. 'But why don't you come over one afternoon and visit us? You can use the Bryncarog carriage; Wyn knows the way. You can meet Mama, and perhaps my brother, Charles, if he is at home.'

'I'd love that, Kate, I find it quiet here . . . there is nothing much to do, other than my riding of course. Thank you, I'll look forward to it.'

After waving goodbye to Kate, Miranda accompanied Gwennie upstairs to the nursery where Olwen was repairing Gwennie's clothes. The young girl leapt to her feet as Miranda entered, her sewing tumbling to the floor as she bobbed a curtsy.

'Hello, Olwen. I wanted to speak to you.'

'Yes, Miss.' Wide-eyed, Olwen stared fearfully at Miranda before dropping her head and hiding her plain face behind a curtain of unkempt hair.

'What exactly are your duties?' she asked the tongue-tied girl.

'I looks after Gwennie, Miss.' Her voice was so low Miranda could hardly hear her words.

Miranda stretched a reassuring hand to the trembling girl. 'Olwen. Surely you're not afraid of me?' The girl shook her head silently and Miranda squeezed her arm gently. 'I won't hurt you – in fact I'd like to help.' By coaxing the information from her, Miranda discovered Olwen came from Swansea, had very little education and received no instructions of any sort from Charlotte regarding her duties.

'I'll see what I can do, Olwen,' she promised. 'And I must say you do very well at keeping Gwennie clean and neat.'

Olwen's heavy jaw dropped with surprise at such unaccustomed praise, and she beamed widely, her face flushing with pleasure. '*Diolch* . . . I mean . . . thank you, Mistress,' she whispered.

Miranda went immediately to approach Charlotte about the subject of increasing the number of servants.

'More servants?' Charlotte exclaimed. 'Whatever do you want more servants for?'

'I should think that it is obvious, Charlotte,' Miranda sighed. 'There are never any servants when we need them. And Ellen is often doing duty as a housemaid, which she should not be . . .'

'It does the girl no harm. You want her to just be your maid? It's hardly enough to keep her busy.'

'I do not wish her employed on other duties. She has more than enough work doing what she is engaged for. I don't wish her employed on other duties,' Miranda insisted sharply. 'She is unused to such work.'

'You've been used to an affluent household,' Charlotte sniffed. 'I'm not saying we don't need them. I would certainly appreciate more servants.'

'Then you agree with me?'

'But how can we afford them? The business is hard stretched. It has to support us all,' Charlotte said petulantly. 'Why don't you ask Luke?'

'Ask Luke? What about asking Huw? I am sure he is concerned for your comfort.'

'Huw? Certainly he is concerned for me.' She gave

her girlish giggle. 'But he is not concerned with household matters. He would consider it woman's business.'

'Then can't you simply say you need a bigger household budget?' Miranda ran a hand through her hair with exasperation.

Charlotte tossed her head. 'I told you before, Luke controls money matters. You must ask him.' She walked away from Miranda and picked up her embroidery. 'This is turning out quite well, don't you think?' Charlotte considered the matter closed.

Infuriated, Miranda turned away. Charlotte was absolutely hopeless, sometimes she seemed to have no sense. Surely Bronwen must have been very different to have attracted and married Papa? But never mind, I have the answer, she decided. I will approach Luke about my idea after dinner.

But Luke did not appear at dinner for almost a week.

Ellen approached Olwen.

'Would you like me to teach you the right way to wait at table for the gentry? You need someone to show you how to do it properly.'

Miranda had told Ellen that poor Olwen had received no training in her duties and had suggested Ellen might like to help the girl. So, on meeting Olwen in the hall Ellen decided to approach her directly.

For a brief moment, Olwen's eyes lifted shyly from under her lashes before she nodded her head. 'Yes please, Miss,' she muttered.

'You don't have to call me Miss,' Ellen chuckled.

'My name's Ellen.'

Olwen looked respectful. 'But you knows so much about quality, like . . .' she dropped her voice to a conspiratorial whisper, adding: 'Ceridwen won't like it though, will she?'

'What has it got to do with her?' Ellen snorted.

Olwen shot an apprehensive glance towards the kitchen fearing Ceridwen might overhear. 'But she's in charge like, isn't she?'

'She is certainly not in charge of me.' Ellen bristled at the suggestion. 'I'll talk to you about it another time, Olwen,' she promised, as Ceridwen came into the hall.

'Miss 'igh and mighty 'erself is it?' Ceridwen sniffed as Ellen pushed past her into the kitchen. 'I never met a maid what thinks she's a lady before.' Her beady eyes gleamed spitefully. 'If you got time to 'ang about talking you can just give me a 'and with the baking.'

Ellen ignored her and lifted her bonnet from its hook in the kitchen closet, tying the ribbons under her chin.

'Did you 'ear what I said?' Ceridwen stood barring her way, her mouth working, a long droplet suspended from her nose.

Ellen's mouth turned down with distaste. 'Get out of my way, you filthy old witch. You have no right to order me about.'

'We'll see about that, won't we? I'll see what Mistress Charlotte 'as to say about this.'

'I am Miss Miranda's maid. Why don't you ask her?' Ellen said scornfully.

Ceridwen decided to back off. 'Where are you off

to, then?' Scowling, her glance raked Ellen from head to foot. 'Done up like a lady, is it? Got ideas above your station 'aven't you, my girl? No good will come of it, you'll see.' She took hold of Ellen's fine green linen skirt, one Ellen had made from a cast-off dress of Miranda's, feeling the material between her thumb and finger.

Ellen snatched it from her hand. 'Leave that alone,' she snapped, smoothing her skirt back into place. 'You put your dirty hands all over it and it will need a wash before I even wear it.' She flounced over to the door and went out, banging it hard behind her.

Once outside, Ellen let out a long breath of frustration, stamping her feet as she walked, hearing them scrunch satisfyingly on the limestone chippings which covered the path. How she hated that crafty, spiteful old woman! Although Ellen's whole life had been spent in service, as had her mother before her, it was her first experience of spiteful, conniving servants, like Ceridwen and her husband, Wyn, who in particular seemed to do as little as possible and seemed always on the lookout for what he could get.

How different it had been at Rushton Hall. As long as she could remember, Ellen's mother had been Mrs Rushton's personal maid, devoted to Miranda's mother as Ellen now was to Miranda. As soon as Ellen was old enough, her mother started taking her with her to Rushton Hall until, at eleven years of age, Ellen had started as a little housemaid. Her work was fetching and carrying, but she was well treated, her duties light and her efforts were always appreciated by the family.

'Ma, I wish I was home with you and all the others now,' she whispered longingly. Tears welled up in her soft blue eyes as she pictured her practical, matter-of-fact mother, imagining those strong arms wrapped around her, holding her close. I wish I had never come to this horrible place where people don't even know how to speak the King's English properly, she thought. Miss Mirry doesn't like it here either. And that silly Mrs Cain! She has no idea how to manage the house and staff. Still . . . I could hardly have left Miss Mirry to come here all on her own. How would she have managed without me?

During her reverie she had been marching briskly up the cliff path and now arriving at the top she stopped to catch her breath and studied the scene below. The sea was calm, with hardly a ripple to disturb its metallic surface, reflecting the colour of the cloudless sky. Three sailing boats, making for the little harbour of Llanmor at the far end of the beach, hung becalmed and listless in the water, their unmoving reflections mirrored as though by glass. A few gulls soared lethargically above them, not even screaming today, and the rest had settled in a little flotilla on the sea, undulating gently with the water.

It's real pretty here, Ellen admitted to herself. If it wasn't for Ceridwen and Wyn maybe I could get to like it. Look at all that lovely sparkling water.

'Ellen!' Hearing her name, she turned, seeing an agile figure bounding lithely up the path, an arm waving wildly. Shading her eyes, she tried to see who it was, as he called again: 'Ellen! Are you not going to wait for an old friend then?'

She drew in a breath, her heart pausing for a single moment before it began fluttering like a wild thing against her ribs. 'Nezer!' she whispered, her face breaking into a delighted smile. She took a few steps to meet him as he raced up, taking both her hands in his, gazing into her face, his black eyes bright with pleasure.

'I knew it was you, Ellen. Wouldn't I know that beautiful face anywhere? Sure it's lovely to see you again.'

Ellen gazed back at him, her eyes prickling again with threatening tears, but this time tears of joy.

'Nezer. I . . . I didn't even know your people were in this area,' she stuttered breathlessly, overcome with emotion. She shook her head, biting her lip. 'I still can't believe it's really you.' Her eyes wandered over him hungrily . . . his lean, swarthy features, his glossy black hair tied back with a leather thong. His full-sleeved homespun shirt, dyed a bright flamboyant red and open at the neck, hung loosely on his spare frame, and was topped by a worn leather jerkin. In one ear was the tantalising glint of a gold earring.

Nezer's face creased in a wide grin, teeth gleaming against his dark skin as he grasped her hands tighter, bright eyes dancing. 'Didn't I hear your mistress had gone to live at Bryncarog and I knew you'd be too soft-hearted to allow her to go alone? We travelled here from Glastonbury only last week and I've been looking out for you ever since.'

'I am glad to see you Nezer, I've been so unhappy. I have no friends here, I miss my Ma . . . and those horrible servants are hopeless and . . .'

'And here I am to cheer you. Where is it you're making for?'

'Nowhere in particular, I just wanted to get away from the house. Miss Mirry is out visiting and I thought I'd take a walk in the fresh air, try to clear my mind of . . . of . . . and all I can do is think about home . . .' Her voice broke on a sob and she covered her face with both hands. Giving in to her misery, she began to cry in earnest, deep racking sobs which shook her whole body as Nezer tentatively reached his arms around her, holding her gently.

'Don't, my sweet, don't cry. I'm here and to be sure I'll never leave you as long as you need me, Ellen.'

Head on his chest, Ellen snuggled up closer to him as he rocked her, at peace for the first time since she had left home. A pleasant, musky smell, mingled with fragrant woodsmoke hung about him as she became aware of the sinewy arms around her. She raised her face to find him gazing down at her, his expression tender. He smoothed one finger gently across each cheek in turn, wiping away her tears.

'Are you better now?'

'Yes. Much better, thank you, Nezer.' She pulled away from him, suddenly overwhelmed with self-consciousness at the nearness of their bodies.

He took her hand in his and together they strolled across the cliffs, the grass springy under their feet. The gorse bushes were smothered with golden blossom and caught at their clothes as they passed. Ellen kept her eyes shyly averted from him, but was well aware that he kept turning to look at her every now and then. He called me 'my sweet', she thought, her heart dancing with joy. He called me 'my sweet'.

''tis sure I've missed you, Ellen, so much . . . and wasn't I afraid you might have forgotten me?' He glanced at her to gauge her reaction.

'Forgotten you?' she cried. 'I could never forget you, Nezer.' She saw his face light up. 'How long did you say you've been here?' she asked, fighting to control her cartwheeling emotions.

He shrugged. 'Only a week. We've come straight from the Midsummer Solstice at Gloucestershire. It is an assembly of grand importance to the Romany clans.'

'What sort of importance?' she asked with interest.

'Marriages to be confirmed, babies given their names.' He stopped to untangle a gorse bush caught in her skirt.

'Then you'll not be moving on again yet?' She held her skirt away from the other grasping bushes.

'Not yet.' He was looking out to sea and screwed up his eyes, shading them with his hand.

'Nezer . . .?' she began, as he stopped walking.

'Look!' He pulled her to face the sea. 'Do you see it there? That's a cormorant.'

'A what?' Her nose wrinkled with puzzlement and she put a hand over her eyes.

'A cormorant. That dark bird, there in the water.' He pointed to the bird bobbing gently on the smooth surface of the water.

'A seagull, you mean?'

'No! Not a gull. 'Tis a cormorant; he'll dive down soon. Watch!'

As Ellen squinted at the sparkling water she saw the bird dive, to vanish beneath the surface. 'He's not come up,' she said anxiously when the bird did not reappear immediately.

'Keep watching. He swims under water and then . . . there he is! Can you see him further out? See!' He gripped her shoulder, pointing again.

Ellen clapped her hands with delight as the bird resurfaced several feet from where he'd disappeared. 'Isn't he clever? Let's see if he does it ag— Oh! Is that another one?'

Nezer nodded, enjoying her pleasure, watching the girl's animated face rather than the birds.

'There's another on the rocks over there. He's got his wings open.' He pointed again to another bird perched on the rocks, both wings held wide.

'Isn't he funny? Why is he doing that?' Ellen chuckled.

'To dry his feathers.'

They sat on the grass, side by side, taking delight in the birds' aquatic antics, taking pleasure from being near to each other.

They were sitting right at the point of the promontory where it jutted into the sea and gazed down at the rocks below at the waves lapping sluggishly. Immediately to their left an inlet in the rocks formed a miniature cove, seemingly inaccessible from land, with tiny limestone islets clustered around its entrance. Further across the cliffs on their left they were able to see the sweep of the larger bay and watched the swell ripple rhythmically up the beach, encroaching on the sand with creamy fingers of lace before creeping back reluctantly.

'Did you miss me when we moved on?' Nezer

asked. Picking a blade of grass, he put it in his mouth.

'I did. Very much, Nezer. And you? Did . . . did you miss me?' Ellen whispered hesitantly.

'Are you needing to ask?' he said simply, his frank gaze finding and holding hers.

Ellen averted her eyes, afraid of her own racing heart. He took her capable hand in his, turning it over, gently stroking the roughened palm.

'Do you read palms, Nezer?'

He laughed, shaking his head. 'To be sure it's work for the women.'

'But do you know how it's done?' she asked, slightly breathlessly.

'Well enough, I suppose.' He grinned, a flash of white teeth.

'Tell me,' she said eagerly.

Smiling, he looked down at her hand still resting in his. 'See this line here?' He traced his finger across her palm. 'It means you have a long life . . .'

'What about love?' she whispered.

He dropped her hand immediately, his smile fading. 'You'd best ask my mother to read it for you.'

Ellen swallowed her disappointment, her gaze returning to the view. 'When we came here I wondered if your people might turn up.' She looked at him again. 'I remember you said you travelled to Wales. You told me how beautiful it was . . . and I wanted to come.'

'It must be as beautiful as anywhere on earth.' His eyes swept round, contemplating the cliffs receding into the distance. Ellen's glance followed his to the opposite horizon where the grey outline of the coast was distinctly visible in the clear air.

She put a hand over her eyes. 'Where's that?' she asked, pointing.

'That's Devon.'

'Really? It doesn't look far away.'

'Pity it's not further, then maybe they wouldn't be bringing the copper ore here to be spoiling everything.' He shook his head sadly.

'Copper?'

'Aye. To Swansea over yonder.' He waved his arm vaguely to the left. ''tis from Cornwall the ore comes, in boats. Though to be sure they get it elsewhere as well now.'

'Why does it spoil things?' Her eyes searched the horizon.

'Because it is thick, green smoke they're making at the smelting works. It stops everything growing,' he said, his expression bitter.

'How awful.'

'Aye. Though I expect the manufacturers would not be agreeing.'

'Why do they bring it here instead of doing it in Cornwall?' she puzzled.

'Because it's coal they're needing, and there is plenty of coal in the ground here. Come on!' Standing, he pulled her to her feet, steadying her, his hands on her waist. He held her for a few minutes before dropping his hands. Stooping, he picked up her bonnet and placed it on her head, gently tucking in wisps of hair from her face. Then he pulled on his own soft brimmed felt hat.

They began strolling across the cliffs again, making their way inland towards the farm buildings in the distance.

'What's happening there?' Ellen indicated across the bracken and bushes towards two men, one of whom was shouting and waving his arms at a dog.

'Let's take a look,' Nezer suggested.

As they drew nearer they could see a large ewe in the middle of the thorn bushes, its woolly coat held firmly on the spikes as it struggled frenziedly to escape. One of the men was shouting at the helpless dog, which was adding to the confusion by barking at both man and ewe.

'Stupid fellow, 'tis frightening the poor creatures he is, making it far worse,' Nezer muttered to Ellen. He shook his head. 'I suppose it's help they'll be needing.'

Once near enough, Nezer called to the men. 'Good afternoon to you, sirs. Is it trouble you have?'

The men looked at him and scowled. 'Trust a gypsy to ask a bloody stupid question,' the elder of them snarled. 'Get in there!' he yelled at the dog. 'Get the stupid thing out!'

The dog cowered and squeezed back under the thorn bushes, reappearing near the sheep to snap at the terrified animal's legs, making it bleat pitifully. Ellen and Nezer could see the fear in its eyes as it thrashed wildly, entangling itself even further in the thorns.

Taking off his leather jerkin, Nezer threw it over the top of the bush, then nimbly leapt up onto it and scrambled across the top of the bushes, coming down near the two animals. The dog spun round, snarling and baring its teeth, but Nezer spoke softly to it, holding out the back of his hand. To Ellen's amazement the dog's antagonism immediately dropped away and it sniffed at Nezer's hand, whining softly, almost as though asking for his help.

Fascinated, they all saw Nezer grab the sheep by its woolly coat and force its head up to face his own. Leaning nearer to the sheep Nezer put his own face close to the animal's and seemed to half whisper, half blow into the animal's nostrils. Even as they watched the fear left the sheep's eyes and it ceased to struggle.

Nezer grinned at his audience. 'I'll just be making a way through for the creature,' he called, and pulling a knife from his belt, began hacking at the bushes. In stunned silence the two men stared and, to her fury, Ellen noticed one make a sign against the evil eye behind his back.

'There y'are sir, one sheep,' Nezer said cheerfully, patting the animal's rump.

'Looks like I owe you my thanks then, don't I?' The farmer's voice was almost resentful. Then relenting, he added more kindly: 'If you call at the farm tomorrow morning, Meadow Farm yonder, you can have some eggs and milk. I'll tell my good lady to have them ready for you, I will.'

'Thank you, sir, most generous. I'll do that.' Nezer touched his forelock.

Ellen gazed speechlessly at Nezer as the men walked away, and seeing her expression, his lips turned up at the corners, his face alive with mischief.

'How did you do it? Was it witchcraft?' she asked fearfully.

'Witchcraft!' He threw back his head, roaring with laughter. 'Don't be silly, girl.'

'But how did you do it?'

'It is something Romanies learn,' he said enigmatically. He slung his jacket over one shoulder.

'All Romanies?' She was still regarding him with awe.

'Well, some are better at it than others, like everything else in this world.'

'That's very clever.'

He took her hand again and wordlessly they began strolling back to the manor.

'Goodness, Nezer, I must have been out ages,' Ellen said with sudden realisation. 'I'll have to go or Miss Mirry will be home before me.'

'Will I see you again?' he asked as they reached the yard gate.

Her face lit with happiness. 'Yes. The day after tomorrow if I can manage it, about the same time.' She turned and ran up the path leaving Nezer gazing after her, his expression troubled.

Six

Kate had sent her groom along with a message, arranging for Miranda to take luncheon at her home the following Friday, and she had included Gwennie in the invitation. Miranda was eagerly looking forward to it, certain she and Kate were going to become great friends.

'It is all right for me to use the carriage this morning?' Miranda checked with Charlotte. 'I did mention it earlier in the week.'

'Of course . . . if you can find Wyn,' Charlotte said, giving her infuriating giggle.

'Find him?' Miranda said, exasperated. 'I asked him to have the carriage outside at half past ten.'

'That doesn't mean he will be there.' Charlotte shrugged indifferently as she preened in the mirror, patting and poking at her hair. 'He's never about when he's wanted.' Then she noticed Gwennie behind Miranda. 'Where do you think you're going, madam?'

Gwennie's face fell and she stared mutely at Charlotte, thrusting her finger in her mouth.

'Well? Cat got your tongue?'

'She's coming to Kate's with me,' Miranda explained.

'She is not!' Charlotte's head wobbled indignantly.

'Why ever not?' Miranda asked. 'The child never goes anywhere and. . . .'

'I hardly ever go anywhere either,' Charlotte retorted peevishly, darting a spiteful glance at Gwennie. 'And she is lucky to be living here at all.'

'For whatever reason she may be here, it surely is not Gwennie's fault,' Miranda flung back. 'Besides, Kate is expecting her,' she added quickly before Charlotte could say any more.

Charlotte clamped her mouth shut, pursing her lips as she glowered at Miranda. But evidently she had no wish to upset the influential Dart family and she flounced away, head bobbing.

Miranda stifled her feelings of guilt. There was nothing stopping Charlotte going out if she so wished; the carriage was always at her disposal. She resolved to try to make it up to Charlotte at a later date: possibly a shopping trip to Swansea next week, with lunch perhaps? I might even be able to persuade her to visit her dressmaker and order some new clothes, Miranda mused, thinking about how shabby Charlotte always appeared. It's strange really, not in character. Charlotte does seem very aware of her appearance, rather vain if anything.

As Charlotte had inferred, the carriage was not waiting outside. Miranda heaved a sigh of frustration and leaving Gwennie in the hall, marched off to find Wyn. There was no sign of him at the stables and the carriage was not even harnessed in readiness.

'Have you seen Wyn?' she asked David, who was cleaning out the stalls. 'He's supposed to be taking me out in the carriage.'

He paused in his work, leaning on his shovel and brushing the back of his hand across his perspiring face. 'No, Miss Miranda. I'm sorry I haven't. I'll harness the carriage ready though, if you like?'

'That would be a help. Thank you, David.' She started to walk away then turned back. 'I must commend you, David. I think you do an excellent job here with the animals. And you're always so cheerful about it.'

His sun -freckled face split in a wide grin. 'Thank you, Miss. It's nice of you to say so. I'll see if I can find Wyn once the horses are ready like.'

'No, thank you! I intend to find where he's hiding and give him a piece of my mind.'

David chuckled. 'Glad it's not me anyway,' he murmured as he moved to harness the carriage, watching Miranda storm off to the kitchen.

She found Wyn sitting on a stool near the huge inglenook fireplace, a large tankard of tea clutched in his hand. The cooking fire reflected on his bald head and the wisps of hair growing around the sides stuck limply to his scalp.

'Just what are you doing?' she snapped, walking towards him.

He turned a surly, unshaven face towards her, perspiration globules beading all over it. 'I'm drinkin' my tea, aren't I? What's it look like?'

She kicked out furiously, catching the leg of his stool, and his tea slopped over his lap, dripping onto the floor. 'Get up, you unmannerly oaf! How dare you sit there when I am talking to you! And how dare you address me in that manner! You are supposed to be preparing the carriage.'

He scowled at her. 'Made me tip my tea now, you 'ave.' As he rose lethargically, Ceridwen pushed the door open, a heavy wooden bucket dragging down her arm. Clattering it down, she hobbled over, scolding and gesturing at the wet patch on the flagged floor, her black eyes full of malice.

'Why is the carriage not ready?' Miranda demanded, ignoring Ceridwen. 'I shall report this to Captain Llewelyn.'

'I forgot, didn't I. Won't take no time,' he whined.

''e's not your slave, is 'e?' Ceridwen said querulously, her chin quivering indignantly. 'You and your fancy maid make a good pair, the two of you.'

Miranda's head jerked round in astonishment. 'No! He is not a slave but he is employed as a servant here and is expected to carry out orders,' Miranda spat, adding imperiously: 'I expect to leave in five minutes!' She spun round on her heel and stamped out, leaving them both staring resentfully after her.

When Wyn eventually turned up at the door, Miranda noticed his eyes alight thoughtfully on Gwennie, lingering on her longer than Miranda thought necessary. Gwennie cringed away from him as he took her arm to help her into the carriage. Miranda studied the child's face, noticing her eyes were wide and dark with apprehension, and realised Gwennie was nervous of him.

As soon as they were both settled on the shabby seats and on their way she questioned Gwennie about her apprehension. The child shrugged, regarding her warily.

'Are you afraid of him?' Miranda demanded.

'No . . . praps a little bit,' she admitted. 'I don't like him.'

'Why not? Has he ever done anything to you?' Miranda asked, grabbing at the strap as the carriage swung wildly around a corner.

Gwennie looked surprised and shook her head, her curls bouncing in time with the carriage's motion.

'Are you quite sure? I thought we were friends, Gwennie? Are you telling me the truth?'

''course I am.' Her lip trembled reproachfully.

'Then why don't you like him?' Miranda repeated insistently.

'He smoothes my hair.' Her hand wandered up to her dark curls.

'That is all? Are you certain?' Miranda touched Gwennie's shoulder gently.

'Yes,' she insisted, winding a curl round and round her finger.

'I see.' Miranda was not sure what of make of this.

Gwennie slid her hand into Miranda's. 'Please Miranda. Will you be my best friend?' Her eyes glowed. 'I love you. Only you and Luke like me.'

'That's not true, you silly goose!' Miranda put her

arms around the child who responded by winding both arms tightly around Miranda's neck. 'Stop! You're choking me,' Miranda wheezed, struggling to release her grasp. 'So you like Luke?' she probed, when she could get a breath.

Gwennie nodded vigorously. 'He's nice. He doesn't scold me. And, sometimes, he tells me stories. About India.'

'Does he indeed?' This was a side of Luke she had not imagined. Evidently he made a far more acceptable father than a brother. 'What sort of stories?'

'Lots of ones. All different ones.' Her eyes gleamed with appreciation.

'Such as?'

'He tells me about temples and . . . and . . . idols. Some are made of gold.'

'Really?'

'And about Indian ladies. They've got silky dresses . . . all colours. And lots of jewels . . . and gold. And I 'specially love the snake charmers.'

'Snake charmers!' Miranda gasped with astonishment.

'Yes, snake charmers. They've got live snakes . . . in baskets . . .' Her face animated, she went on to describe this miracle to Miranda. '. . . and the snakes come out when the men play music. And they don't bite the men.'

'It sounds intriguing,' Miranda conceded.

'Sometimes he brings me presents.' She put a hand to her mouth and giggled, her eyes dancing mischievously. 'Mrs Cain gets cross.'

'Poor Charlotte.'

'Why?' Gwennie asked with surprise.

Miranda paused. 'Because she doesn't go anywhere or do anything,' Miranda sighed.

'Why doesn't she? Grown-ups can do what they like.' Gwennie looked puzzled.

Miranda chuckled. 'They can't, you know. We all have to do things we don't want sometimes.'

Gwennie's expression was incredulous. 'Really?' She turned her face to the window, nose glued to the grimy glass. 'Please can I open the window, Miranda?' she asked. 'I'm very hot.'

'If it will open.' Miranda regarded it dubiously. The bright sunshine streaming in through the panes served only to emphasise the dirt on them; obviously they had not been cleaned for some time. But with a few tugs, Miranda successfully managed to open a window.

'Kate's carriage is nicer than this,' Gwennie commented, bouncing experimentally on the seat and running her hand over its worn tapestry. 'Hers is bouncy.'

'Have you been to Kate's home before, then?'

'Oh yes. Miss Kate's taken me. In her carriage. I like her house lots . . . and her mother.' Gwennie stood up and leaned out, one hand tightly clasping her bonnet to her head. She looked back along the road they had travelled, her black hair flapping in tendrils across her face.

Miranda smiled, enjoying her enthusiasm, looking forward herself to meeting Kate's mother. She moved back slightly, away from the draught, not wanting to arrive with frizzy hair tangled into red-gold knots. Just then, two men rode past on horses, raising their hats in salute to the occupants of the coach, reminding Miranda of another idea she had been mulling over.

'Have you done any riding?' Miranda asked Gwennie, when she flopped back onto her seat. Gwennie shook her head. 'Then perhaps we can give you a few lessons. I was younger than you when I learned to ride.' Miranda held her face up, enjoying the cool breeze blowing through the open window.

'Really?! Will they let me?' Gwennie's eyes grew enormous, her face flushed pink at the prospect.

'I think we'll ask Luke,' Miranda promised, sure he would be amenable where Gwennie was concerned.

'But he's gone away,' Gwennie wailed.

'When he returns.' She patted Gwennie's hand.

Gwennie leaned over and kissed Miranda's cheek, nuzzling against her shoulder, reminding Miranda of something else.

'You told me you don't know your mother, Gwennie? Is that right?'

'Yes.' Gwennie looked up at her. 'She didn't want me,' she whispered. 'Ceridwen said.'

'Gwennie darling. You mustn't listen to her, I'm sure that's not true. Ceridwen's making up stories. Tell me . . . how long have you lived at Bryncarog?'

'I don't know. I don't remember 'bout before,' she said miserably.

Miranda did not press any further as it was obvious Gwennie was getting upset. I'll speak to Luke about this, she decided. I must find out if he is aware of Wyn's interest in the child and what she's being told by the servants.

Kate, delighted to see them, embraced them both warmly. 'I am pleased you decided to come. I was hoping my brother, Charles, would be here. I've so sung your praises to him he wanted to return home for luncheon especially to meet you. He and Papa were too busy though,' she said, pulling a face. 'But do come and meet Mama.'

Miranda loved the house, a modern regency-designed building, with spacious, well-proportioned rooms and graceful bow windows, all decorated with perfect taste. Glancing around, she realised the lack of money which plagued Bryncarog was evidently not an issue here; only lavish expenditure could have purchased such elegant furnishings.

Miranda took an immediate liking to Kate's mother, who seemed an older version of her daughter, sharing the same serene looks and manner and exquisitely dressed, as Kate always was. Her full-skirted dress, of pale linen, was sprigged with brown flowers, complementing her pale beauty and rich brown eyes. Made in the latest fashion with huge sleeves, the dress had a tiered collar of deep, creamy lace, making Miranda even more impatient with her own unflattering black dresses.

'Miranda, my dear. I have so been looking forward to meeting you.' She kissed Miranda's cheek and, taking her by the hand, led her into the drawing room, revealing a similar lack of formality as Kate had.

After lunch, they sat out on the velvet lawn to enjoy the warm July sunshine. It overlooked the splendid sweep of Swansea Bay. The only blemish on the scene was a dark shadow glimpsed to the east, suspended low over Swansea town which was situated at the furthest end of the bay.

'What is that black cloud?' Miranda asked, pointing a finger.

'It is caused by the copper smelting industry carried on at Swansea,' Kate explained.

'How awful!' Miranda was appalled.

'Yes. But Papa tells us it is for the good of the area,' Kate remarked.

'Good of the area?' Miranda exclaimed. 'All that horrible smoke!'

'I didn't mean that,' Kate said, flushing slightly. 'I think what Papa meant is that more coal is required for the copper-smelting process. It brings much wealth to the area,' she added defensively. 'It means more work for the poor people living here.'

'Yes, of course,' Miranda agreed, rather uncomfortably. 'You must realise any industry is foreign to me; I'm only used to agriculture.'

She watched an assortment of sailing craft making their way across the bay towards the docks, their sails seeming to glow as they reflected the sunlight.

Miranda was enjoying her visit immensely, and felt thoroughly at home and relaxed. The only flaw was that the well-run household poignantly reminded her of life at Rushton Hall.

When the time came, she was reluctant to leave.

'Thank you so much. Gwennie and I have indeed enjoyed ourselves,' she said.

'You must all come and spend a weekend with us,' Mrs Dart said. 'We can ask a few other house guests also.' Her eyes slipping thoughtfully towards her daughter, she added: 'Perhaps when Luke has returned?' she suggested.

'That would be lovely,' Miranda said, giving both ladies a big hug.

Seven

Hot and sticky from the blazing sun, Miranda raced up the stairs, looking forward to a bath before changing for dinner.

'This room is stifling, Ellen. Can we have a window open please?'

'No, Miss Mirry. I have tried to open it but the stupid thing is stuck fast.'

Miranda wrinkled her nose as she examined the rotten frame and surround, with its peeling paintwork. 'No wonder it doesn't open. Just look at it!' She climbed up onto the cushion, which covered the wide sill in front of the window. She often used this as a seat. Balancing on it, she reached up, banging at the wood with her fist. It remained wedged shut. 'Pass me the poker,' Miranda ordered.

'Careful, Miss. You could easily fall through if it opened,' Ellen warned.

As Miranda hammered at the latch with the iron poker it began to ease and with another bang, came free, allowing the window to open and a cooling breath of fresh air into the room. 'That's much better,' Miranda sighed. 'I'll take my bath now, Ellen. Cool, if you please.'

Refreshed, Miranda considered the hated black dress Ellen had laid out ready for her, and suddenly rebelled. 'I am not wearing that dress, Ellen! It's far too hot and sticky for black and I've decided I've had more than enough of those dreadful clothes. You can take it away!'

'Take it away? But Miss Mirry . . .'

'I refuse to wear it any longer, Ellen. I should never have allowed Mrs Langdon to persuade me to order dresses in that appallingly immature style in the first place. I was so distraught after Papa died, I wasn't thinking clearly. Get rid of it . . . all of them in fact!'

'All of them?' Ellen's face was shocked. 'All your new mourning clothes, Miss Mirry?'

'Just look at it, Ellen!' She snatched up the loathed black gown, holding it against herself, regarding her reflection in the mirror. Her mouth turned down in disgust. 'Apart from the childish, old-fashioned style, black does nothing for my colouring. Nothing! I know Papa would have hated to see me wear it. I will have the brown linen instead. Now, please, Ellen!' she added firmly, before her maid could object.

'Just as you say, Miss Miranda.' Back stiff, Ellen marched over to the closet, and flung back the door, disapproval apparent in her every movement. Miranda ignored her reaction; at least she would be wearing her own lovely clothes again.

Ellen helped her step into the petticoats, which the style required. Then she wriggled into the nipped-waisted dress and stood as Ellen fastened the boned corset which attached to its fashionably fuller skirt.

'That's much better,' she sighed, as Ellen knelt to pull on her matching pumps and tie their ribbons. 'Now I feel like me again.'

Standing behind her, brush in hand, Ellen's face softened when she saw Miranda's reflection in the long mirror.

'Well, it is a sort of dark colour, Miss Mirry, and brown is considered half mourning,' she capitulated. Taking her hair back from her face, Ellen, always more than proficient with the latest hair fashions, expertly parted it, piling a bun on the top of her head, a small plait coiling around it. Then she arranged ringlets to hang down on either side of Miranda's face. With her naturally curly hair Miranda never had to submit to having her hair crimped to form curls. With a last little twitch, Ellen adjusted a ribbon, then stood back critically, well pleased with the results.

'That should do you nicely, Miss Mirry. I bet Master Huw will be dancing in attendance tonight,' she remarked perceptively.

Miranda turned back from examining her reflection to look at Ellen. 'Do you think so?' Miranda's voice was deceptively casual, then her face dimpled in a companionable smile. 'He is rather attractive, don't you think? I am so sick of being hidden away in Bryncarog.'

Ellen nodded in complete agreement. 'Me too, Miss,' she admitted.

Hearing her wistful tone, Miranda put a concerned hand on her arm. 'Are you getting on any better with the servants now?'

Ellen shrugged. 'That miserable pair will never be friendly but I take no notice. They don't worry me none, Miss Mirry.' Then she grinned conspiratorially. 'And guess who I met a few weeks ago? Nezer. It was lovely to see him again.'

'Really?' Miranda pursed her lips, a glint of compassion in her eyes, not quite sure how to view this development. 'Ellen. Please remember, his people are . . . well . . . different from the rest of us. I love you a great deal and I'd hate you to be hurt.' Her expression was serious.

Ellen's grin faded. 'Yes, Miss. I understand what you mean.'

'Another thing.' She took both her hands. 'If you ever decide you would rather go back home, please do tell me. I never want to you be unhappy.'

Ellen bit her lip. 'Don't be silly,' she said gruffly. 'But thank you for your concern. I'll remember what you've said.'

Miranda hugged her and Ellen returned the embrace, though rather cautiously. 'Mind we don't crush your dress,' she warned.

'Now that I have discarded those dreadful clothes we'll have to look through the remainder of my wardrobe. It might be a good idea for me to order some new dresses,' Miranda mused thoughtfully. 'I'll ask Charlotte about her dressmaker.'

'It would be better if you asked Miss Kate.' Ellen pulled a face. 'Mrs Cain's clothes are very out of fashion.'

Miranda laughed. 'You're right as usual, Ellen. Thank you, I'll do that. And I must ask Luke about those new servants. I believe he will be home this evening. I will not have you doing other servants' work and I don't want you working harder than you should.'

Charlotte was astonished when she saw Miranda's attire. 'My goodness! The real lady tonight!' she said archly. 'I kept full mourning for much longer, both when Papa and my dear husband passed away.'

Before Miranda could reply Huw came striding into the room. 'Good evening, ladies.' Bending, he dropped a kiss on his mother's cheek as she dimpled with pleasure. His glance washed over Miranda, his appreciative eyes widening in surprise before lingering for a moment at her v-shaped neckline.

'Well, I must say, this apparel does you more justice than the gowns you have worn previously, Miranda.' He leaned towards her. 'Am I allowed to kiss my . . . cousin?' His voice was low and mischievous, and he brushed his mouth against her cheek, his lips warm and teasing. 'You smell as good as you look . . . divine,' he whispered in her ear, just loud enough for her to hear.

'Good evening, Huw.' She kept her voice light, though her cheeks coloured slightly. It was pleasant to have an admiring male in attendance again.

Charlotte was watching, a little smile playing around her mouth. 'You wicked boy,' she said, her tone indulgent. 'Whatever will Miranda think of you?'

'Yes, what will she think?' he chuckled. His eyes,

dancing with amusement, regarded Miranda quizzically. 'Will you take a sherry, Miranda?'

'Greetings, all!' Luke said, appearing as they were about to take their places at the table. Miranda saw him also gaze at her new attire. His eyes swept back to her face, lingering there; then realising she was aware of his scrutiny, he gave a polite smile before turning away.

Miranda was vivacious and entertaining over dinner, exhilarated by her re-emergence into society, as she felt it to be. Both men responded, and for the first time since she had arrived, she fully enjoyed the meal as a social occasion. They leapt to their feet as she and Charlotte rose to retire to the drawing room. Obviously they have now decided I am no child, she thought with gratification.

'I think you impressed Huw tonight, my dear,' Charlotte said with evident satisfaction. 'You certainly sparkled. I think you were right. It was time for you to discard your mourning.'

'I looked so drab,' Miranda giggled. She had taken rather more wine than usual. 'Quite unlike myself. I should never have let Mrs Langdon persuade me to order those dreadful garments. I felt like a child in those dresses she chose.'

'Well no-one could mistake you for a child tonight,' Charlotte stated silkily.

After finishing his brandy Luke put in a brief appearance in the drawing room to excuse himself. 'Please forgive me, ladies, but I have work to do.'

Huw joined them though, and stood, glass in hand,

by the piano as Miranda played. Putting his glass down, he began picking out the tunes with his right hand. Miranda gathered up her skirts, sliding along to make room for him on the stool alongside her. Then, with Huw playing the right hand, she played the left. After a few tunes, she broke off, laughter rippling through her.

'That was fun,' she chuckled. 'I didn't know you played the piano, Huw.'

'Not very proficiently, I'm afraid. My mother was too indulgent. Never made me practise enough.' He smiled down at Miranda and she noticed, once again, how handsome he was.

'I feel you disguise your talents, Huw,' she teased. 'I wonder what others you have concealed?'

'You will have to find that out for yourself,' he quipped with a lazy grin and a glint of desire in his eyes.

After a few more pieces Miranda decided to retire. As she left the drawing-room Huw followed her.

'I never realised you were such an exquisite woman, Miranda.' His hooded glance slid across her again, his smile teasing. 'You've been masking your beauty under those awful clothes these past weeks. David tells me you often go riding. Perhaps we could ride together sometime?'

'That would be lovely, Huw.' She put a foot on the first step but he caught her arm to restrain her. She couldn't help noticing how soft his hand was on her bare skin, compared with Luke's calloused ones; but his grip was firm as he gazed down at her. 'Would tomorrow afternoon suit you?'

'Quite suitable. Shall we say two o'clock?'

As she tried to withdraw her arm, his hand slid down to her hand, and lifting it to his lips, he kissed it. 'Until tomorrow,' he drawled.

Miranda looked at him uncertainly, realising he was flirting with her. 'Good night, Huw,' she said coolly, turning away as he returned to the drawing-room. Half way up the stairs she hesitated, suddenly remembering her intention to speak to Luke. He would be in the library.

The library, situated as it was on the east side of the house, received no evening sun, and its gloom was intensified by the dark wood panelling and leather-covered books lining the walls. The top of the huge mahogany desk was littered with papers and ledgers Luke was working on. He pulled a ledger towards him, flicking through it until he came to the entry he was seeking and continued working.

His attention was interrupted by a light tap on the door, and Miranda popped in her head. 'May I have a word with you please, Luke?' she said.

'Miranda! Of course!' He rose to his feet and, reaching behind him, took his jacket from the back of the chair and pulled it over his muscular shoulders.

'There are a few matters I wish to bring up.'

He nodded, remaining standing until she was seated, before slumping back down behind the desk. 'Nothing is troubling you, I hope?' he asked.

'No . . . at least nothing that cannot be put right.' Her smile was deceptively innocent, he thought.

'I wish to employ more staff.' Head on one side, she

looked up at him from beneath her lashes, her expression beguiling.

'Staff?' His eyes widened, his mouth twitching with amusement.

'Yes, staff! Surely that is easy enough to arrange?'

He took a breath, drumming his fingers on the scuffed surface of the desk. 'What sort of staff?' he sighed. 'Another lady's maid? I'm afraid the household expenses are fully stretched . . .'

'But I do not wish your household to pay for them.'

He clenched his jaw, contemplatively. 'What exactly do you lack now?' There was more than an element of sarcasm in his voice.

'I have my own allowance, I wish to pay for two more servants.' Miranda was now using her most imperious tone, he realised, with irritation.

'May I be allowed to know which servants?' he asked with excessive politeness.

Looking down, Miranda examined a mark on her skirt, taking her time. 'Ellen should not be expected to do the work of a housemaid, which she has been doing.' She looked up at him. 'She was never employed in that capacity.' He nodded his agreement. 'So I would like to employ a housemaid. Also, I would like an under-housemaid to help in general, including in the kitchen.'

'Help in the kitchen?' he yelped. His teeth flashed in a wolfish grin, the stern lines of his face disappearing. 'Good God! Don't tell me Ceridwen has found a friend at last? Have you mentioned it to her?'

'Ceridwen? Why on earth would I ask a servant's opinion?' Miranda regarded him with astonishment.

'Because she is a miserable old . . .' He paused, having second thoughts about the word he was about to use. 'Because she has charge of the kitchen and might not take kindly to someone else. What makes you think she requires help?'

'Because there is never a servant around when needed,' she explained.

'Of course. I should have realised,' he said cynically. His mouth twisted. 'You cannot possibly be without a servant when you want one. Have you approached Charlotte about this matter?'

'I have. Charlotte is . . .' Miranda paused. 'Charlotte seems uninterested.'

Luke's face was impassive.

'She said to approach you. Does Huw have no say in the financial affairs of his mother's home?' Miranda asked.

Luke gave a sardonic laugh, shrugging his shoulders eloquently.

'Are you not equal partners?' Miranda continued.

Luke slammed closed the ledger he had been working on and stood up. 'No!' His expression did not invite discussion.

'So you make all the decisions?' she persisted, looking up at him.

'You can put it that way,' Luke assented.

He leaned towards her, both palms flat on the desk. 'Look Miranda—'

'So will my allowance run comfortably to these servants?'

'Yes,' he admitted with reluctance, 'though I am not happy about you funding servants for—'

'It is for my own comfort.'

'I comprehend that,' he said dryly. He straightened again, running a hand through his unruly hair, rumpling it further.

'Thank you, Luke. The second matter . . . is it possible for me to have my own horse, Star, brought here?' Her expression was wistful. 'It would be a great comfort to me. I've really missed him since I've left home. He's been with me since he was a foal; riding is not the same without Star.'

'I'm sure it is not.' There was a glint of compassion in his eyes. 'That's easily solved. I'll bring him back with me when next I go to Rushton Hall.'

'Are you going soon?' Miranda's face lit up. 'How often do you go? I would really love to see everyone again. No! On second thoughts I couldn't bear that horrendous journey . . . and twice over.'

Luke gave a wry smile, grateful she had reached that decision. 'I have been once before – I should have thought about bringing your horse then. It was remiss of me.'

'And all is well? How are they all? The staff?'

'Everyone is keeping well enough.'

'And Eliza, Ellen's mother?'

He shrugged. 'I believe Eliza misses her daughter,' he admitted.

Flooded with guilt, Miranda's face clouded. 'She must do, I know I'd miss her dreadfully.' She sighed. 'Have you spoken to Ellen about her mother?'

'Of course,' he said quietly.

'I need not have asked you that,' she murmured. She frowned thoughtfully. 'But you knew Eliza, didn't you? When you were a child?'

His eyes flashed across her face. 'I did.' His mouth twisted slightly. 'I knew her well. Ellen has inherited a similar dependable character. Both unswervingly loyal.'

Miranda was silent for a few minutes and Luke broke her reverie. 'So next time, I will return with Star.'

'I would be truly grateful. When are you likely to go?' she asked eagerly.

'I am not sure. Probably early in October.' He understood her enthusiasm.

'That will be wonderful!' She began to rise, then hesitated. 'Luke . . . have you realised Gwennie doesn't like Wyn?' she asked, remembering her intention to bring up the subject.

She held his full attention now and he frowned. 'Has she any reason for her dislike? After all, I don't think any of us are particularly fond of Wyn,' he said dryly.

'She said not, except that he keeps smoothing her hair.'

Luke pulled a face, rubbing a hand across his chin. 'To tell the truth I believe he is genuinely fond of the child,' Luke said thoughtfully. 'Though I agree she does spend too much time with the servants. I'll get Olwen to take her out more. Thank you for—'

'May I teach her to ride?'

His eyes glowed. 'That is a marvellous idea. Why didn't I think of that? Certainly. I'd be pleased for you to do so. Get David to help you, he has a lot of patience.'

'Good. I thought you would agree; I heard you

liked riding as a child. How old were you when Papa taught you to ride?'

He regarded he quizzically. 'He never taught me,' he said flatly.

'He didn't? But who . . . eh . . . I assumed . . .' She let the sentence trail off uncomfortably.

His face was hard and his gaze dropped for a few seconds, as though he was looking into the past. His eyes rose again, to meet hers. 'Little Rosie is a placid pony, and not too big,' he mused. 'Perhaps we might get Gwennie a pony later on.'

'That would be lovely. She's a dear little girl, very loving. Now what do we do about getting the staff? Do you wish me to . . .'

'I'll have a word with Charlotte. You could interview the girls she selects if you wish to make a final decision, perhaps?' He hoped she would agree. He didn't want to step further on any toes at Bryncarog; life was difficult enough as it was.

'Yes, of course. I understand.' She threw him a warm smile; for once they were in agreement. 'Will you be able to arrange it soon?'

'I will do my best.'

'And you will arrange the funding from my allowance?'

He hesitated slightly before answering. 'Yes. I can do that.'

'You sound unsure?'

'There will be no difficulty,' he insisted. He stood up as she rose to leave, his eyes dropping back to his papers. He sighed soundlessly as she turned back again.

'There is one more thing, Luke. The window in my room is very hard to open. I have asked Wyn several times to look at it but as usual get no response.'

'I'll have a word with him about it before I leave for Bristol,' he promised, opening the ledger and flicking through the pages.

'Thank you. It is so terribly hot. Then I'll leave you to your work.' She threw him another sunny smile.

What a change to be in harmony for once, he thought, as she closed the door. I wonder if we will ever permanently see eye to eye, Miranda? he pondered, and if you will ever stop resenting my supervision.

Taking responsibility for Miranda was proving harder than he had anticipated. This evening, he had been made fully aware she was certainly not the child he had mistaken her for when they first met. She is a woman with beauty and confidence . . . and is also very spoiled and self-willed, he thought with impatience. But what exactly had he expected? Having bitter personal experience of Stanton's volatile and complex personality, Luke probably understood him better than most people. So why expect Miranda to be a conventional woman?

Miranda knows what she wants and makes sure she gets it. Luke was unhappy at the idea of her paying for servants at his home. It could appear that he was misappropriating her money and the briefest audit would show he was very short of funds. Who would believe a disinherited heir? he thought bitterly. I could certainly make good use of just a little of that Rushton fortune.

There was no doubt about it, Llewelyn Shipping was definitely reaching a crisis point and unless something extraordinary happened it would soon fall into bankruptcy. I can't keep pumping my own savings into the firm, otherwise I'm going to end up in the same state, he decided. We need some new ventures, trade in the channel is changing so rapidly. I'll see what might be suitable, when I'm in Bristol. Arrange a loan perhaps? he considered.

His face pensive, he took a deep breath, leaning back in the chair. He stretched his long legs in front of him, running his hands through his dark curls again as he stared up at the ceiling.

'It's no good, we'll just have to risk another run. We need one badly,' he muttered under his breath. 'As soon as I return, I'll set it up ready for October.' But runs were becoming increasingly dangerous to arrange. The new Coastguard Service, so recently inaugurated, was proving very successful in this part of Wales. As well as patrolling around the Gower coast, its officers were keeping periodic surveillance over vessels moored in Swansea harbour, especially those known to trade with Ireland, which might be suspected of carrying contraband.

We can't afford to take any chances, he mused, recalling Jack Nichols' recent show of interest in the *Windrush*. The *Windrush* had been purchased as a joint venture by a partnership of four, Llewelyn Shipping owning two parts. Although it was gradually beginning to pay its way, most of which was being reinvested wisely, it was a slow return when divided between four.

Trading legitimately between Swansea, Bristol and Ireland, the official captain of the *Windrush* was not above receiving a little extra to turn his back on smuggling activities organised by Luke. Ostensibly as a passenger, or even aboard unofficially, Luke would detour the cutter to pick up contraband, and on its return home, use his expert navigational skills to land the cargo on the treacherous Gower coast. Many a ship had been wrecked in such an activity. Sometimes the *Windrush* would meet up with a ship returning to Bristol from the colonies, loaded with rum, sugar and tobacco. At other times they detoured to Rush, a traditional contraband port in Ireland, which received brandy, wine and geneva from the French ports. This contraband was stacked away in secret compartments, specially constructed in hollow bulkheads on the *Windrush*. It had proved successful in the past but how long could this continue with a more sophisticated Coastguard Service?

Luke sighed, chose a quill for his pen and began trimming it in readiness to start writing. It was going to be another late night.

Eight

Huw, already at the stables when Miranda arrived, lifted his hat to her, smiling warmly. Cariad and Dancer, already saddled, stood waiting patiently, with David stroking Cariad's muzzle.

'I'd like to go over to the harbour at the other end of that long beach,' Miranda said as they left the yard. 'Is the tide suitable today? David told me you have to allow plenty of time.'

Huw hesitated briefly. 'Yes. It is all right today . . . but the path goes inland for a while, through the trees. Wouldn't you prefer to go up onto the cliffs and look at the view from above?'

'No. The idea of going to the village appeals to me.' She waved her hand to the left. 'I've wanted to go there for some time. Does it make any difference to you?'

'Not at all,' he said as they cantered off. 'What interests you in Llanmor?'

'I'd just like to see it. What did you say it is called? Ll . . . anmor?' Miranda giggled, trying out the unfamiliar pronunciation.

The trail led first across the cliffs, where the gorse flower was already beginning to shed golden showers as they brushed past. Tangled amongst the gorse, the last of the blackberries weighed down the bramble branches. Huw tapped Dancer's shoulder lightly with his crop, turning her head towards the track leading to the woody glade. He sat easily in the saddle as Miranda followed behind him. As they descended towards the woods, a slight breeze came rustling through the leaves, ruffling the horses' manes and lifting Miranda's ringlets away from her face. Huw stooped beneath a low branch, then held it to one side for Miranda to pass beneath.

They emerged to skirt the edge of the golden sand of the beach. This end, nearest to Bryncarog, was extremely craggy, its surface covered with jagged fingers of rocks. Once beyond this area, Miranda and Huw picked their way off the path, crossing onto the beach and riding the horses down to the firm sand.

'What is Llanmor? A fishing village?' Miranda asked, once they were riding alongside one another.

'A bit of everything really. But mostly oyster fishing in the winter and the limestone trade in the summer.' He put a reassuring hand down to Dancer as a stone kicked up under her hoof.

'What's the limestone trade?' Miranda asked.

'Limestone is our local stone; most of these rocks are limestone. I'm told lime is an excellent fertiliser for farming. It's shipped from Llanmor.'

'Really? Does Llewelyn Shipping export it?'

'Unfortunately not.' He shook his head ruefully. 'I wish we did. The ships come from Devon and Cornwall. It seems they have a singular lack of lime in the soil over there. The Cornishmen own most of the boats and the ship owners have agreements with local men who quarry and transport it ready for shipping.'

'So, if you don't own those village boats, what does Llewelyn Shipping do?' Miranda brushed a hand through her hair as the wind flicked a strand across her face.

'We do own a few oyster dredgers in the village, but our main trade is with coastal traders in the channel.' He pointed across the water. 'They either bring copper over from Cornwall or transport coal within the channel . . . there's no tax now on shipping coal between the channel ports. We also have part shares in the *Windrush*; she's a cutter.'

'Do you ever go to sea?' She threw him a speculative glance.

'Not if I can help it.' He shrugged laconically. 'I leave that to my cousin, he's the sailor in the family.'

'Do you mean Luke goes with the boats?' Miranda was surprised.

'With the *Windrush* sometimes. Luke believes nothing can be done as well as he does it himself.' A dismissive expression crossed his handsome features. 'I suppose he can be forgiven. He probably misses being an important captain at sea.'

Miranda caught his sarcasm. 'Your mother told me about Luke coming to Wales and more or less taking over the business. It seems unfair on you, Huw, and you accept it with such good grace,' Miranda sympathised. 'I'm sure I never could.'

'Live and let live is my motto.' He smiled lazily.

'It must have hurt you most deeply when your uncle included Luke in his will.'

He nodded, looking away over the sea. 'Perhaps,' he admitted ruefully. Miranda was struck once more by his unruffled demeanour, his good-natured humour.

As they drew near the village on the opposite end of the beach, they returned to the path, which ascended steeply, to arrive at the top of a long, narrow street lined with whitewashed cottages. An ancient stone church, squatted amongst the cottages, almost hidden by trees. The street wound its way down to a small, stony harbour on the beach.

'Pretty ribbons, mistress,' a young gypsy girl called, waving a bundle of bright colours near Cariad's head. The horse snorted, tossing her head, wide eyes showing white, and pranced a few steps to show her displeasure.

'Careful, girl. Would you unseat me?' Miranda cried. She leaned forward over the horse, stroking her neck reassuringly. 'It's all right, my beauty,' she whispered in Cariad's ear, soothing her panic. 'It's all right.'

Entering the busy little harbour, a powerful smell of fish overwhelmed even the pungent odour of hot melted tar, which a man was stirring in a vessel over a fire. A woman passed, a heavy basket balanced on top of the flat straw bonnet she wore on her head. Everyone bustled about, engrossed in their work, all clothed in garments in assorted shades of red, black, grey or undyed wool. Most of the women wore striped or checked flannel aprons over their skirts, feet bare in their wooden clogs.

A few of the villagers turned their heads, the men touching their forelocks and the women bobbing a respectful curtsy as they scrutinised Miranda with curiosity. Many of them acknowledged Huw, calling out a greeting.

Boats, apparently stranded by the tide, were resting on the pebbled beach, positioned between high parallel lines of quarried limestone. Barefooted, men and women, skirts and trousers tucked up, were loading the stones into the boats.

'How do they manage to get the boats back out?' Miranda exclaimed.

'They refloat them. The bow is left attached by a line to a buoy floating out there. Can you see it?' Huw pointed. 'When the tide comes in the boat refloats itself and they can haul it out again. Talking about the tide, we had better make our way back; it has already turned and we don't want to be caught by it.'

On the way home they allowed the horses their heads for an exhilarating gallop along the hard sand, the wind tangling Miranda's hair into a riot of curls. Returning to the Bryncarog end of the beach they slowed down to a canter. Huw regarded her with new respect.

'You're a very proficient horsewoman, Miranda. I've yet to see a woman who rides as well. We must make a point of joining the hunt one day.' He threw back a blonde lock, which had flopped over his forehead again.

'Is there one? Marvellous! I love riding to hounds. The one drawback is I always feel sorry for the poor fox,' she admitted, pulling a face. 'I never want the hounds to catch him.'

'Miranda!' Huw laughed, his shoulders shaking. 'You are incorrigible. I've never heard such a thing. The fox has to set the trail.'

'Yes. Poor, clever little fox. Satan would be the horse to follow the hunt.' Her face was animated as she imagined it. 'He could jump any obstacle. Such a beautiful animal . . .'

'Never attempt to ride him!' Huw barked. 'The horse is half wild, quite uncontrollable. But Luke will not listen; he has his own way as usual. The horse is a danger.'

'I don't agree. I know I could ride Satan.' Her expression was stubborn.

Huw reined in Dancer, catching Cariad's reins, anxious to impress his warning on her. 'Don't even consider it, Miranda, I beg you. I couldn't bear you to come to harm.'

Touched by his concern, Miranda reached out, placing her small hand over his. 'Thank you, Huw. I will remember what you've said.' But she made him no promise.

Going straight up to change, Miranda discovered Ellen was missing. Shrugging out of her jacket she began fumbling to undo the buttons on the back of her riding skirt. 'Bother!' she snapped, hot and frustrated with the row of tiny buttonholes.

'I am so hot,' she murmured, rubbing a towel over

her perspiring face. She glanced at the window, groaning to see it firmly shut once more. Furiously, she leapt up onto the window seat to open it. The latch seemed even stiffer than previously, as she wrestled with it, struggling to force it up, simultaneously thumping and pushing at the window. She screamed as the latch suddenly came free and the window shot completely out from its surround. It would have taken her with if she hadn't snatched frantically and grabbed hold of the curtain. Her full weight dragged on it, which broke her fall as she half fell out of the window. She was left dangling across the sill as the pole came plummeting down, the material tumbling in folds around her. Holding her breath, she clawed at the sill and held onto it, just managing to prevent herself falling right out. Blood pounding, knuckles white, she held on stubbornly. Gingerly she managed to push herself back in and down onto the window seat. Trembling, she sank to her knees, chest heaving in ragged gasps.

'Dear God!' she panted, almost in tears, realising how close she had been to falling out and furious with her own stupidity. 'You idiot! You stupid, stupid idiot!' she whispered.

When her heart rate returned to normal she examined the window frame. There were little pieces of splintered wood on the window ledge outside and flakes of paint scattered over the floor. Someone had been working on it. That stupid Wyn! The screws were missing, having been pulled completely out as the window fell . . . or had they been removed? Still trembling, she splashed water into the bowl on her washstand and pulled off the rest of her clothes. Sand had stuck to her perspiring body as they had galloped along the beach, and she sponged herself in the cool water, leaving a sprinkling of sand in the bottom of the bowl. She finished changing and hurried from her room, almost bumping into Olwen, who was carrying a basket along the corridor.

'Sorry, Miss,' the girl murmured, blushing a deep crimson.

'Not your fault, Olwen. Do you know where Ellen is?' She peered past her up the corridor.

'I'm not sure, Miss. I . . . I think she went out,' she admitted reluctantly. She hoisted the basket, which was laden with clean linen, higher on her hip.

'Of course! I remember now. She asked me if she could, this morning.'

'Did you want anything, Miss Miranda? I can . . .'

'No. It's all right . . .' Miranda started to turn away, then stopped. 'But wait a minute! You may be able to help. Do you know if Wyn has been repairing the window in my room?'

'Don't know about Wyn, Miss.' She deposited her load onto the floor. 'The Captain was here though. He spoke about the window.' Her deep set eyes peered at Miranda from beneath heavy brows.

'The Captain?' Miranda said, startled.

'Yes, Miss. He was knocking on your door and he asked if you or Ellen were inside.' She lifted her basket again. 'He said he wanted to look at the window. He went in to see, when you weren't there.'

A tingle crept slowly along Miranda's spine, lifting the hairs on her neck. 'I see. Thank you, Olwen,' she whispered.

Disturbed, she returned to her room, pacing restlessly across the carpet. Luke has been in my room? Not Wyn? She bit her lip, sweeping a hand through her hair. But Luke would never be so stupid, she thought. He would never leave it in a dangerous state like that. I could easily have been killed . . .? A bolt of alarm sent every nerve jangling. Killed? Uneasiness gnawed at her. I could have been killed! Was . . . was that Luke's intention?

'Oh God!' Her knees like jelly, she sank down on the bed, trembling and icy cold. If I were dead, would Luke inherit? 'Luke isn't like that,' she whispered to herself through stiff lips. 'He would never . . . ' A niggle of doubt squirmed again. Would he? The firm is short of money. Who would inherit if . . .? 'I don't know,' she muttered. 'But I shall find out.'

She rushed over to her secretaire, pulling paper towards her and dipped a quill into the ink. She wrote decisively for several minutes, the pen scratching as she quickly covered the page. Then she scanned her writing and nodded with satisfaction. Sanding it, she put the letter in an envelope and addressed it to William Langdon Esquire. Lighting her candle, she melted wax, dripping it onto the envelope, then sealed it firmly. She took it downstairs with her to ask Wyn to take it to the Post House at Swansea.

'Ceridwen. Do you know where Wyn is, please?' She walked over to the scrubbed, wooden table, where Ceridwen was scraping carrots.

''aven't seen him all morning,' was her flat reply, without looking up.

'Has he been repairing the window in my room?'

'Window?' she snapped waspishly. ''ow would I know?' She threw a carrot into a saucepan, splashing water over Miranda.

Miranda took a sharp breath, moving back out of the way. 'Well, do you know if Captain Llewelyn asked him to repair my window?'

'I dunno. Why don't you ask Wyn? Anyway, the Captain's gone again.' She threw another carrot into the saucepan.

'Well, when you do see Wyn will you tell him my window is smashed on the ground outside. I need it repaired as quickly as possible. Also I have a letter for him to post.'

Ceridwen grumbled irritably in Welsh, and began turning away.

Miranda grabbed her arm. 'You did hear me, Ceridwen?'

'I 'eard,' she snapped, tugging her arm free.

Nezer was waiting inside the stable compound as Ellen left the kitchen. He waved and climbing the gate, landed catlike, lithe and silent on his feet on the other side. Then he walked over to join her. He strolled at her side until they were out of sight of prying eyes from the manor, then giving a whoop of joy he grabbed both her hands in his and swung her round and round in a joyful circle.

'Stop it!' Ellen shrieked, laughing. 'Stop! Or I'll be dizzy.'

He stopped abruptly, his black eyes alive with mischief. 'Have you never danced then, my girl?' he teased. 'It's some good stirring Romany music you need, to excite you.'

'Of course I've danced,' she chuckled, pulling off her bonnet, which had become tilted down over one eye during the carousel. 'But never like that.'

Nezer took her hand and they wound their way up the track leading to the cliffs.

'I thought we could . . .' Ellen stopped as a shadow gliding silently through the bracken alongside them, caught her eye. Her sharp eyes scanned the undergrowth, but nothing moved. 'I was sure I saw something moving in the bushes,' she said as they continued walking.

'A fox perhaps?'

'I suppose it could have been . . . there is something,' she exclaimed. 'I saw it again. Don't stop walking,' she whispered. 'There. Did you seen it?' She pointed to a shadow trailing them discreetly. 'It's a dog!' she chuckled. 'Here boy,' she called. 'Come on.' It ignored her and, slinking back into the bushes, disappeared.

'What dog?' He looked around him, pretending to be puzzled. 'I can't see a dog.' Then she realised his eyes were gleaming with fun.

'You fibber.' She pushed him and he gave an extravagant stagger sideways.

'Do you like dogs then, my sweet girl? I'll call her to meet you.' He gave a low whistle and a lean, mud-coloured dog slunk out towards them, its wagging tail tucked tightly between its legs. About two yards from them, it crouched down on its belly, head on its paws, eyes glued firmly on Nezer.

'Is it really your dog?' She held out a hand, which it ignored.

''tis an' all. Her name's Richi.'

'Whatever sort of name is that for a dog? And what sort of dog is it? It acts a bit like a sheepdog, the way it's crouching, but it's such a skinny thing. And a funny colour . . . an unusual colour,' Ellen hastily corrected herself.

Nezer laughed aloud, his head going back and the gold ring in his ear glinting as it caught the sun. 'So it's funny you think she is?' Nezer gave only the slightest movement of his hand and the dog rushed over to sit at his feet, eyes fixed adoringly on him. He rubbed the dog's ears, grinning at Ellen's red face.

'That's not what I meant,' she protested. 'I just . . .'

'Richi's a lurcher. And to be sure you're right, isn't she a cross between a sheepdog and a greyhound.'

Nezer uttered a word, which Ellen didn't catch, and the dog stood up sniffing at Ellen's skirt and wagging her tail. Ellen tickled the dog's ears and immediately the animal collapsed onto the ground, turning her belly up for more.

'She's lovely. Why does she hide?' Ellen asked curiously.

He grinned. 'Do you need to ask? All Romanies teach their dogs to hide. How else would they be useful for poaching?' His voice was teasing.

'Poaching?' Ellen tried to sound shocked. 'You don't go poaching!'

'If I have a need to, I do.' He picked a blackberry off the bush and popped it into his mouth.

'But poaching is stealing,' she said primly.

'Rubbish! Aren't Mother Earth's creatures there for all men? Just like these are.' He indicated the blackberries. 'I don't see how any one man can lay claim to them.'

'But it's breaking the law.' Her voice lacked conviction.

'Sure it's an unreasonable law.' He picked more blackberries, holding them out on an open palm. 'Do you want one?'

Her forehead puckering in an uncertain frown, she took one, tasting the sweet juice as she bit it. 'It is still the law,' she declared.

'Then it's a law just begging to be broken.' He placed three more berries in her hand.

'Nezer! What a thing to say!' She tossed her head, chewing the fruit.

'Everyone breaks the law sometimes.' He grinned wickedly with a flash of white teeth.

'Not everyone. I don't.'

'Most people do,' he amended, shrugging nonchalantly. 'Even the gentry.'

'How do they?' she demanded.

Taking off his neckerchief, he began filling it with fruit. 'Let's see,' he pondered, chewing. 'Well, what about smuggling?'

'Smuggling? Whatever are you talking about?' Her mouth dropped open in amazement.

'Aren't all the gentry involved in smuggling? And sure isn't that stealing from . . .?' He stopped questioningly, scratching his head, then lifted his shoulders. 'I don't know,' he admitted. 'But to be sure they are breaking the law.'

'Do they go smuggling? Really?' Her eyes were like saucers. 'How do you know?'

He laughed, giving Ellen his neckerchief to wipe her stained fingers. 'The whole world knows, even the Coastguard. But they can't catch them.'

'How does everyone know?'

'Because everyone gets a share. As well as the sailors there are . . . the porters who carry the cargoes, drivers for the wagons . . .'

'Have you ever done it? Carried the cargo, or driven horses, I mean?' she said tremulously.

'And what would you say if I had?' he said, mocking her again and throwing a stone along the path for the dog to chase. 'Am I stealing?'

'I don't know,' she admitted. 'I've heard of smuggling, but I've never thought about it like that. It always seemed . . . well, romantic somehow.'

Richi dropped the stone at Nezer's feet, waiting for him to throw it again. 'Have none of the servants said anything about it?' He eyed her quizzically.

She shook her head. 'They don't talk to me much, only David . . .'

'David?' He frowned slightly, his eyes narrowing speculatively. 'It is much you are seeing of David then?'

'Oh yes. Lots.' She giggled when his eyes widened anxiously, her face teasing this time. 'Every day at breakfast. Why do you ask?'

'Just curious,' he said, his voice studiously nonchalant. He paused for few moments then added: 'Are you growing fond of him then?' A note of concern had crept into his voice.

Ellen caught his hand. 'I like him, that is all.' He let out his breath, which he had been holding, and grinned at her.

'Tell me! Are the servants part of it then? The smuggling I mean?' she asked.

Before he replied another thought struck her. 'What do you mean by the gentry? Not the Captain? He would not be part of it?'

'Well now, perhaps I should be saying no more,' he hedged, bending down to pick up the stone. 'You'll learn soon enough from the servants themselves.'

She came to an abrupt halt. 'Nezer, you know I won't tell anyone,' she protested.

He threw the stone across the grass and Richi raced after it, crouched low to the ground. 'You might tell Miss Miranda,' he said, turning back to her.

'I wouldn't.' She bristled with indignation.

'You could let it slip.' He took her hand, squeezing it gently. 'Where are we going? Anywhere in particular?'

Realising he was changing the subject Ellen allowed him to, determined she would learn more at a future date. 'I'd like to buy some lace and some ribbons,' she said. 'Do you know where there's a shop selling some?'

'That I wouldn't. But some of the Romany girls sell them, we can walk to the village and take a look. Is it for your hair you're wanting the ribbons?' He took a lock of her hair, feeling its silkiness between his fingers. 'You are beautiful, Ellen, like the summer itself. Those rose petal cheeks and cornflower eyes. And to be sure your hair is the colour of warm honey,' he said softly. He let his fingers trail onto her cheek, smoothing it gently.

152

'I suppose you see it is so different from . . .' She broke off, her face flushing with embarrassment.

'From the gypsy women's?' he said perceptively. 'Aye, it is that. My own mother has hair as glossy and black as a raven's wing.'

Her eyes softened. 'You always see things, describe things, in a different way from other men.'

'Is that good?' he asked, smiling.

'I like it,' she said simply. 'And I don't want ribbons for my hair, it's for something else. Miss Mirry gave me all her black dresses to make over for myself. I gave Olwen one and I've already made two new skirts for work, but I thought I could brighten the silk one up for best, with some lace woven with coloured ribbons.'

'Is your mistress no longer in mourning then?' Nezer asked with surprise.

'She mourns in her own way, she has no need for show,' Ellen defended. 'She really misses her Papa, she loved him very much. She knows he wouldn't like her in black . . . I think she's right too.'

'So she has discarded the black?' He raised his eyebrows at this lack of convention in the gentry.

Ellen nodded. 'She brought grey and brown dresses with her, and a dark blue one, they are like half mourning,' she defended stoutly. 'She's wearing those now until she has new ones made up.'

Hand in hand, they walked on in silence for a while, then Nezer asked: 'Do you ever resent all she has?'

Ellen looked at him in amazement. 'Resent Miss Mirry? Why ever should I? I love her, Nezer.'

'Well perhaps envy would be the better word?' His dark eyes regarded her seriously.

Ellen began to shake her head, then paused thoughtfully: 'Perhaps sometimes,' she admitted honestly. 'Sometimes it would be lovely to go out and just buy anything I wanted. New clothes or a present for my mother . . . ' She sighed. 'Just to go home and see Ma would be lovely too.'

'Have you told Miranda you're wanting that?'

'Miss Miranda, Nezer,' she corrected primly. 'No, I haven't, not really. But Miss Mirry isn't happy at Bryncarog either.'

'Why not? There is so much beauty here, sometimes I feel I could stay here for ever.' He was gazing out over the sea as he spoke, his face pensive.

'But gypsies don't stay anywhere for ever, do they?' she said lightly, though she felt the blood pounding through her veins.

He turned a solemn face to her, his eyes holding hers, but didn't reply.

'When are you moving on?' She tore her glance away.

'The family will be moving on in the next month or two. To the west coast of Wales. I have a mind to stay here until they return.' His eyes flashed to her face, gauging her reaction.

'Really? Have you ever done that before?' She kept her voice studiously casual.

'I have not. To be sure there is a first time for everything.' He offered no explanation.

Ellen turned away from him. 'I'll never get to the village at this rate. Come on!'

A heavy, salty smell rose from the seaweed on the shore, hanging heavy in the air as they wound down the lane into the village. The whitewashed cottages reflected the autumn sun. Many of them were fronted by small patches of land enclosed by a low wall, also washed in white.

'Don't they all look lovely and clean.' Ellen exclaimed with pleasure. 'What's this white stuff covering them?' She explored the low wall with her hand, feeling the surface texture.

''tis lime,' 'Nezer told her, 'kilned from the limestone rock. They dissolve it in water to make a wash.'

'Isn't that a good idea,' she approved. She picked up a loose flake, crumbling it in her fingers.

'Aye. Come on!' He took her hand. 'Let's see if they have some lace, I've a mind to buy you some.'

'You couldn't do that, Nezer. It wouldn't be . . .'

'I can do what I like. I belong to no man,' he said cheerfully.

Or woman, Ellen thought sadly.

Nine

When Ellen returned, Miranda spoke to her about the window, explaining what had happened.

'The stupid man. You could have fallen out,' Ellen exclaimed, her face horrified.

'Did you hear Captain Llewelyn ask Wyn to repair it?'

'No, Miss. But knowing Wyn, it's nothing new if he didn't do it properly,' Ellen said, examining the gaping window frame. 'The man's a fool leaving it like that. You could easily have been killed.'

Miranda shot her a reflective glance, wondering if Ellen had any suspicions similar to her own, but the maid's face expressed only contempt.

'I'll go and give him a piece of my mind,' Ellen declared. 'I'll get him to mend it right away.'

Wyn stamped up to the room later, his arms full of wood. 'Not my fault. I don't know nothin' about it,' he whined, dropping the wood on the floor.

'Well, how did the hinges become loose if you didn't unscrew them? Captain Llewelyn told me he would ask you to see to it.'

'I don't know nothin' about it. Not my fault. It must 'ave been loose and broke,' he insisted, turning his back on her to hammer a nail into wood. He continued thudding so loudly on the nails that Miranda was unable to question him further. 'This'll 'ave to do 'til we gets a new one made,' he muttered when he had boarded up the opening.

Miranda considered it in dismay. 'But that certainly will not do! You can't leave it like that!'

'Not no carpenter, am I?' he grumbled. 'Got enough to do as it is, I 'ave.'

'Well please find someone to make another immediately,' Miranda directed. 'I can't manage with it like that!'

He flashed her a sulky look but said nothing, his feet plodding noisily back down the corridor.

The humid October night air hung torpid and brooding, with not a breath of wind to stir the net curtains. Thunder, rumbling somewhere in the distance, rolled ever nearer, with transient lightning blazing fleetingly on the horizon, as Miranda tossed restlessly in her bed. The feather mattress beneath her was lumpy and uncomfortable. The sheets clung to her as she twisted and turned uneasily, tangling hopelessly around her. A streak of lightning speared the sky almost outside her window, illuminating the whole room. It was immediately followed by an ear-splitting explosion directly above, which reverberated around the house.

Miranda jerked awake and sat up wide-eyed as another crack of thunder blasted above. Realising it was only a storm, she relaxed back against her pillows.

'I'm so hot!' she murmured, passing a hand over her face. Throwing back the clothes she climbed out of bed, yanking the top sheet and blanket into a crumpled heap on the floor. She padded over to the small table, and removing the beaded cloth from the pewter jug, poured herself a glass of water. She gulped it down thirstily and poured a second, carrying it over to gaze out at the storm.

Wind suddenly whipped from nowhere, hurling her window, which she had left ajar, back against the casement. Rain, pounding the ground outside, now also beat in on her window seat. The wind, repeating its manoeuvre, flung the window back again, crashing it against the wall. The net curtains, already soaked by the rain, billowed into the room and she reached out to grasp the window to prevent it from banging against the wall again.

Leaning on the sill, she waited to see if the dramatic aerial display she had witnessed from her bed would be repeated. She could hear the waves thundering onto the rocks below and imagined the scene as the turbulent sea erupted onto the shore. The storm seemed to be passing on as the thunder diminished to an occasional grumble. She was about to turn away when one final glow lit the sky and in that brief instant she thought she saw a ship in the bay below.

Unable to believe it could possibly be true, she was

staring hard into the savage blackness when two thin beams of light suddenly pierced the night. That's not lightning, she thought, frowning. Then it came again, a distinct double flash penetrating the darkness over Pentrebach Bay.

What on earth can it be? Miranda wondered. It can never be a ship this near, right in the bay? Filled with apprehension, she gave an involuntary shudder at the thought of any boat being off course in that hostile, violent water, threatened on both sides by those ominous rocks. She stood watching for a while longer but the light was not repeated. What if it's a ship in trouble? she reflected.

Decisively she snatched up the flint and lit the candle on her bedside table. Then she tugged on her housedress and went out into the corridor. She peeped over the banister and saw a crack of light shining on the carpet in front of the drawing room door. Huw must still be up. Running lightly down the stairs in bare feet she pushed open the door. Huw was slumped in a chair, legs stretched out in front of him, a glass of brandy in his hand. He turned in surprise as she entered.

'Miranda. I thought you were in bed.' He rose as she hurried over to him, almost tripping on her housecoat. 'Is anything wrong?'

'I saw a light! In the bay.' She gestured at the window.

'A light? You saw a light?' His expression was indulgent.

She pulled her housecoat tighter around her, eyes wide with anxiety. 'Yes. I definitely saw a light flashing.'

'It was lightning. I saw that myself . . .'

'No! I saw a light before that! Then I thought I saw a ship . . .'

'A ship? But you couldn't have, it's dark! There's no moon tonight.' He chuckled with amusement.

'When the lightning flashed! I saw it then!' She shook his arm in exasperation. 'We must do something!'

'I am sure you've made a mistake . . .' he began in a soothing voice.

'I have not made a mistake,' she exclaimed. 'Certainly not about the light. Do you think it could be a ship in trouble? Perhaps trying to signal us? You must do something!'

He sighed deeply, his mouth turning down with displeasure. 'Really, Miranda I think you are making a fuss about nothing . . .'

'If you won't go to investigate I shall go myself,' she exclaimed scornfully.

'Wait!' Huw caught her arm. 'If I go out and take a look, will that please you?' He grinned disarmingly at her. 'Anything to please you. You can go back to bed.'

'I'll wait here.' She plonked herself down on the chair Huw had vacated. He would have argued but, seeing her determined face, shrugged and turned away.

'Please yourself.'

Miranda curled up in the chair, legs tucked up under her. She yawned as her eyelids began to droop and, however hard she struggled, kept closing. When Huw returned she was fast asleep.

'Come on! Up to bed, young lady,' he said softly.

Miranda blinked sleepily, rubbing her eyes like a

child. Then remembering why she was here, looked up expectantly. 'Well? Was it a ship?'

Huw shook his head. 'Nothing to worry about. Someone was down on the beach looking for his horse,' he said easily. 'It was frightened by the storm.'

'No ship?' She wrinkled her forehead, pushing her tumbled hair back from her face.

'No ship. Now back to bed or it will be time to rise before we get any sleep,' he chuckled.

'I could have sworn . . . I am glad it wasn't a ship anyway. Imagine being out in that storm.' She shivered theatrically, rubbing her arms.

He shrugged, unconcerned.

'Thank you for putting me at ease, Huw. I'm sorry I disturbed you.' Her smile was beguiling.

'My pleasure,' he murmured, his hooded eyes sliding down to her bare legs as she uncurled them from under her.

'Good night, Huw.'

Luke was alone in the dining room when Miranda arrived. 'You've returned home, then?' she said coolly.

He turned towards her smiling. 'I have. Good evening, Miranda.' He studied her face. 'You look displeased?'

Miranda marched over to him. 'Have I reason to be?' she demanded.

'I don't understand the question.' He picked up a glass from the sideboard.

Her eyes flashed fire at him. 'The window in my room—?'

'What about your window? . . . No! Don't tell me!

Wyn didn't repair it,' he sighed, pouring a sherry and holding it towards her.

She ignored the proffered glass. 'You could put it that way. Did you ask him to?'

'If I say I will do something then I always do it,' he snapped, irritated by her tone. He thumped the glass back on the sideboard.

'Then you didn't repair it yourself?'

'Don't be ridiculous! Did you expect me to?' he asked, astonished. 'I certainly didn't say I would do it myself,' he barked. 'I told you—'

'Then why were you in my room?' Miranda's voice rose, her colour draining.

'Miranda, will you please stop talking in riddles.' His eyes narrowed.

Discourteously, she enunciated each barbed word carefully and slowly. 'I-am-asking-what-you-were-doing-in-my-bedroom-on-the-morning-of-your-departure?'

Luke clenched his jaw. 'You are the most infuriating woman,' he hissed through his teeth. 'What are you afraid of? That I might pilfer something?' There was a steely glint in his eye, and he clenched one fist, thumping it into his other hand. 'Why the hell do you think I went into your room? To look at that bloody window,' he fumed.

'Please do not use your abusive seaman's language to me, sir. Wyn says you didn't mention the window.' The air crackled between them as they glared at one another.

'What? Anyway does it matter about your bl . . . your damned window not opening? Does it matter if you suffer a little discomfort for once in your cosseted life?' he roared. He twisted away impatiently, grabbing a decanter, clinking it on the glass as he sloshed brandy into his sherry glass, splashing it over the sideboard.

'It matters when I nearly fall out of the window to my death,' she flung back caustically.

He spun back. 'What do you mean?' His voice was suddenly very quiet, his eyes steel slits, his face stern.

'Exactly what I said. The hinges were unscrewed.' Her voice was low.

'Unscrewed?' He gestured with the hand holding the glass, spilling the golden liquid onto the floor.

'Yes, unscrewed! When I leaned against it, it fell out!' Her voice broke, wavering on the last words and she swallowed hard, pressing her lips together.

Neither of them turned as the door opened and Charlotte fluttered into the room. 'Good evening, Miranda. Luke. A successful trip, I hope?'

Luke seemed not to hear, his face hard as he directed his steely gaze at Miranda's face.

'Luke?' Charlotte's little eyes scanned both of them inquisitively, sensing a tense atmosphere. Ignoring her, Luke banged his glass down, stalking from the room, with long purposeful strides. 'What's upset him?' she chirped.

Miranda shrugged, her emotions in turmoil. Luke had appeared surprised, but had not directly answered her questions. If anything, she believed he had avoided them. She swallowed hard, her appetite vanishing; only this morning she had received the disturbing answer to her letter. William Langdon had informed her that Luke would indeed inherit the whole Rushton fortune should she predecease him!

They were all seated at the table when Luke returned to the room, striding over to Miranda. 'Miranda, come with me!' he commanded.

'I am having my meal.' She tossed her head, picking up her fork. It dropped clattering to the floor, as he grabbed her arm roughly, yanking her from her chair. 'How dare you—' she began.

'It will take but a few minutes.' His manner was domineering.

Huw rose to his feet, his face baffled. 'What on earth are you doing?' he barked.

'This is between Miranda and me.' Face twisted in fury, Luke silenced Huw with an intimidating glare and continued to drag Miranda, from the room and along to the kitchen.

'Wyn!' he roared, his voice reverberating from the walls. 'Did I ask you to repair the window in Miss Miranda's room?'

Wyn's face went grey as he stumbled to his feet, regarding Luke fearfully. 'I . . . I . . . Yes. Yes, Captain,' he stuttered, saliva gathering on his lips. 'I think you did, sir.'

'Think? Damnation! I—'

'You did, sir. Yes, sir, you did, Captain.'

White-faced, Miranda flashed hard, bright eyes at Luke and wrenched her arm free from his bruising fingers. 'Are you quite finished? May I go now?' she said, her voice controlled, though tears of rage filled her eyes.

'Are you satisfied?'

Miranda regarded him silently, then walked away rubbing her arm, leaving him scowling after her.

Miranda avoided Luke for the next week, still unsure what to believe. Certainly, when confronted by Luke, Wyn had admitted he'd been asked to repair her window; but he had been so terrified of Luke's anger he could have agreed to anything Luke suggested. Miranda had even confronted Wyn about the perplexing subject.

'You told me you knew nothing about my window,' she accused him.

'I was afraid I'd get into trouble, wasn't I?' he whined, his expression agitated. He pulled nervously at the neck of his shirt. 'Didn't mean no 'arm.'

'But you did unscrew the window?'

His eyes slid away from her. 'I was very busy like. I don't remember exactly what the Captain said.'

Miranda let out an exasperated breath. 'But you must remember whether you did anything to the window?'

Wyn cringed away from her.

'Never mind, you're hopeless.' She was left just as suspicious as before.

'Bye, Kate. Miranda.' Gwennie bobbed a polite curtsy to them and ran along the passage to find Olwen, leaving Kate and Miranda chatting in the drawing room.

'. . . soirée. You are all invited,' Kate was saying, 'so I do hope everyone will accept.'

'A soirée! How lovely,' Miranda exclaimed, with delight. 'I haven't been to one since I left home. It will be such a change.'

'Mama has been planning to have one for a while, so she thought it might as well be a pre-Christmas one. Do you think Charlotte will accept?'

'I know she'll be thrilled. She hardly ever seems to go anywhere.' Miranda pulled a face. 'I have managed to persuade her to come out with me a few times but that's all.'

'What about Luke? Will he be away?' Kate's face coloured slightly as she met Miranda's eyes.

'I have no idea,' Miranda said abruptly. She sprang to her feet, turning her back on Kate, fidgeting with an ornament on the mantelpiece.

'You're not on good terms again?' Kate asked, noticing her rigid stance.

Miranda said nothing for a few minutes, considering whether to admit her suspicions to Kate. She longed to share her feelings with someone, rather than bottle it all up, and Kate was a very dear friend. She replaced the ornament carefully, turned towards Kate. 'Kate . . .' she began slowly. She paused again, taking a deep breath.

'What's wrong?' Kate got up, taking her hand.

Miranda looked straight at her face. 'I haven't told this to anyone else but . . . I . . . I feel I must tell someone . . . And I would like your opinion,' she ended decisively. She proceeded to tell Kate about the accident with her window.

'How perfectly awful! You could easily have been killed!' Kate was aghast.

'Precisely!' Miranda's gaze fixed on Kate's face.

Kate's brow furrowed, her face puzzled. 'I don't understand. What are you trying to say, Miranda?'

'Do you think it was deliberate?' Her face was tense as she gave voice to her apprehension.

'What?' Kate's gasped, her eyes wide with shock. 'Don't be silly! Nobody would deliberately try to harm you.' She put an arm around the younger woman's shoulders protectively. 'You poor girl, you really have had a fright.'

'Yes. I was, and still am, very frightened.' Her eyeswere bright with unshed tears as Kate hugged her.

'It's obvious that witless Wyn was at fault.' She patted Miranda's back. 'He is appalling, so unreliable. Charles tells me Luke is very intolerant of him, but in Luke's position it is extremely awkward for him to fire Charlotte's servants.'

'I hadn't thought of that,' Miranda admitted, brushing the back of her hand across her eyes.

'Now you really must put this notion out of your head.' She drew Miranda back to the settee, settling alongside her, still holding her cold hand. 'And you must speak to Luke about it.'

'Luke?' Miranda bit her lip, realising Kate would never see her point of view.

'Of course. I know you don't always see eye to eye with him . . .'

'I cannot tell Luke.' Miranda's face drained of colour.

'Why not? Miranda! You're not trying to tell me you suspect Luke?' Kate's voice rose incredulously. She shook her head vehemently, staring at Miranda. 'How could you? Luke of all people? He really is a caring man. What possible reason could you have to suspect Luke?'

Miranda shrugged dismissively, unwilling to admit her fears. 'I'm just being silly,' she murmured, trying to dismiss the subject and sorry now that she had mentioned it.

'I'm sure you are. And you really must discuss it with him. Luke is so capable and . . . and . . . I know he will reassure you.'

Luke came from the rear of the house into the hall in time to meet Miranda and Kate leaving the drawing room.

'Good afternoon, ladies.' He swept his top hat off, nodding his head.

'Luke! I was about to take my leave.' He noticed Kate flush slightly as she addressed him, lending an attractive rosy tinge to her creamy skin. 'I've been issuing an invitation to a soirée at our home. I hope you will be able to attend.'

He returned her smile warmly but shook his head. 'I would be most happy to accept but I am about to leave for Rushton Hall in the morning.'

Her face fell. 'How long will you be away? It is a pre-Christmas soirée and not until next month.'

'Then I accept. It is but a flying visit. I most certainly should have returned before then.'

Her face lit up again and she beamed widely. He regarded her with pleasure, not for the first time thinking how pretty was her delicate complexion and how sunny and uncomplicated her nature. His glance strayed to the defiant form of Miranda alongside her: Miranda of the temper tantrums. Her flashing eyes were regarding him coldly as usual. I believe she really does regard me as her enemy, he reflected.

'I will look forward to dancing with you,' he said, returning his glance to Kate. He took her hand as she held it forward.

'Until next month, Luke.'

'You won't forget your promise to return with Star?' Miranda asked reluctantly, unwilling to put herself in his debt.

'When I make a promise I never forget,' he said coldly.

'Luke is to bring my own horse, Star, here,' Miranda explained to Kate. 'Will Huw be home soon?' she asked, as Luke moved to pass. 'We were to go riding again together. I hope he has not forgotten.'

Luke hesitated, knowing Huw was still in a tavern at Swansea. 'I think he has been held up,' he replied gallantly. 'If you wish for company I would be pleased to accom—'

'It is not important,' Miranda dismissed him.

Luke smiled wryly, his eyes meeting Kate's thoughtful ones, and he noticed Kate press her lips together disapprovingly. 'As you wish. But take care, it will be dark soon.'

'I am not a child, Luke, even though I know you still consider me as one,' she snapped, raising her chin in her typical manner.

'I am responsible for you, however capable you may be,' he rebuked her brusquely. 'If you will excuse me ladies. Kate. Miranda.' Luke nodded and left them, ascending the stairs two at a time in effortless strides. As he passed along the landing, he heard Kate's voice.

'That was very uncharitable, Miranda.'

'Fiddlesticks! He cares not. He thinks I am an uncontrollable child and he cannot bear not to be in control.'

He pushed his bedroom door closed, shrugged out of his jacket and tugged off his cravat, flinging them on the bed. Pulling a leather bag from his closet he gathered together his shaving things and tossed them into the bag, still annoyed with Miranda. He topped these with spare shirts and linen in preparation for his journey the next day.

Miranda understands me well: I do like to be in control, he mused, considering her words. And she is certainly a law unto herself. She must have been ridiculously spoiled by Stanton, always had her every wish granted. Very different from the harsh treatment he administered to me, he thought cynically.

After all these years, he could normally reflect on his childhood without bitterness. However, sometimes he remembered Stanton's indifference to him so clearly, and his fruitless struggle to gain his father's approval. From a man's viewpoint he could better understand, if not condone, Stanton's animosity at being left with an offspring in place of a beloved wife. Perhaps he could even accept the initial rejection, but to continue to reject a child was unforgivable. He could hear his own treble voice, a lonely four-year-old longing for acceptance . . .

'Papa, will you come and see how well I can ride?' He'd gazed up with pleading eyes.

'I have no time.'

'Please, Papa.' He had clung to his coat. 'Please. Just for a few minutes . . .'

'Do get out of the way, boy, you're like a puppy around my legs. I have a call to make,' an irate Stanton had snapped, pushing him aside irritably.

'Then may I come with you, Papa? I can keep up, really I can, Papa. Stuart says I ride very well and—'

'I said I am busy! Will you not listen to anything I say?' He had been shaken roughly and thrust away as usual, his eyes shining with tears as he watched his father depart.

He learned to become adept at hiding his feelings, displaying only surly indifference and defiance. Seeking consolation in his love of horses, he lavished his affection on them, learning to ride recklessly any mount, however wild and untamed; though this seemed not to please Stanton any more than it did before. He'd rebelled by challenging authority, mutinously disobeying orders, to produce some reaction, even if wrath. In the end he had gone too far, he realised bleakly, provoking Stanton into that last violent dispute, the final enraged beating . . .

Still, if I had not run away from home I would never have ended up as a captain in the service of John Company, he thought, using the colloquial name for the East India Company. And although he would never admit it to any person, that commission had given him great personal satisfaction. Clawing his way up the hard way through the ranks was proof of his own tenacity, his own ability; something he had achieved entirely alone, without help from his discarded Rushton name or fortune.

I wonder how Miranda and I would have fared had I remained at home? I suppose we are alike, in many ways, he acknowledged, a twitch of amusement crossing his face. Miranda is also a fighter; she would never give up easily either.

He glanced through the window to see Kate's graceful figure climbing into the carriage, her immaculately liveried driver cracking a whip over the horses and driving away. Luke sighed deeply. Kate made it transparently obvious she cared for him and he had no wish to hurt her. He should be thinking of taking a wife, but until now the only woman to whom he had been truly drawn was unobtainable, he reflected, a trifle bitterly.

He had been giving serious consideration to paying court to Kate. As well as being so beautiful, she was intelligent and sweet-natured, would make a perfect wife . . . you're a fool, Luke. What else could you expect from a wife? Once again Miranda's mutinous face flashed into his mind and he dismissed the subject impatiently, giving his concentration to his packing.

He buried himself in work in the library for the next few hours, determined to finish off any loose ends before his trip to Rushton Hall. Finally completed, he tidied the papers away in a desk drawer and reached to blow out the candle.

Ten

Ellen rushed into Miranda's bedroom, hardly able to contain herself before bursting out with her news. 'Miss Mirry, Captain Llewelyn has taken Nezer on for a while to help out with the horses.' Pink with excitement, Ellen beamed at Miranda. 'He's very good with horses, so David tells me, and the Captain thought he would be handy helping out in the stables.'

'That is good news, Ellen, Nezer is excellent with horses,' Miranda agreed, pleased for him. She walked over to her washstand as Ellen poured warm water into the china washbowl. 'I remember how well he handled Star at Rushton.'

'He has a way with animals, Miss Mirry. I've seen him coax one of those silly sheep out of the gorse bushes on the cliffs, when everyone else had it struggling in further . . .' She broke off, her face flooding with colour as she suddenly realised what her words implied.

'Have you indeed?' Miranda raised teasing eyebrows and waggled a finger at Ellen. 'And what were you doing on the cliffs with Nezer, I wonder?'

'Nothing, Miss Mirry.' She shook her head vehemently. 'We were walking. Just walking and talking.' Her frank gaze scanned her mistress' face. 'I could listen to him for hours; he sees everything differently from other people. He knows such a lot of unusual things too.'

'I suppose he does,' Miranda reflected. 'He is certainly widely travelled. What about his family? I thought they had moved on.' Her smile was fondly teasing, as she was well aware of her maid's fondness for the Romany man.

Ellen glanced at Miranda, her colour rising again. She thrust a fluffy towel towards Miranda. 'I don't know, I'm sure, Miss . . . maybe he's had enough of travelling?'

'I take it you would not wish to travel, Ellen?' Miranda said, still teasing. She buried her nose in the lavender scented towel.

Ellen's expression was horrified. 'Travel? Good gracious, you don't mean that, Miss Mirry?' A little frown crept over her face. 'But sometimes people change. They do, don't they, Miss Mirry?'

Miranda, realising Ellen was serious, gave her arm a squeeze. 'Of course they do, Ellen. But I am uncertain whether a gypsy can change his ways easily.' Observing Ellen's troubled expression she added: 'But if anyone has a strong enough reason to want to change, he will.'

Still not quite reassured, Ellen held out Miranda's

riding coat, ready to help her on with it, but Miranda spun around to face her.

'Ellen. The Captain left early this morning, didn't he?'

'Yes, Miss Mirry.' She held the jacket out again. 'Wyn drove him to Swansea to catch the Post Coach.'

'That's what I thought.' Miranda had a satisfied gleam in her eye. 'I have a mood to wear my boys' riding apparel instead, today. Will you bring that to me, please, Ellen.'

'But I thought you had given up those—' she began objecting.

Aghast, Miranda's jaw dropped. 'You do still have them?'

'Of course I have, Miss. I wouldn't get rid of them without you saying so,' Ellen reproached her. She laid the jacket on the bed with a last regretful glance.

'I know that, I'm sorry, Ellen. Are they easily to hand?'

'Yes,' she admitted with reluctance. Ellen walked over to the closet and brought out the neatly folded clothes. 'Here they are, Miss Mirry.' She helped Miranda into them, her mouth set in a disapproving line.

'Just tie my hair up out of the way, please.' Miranda dropped impatiently onto a chair. She allowed Ellen to pull back the tumbling cloud of bright curls, secure them with a ribbon and then pin them up in a knot on Miranda's head.

Miranda jammed her hat on top, thrusting in any escaping tendrils with her fingers and nodding with satisfaction at her reflection. 'I had better see how well

Nezer's been managing those horses,' she chuckled as she went out.

At the stables Miranda found the door was no longer hanging loose, the hinge having been repaired and now securely in place. A pleasant smell of beeswax polish lingered in the air, muting the all-pervading, heavy odour of animals and horse dung.

'Good morning, Mistress.' David appeared from the tack room, gleaming harness and a brush still held in his hands. His eyes widened as he noticed her attire, but he immediately hid his surprise with a broad smile.

'I see you've been busy, David. Everything looks sparkling here.'

'Aye, Miss. Nezer's working with me now and there's a great help he is.' He gestured to the gypsy who had followed him out. 'Nezer. Do you know Mistress Rushton, the Captain's sister?'

Nezer leaned one arm against the wooden upright, beaming. 'To be sure. Haven't our people camped on Rushton lands often enough? It's many a time I've seen Miss Rushton enjoying a gallop over the heath ever since she was but a little thing. She's a real lady for the fresh air. She's no weakling, afraid to let the breeze blow on her.' His voice changed, taking a serious note. 'It's sorry I was to hear of your father's passing on, Miss Rushton. A great man he was, a great man indeed, Miss.'

'Thank you Nezer,' she whispered, swallowing the lump that rose in her throat. She fiddled with a harness to mask her feelings.

'He's mourned by the Romanies, Mistress. Our

whole tribe mourned for his passing.' His expression was sincere, full of sympathy.

'I miss him too, Nezer, so very much.' Making an effort to shake off her distress she asked: 'Have your people moved on yet, Nezer?'

'They have indeed, Mistress. Further west. But they'll be making their way back soon. It will be on the way to Glastonbury they'll be travelling, for a meeting of the clans at the winter solstice.'

'Will you want to stay on here?'

'If I feel the need to linger, Mistress.' He regarded her quizzically, lips turned up at one corner. 'Not that I'm lonely . . .' then hastened to add: 'I've my dog for company. I'm thinking I wouldn't be staying without her.' His dark eyes danced with mischief, his grin infectious as Miranda and David caught his mood and returned his smile.

'Where do you live?' Miranda pulled some grass for the horses, who were turning their heads around towards her.

'Live?' he said with surprise.

'Now that your family wagons have moved on.' She fed Cariad and pulled some more grass.

His face cleared. 'Under the stars, Mistress, where else?' He picked up a stiff broom and began vigorously sweeping out a stall. 'The weather has not been that cold yet, and I've a fine tent of sackcloth which has served me well. I've a mind to be building my own wagon . . . or even to take a cottage maybe.' He threw her an enigmatic look.

'In the village?' Miranda asked, wondering how the villagers would view that.

He lifted his shoulders. 'Maybe, Miss Rushton. Maybe.' And his grin flashed again, teeth sparkling against his dark face.

'I thought Romanies never lived indoors?'

He pursed his lips, head on one side. 'Not many,' he agreed. 'But to be sure there's a first time for everything in this world. I've a mind to try it.'

'I wonder why,' she chuckled.

His expression was bland. 'I'll have to be getting on with my work if you'll be excusing me, Mistress.' He turned away, whistling as he swept.

David had been lifting a saddle from the rack as Miranda was talking to Nezer. Noticing, she caught his arm.

'I don't want a side-saddle today, David,' she told him.

Surprised, David paused, still holding the saddle. His glance dropped to her boys' riding breeches. Hearing a snicker behind them, they turned to see Satan stretching his head towards Miranda.

'Hello, my fine fellow. Haven't I paid you attention today?' Watched by the two men she took another handful of grass and sidled alongside him into his stall, feeding the horse with it as she stroked his velvet nose.

David replaced the original saddle and took down the one she had requested. By this time he was well used to seeing her enter Satan's stall and could accept her capable handling of the horse without apprehension. However, she had never asked for a man's saddle before.

'You are a beauty, indeed,' Miranda whispered in the horse's ear. 'You want to go out, I know you do.

David,' she called softly. 'Has Satan been out today?'

'No, Mistress. The Captain—'

'So he needs exercising?' She studied the horse, a gleam in her eye.

'Yes, Miss. I'll have to take him out presently.' He pulled a face, eyeing the horse without pleasure.

'You ride him then?'

'Not unless I have to, Miss. Don't really trust him. He's thrown me a few times . . . and Mr Huw. Not that I mind taking a tumble like, had enough of those, haven't I?' His plain face crinkled in a grin. 'He's really the Captain's horse. They understand one another.'

'Is that a fact?' Miranda eyed him speculatively.

'I often take him on a lead rein but Nezer can ride him easily, mind you. He can ride anything. He charms him, same as everything else, whispering sweet words in his ear.' Behind Miranda's back David grinned, nudging Nezer in the ribs with his elbow, giving him a knowing grin.

Miranda turned to catch the two lads' guilty expressions and Nezer's dark skin took on a rosy hue.

'Then saddle Satan, not Cariad, please David.'

David's mouth fell open and he regarded her with horror. 'Miss Miranda . . .' He swallowed hard. 'You're not considering riding Satan, are you?' His voice rose anxiously.

'I am certainly not considering it.' As David exhaled a sigh of relief she continued: 'I have already decided.'

'What?' Adding hastily: 'Miss.'

'I will ride Satan.' She stood back to allow David to enter the stall.

'Satan?' he yelped.

'Surely you can understand English, David? I am afraid I have no Welsh.' She smiled at her own joke although the groom was unamused.

'But, Mistress, the Captain . . . he'd skin me alive he would.'

'Would he indeed?' Miranda said coldly. 'Did he instruct you that I am not to ride Satan?'

'Well Miss . . . not exactly like,' he admitted unwillingly. 'But there's mad he'll be.'

'Why? Because someone other than he can ride Satan?'

David stared at her with shocked disbelief. 'No, Miss. But what if he threw—'

'Herself can ride anything,' Nezer interrupted him. 'You should see her own horse.'

'The matter is not open for discussion,' Miranda said firmly. 'I want you to saddle Satan! Now, please, David!' Her authoritative tone left no room for argument and David moved reluctantly to comply. 'And finish saddling Cariad and one of you can ride with me to give her some exercise.'

Nezer took Satan's head, all the time whispering in the horse's ear, as David saddled him. The words, if they were such, were inaudible to either Miranda or David, but Satan, who always hated having the bridle and bit put on, seemed to calm at his words, and pranced less restlessly.

Harnessing completed, David stood back, his white face puckered fearfully. Miranda raised her chin imperiously, waiting for him to assist her to mount.

'Mistress—'

'A hand if you please, David!' Her authority was not to be challenged as she gripped the saddle.

David cupped his hands and, stepping into them, Miranda swung her leg lightly over into the saddle. The horse rolled his eyes, whites showing, and Miranda leaned forward, stroking his gleaming, black-satin neck.

'Easy, my beauty. Easy,' she soothed, settling herself into the saddle. 'We'll get on very well together. Thank you, Nezer.' She nodded to the gypsy who carefully released the horse's head. Satan took a few prancing steps, but his eyes were calm now as Miranda sat comfortably in control.

'Well, who's coming with me?' she asked, her face alive and glowing with anticipation. 'I think Satan is eager to be off.' The saddle leather creaked beneath her and the harness clinked as the horse pranced restively.

'I'll come, Mistress. If I can just finish saddling Cariad, like,' David hurriedly grabbed a saddle and flung it onto the horse's back.

'We will just take a turn around the yard.' Miranda pressed her heels gently against Satan's sides and he danced forward, lifting his feet. Miranda felt the latent power of the horse surge beneath her as he trotted eagerly around the yard. David vaulted into the saddle, his face grim.

'I believe Satan often jumps that gate with my brother? Isn't that so?' Miranda said, pointing her crop at the gate on the outer yard.

David gave an anguished gulp and clenched his teeth.

'David? You are strangely deaf today. Did you hear my question?'

The groom shook his head with despair. 'No, Miss.' He turned away as he spoke, avoiding her eyes.

'I've seen Captain Llewelyn jump the gate more than once,' she accused. 'I think you are not speaking truthfully?'

'Maybe the Captain does, but no-one else. Please, Miss. Don't try it,' he begged. 'For my sake if not your—'

Before he could finish the sentence Miranda tapped her heels into Satan's sides, urging him forwards. She lifted in the saddle and leaned over his neck as the horse surged confidently towards the gate, soaring effortlessly over and thundering on towards the path.

Drunk with elation Miranda leaned forward, patting the horse's neck, congratulating him, coaxing him to further efforts as, with a look of utter disbelief, David tore after them.

Miranda heard the gypsy's whoop of exultation following her as she rode away.

Eleven

Miranda was dreading the coming festive season. The thought of a Christmas, which included neither her adored Papa nor Mama, was intolerable. It had been bad enough these last five years since Mama had passed on, but she had gradually learned to accept her mother's absence, binding herself even closer to her father to compensate. Without his dearly loved face full of indulgent expectancy as she opened her numerous gifts, how would she bear it? And although she managed to hide her misery quite successfully, nothing really took away the knot of desolation inside her.

She decided to concern herself in Gwennie's anticipation instead, but was surprised at the child's lack of excitement for the approaching festival.

'What presents do you hope to receive, Gwennie?' she asked.

'Me? . . . I don't know.' Seeming without interest, she skipped over to the fireplace and knelt down in front of it. 'Ceridwen says I won't get any. She thinks I'm too naughty.'

'Gwennie! Why do you listen to that horrible old witch?' Miranda leaned forward warningly as a glowing coal fell out into the hearth and rolled towards Gwennie. 'Mind you don't get too near,' she cautioned the child.

'Do you think she's a witch? A real witch?' Gwennie's sapphire eyes opened even wider with superstitious horror. 'She looks like a witch.' She dropped her voice. 'Olwen thinks she is. And, when she was cross once, Mrs Cain called her a witch . . . .'

'Of course she's not, you little goose. There aren't any real witches, those are just tales told to frighten children and make sure they behave.' Miranda prodded the coals in the fire, making them into a more stable pile.

Gwennie glanced furtively around over her shoulder. 'There's a wise woman in Llanmor.' She nodded solemnly. 'Olwen told me,' she confided in a whisper, her hand shielding her mouth. 'She went to her . . . to make her mother better.'

'What was wrong with her mother?' Miranda's disbelief was evident. Miranda put the poker back in its stand, returning to her seat. 'Did it work?'

'I don't know. She didn't tell me. But I'd like to see a wise woman.' She gave a shudder of mock terror. 'Would you, Miranda?'

Miranda laughed. 'What do I want to see her for? I believe you see far too much of those servants. We must make sure we spend more time together so we can have some fun.'

Gwennie's angelic face lit in a smile, and she scrambled to her feet, rushing over to Miranda, grasping her around the knees. 'I love you, Miranda. You always talk to me . . . like I'm grown up.'

'I love you too, Gwennie.' Miranda hugged her, dropping a kiss on her curly hair. 'You must never underestimate yourself, Gwennie, never. Do you hear me?' She bent down, studying the child's face.

'What's underest . . .?' Her voice trailed off in a question.

'Underestimate? That means not thinking highly enough of something. You are a very pretty young lady and are certainly not wicked. You must always remember you are as good as anyone else. Anyone!'

'I'll 'member, Miranda.' She nodded, her expression earnest. Dropping her head, she peered up coyly through those tangled, sooty lashes. 'Do you really think I'm pretty?'

'I do. But no more of that now.' Miranda changed the subject, not wanting to make the child too aware of the extraordinary beauty she obviously shared with her grandmother. 'Now what about Christmas shopping?'

Gwennie's face lit up expectantly. 'Can I go? I've never been.'

Miranda nodded, smiling. 'Do you get an allowance, Gwennie?'

Puzzled, Gwennie frowned. 'A 'llowance? I don't know.' Never still for long, she began flitting about the room again. 'What's a 'llowance?'

'I mean, do you receive any money of your own?

To spend as you wish?'

Gwennie came to an abrupt stop, shaking her head. 'Who'd give me money?' she said with genuine surprise.

'You should have something.' Miranda pursed her lips, her thoughts racing. After all this child was her niece. 'I shall make you a small allowance each month and you can do just as you like with it.'

Gwennie clapped her hands, her face alive with excitement. 'Money? You mean money of my own?'

'I do,' Miranda agreed, her face alight with laughter at Gwennie's astonishment.

'And I can buy anything I like? In the whole world?' Delighted, she jumped up and down on the spot, clapping her hands again.

Miranda shared the child's pleasure. 'Yes. You may decide. But . . . you will need to save if you wish to buy something expensive.' Miranda looked around for her reticule.

'What's ex . . . what's that?' Gwennie asked.

'Something which costs a lot of money.'

'I couldn't buy a pony then?'

'A pony!' Miranda's brows arched. 'You certainly could not. A pony is very expensive.' Miranda had been giving Gwennie riding lessons and she was becoming quite accomplished. 'Of course you might want to buy a present for someone else?'

Gwennie nodded, her eyes sparkling. 'Oh yes! For Olwen. And Kate. I like them, and—'

'Just a minute!' Laughing, Miranda held up her hand. 'Before you can decide, you need to know how much you have to spend. I shall give some thought about how much allowance you will get. Then you may receive it on the first day of each month . . .'

'The first day?' Her face dropped. 'But that's . . .' She broke off, colouring with guilty embarrassment, but her disappointment was obvious.

'The first of October is already well past.' Miranda finished the sentence, understanding her reasoning. 'Is that what you thought?'

Gwennie shook her head, looking down at the floor.

'Gwennie, don't ever be afraid to tell me the truth.'

'Yes. I did think that,' she whispered.

'Little goose. It doesn't matter. I had already considered that. I'll tell you what I'll do. Because I have been here . . . let me see . . . how long is it? Yes, over seven months already, counting this month, I shall give you your allowance for each of those past months, so it will be as though you had already saved it for seven months. And as it is Christmas I shall give you a little extra, for December only . . .'

Gwennie threw her arms around Miranda's neck, squeezing hard. 'Thank you, Mirry. I've heard Ellen call you that,' she explained. 'Can I?'

'Stop! You're choking me. Of course you may call me Mirry. Most people close to me call me that.'

'And I'm close,' she exclaimed. Her brow furrowed. 'But Ellen's only a maid . . .'

'I don't want to hear you say things like that!' Miranda corrected her sharply, giving her arm a little shake. 'Not ever! Maids must not be belittled. They are people with feelings too.'

'I'm sorry.' Gwennie's voice was crestfallen and tears shimmered on her lashes.

'Don't cry . . . just remember it, Gwennie,' Miranda's voice softened. 'It is very important. But in any case, Ellen is also my friend. We love each other dearly.'

Gwennie nodded solemnly. 'I'll 'member.' She regarded Miranda thoughtfully. 'Olwen loves me too, Mirry.' They smiled companionably at each other.

'So the next thing is for us to go shopping; to Swansea I suppose.' She fumbled in her reticule. 'I'll give you your allowance later today, and in the meantime you can make out a list of those you wish to buy presents for.'

'Will you help me? I can't spell all the names.'

'We'll do that later. In the meantime you think about it and do your best.' She gave the child a gentle kiss on the cheek.

'Charlotte. Do you go into Swansea to do your Christmas shopping?' Miranda asked, as she spooned a portion of scrambled egg onto her breakfast plate the following morning. She scanned the sideboard and sighed. 'No toast again.' She yanked at the bell cord and poured herself tea before carrying her breakfast to the table. Thinking Charlotte had not heard, Miranda turned to her, repeating her question.

'I suppose so,' Charlotte said bleakly.

Miranda regarded her more closely, thinking Charlotte appeared older and more crumpled today. 'Is something wrong, Charlotte? You look worried.'

Charlotte raised her shoulders in a shrug. 'Nothing's wrong.'

'I'm sure there is.' Impulsively, Miranda walked

over, putting an arm around Charlotte's shoulders. For a moment the older woman did not respond, leaning away from Miranda, her dumpy, little body rigid. Then she relaxed, and turning towards Miranda, she patted the hand on her shoulder.

'Thank you for your concern. You are a kind girl, Miranda. I'm afraid it is just the time of the year.'

'I know exactly what you mean, I understand why you feel unhappy,' Miranda exclaimed, with a rush of sympathy. 'I am so missing my dear Papa and at times like this you miss your . . . husband,' she ended lamely, realising Charlotte's husband had been dead for many years.

Her eyes flashed at her reflectively. 'Yes,' she replied, lacking conviction.

'That's not the main reason though?' Miranda said perceptively.

Charlotte gave a little sigh. 'I become anxious about how I shall manage . . .' She broke off, biting her lip. 'There, you have coaxed it from me. I had no wish to tell you.'

'You're short of money? Don't you receive a bigger allowance to cover Christmas?'

Charlotte grimaced. 'From where? The firm is very hard pressed to hold its own, or so I am told.' She glanced down at her dress with distaste. 'Do you think I enjoy wearing old garments? Kate has invited us to a soirée. What shall I be wearing? The same dress I have worn for the last . . .' Her voice ended in a choked quiver. 'Never mind. I am sure it must soon improve.'

'You rang, Miss?' Nia, the new housemaid, appeared at the door.

'More toasted bread please, Nia, ' Miranda said, returning to her place at the table, uncomfortably aware of Charlotte's embarrassment. Both women sat in silence. Charlotte snatched up the paper, rustling it ostentatiously.

Miranda considered what Charlotte had revealed. It was apparent that Llewelyn Shipping was in a worse condition than she had thought. Luke must be desperate for money. Her skin prickled slightly at this revelation; she was still uncertain of what to believe about her window, but she pushed that thought away. Huw is always fashionably well-dressed, as is Luke, she mused. Neither man seems to lack funds. Why should Charlotte be the only one to suffer, she thought cynically.

Miranda wondered how she could buy Charlotte a new gown without offending her pride; it needed some deliberation. The grandfather clock chimed the hour and Charlotte peered anxiously at it over the paper, tutting:

'Dear me! Where is Huw? He will be very late for work unless he appears soon,' she remarked. 'I hope Luke doesn't get home before . . .' She let the sentence trail off, suddenly realising what she implied.

'Luke is expected to return today?'

'So I understand.'

'I hope he has Star with him, I'm so looking forward to seeing him. I've had him since he was a foal.'

'I never could understand any lady's passion for horses.' Charlotte wobbled her head. 'I never wanted to partake in any sport. I was always much too feminine,' she added, preening slightly.

Miranda concealed a smile at the thought of Charlotte on a horse. 'Did Luke's mother ride? Or does he inherit his love of horses just from our father, as I did?'

Charlotte glanced speculatively at her. 'Yes. Bronwen adored riding. She enjoyed following the hunt too. Horrible smelly things, horses.' She pulled her mouth down.

'Is that how she got to know Papa? At Bath, I believe you said previously?'

'Yes. Perhaps I should have tried it,' she said archly.

'Whom did you say you were visiting?'

'I am uncertain now. Probably Lord Mark.'

Miranda nodded. 'Papa and I stayed at his estates a few times, it was quite a while ago.' She noticed Charlotte peer at the clock again. 'I am to ride with Huw this afternoon; perhaps I'll have Star before then.'

Charlotte flashed an approving smile. 'You and Huw seem to spend much time together. I believe he is becoming very fond of you.'

'I like Huw, he's good fun and I enjoy his company. He rides well too.'

'He does. He is every bit as accomplished as Luke.' Charlotte snorted. 'Though I doubt Luke would agree.'

Miranda didn't reply, realising she did not agree either. Even though she disliked Luke, she fully appreciated he was an outstanding horseman, equalled only by their late father. Papa probably taught him to ride as he had taught . . . no! Luke told her he hadn't. Her reverie was broken, as she heard Luke's resonant voice in the hall. She pushed back her chair, hurrying out eagerly to hear about Star.

'Good morning, Luke. Did you have a good journey?'

'Good morning, Miranda. You seem unduly anxious to greet me!' He grinned sardonically, not taken in by her words. 'I wonder why?'

She tossed her head. 'You malign me, brother. I merely expressed concern over your—'

'Yes, I have brought Star. He is a wonderful—'

'Oh thank you, Luke.' He seemed astonished as she flung her arms around his neck, pressing a kiss on his cheek, noticing for the first time the sharp, spicy smell of his cologne. But he didn't respond to her embrace, regarding her with detachment, his eyes enigmatic sapphire pools. He does resent me, Miranda thought, pulling away peevishly. Then she became aware of another man entering the hall, canvas valise in his hand.

'Miranda, allow me to present a very good friend of mine, Captain Will Owen of the East India Company. Captain Owen, my sister, Mistress Miranda Rushton.'

'At your service, Miss Miranda.' He swept his hat off with a flourish, leaning gallantly over her hand. His clear grey eyes rose to meet hers, a twinkle dancing in their depths as he smiled down at her. Not quite as tall as Luke, he seemed equally as well muscled, moving with the familiar agile grace which seemed a common denominator of a life spent at sea.

'I am very pleased to meet you, Captain Owen. Are you a serving member of the company?'

'That I am, though at present on extended leave.

My grandfather passed away during my last voyage. Being his only living heir, I have been given six months leave of absence to sort out affairs for my grandmother,' he explained frankly, a Welsh lilt noticeable in his speech.

'We met by chance at a coach-house in Bristol,' Luke explained. 'I invited Will to be our guest for a few days. I must see Charlotte about it; is she still at breakfast?' he asked, turning away, leaving Will with Miranda.

'Have you eaten this morning, Captain Owen?'

'Indeed. Many hours since, Miss Miranda.' He grinned engagingly, his even teeth white against the deep tan of his face. 'I would not refuse a of cup of tea, though.'

Taking him into the drawing room, Miranda rang for refreshments, seating herself as he waited to take a place opposite. 'Were you and Luke together at sea?' Miranda asked curiously.

He chuckled. 'Aye! Many a year. As boys we were midshipmen on the same ship and saw some good times together. We were split up for a while as lieutenants. Then I was lucky to be posted as his second mate on *The Indian Princess* – his command, you understand. I served as his first mate for the last two voyages after Horace Mortimer was killed.'

'Killed? At sea?' she exclaimed.

He hesitated. 'Aye.'

'What happened?'

He shrugged. 'A battle with pirates; it happens sometimes, Miss Miranda. I was more than sorry to see Luke leave the Service,' he said, leading her away from the subject.

'But surely it is more satisfying to be a Captain with your own command?'

'True. But I sorely missed him.' He glanced quizzically at her. 'I understand you and Luke have not long been acquainted, so you would not realise your brother was a first-rate seaman and commander. He's a good man to have at your back, pulled me out of more than one tight spot, I can tell you . . .' He paused as Nia came in with the tea-tray, placing it on the low table and Miranda was pleased to see her give a little curtsy. Ellen was doing an excellent job; the staff were certainly improving. Ceridwen and Wyn, however, would never improve, she knew.

'You also are Welsh, Captain Owen?'

'I am. Our family is from the Porthcawl area, so I always lived near the sea as a child.'

'Is that where your grandmother lives at present?'

'Aye. My home too.'

'Was it your close proximity to the sea that influenced your choice of career?'

'Probably. Though my maternal grandfather was also a seafaring man . . .' He broke off as Luke entered, giving him a surprisingly informal wink.

'All settled.' Luke pulled a face and, dropping his voice, added, 'You will recall Charlotte's lack of warmth towards visitors from your last stay here. I am afraid there is nothing to be done about that.' Both men laughed but Miranda, remembering Charlotte's confession, realised this was another burden for Charlotte's budget. She must mention it to Luke at a more convenient hour.

Miranda could hardly wait to escape and go out to see Star. Holding up her skirts, she ran to the stables, and dashed inside.

'Star, my beauty,' she called. 'Where are you?' There was a loud whinny as she hurried towards the stalls. Star turned his head, extending it back as far as he could to reach her.

Miranda rushed into his stall, stumbling through the straw in her eagerness to see her horse. Throwing her arms around his neck, she kissed the white star-shaped mark on his velvet nose, over and over, the mark he was named for, and kept smoothing him, whispering endearments all the while. Tears filled her eyes, as she rubbed her cheek against him, still murmuring to him.

'To be sure you'll want him saddled, Miss Miranda?' Nezer asked with a smile, already holding her saddle in his arms.

'Thank you, Nezer,' Miranda murmured. She beamed at him. 'I can't wait, but I'll have to change first.'

'He knew you were near,' Nezer continued. 'Didn't he keep turning his head, looking for you.'

Excited, Miranda flew back inside and up the stairs. Flinging open her cupboard, she grabbed the nearest riding habit and pulled it on before racing back to the stables. Star, already saddled and in the yard, snickered another greeting, and she fed him a sugar lump from her pocket.

'That didn't take long,' she chuckled to the two young men who were both grinning.

'I don't blame you, Miss Miranda. He's a really

beautiful animal,' David said as he held a hand for her to mount. She swung up easily in the saddle, the metal clinking on his bridle as Star pranced, restless to be off. Watched by Nezer and David, she cantered through the yard and out, making for the path towards the long beach.

'Have a good ride,' Nezer called after her.

She waved a hand in the air in acknowledgement. At last I have my Star back, she thought. I'll not leave you again, my friend, she vowed.

Miranda decided she would buy a new dress for Charlotte as a Christmas present. In that way she could hardly consider it to be charity. But the main problem was how to go about getting her measurements to give to the dressmaker. Without revealing Charlotte's true circumstances, Miranda took Ellen into her confidence.

'We could find out who her own dressmaker is, Miss Mirry. She would have all her measurements,' Ellen suggested, busy rearranging clothes in the cupboard.

'But as you have previously pointed out, the styles she presently wears are terribly out of date.' Miranda slipped an earring through her ear lobe. 'In any case, I don't believe she has had any new dresses made for quite some time.'

'It certainly looks that way, Miss Mirry. Why ever not, I often wonder? She can't care much what she looks like.' Having always been in service with the wealthy Rushton family, Ellen would never even consider that any member of the gentry might be unable to afford a new dress.

'Perhaps she feels she doesn't go out enough to need them. Anyway, I wish to engage my own dressmaker.' She poked in her jewellery box for the matching earring.

'I could ask Nia to bring one of Mrs Cain's dresses. She could make the excuse she was taking it to launder or repair.'

'That is an excellent suggestion. Write down all the measurements for me and I'll take them with me. Tell Nia it is to be kept a secret between us three. Explain it is for Mrs Cain's Christmas present.' Ellen brushed some fluff off Miranda's shoulder as she rose to leave.

'I wish you to make a new dress for my aunt,' Miranda informed Mrs Baker, as an assistant placed a cup of tea alongside her. 'Is it possible to make it from these measurements? She can't attend in person as I want it to be a surprise present.'

'What a lovely idea, Miss Rushton.' The dressmaker's eyes gleamed as she held up the pair of wire glasses, suspended on a ribbon around her neck, and peered down her long nose to scan the figures. She was more than pleased to receive wealthy Miss Rushton's aunt as another prospective customer. 'There should be no difficulty with these measurements, Miss Rushton. They are quite comprehensive.'

'There is another stipulation. I need the dress completed by next Wednesday? Will you manage that?'

'I am sure we can manage that,' she purred, placing the list on a table cluttered with pincushions, tape measures and samples of material. 'I will have my assistants work solely on this dress until its completion. Have you some idea of the style you require?'

'I will be guided by your expertise in that matter, Mrs Baker. Obviously it will need to be suitable for my aunt's mature years. She is in her fifties, but I also want it to be pretty and fashionable.' Miranda sipped her tea from its bone china cup.

'I understand perfectly, Miss Rushton. As you know I make all the clothes for Mrs David Dart as well as for her daughter, Miss Kate. I believe they recommended me?' she added smugly. 'You would like to see some fabrics?' She waved an imperious hand at her hovering minions. 'Have you a colour preference?'

'A soft blue or pink shade would suit her, I believe. And it must be a good warm material,' Miranda added, reflecting on draughty Bryncarog.

She examined the bolts of cloth held out for her, fingering them, finally narrowing it down to two. 'Which do you like, Gwennie?' she asked, unable to make up her mind between a downy wool, in a pinky-lilac shade and a soft sapphire-blue velvet.

'This one.' Reverently Gwennie stroked the sheeny velvet. 'It's so lovely and smooth.'

Miranda's eyes narrowed thoughtfully. 'I will take the lilac,' she decided. 'The other one would suit you, Gwennie. It is the exact colour of your eyes.'

Mrs Baker smiled indulgently down at Gwennie. 'Such beautiful eyes. A dress for this little lady too?'

'Yes. The velvet please.' She grinned at Gwennie's expression of delight, receiving as much pleasure as the child. 'And I also want an evening dress for myself.'

By the time Gwennie's measurements had also been taken, Miranda was far later returning home than she had expected and Kate's carriage was already standing outside. They hurried up the steps and into the hall as Charlotte fluttered down the stairs towards them.

'Hello, Charlotte. We are rather late, I'm afraid. You run and have a quick glass of milk and some oatcakes, Gwennie,' Miranda urged her towards the kitchen. 'I shall explain to Kate.'

Charlotte sniffed disapprovingly. 'Kate has been here some time. Wherever have you been?' She lifted her fob watch to see the time.

'Gwennie and I have been to the dressmaker,' Miranda replied without thinking. As she spoke she groaned inwardly, noticing Charlotte's face take on a dismal expression.

'I see. I suppose you feel you need new clothes for Christmas,' she said bleakly.

'Excuse me, Charlotte, but I must see Kate,' Miranda put her hand on the door knob.

'You have no need for concern. Kate seems well entertained by Captain Owen.' Charlotte's voice was cool and she fluffed her shawl around her like a bird ruffling its feathers. 'They had little need of my company.' Laughter bubbled through the unopened door as if to prove her point.

'Good afternoon.' For a few moments neither of the occupants were aware of Miranda's entry as they continued engrossed in animated conversation. 'Good afternoon,' she repeated, approaching them.

'Miranda!' Kate's wide mouth positively beamed at her as Captain Owen scrambled politely to his feet.

'Kate. Please accept my apologies for detaining Gwennie . . .' Miranda began.

'No need. I didn't even notice.' Kate waved a nonchalant arm, brushing away her apology. 'Captain Owen has been keeping me well entertained.' She directed her attention back to him as he stood returning her gaze with evident pleasure. 'He has many interesting tales to impart.'

'It seems you have done me a service, Captain.' Miranda was disconcerted when he did not respond immediately, only to start and tear his eyes away from Kate with obvious reluctance, when she repeated: 'Captain?'

'Miss Miranda?' Obviously, he had not even heard what she said.

'I said it seems you have done me a service in entertaining Mistress Kate,' she repeated, sinking down on a chair.

'It has been my pleasure, Miss Miranda. Though in truth the time has passed swiftly.'

'I am sure it has,' she said tartly with a sudden empathy for Charlotte. Miranda was not used to inattention from any man. 'Have you received refreshments?'

'Refreshments?' he said vaguely, his eyes still on Kate as he sat back down alongside her.

Miranda sucked in an exasperated breath and walked over to the bellpull.

'Captain Owen has agreed to attend our soirée on Friday week. You must make sure you do not forget, Captain,' Kate said gaily, giving him an unusually coquettish glance.

He grinned at her. 'I assure you, I will not forget, Miss Kate.' He added softly: 'I look forward to it.'

As they carried on talking, Miranda studied the two of them. They were oblivious to her presence, still very engrossed in each other.

'My goodness! Gwennie! I had completely forgotten about her,' Kate exclaimed. 'You will please excuse me, Captain?' she said with obvious reluctance.

'If I must,' he said wryly. 'Could we go for a walk perhaps, later?'

'I am sure Gwennie would like to go,' she murmured. 'That would be lovely, Capt—'

'Will. Please call me Will. How often do you call to teach Gwennie?'

She beamed, her face flushing prettily. 'I will be here again on Thursday.'

'May I see you then?' he said eagerly.

I think my brother has left it too late, Miranda decided, as Kate opened the door and left the room. Kate's heart has been captured by another.

Twelve

The sea was rough, its surface bristling in angry-looking peaks. A four-masted sailing ship passed quite close inshore, its sails flattened, beating hard against the wind. Its bow thudded into each wave with a shuddering jar. A flock of gulls hung above it waiting for waste to be jettisoned, calling and screaming to one another as they effortlessly swooped and dived on the wind's currents.

'I'd like to see the water up real close,' Ellen said. They were watching the encroaching waves crash onto the limestone crags below, sending high white plumes of water into the air. 'It would be lovely to walk on the beach. Do you think we could go down?'

'That's where we're going, my girl,' Nezer said. 'Does it matter to you which bay? 'tis easier to get down into the valley. Llanmor is quite a walk away, and to be sure the tide would be well up the beach when we got there.'

Ellen shook her head. 'I don't mind which. I thought we could walk on the sand and just look at the water.' She grabbed her bonnet as a swirl of wind would have stolen it.

Keeping her hand in his, Nezer led her across the cliffs to their left. 'There are old wooden steps near here. We have to take care though, as they are in poor repair.'

Ellen hesitated on seeing the rotting wood of the steps, which clung precariously to the cliff-side, winding their way down.

'Are you sure they're safe?' she queried, pulling back, reluctant to commit herself to them.

'I've been down them many a time,' he reassured her, holding his hand out to her. 'It's just careful we have to be. Pick our way.'

'What if my bonnet blows off?' She had one hand firmly jamming it on her head.

'Give it to me.' He held out his hand and, tying the ribbons together, hung it over one arm.

Nezer went first, carefully testing each board with his foot before putting his weight on it. Ellen held her skirts back in one hand, preventing them snagging on the splintered wood as she ventured onto it. They picked their way down the rickety steps which lacked even a handrail in places, making Ellen even more apprehensive when she viewed the long drop down to the beach.

'Here! Put your feet where I tell you,' Nezer said, gripping her arm. 'Do you think I would let my own sweet girl fall?'

The steps ended halfway down the cliff, emerging onto the path taken by the horses, and Ellen stepped onto the sand with a sigh of relief.

'There's a proper path going up there,' she exclaimed, pointing. 'Why did we need to take those awful old steps?'

'Because they were near where we were walking. The beginning of that path is way back the other way, not far from the manor.'

Ellen gazed around the beach with pleasure. 'It's real pretty down here. What are these old steps for anyway? Does anyone use them?' She glanced up at them again curiously, thinking how unsafe they looked.

Ellen watched as Nezer stopped, tugging off his soft leather boots, to walk on the wet sand with his bare feet. 'I think it's the smuggling they were used for in times past,' he said, answering her question. 'There was a cottage or something on the cliffs at one time, I am told.'

Ellen flashed him a quick sideways look. 'Is it used now?' She caught up her skirts as they dragged in the sand.

Nezer laughed. 'Never. To be sure anyone carrying a load up there would fall straight through the boards.'

A flock of gulls rose screaming from the beach as they approached them, landing with a flurry of wings further along. A separate group of sandpipers raced away.

'How do you know so much about what goes on with smuggling?' Ellen probed. She had been worrying that Nezer could be involved.

'Romanies know everything,' he teased, his fingers reaching for her hand again. 'We need to!'

'And do the smugglers use the path now instead?' She followed the path up with her eyes. 'It doesn't look very big.'

'That they do! No horse would go down those steps. Even I could not get one down there,' he said, bragging a little.

'I don't know much about horses. They frighten me.' Shading her eyes with her hand, she gazed inland to the rivulet's mouth. 'Is that the other village? Pentrebach?' she asked, pointing at the little hamlet crouched in the valley.

'Aye. Though it's not exactly a village, more like a hamlet. But about horses . . . 'tis gentle animals they are if they're treated right.'

'They are so huge and smelly,' she said, wrinkling her nose. 'What about Satan? I've heard David talking about how wild he is.'

'Satan is a stallion; they are always harder to control. He is free spirit, knows his own mind.' He curled his bare toes around a worm cast, flattening it. 'And to be sure Luke likes it that way. He rides Satan without any problem . . .'

'But Miss Miranda has ridden him. She told me she had.' Her eyes widened. 'Was it very dangerous for her?'

Nezer laughed. 'Not for that young lady. Herself can ride anything as well as her brother.'

'I think she wanted to foil the Captain,' Ellen chuckled. 'She does get cross with him.'

Nezer smiled, shaking his head. 'Luke is all right,' Nezer defended. 'He—'

'You should call Luke "the Captain",' she declared before Nezer could finish.

Nezer shrugged, sticking out his chest and lifting his chin. 'I am as good as any man,' he declared without false pride. 'In front of others I may bow to convention, but it is because I wish to and for no other reason.'

Ellen regarded him uncertainly. 'You truly mean that, don't you?'

'I do,' he said simply.

They walked on silently, Ellen digesting his words. 'Why can the Captain and Miss Mirry ride Satan and not anyone else?' she asked, coming back to a safer subject.

'Because horse and rider understand each other. The horse knows both Luke and Miranda have no wish for submission, just . . . perhaps a friendship, or even partnership, might be the word.'

'Miss Mirry is a good rider, isn't she?'

'That she is. She takes after her brother . . . and her father who was a great horseman. She loves horses. Star still has his spirit. She's not wanting to break the poor creature's spirit to ride, as so many do.'

They followed the river up the valley until they reached the soft sand. Ellen stooped to pick up a handful of the fine grains, allowing them to trickle slowly between her fingers. 'It's as fine and soft as ground flour,' she said in wonder. 'It looks like . . . like . . .?' She searched vainly for words to describe it.

'Grains of pure gold?' Nezer suggested poetically. 'Come on!' He tugged at her hand and they raced like two children across the sand, level with the high tide mark, Nezer's boots banging against his side. Here the beach wore a necklace of seaweed and tiny shells, the salty smell of rotting seaweed strong in their nostrils as they crunched the shells under their feet.

Turning towards the sea they carried on running across the ripples of hard damp sand, right down to the water's edge to where the rollers thundered onto the beach, ending in small waves, hurrying across the sand before trickling back with a reluctant sigh. Breathless, Ellen stopped to watch them, catching her breath.

'Do you want to walk in it?' Nezer had noticed her fascination with the water before. 'Take off your shoes and stockings.' He threw his boots back on the beach, away from the water, and sat down at her feet, reaching for her foot. After a moment's hesitation Ellen bent to sit on the sand to remove her shoes.

'The sand is soaking wet,' she exclaimed as she put her hand on it. 'I can't sit on that, I'll get my skirt all wet.'

Nezer stood up, taking her hand. 'Lean against me.'

Standing on one leg, she tugged off one shoe, then began tugging at her stocking but lost her balance. As she would have fallen, Nezer grabbed her around the waist, steadying her, his face close to hers. He looked into her blue eyes, pulled her closer, pulling her hard against him. He bent his head towards her, pressed his lips gently against hers, a soft, butterfly caress. As he lifted his head, she became aware of his warm, herb-smelling breath on her face, of her breasts pressed against his sinewy body. She gave a whimper of protest and heard him take a deep breath as he released her abruptly, still staring down at her.

Ellen realised she was breathing hard herself and pulled away from his hands. Turning, she walked rapidly away from him along the wet sand, regardless of one stockinged foot, her thoughts in turmoil.

He came after her. ''Tis sorry I am, Ellen.' She ignored him, carried on walking and he grabbed her hand, yanking her round to face him. 'Ellen . . . my heart ruled my head,' he said frankly. 'Truly I am sorry.' He bit his lip, his face crumbling. 'What am I to do?' he whispered, anguish in his voice.

Ellen's heart thudded even harder as she regarded him in silence. She dropped her eyes, afraid he might read her love for him in them. 'My stocking is wet now,' she muttered irrelevantly.

'Ellen. Will you come and visit my family?' His whisper was just loud enough to hear over the waves. 'My mother . . . I want my mother to meet you,' he stuttered.

Ellen's heart sank like a stone, leaving her cold. 'Meet your mother, Nezer? I don't know,' she said helplessly.

'Because we are gypsies?' he spat harshly, his face tight with hurt.

'No, Nezer.' She shook her head. 'That's not why.' She lifted her foot listlessly, feeling her wet stocking.

'Then why?' he demanded, his eyes flashing dark fire.

'Because what good will it do? We are different people, our ways are different . . .' Her voice broke off uncertainly, tears shimmering in her eyes.

'Ellen. My own sweet girl.' His voice was ragged and desperate. 'Ellen, you must be realising what my feelings are for you? It's wild I am about you . . . I think you might feel the same way but . . .?' He stopped, his questioning eyes travelling eagerly over her face.

'I do feel the same,' she whispered softly.

He took her face in his brown hands, smoothing her cheeks gently. 'I have never told you before because . . .' He broke off with a loud groan of despair.

'Why?' She gripped the front of his jerkin, her voice demanding.

'Why? Because my darling girl, the Kriss, our Romany law, does not allow us to marry Gaujo.' He stared over her head at the sea, not looking at her face.

Fastening first on the word marry, her heart danced for a minute . . . then it paused. 'Gaujo?' She released his jerkin.

'Non-Romanies.' His troubled eyes returned to her face.

'Not allowed?' The words trembled on her lips. 'And I am a Gaujo?'

He swallowed hard, looking away from her again, and nodded his head, his earring glinting.

Putting both hands on his chest, catching him unaware, she pushed him hard, so that he staggered and almost fell. 'Get away!' she screamed. 'Get away from me! What do you think I am?'

His eyes widened. 'I think you're my very own sweet—'

'But I am not your girl, am I?' she said bitterly, adding in a low whisper. 'And I never can be.'

'Ellen, I love you. I love you more than my life.' He chewed his lip, rubbing a hand through his dark locks.

Brow furrowed, she studied his face, reading the truth, reading his misery. She reached and put her arms around him, rocking him gently. 'I love you too, Nezer.'

'If I stayed here always would you marry me?' His face was hopeful.

'But you cannot . . .' She put her head on his chest, felt his heart beating strongly.

'I can if I want. My life is my own.' He rubbed his chin on her hair.

'But your family? What about your family?' She looked up uncertainly.

He took a sharp breath, his face pale beneath his tan. 'If we wed I would be excluded. I'd have no right to call myself a Romany,' he admitted. 'You mean more to me, Ellen.'

'You would give up your own people to marry me?' she asked faintly, her heart trembling with mixed emotions.

'I would give up my life for you, Ellen.' His voice was solemn. 'If we were to wed, Ellen, you would be my family.'

Ellen drew away from him, bent to retrieve the shoe she had dropped, hiding her tear-filled eyes. Why had she allowed herself grow to love him? She had known there would be problems. Miss Miranda had warned her Romany ways were different. What future could there be for either of them?

'Ellen?' He raised her chin gently.

She studied each detail of his downcast face, so alien to his normal laughing one, his sad eyes devoid of their dancing spirit. 'It's no good, Nezer. In time you would grow to hate me.'

'As long as there are stars in the sky will I love you, Ellen.' He tried to take her hand but she snatched it free and walked on blindly across the beach. He ran after her again. 'If you love me, tell me you're willing to think about it?' he pleaded.

'I don't know . . .' Her eyes roamed his face and she shook her head sadly. 'I don't think so, Nezer. Perhaps it would be better if we accepted it now? Accept that we must forget that we . . . that we love each other . . .'

'Never.' Normally so graceful, his feet seemed to flounder as he stumbled alongside her. 'It's stay behind I will when my clan move on again. I have done it twice already. I am getting used to being here without them.'

'I don't think you should, Nezer. I never want you to be unhappy. Never want to know it was my fault.' She rolled a shell under the sole of her shoe.

'And do you think I could ever be happy anywhere without you, Ellen?' He turned away, releasing his frustration by kicking at the sand.

Her face crumpled, tears overflowing. 'I don't know,' she whispered.

'We have a few weeks to think on it.'

'It's late, Nezer, I'll have to go home.' She pulled a face as she felt her wet stocking and tugged it off, putting her shoe back onto her bare foot. 'We have that steep climb to make before we get back. We'll have to hurry.'

Nezer led the way back to the house.

Ellen could hardly wait for the opportunity to pour it all out to Miranda, the words tumbling out in a wave of misery. 'And he wants me to marry him, Miss Mirry. But his Romany law forbids it. He would be an outcast from his own people. What can I tell him?'

Miranda sucked in her breath, at a loss for the best advice. 'Ellen. The first question to answer is: do you want to marry him?'

'Yes. Yes I do, Miss Mirry. I love him with all my heart, I know that. I could marry no other.' They were sitting side by side on Miranda's bed, Ellen's shoulders slumped. Miranda took her sturdy, work-worn hand, looking into her eyes.

'And . . . I have to ask you this . . . you don't mind that he is a gypsy?' She paused reflectively, before adding: 'and that some people might look down on you as well?'

Ellen's colour faded but she shook her head firmly. 'People who think like that don't matter. I know what he is, how good he is.'

'Good!' Miranda nodded her approval. 'I'm glad you said that, it is exactly how I feel too. The next question is: what about his people? Can he bear to be cast out from them?'

'That's what worries me: that he could grow to hate me for it,' she admitted. She closed her eyes, but tears squeezed past her lids, trickling down her cheeks.

'I think that's your biggest problem, Ellen. But if Nezer himself is certain then you must accept that.'

Ellen's eyes lit up hopefully. 'Then you wouldn't mind if I marry him? You think it could work?'

'If you are certain it is what you want, Ellen.' Miranda got up and paced around the room. 'I like Nezer very much, I admire his spirit and I'm sure he loves you. He has already stayed on here when his people moved on, hasn't he? I believe he's been trying it out.'

'I never thought of that. The Captain told him if he wants it, he has a permanent position here with the horses.'

Miranda turned back. 'That is good, but I'm not surprised. He and David get on well together.'

Ellen beamed. 'Yes, Miss, they do.' She jumped up, hugged Miranda, her face tight with excitement. 'He wanted me to meet his family. I'll tell him I'll go.'

Charlotte's dress was delivered to the house in plenty of time. Miranda hoped Charlotte would wear it to Kate's soirée. She tapped on the door of Charlotte's bedroom, entering at her bidding.

'Hello, Charlotte.' Charlotte looked around in surprise as Miranda approached her, suppressed excitement on the younger woman's face and a large box filling her arms. 'I would like you to have your Christmas present early, Charlotte.' Miranda smiled expectantly as she placed the box in Charlotte's hands.

'A Christmas present for me? So early? Whatever can it be?' Charlotte's pale eyes gleamed as they flashed enquiringly at Miranda. 'It looks very elegant.' Carefully she picked at the enormous red satin bow and tugged off the ribbon, her face pink with excitement. She drew a sharp breath as she saw the soft lilac-coloured material. 'It is a beautiful shade. Is it a shawl? . . . Oh! It's . . . it's a dress!' she stuttered, as she raised it up in the box. She darted an uncertain glance at Miranda and her hands trembled slightly as she lifted it from the box to tumble around her in soft folds. Hardly daring to breathe, she held it up, tears filling her eyes. 'It's beautiful,' she whispered. 'Absolutely beaut . . .' her voice ended on a sob and she turned away, her body shaking.

'Charlotte. Don't cry. Please don't cry.' Miranda hugged the plump shaking body against her. 'You do like it? I thought it should suit you.'

Charlotte dabbed at her eyes with a lacy handkerchief. 'Of course I like it. You know I do.' Biting her lip, she flashed another agitated glance at Miranda. 'But you can't do this. I cannot possibly accept it.' Her voice wobbled again at the end of the sentence.

'Why not? I get much pleasure from giving it, Charlotte. You've been very kind and made me most welcome in your home. For my sake, please accept it, Charlotte.'

Charlotte's eyes were drawn longingly towards the dress, and she crushed the soft wool in her fingers. 'So soft,' she murmured, 'so pretty . . .'

'Try it on!' Miranda prompted.

Charlotte's eyes sparkled. 'Shall I? . . . but I shouldn't really accept it.'

'Please do. I very much want you to have it.' Miranda began opening the tiny buttons on the dress. 'It should fit you, I took your measurements from one of your dresses.' Miranda prudently omitted to mention the part the two maids had played in the episode, wanting to avoid embarrassing the older woman.

'Did you really?' Charlotte slipped off her robe and

stepped into the new dress, and Miranda fastened the buttons at the back.

'Come and look in the mirror.' She caught Charlotte's still trembling hand, leading her to the long mirror where both women regarded the reflection.

'It is perfect,' Charlotte whispered, blinking back her tears. 'It is one of the loveliest dresses I have ever had,' she murmured, dabbing at her eyes with her handkerchief.

Mrs Baker had done her work superbly. The dress was a faultless fit, the lines flattering Charlotte's dumpy little figure. The shade lent a subtle glow to her drab complexion, having just the effect Miranda had hoped for.

'It really suits you, Charlotte. I'm delighted with it.' Miranda's expression mirrored Charlotte's enjoyment and Charlotte turned to her, hugging her warmly.

'Thank you so much, Miranda. I know I should refuse it . . . but . . . how could I refuse such kindness?' Her voice choked in her throat again.

Miranda kissed her cheek lightly. 'And thank you for giving me the pleasure of your acceptance of my gift. Now you will look as fashionable as any lady present this Christmas,' she added with satisfaction.

Charlotte preened in front of the mirror, turning to view the back of her new possession. 'I still can't believe how beautiful it is. How perfectly it fits.'

'I think I shall ask Ellen's advice about your hair,' Miranda deliberated. 'She always manages to produce all the latest styles,' she continued hastily, as Charlotte would have interrupted. 'We ought to get her to show Nia, she seems a bright girl.'

'That is a good idea,' Charlotte agreed. 'I haven't had a lady's maid since I was young.'

'When are you going to wear it?'

Charlotte's face screwed up with excitement. 'To Kate's soirée of course. It will be perfect.'

Miranda left her fluttering in front of the mirror, well pleased with the results.

Lanterns flooded the long drive leading up to Westfield Manor. Curtains, left undrawn across the elegant bowed Georgian windows, allowed the light to spill out as their coach drew up before the sweeping steps. Music drifted down, and liveried servants rushed forward, lanterns held aloft, to help them down from the carriage. Yet more servants relieved Luke, Huw and Will of their overcoats and showed the ladies to the rooms set aside as dressing rooms upstairs.

Charlotte's lips quivered with excitement as she was assisted out of her cloak and she fluttered over to the long mirror, turning her head this way and that as she preened in front of it.

'Miranda, my dear. I am so pleased with your lovely present,' she whispered, her eyes shining as she studied her reflection. 'It really is the most beautiful dress.'

Miranda smiled in return, enjoying Charlotte's pleasure but gave merely a cursory glance at herself in the mirror, knowing her new dress did her justice. The off-the-shoulder bodice of the deep green velvet dress showed off the smooth skin of her neck to perfection

Its enormous puffed sleeves and full skirt stood out, emphasising her small waist, with a profusion of paler green embroidered flowers tumbling down the front to continue on in a froth around the hem line. The emerald earrings her father had bought for her mother dangled almost to her shoulders, catching the light and needing only the slightest movement of her head to sparkle. They had been Mama's favourite, bought for her tenth anniversary, and the matching necklace adorning Miranda's slender neck had been purchased the following Christmas.

The two women descended the stairs to join the men who had waited in the hall below for them. Miranda thought how handsome they all looked in their evening suits. The three of them sported the latest cut-away jackets with contrasting reveres, with low-cut waistcoats over frilled, high-collared shirts. Straight white trousers, stirruped under their patent leather shoes, completed their outfits.

They entered the drawing room which had the doors at its furthest end folded back, doubling the size of the original room. Hundreds of candles flickered from a profusion of candelabras, reflecting in the mirrored panels which lined the room extension. A few heads turned towards them as they entered the room, where an enthusiastic quartet on a tiny rostrum provided the music. Miranda saw Will's eyes eagerly scanning the room for Kate. Obviously having been watching for their arrival, Kate waved and had a quick word with her mother who hurried over to greet them, closely followed by her daughter.

Will's eyes lit up, his gaze firmly fixed on Kate and

Miranda agreed she did look striking. Her dress of wild silk was a rich cream and its cross-over, pleated neckline of a shimmering gold material was nipped at the waist, leaving her shoulders bare. A coffee-coloured panel, pleated down the front of the wide skirt, was edged with a froth of gold embroidery laced with tiny pearls. Kate's eyes, secured on Will, shone like the gold embroidery on her dress, her face radiant.

'How lovely to see you. So pleased you could come.' Mrs Dart took each of their hands in turn and then she came to Will. 'And you, sir. We meet yet again. I feel we are old friends already,' she said with a smile. 'Delighted to see you this evening, Captain Owen.' Her eyes swept towards Luke, lingering briefly on him before returning to Will. Was it her imagination, Miranda wondered, or did she see regret in Kate's mother's eyes?

'You must meet my brother,' Kate declared, linking an arm in both Miranda's and Will's and leading them off. Although both of them had been to Kate's home on many occasions, Charles had yet to be there when either of them had called. They picked their way through the crowded room, Kate pausing to make introductions as they went. She stopped near a group of people, tapping a thick-set young man on the shoulder. 'Charles, I have two people I particularly want you to meet.'

He turned with a smile, revealing an open, good-natured face, sprinkled with freckles, and mousy fair hair curling around his cheeks.

'This is Miss Miranda Rushton, Luke's sister.'

His humorous eyes appraised Miranda and he gave

a little bow over her hand, blushing hotly as he addressed her. 'My pleasure. I have heard much about you, Miss Miranda.'

'And this is—'

'Will! Good to see you again.' Charles extended his hand. 'Will and I have met previously in Luke's company,' he explained to his sister.

'I didn't realise.' Kate smiled, leading Will away and leaving Miranda with Charles. She soon realised he was bashful and, taking a liking to the young man, did her best to put him at his ease. He was soon completely captivated.

'Luke tells me you love riding,' he remarked eagerly. 'You obviously follow your brother: he is a superb horseman.'

'In that respect, if no other, we take after our dear Papa.' She tapped his arm with her fan. 'He was reputed to be the best horseman in the county.'

He nodded, his eyes contemplative, making Miranda wonder how much Luke had told him of their past circumstances. 'I also enjoy riding. Would it be acceptable for me to call some time and accompany you, Miss Miranda? I would ask your brother for his permission first, of course.'

'I do not need his permission,' Miranda flashed, but seeing him flush uncomfortably, softened her manner. 'But I would be pleased to accept your invitation, Mr Dart.'

'Please! Do call me Charles,' he protested. As they were talking Huw appeared at her side, nodding amiably at Charles. 'You don't mind if I steal Miranda away from you for this dance, do you, old man?'

'No! Not at all,' Charles responded politely, his face crestfallen.

'But I will be disappointed if you don't ask me for a later dance,' Miranda invited, seeing his disappointment.

'I thought I would help you escape,' Huw whispered in her ear. 'I believe the ladies can find Charles a bit staid.' His good-natured grin, as he said it, robbed the words of their sting.

Charles, however, was not deterred and made a point of rejoining Miranda when she left the floor. Huw was immediately beckoned by two young women, one of whom was particularly attractive with bold laughing eyes and who had addressed him enthusiastically earlier. Miranda felt a little pang of jealousy when she saw the girl put her hand on Huw's arm and flutter her eyes at him, flirting outrageously. She was further irked to see Huw returning the flirtation with interest, and quickly dragged her eyes away, returning her attention to Charles. He blossomed under her encouragement and they were both laughing together when she caught Charlotte watching them from the opposite side of the room. Her face was dragged down in a petulant scowl and she tossed her head away dismissively when she caught Miranda's eye. Now what's upset Charlotte? Miranda wondered. Surely she didn't expect me to remain with her all evening?

Once she had the opportunity, she made her way over to Charlotte, determined the older woman would enjoy this evening. 'Are you enjoying yourself, Charlotte?'

'Yes,' she snapped, fluttering her fan agitatedly. 'You seem very preoccupied with Charles,' she declared peevishly.

'He is charming,' Miranda admitted, comprehending Charlotte's pique. 'Just like the rest of the Dart family.' Charlotte's eyes strayed over her shoulder to Huw, still with the pretty, fair-haired young woman.

'Who is that girl with Huw?' Miranda asked, a trifle maliciously.

Charlotte's eyes flashed a searching look back at Miranda. 'One of the Tally girls. Their father is in trade,' she said waspishly.

'The fair one is very pretty.'

Charlotte pursed her lips, tossing her head with disapproval. 'She is always chasing after Huw.'

To Miranda's relief Kate's parents came to talk to Charlotte, allowing Miranda to escape. Feeling very hot in the crowded room, Miranda decided to go upstairs and splash her face with water. She passed along the landing and had nearly reached the open door when she heard young women's voices talking and giggling together inside. She paused, listening, as she heard Luke's name mentioned, the smell of perfume wafting from the room.

'Well, you choose who you wish, I will have Luke. Please!' the young voice intoned dreamily. 'He is so masculine. He makes me shiver just to look at him.'

'I suppose you're right about that,' the second voice agreed dubiously. 'But he seems so aloof. I mean—'

She was interrupted by a third.

'Aloof! Is that what you call it? Never! I call it

exciting. Have you ever really looked into those wonderful smouldering eyes? It makes me squirm to wonder what they hide.'

Someone else was coming up the stairs so Miranda could wait no longer. The three girls started as she went in, heads all swivelling towards her.

'Good evening!' Miranda smiled, nodding at them. They stared at her for a few minutes, before answering, one girl's face flushing a bright pink. Then one of them came over to her.

'Someone told me you are Luke's sister,' she said, her glance briefly scanning Miranda. 'I didn't know he had one. You are not much alike.'

Miranda nodded. 'He's my half-brother. Our father passed away, and I have since moved here.'

Her eyelids fluttered. 'He is dashingly handsome,' she said a trifle wistfully. 'You must agree even though he is your brother?'

Miranda laughed. 'Yes. I must agree; though I think he is quite unaware of it. I'm sure if he knew anyone had been saying so he would be greatly amused.'

'Please don't tell him,' she yelped with dismay.

'I won't. Your secret is safe with me,' Miranda promised, chuckling.

The other two crowded around. Miranda had made some new friends and was soon giggling and chatting, entertained by the three girls.

Exhausted but content, Miranda and Charlotte wearily ascended the stairs on arriving home, leaving the men to take a nightcap in the drawing room.

Everyone had unanimously agreed that the evening had been a huge success and Will appeared to be walking around with his head in a fog, entirely preoccupied, a bemused expression fixed on his face.

Miranda had difficulty sleeping when she finally got to bed. Tossing and twisting restlessly, she tried to organise her troubled thoughts which were as truly tangled as the sheets around her body.

When they had gone riding, without putting it into actual words, Huw had made it plain that he was interested in her as his future wife. Flattered and excited at the prospect, she was in a turmoil. Is this positively what I want? she asked herself. I am not certain it is. I always enjoy Huw's company. He is entertaining and charming, as most women would agree, she thought, ruefully recalling the feminine attention he had received the previous evening. He enjoys flirting, Miranda realised. But can I truly expect otherwise? . . . He is a particularly handsome man. But his pleasing little asides, whispered in my ear alone, are all for me, she thought with satisfaction. Remembering some of the things he had whispered stimulated delicious tremors of excitement and sent blood rushing to her cheeks.

He tells me I am beautiful, she thought, and is disparaging about other women in comparison – even the lovely fair-haired girl with the tantalising eyes who'd been pursuing him so persistently at Kate's soirée. Yes. Huw is definitely paying me court, but I am not sure of my own feelings. Yet it is more than physical attraction I feel for him. I admire his easy-going tolerance, especially the situation with Luke and his unruffled acceptance of life as it comes. But is that enough basis for marriage? I know life cannot truly imitate a romantic novel, but what do I expect? She groaned, thumping her pillow.

Women also find Luke very attractive . . . 'masculine' was the word she'd heard used. Even though he never appears to give any encouragement, she mused, picturing again the expression on that girl's face when she spoke of Luke. He has an air of detachment, a sort of brooding mystery; as if . . . he has hidden depths, Miranda judged. There was also Kate's initial adoration, though now I believe he has lost her to Will. He shouldn't have been so self-contained and distant, Miranda thought, with a tinge of regret. He should have married her whilst he had the chance, she decided, dropping off to sleep.

The following morning Will went off quite early, telling them he was on his way to visit Kate.

'Please convey a little note of thanks for me,' Miranda requested. 'I have already written one and intended asking Wyn to take it.'

Charlotte's eyes gleamed spitefully as he left. 'I think Luke has lost Kate,' she smirked. 'If you ask me, Will is besotted with her.'

Miranda didn't reply, being of a similar opinion herself, and wondered if Luke would regret it. Had he intended to take Kate as a bride? He did seem fond of her.

'Serves Luke right if he does lose her,' Huw chuckled. 'The man is so thoroughly arrogant. I believe he thought he could keep her hanging on his whim.'

Thirteen

At the beginning of December Miranda decided to take Gwennie into Swansea to do their Christmas shopping. She helped the young girl to prepare her shopping list from the one she had already attempted to write out with chalk on her slate.

'How about a lavender pin cushion for Charlotte?' Miranda suggested, studying the slate over her shoulder.

'Charlotte? But I'm not getting her a present.'

'I think you should. What have you put down for Olwen?' Miranda continued, making subtle suggestions where necessary, as Gwennie wet her finger before carefully rubbing out the chalk and rewriting the words.

'And Luke? What can I get him?' Her brow puckered in thought.

'Let me see?' Miranda pondered. 'I think he would

like a new quill pen.'

'Oh yes!' Gwennie clapped her hands gleefully. 'That's a good idea. He will be surprised.' She grinned impishly. 'He never gets presents . . . 'cept from Kate. Last year she gave him a book.'

Miranda felt another surge of guilt at the words, remembering how many presents she had always received.

Once the list was completed Miranda assisted the child to copy it onto a sheet of paper. The quill spluttering tiny ink specks as she laboriously scratched out the letters. 'Oh no! I've got a big blob,' she shrieked.

'Here, quickly!' Miranda snatched up the sander, sprinkling fine sand over the paper which soaked up the ink before it could smudge. 'There, it's all right,' Miranda consoled her. She tipped the sand off into a ceramic bowl. 'See, it hasn't smudged.'

She hugged the anxious child, and vowed to make sure their forthcoming journey would be fun for Gwennie.

'Where shall we go first?' Miranda asked as they alighted from the coach. 'Perhaps the haberdasher? You can buy the lace handkerchief you wanted for Olwen there.'

The two of them spent an enjoyable morning poking in the shops in Wind Street, ending in good time for luncheon at the Mackworth.

Gwennie stared around, her eyes round. 'I've never been here before,' she confessed. 'It's like being grown-up.'

'You don't want to grow up too soon,' Miranda laughed.

'I just want to be like you.' She laid her head on Miranda's hand, which was resting on the table and Miranda rubbed her hair affectionately, touched by the child's remarks.

'Can we go to the office later?' Gwennie asked, popping another potato in her mouth.

'You mean Llewelyn Shipping?' Miranda was busy spreading butter on her bread.

'Yes. I love seeing all the ships.'

'Yes. I expect I would too,' Miranda agreed. 'I've never been to the docks. Who did you go with?'

'Olwen took me there once. We went to her mother's, then we took a letter to the office. The *Windrush* wasn't there, though. It was at sea.'

'Well, it should be there today. Let's find out,' Miranda said, brushing crumbs off her skirt.

Miranda made enquiries about directions to the dockside, which was beyond the old Norman castle. A salty smell filled the air, coupled with an acrid smell of burning. They discovered where the latter came from as they rounded a corner and found a fire blazing in an iron brazier on the quayside. Chestnuts were roasting on a metal tray on top of it. A gang of ragged urchins, their faces pinched with cold, were warming themselves near the fire, looking on longingly. They turned hopeful eyes toward Miranda and Gwennie.

'Got an 'a'penny to spare, missus?' the cheekiest of them asked.

'Give them a portion each, please,' Miranda said to the vendor, slipping him a coin.

They crowded around delightedly. 'God! Thanks missus. ''appy Christmas,' they chorused. Seeing the shivering children, their bare feet blue and chapped with the cold, made Miranda acknowledge how lucky she and Gwennie were to be tucked up in their warm, fur-trimmed cloaks and muffs.

Walking along, they needed to keep firm hands on their bonnets to prevent them being carried off in the gusts of wind. Gwennie skipped excitedly as they made their way to the office of Llewelyn Shipping. The tide was out, leaving all manner of ships squatting dismally in the thick, grey-looking mud lining the docks. Seagulls strutted about in it, their eager eyes searching for scraps. Reaching the Llewelyn sign hanging outside, they entered the outer office where a middle-aged man was seated on a high stool, busy working on a thick ledger. He looked up from his work and rose politely to his feet.

'May I help you, Madam?' he said courteously. Then he noticed Gwennie. 'Ah! It's little Gwennie, I believe,' he observed, smiling at her.

'It is, sir. And I am Captain Llewelyn's sister. Is either he or Mr Huw inside?'

As he pulled up a chair for her, he informed them that neither partner was in but that Luke was probably on board *Windrush*. 'I'll fetch him for you, Mistress Llewelyn.'

Miranda didn't correct his natural mistake. 'No need. We will take a walk along the quayside. Is the ship far away?'

They picked a careful path along the wharf,

stepping over the clutter of tarred ropes which reached across the quay from the stranded boats in the mud. They found the *Windrush* moored close alongside the quay.

Gwennie almost jumped up and down with glee. 'I'd love to go on the ship. Do you think we're allowed?'

'I don't know,' Miranda admitted. 'Maybe someone will see us. Hello there!' she called, waving a handkerchief. Gwennie quickly imitated her and a sailor appeared on deck, coming over to the side.

They were helped across a narrow gangplank, one at a time, Gwennie being carried and another sailor firmly holding Miranda's hand. She glanced down with distaste at the viscous mud below them, imagining the horror of falling into it. Luke took her hand as she arrived on board, a quizzical look on his face.

'To what do we owe this pleasure?' he said.

'We were in town shopping,' Miranda explained as they stared around in fascination. The tall masts towered above them, with apparently hundreds of ropes reaching up to them from all directions. The canvas sails were tightly furled and a few gulls perched on the cross members, most of them fixing a beady eye on deck.

'What are all the ropes for?' Gwennie asked, craning her neck to see where they went.

'They are called halyards,' Luke told her. 'And they control the sails.'

'But there's lots. How do you know which one to pull?' She walked over, reaching up to feel them, her lip curling with disgust when she found tar on her hand.

Luke laughed at her distaste. 'You have to learn. Just like learning to read.' Picking up a piece of sacking he rubbed her hand.

'Is this ship like the one you sailed in to India?' Gwennie asked Luke with awe.

Luke smiled down at her. 'Let's say it was quite a bit bigger than this,' he chuckled. He took her hand and led her around to show her, lifting her up when she wanted a closer look at something out of her reach. Miranda trailed along after them, looking at their dark heads so close together, their hair so similar in texture and colour, their eyes the same arresting blue.

Luke saw her watching them and smiled, putting Gwennie down. 'Thank you for taking Gwennie shopping. She seems to have had a wonderful time. Also for bringing her along to the *Windrush*. I should have brought her here before.'

When they eventually returned to their coach Miranda decided it had been exceptionally enjoyable. And for once she and Luke had not been at loggerheads with one another.

'They hold a Christmas fair in Llanmor village, Miss Mirry.' Ellen's face was alight with anticipation. 'David was telling me about it at breakfast. It's two days before Christmas. Wouldn't it be lovely to go?'

'That would be fun,' Miranda agreed. 'We could take Gwennie, she'd enjoy it . . . unless you'd rather go on your own? With Nezer, I mean?' Miranda asked, realising Ellen would enjoy the treat even more with Nezer.

Ellen placed Miranda's pumps on the floor in front of her, beaming, her apple-red cheeks glowing with delight. 'May I really, Miss Mirry? If you don't need me I would like to go with Nezer. But who will you and Gwennie go with then?'

'Huw, I suppose. Perhaps Charlotte will come?' Miranda pulled on her pumps.

Ellen looked doubtful. 'I don't think she will.'

'What makes you say that?'

'I just think it,' Ellen said, bustling away as she spoke. She picked up a dress from the bed and shook it energetically. Miranda's brow puckered, wondering why Ellen had reached that decision; she seemed so positive about it. But before she could question her Ellen went out, taking the dress with her.

As Ellen had implied, Charlotte shook her head firmly when Miranda suggested going to the fair. 'No, my dear. I have no wish to go. In any case it will be mostly village people and I never mix with the villagers.'

'Why not? It will be fun and a nice change for you,' she coaxed. 'Gwennie and I are looking forward to it.'

'Gwennie?' Charlotte exclaimed, shaking her head again. 'No! Thank you for asking me but I don't wish to go.' She pursed her mouth primly. 'And I really consider it a most unsuitable place for you to go.'

'Why? I'm hoping Huw will come with me.'

'Huw will not go. And I am sure Luke will not approve of—'

'I don't intend asking Luke,' Miranda snapped. But Charlotte tossed her head, walking away. As usual, when Charlotte did not approve she would not discuss the subject. Miranda received little more enthusiasm from Huw when he arrived home.

'Llanmor? Why on earth do you want to go there?' he inquired, handing Nia his hat and shrugging out of his heavy, caped topcoat.

'I've just told you. They are holding a Christmas fair. Do come with us . . .'

'Us? Who else is going?' He pulled down the sleeves of his jacket.

'Only Gwennie. I thought—'

'No! I'm sorry, Miranda, but the answer is no.' His chin dimpled winningly as he smiled and took her hand. 'In any case I'm afraid I have a previous engagement. You would not wish me to break it?'

'I suppose not,' Miranda pouted.

'And you cannot possibly go unaccompanied,' he said with studied remorse, flinging a blond lock back out of his eyes.

Miranda raised her eyes to the ceiling. 'Why not? You are as bad as your mother.'

'On this occasion I agree with her.'

Luke approached Miranda when he came home the following evening. 'Miranda. Gwennie tells me you were both hoping to attend the fair at Llanmor but have no-one to accompany you?'

Miranda shot him a disbelieving look. 'You're not saying you will come?'

He gave a lopsided grin. 'I'm afraid you will have to put up with me if you wish to go. You cannot go unaccompanied . . .'

'I thought Wyn could take us in the coach.'

'Wyn?' he barked, his face darkening. 'Are you telling me you'd feel safer with Wyn than with me?'

Miranda scowled at him. 'You know that's not what I meant.'

'Well if you cannot tolerate my company I am afraid you and Gwennie will have to cancel your treat,' he said coldly. He made to move away but Miranda darted in front of him.

'I'm sorry, Luke. I didn't mean it like that at all. I appreciate your offer and accept gracefully.' She gazed up winsomely.

He was not taken in, his eyes blazing as he stared silently at her.

The smile slid from her face. 'You have withdrawn your offer?'

He sucked in a breath, through clenched teeth. 'No! Much as I would like to. But Gwennie would be disappointed. Let me know what time you wish to leave, nearer the time.' He stalked away, leaving Miranda mortified.

'He's only coming for Gwennie's sake anyway,' she muttered.

Miranda thought Luke was avoiding her and hardly spoke to him for the following week. But the day of the fair dawned fresh and crisp, and for once Wyn had the coach already waiting outside after luncheon. Gwennie's face was beaming as Luke helped them into the coach. Well wrapped against the icy air, Miranda and Gwennie huddled together with eager anticipation, their hands thrust into fur muffs, a rug over their knees.

'I've never been to a fair in Llanmor,' Gwennie

admitted, kicking her legs beneath the blanket. 'I went to one with Olwen once. In Swansea. But she said the Llanmor one is the bestest—'

'Best,' Luke corrected her.

'Best,' she repeated obediently. 'Wyn was talking 'bout it. He wanted to go too.'

'No wonder he was ready,' Miranda chuckled, her breath clouding out in front of her in the unheated coach.

'He said they've got everything. Even a strong man last year. I bet they haven't got an Indian rope in the air . . . with a boy climbing it,' she giggled, looking at Luke.

Luke laughed. 'I doubt it.' He grinned at Gwennie. 'I expect there will other interesting things though.'

'Lots of stalls, Wyn said. And I still have some allowance left,' she confided. She wriggled from under the shawl, leaning her head against the window to peer out.

'Allowance? What allowance?' Luke frowned, then turned to Miranda with comprehension. 'You give her one,' he said.

Miranda nodded. 'I hope you have no objection?'

He gave a rueful grin. 'None at all, I'm grateful. It seems once again you have thought of something which I overlooked.' He studied her face frankly. 'You are more than kind to Gwennie.'

'I am truly fond of her.' Her glance wandered to the child who was listening to this conversation, watching them both, wide-eyed.

'I love Miranda,' Gwennie whispered to Luke, her finger straying into her mouth.

'I can see why,' Luke agreed thoughtfully.

'And I love you too.' She flung both arms around Luke's neck, kissing him on the cheek and squeezing him tightly. He smiled, returning her hug, looking slightly embarrassed as he caught Miranda's eye.

'Are we nearly there?' Gwennie bounced back onto her seat. 'Do you think I will buy something?'

'I think it most likely,' Miranda agreed.

They had to leave the coach at the top of the road leading down through the village, as it was too steep for the coach and horses to negotiate. Alighting to walk down, Miranda and Gwennie began laughing as their feet crunched on the frost-covered ground.

'Careful! Or else we will go sliding down the hill,' Miranda yelped as her foot slipped.

'I think you ladies had better take my arm,' Luke grinned, holding out an arm for each of them.

The smell of fish, strangely mingled with other unrecognised scents, hit them as they approached the little harbour. Crowded together were wagons, hand-carts and trestle-tables, all strewn with branches of yew, their dark green needles offering effective background for the carefully arranged wares for sale. A number of people were displaying their goods on the ground; women stood beside wicker baskets piled high with oysters, coaxing everyone to try one. Miranda was surprised to see many of the women's white-woollen stockings were footless, leaving their feet bare though many wore stout boots rather than clogs.

A cacophony of sounds encompassed them. Vendors called out their wares and a gypsy violinist walked amongst the crowd playing a plaintive tune accompanied by a dark-eyed little girl rattling a tambourine for pennies. A pieman carried around a tray from which a mouth-watering smell of hot pork-pies wafted as he sang out persuasively: 'Hot pies. Who'll buy my hot pies?'

'How delicious they smell. It's a pity we've had our luncheon,' Miranda remarked, licking her lips.

Cinnamon sticks and candied fruit were piled high on another stall, and at the furthest end were pomades, oranges stuck with cloves, which further added to the strange blend of smells. They stopped near a tent set up over a cart, to watch and listen to a man extolling the virtues of his medical concoctions.

'Try my Pectoral Elixir,' he coaxed, waving a bottle in the air. 'Wonderful for curing all your chest ailments. Coughs, breathlessness, wheezing, rashes, aches. You will have no need to visit an apothecary again this year. You, sir,' he waved at Luke. 'I am sure you will buy one.'

Luke shook his head. 'Thank you, sir. But I am in full health,' he chuckled.

'What about some Embrocation?' they heard him call as they left. 'You need to rub it in for all aches and pains in the joints or the back. You'll take one, Mistress? You will not regret it.'

Pipes and drums sounded, and they followed the crowd to where acrobats were balanced into a high pyramid: a small boy no bigger than Gwennie stood right on the top, arms outstretched. The crowd shrieked as the whole pyramid toppled towards them but the pipe player stepped forward in a well rehearsed manoeuvre, to catch the boy safely as the others agilely somersaulted unhurt across the ground. Another performer stepped into the middle and putting a hand to his mouth, began breathing out fire, long orange flames licking out from his mouth. A woman screamed and the audience gasped and stepped back apprehensively as he lit a torch from the flames. Then he thrust the blazing brand into his mouth to put it out.

Moving on, they saw Ellen and Nezer in the crowd, holding hands as they walked, engrossed more in each other than watching the scene. Luke gallantly doffed his hat to Ellen and she dimpled, bobbing a curtsy in return.

On the seashore a brazier burned, on top of which a woman stirred a sticky concoction in a pottery vessel. The smell of burnt caramel was very tempting. On a stool alongside her, a plate of toffee apples thickly coated with the sugary mixture reflected the fire, shining invitingly. Another basket of rosy apples, already speared with sticks, was on hand to prepare further supplies.

'Would you like one?' Luke asked Gwennie.

'Yes, please.' Her eyes shone.

'One please,' Luke said, then seeing Miranda's face, amended. 'Make it two.'

Miranda giggled. 'One for me? I feel like a little girl again,' she added, grinning as he handed it to her.

By this time it was growing dark and the stall holders had lit candles, which glowed and flickered in containers of all shapes and sizes. The nearby cottages had placed lights in their windows and most of the boats drawn up on the beach had done the same, turning the scene into magical fairyland. A huge bonfire blazed on the beach and everyone began dancing to the music of the gypsy's fiddle and a concertina played by an old ex-seaman with one peg-leg. Luke stood next to this man, talking to him and Miranda noticed that before walking away he slipped a coin into his hand, doing the same to the gypsy.

'Have you had enough?' he enquired of Miranda but looking at Gwennie, who was rubbing her eyes and yawning.

'I have, thank you. I'm sure Gwennie is tired.'

'I'll find Wyn. Don't move from this spot.

Returning, he took the monkey-on-a-stick toy from Gwennie's hand, thrusting it in his pocket, and swept the child up in his arms. She snuggled her head against him, falling asleep almost immediately.

'It has been wonderful.' Miranda took his arm as they walked up the hill. 'Thank you for sparing us the time.'

'My pleasure,' he said blandly.

Returning from the tiny church at the hamlet of Pentrebach on Christmas morning, they were delighted when Kate and Will turned up to visit. Kate's mother had invited him to spend the Christmas holiday with the Dart family and Will had enquired if Luke had any objections before accepting the invitation. Will was jubilant, his face beaming.

'I have some wonderful news,' he told them, keeping a firm grip on Kate's hand as he spoke. 'Kate and I are betrothed. She has done me the honour of accepting my hand in marriage. Her father has given us his consent and blessing,' he said with evident satisfaction.

As everyone congratulated them, and as Huw slapped him on the back, Miranda studied Luke's reaction. He doesn't seem unduly concerned, she thought, and this seemed confirmed when he produced a bottle of champagne.

'How did you know?' Will chuckled. 'I told no-one my intentions. '

'I guessed,' Luke admitted, with a grin. 'I bought it last week in anticipation.' He raised his glass. 'Congratulations to you both. I wish you a long and happy marriage. You are a lucky man, Will.'

'You never said a truer word,' Will said fervently, turning an adoring gaze at Kate.

'So have you set a date?' Luke's eyes travelled between Kate and Will.

'No. It cannot be for some time. I must return to Bristol, to commission a new command . . . it means I will be able to travel here easily enough. Kate is coming to visit my mother and the rest of the family after Christmas. I know they will love Kate. Everybody does,' he added simply.

Kate was thrilled when Gwennie presented her with her gift, a fine-linen handkerchief edged with lace.

'How beautiful, Gwennie. I'll treasure it always. I think I'll keep it to use on my wedding day,' she said considerately, knowing this would please Gwennie. 'And now I have a great favour to ask of you. Will you be my flower girl at our wedding?'

'Me?' Gwennie gasped, going pink. 'Really?'

'If you will?' Kate smiled at her.

'Yes, please,' Gwennie whispered, her eyes enormous.

'Thank you, I am pleased. We can arrange about seeing my dressmaker sometime later on, when we set a date. Now here is our Christmas gift for you.' She handed Gwennie a parcel wrapped in pink tissue paper. Inside it was a soft fur muff.

The family were to eat dinner at midday so that the servants might have the rest of the day off. Kate and Will could not be persuaded to stay but they all enjoyed a pre-luncheon toast of piping hot mulled wine before they left. The whole family waved as they eventually drove off.

Gwennie, Charlotte and Miranda had gifts for everyone. Huw gave only to his mother and to Miranda, who was disappointed to realise he had not included Gwennie. For once Luke was caught unawares when Gwennie shyly gave him a present.

'This is for me?' he said with obvious astonishment. 'Thank you, Gwennie.' His eyes glowed blue and he gave a lop-sided grin before unwrapping it self-consciously as they all watched. 'A new quill pen. Just what I need,' he said gruffly. 'Thank you very much, Gwennie.'

'Miranda thought of it,' she said gleefully. 'She said you'd want it.'

'A very good idea,' he agreed, his eyes straying to Miranda. 'And now, Gwennie, I have a surprise for you.' His eyes danced. 'But you will have to come outside to receive it.' He led the child outside where a plump little pony was tethered, contentedly chewing at a mouthful of rye.

'A pony? For me?' she screeched. She rushed down the steps and in her haste would have fallen had Luke not grabbed the back of her dress. 'It's lovely.' She rubbed her head against the pony who nuzzled at her in return. 'Thank you, Luke. It's the bestest . . . best present I ever had,' she sobbed, tears streaming down her face.

Luke crouched down alongside her. 'Don't cry, poppet,' he said softly. 'You lead her around to the stables and I'll follow on.'

Charlotte's eyes darted disapprovingly at Luke as Gwennie led the pony away. 'I am not sure this was wise,' she snapped.

Luke's eyes turned to steel. 'She is my . . .' he began, but broke off the sentence, leaving it unsaid.

Charlotte stared at him, her face going bright pink and she spun on her heel, flouncing away.

'I think it was a lovely idea,' Miranda whispered.

He shrugged. 'I have upset Charlotte yet again,' he sighed.

Later, as Miranda opened her package from Luke, her eyes brimmed with tears when she found a tiny miniature painting of her father. 'Luke. How thoughtful.' Her voice was choked. 'How did you . . .?' She rushed out of the room as they all stared after her.

'Trust you to upset both Miranda and my mother on Christmas Day?' Huw commented spitefully. 'You always manage it.'

Luke shot him a scornful look and went after Miranda. He found her in the library, curled up in his chair behind the desk, sobbing softly. He sat on the edge of the desk, swinging his leg, wondering if he should attempt to comfort her.

'It seems my gifts have upset everyone,' he murmured.

Miranda looked up, dabbing at her eyes with a soggy handkerchief. 'No. It's just that I truly miss dear Papa. Sometimes I can't bear it without him. It's a beautiful gift, Luke, I love it. And it made me realise you must have loved Papa too.'

Luke raised his eyebrows, not having expected that reaction. He had commissioned it only because he believed it would give Miranda comfort to have her father's portrait near at hand. He said nothing, keeping his own counsel.

Miranda rose, putting both arms around Luke's neck and he returned the hug. 'I must remember this next time I am furious with you,' she whispered, her head against his chest. She was not aware of him looking down at her tenderly.

Fourteen

Satan's hooves clattered across the cobbles as Luke trotted him into the courtyard of the Mackworth Arms in Wind Street. Swinging an athletic leg over, he leapt down and a young ostler scuttled across to take charge of the horse.

Unfamiliar with the boy, who had only recently started there, Luke exclaimed: 'No, lad!' as the boy reached towards the horse's head. The youngster backed away hastily seeing Satan bare his teeth. Retaining the reins in his own hand, Luke explained: 'Satan does not take kindly to strangers. Where is Tom? He usually handles Satan for me.'

'In the stable he is, sir. I'll fetch him now, sir.' Sidling fearfully past Satan, whose ears were laid flat, he raced back to the stables as Luke followed. He led his horse around the perimeter of the busy yard where a stagecoach was disembarking its passengers.

From the top of the coach, one coachman was throwing luggage down into the waiting arms of porters as another assisted the last of the passengers from inside the coach.

'Morning, Captain!' Tom, grey-haired and calm in manner, emerged from the stables, approaching the horse confidently. 'There you are, my beauty,' he murmured to Satan. 'Old friends, aren't we? Come by here, Satan, and we'll have some nice oats.'

Content to leave Satan in Tom's capable hands, Luke ducked his head to enter the low passageway and walked through into the foyer, rubbing shoulders with the stagecoach passengers who were milling around waiting for attention. He caught a pot-boy's arm as he dashed past, giving him his order and then went into another room.

'Luke, there you are. We wondered where you had got to?' Charles Dart called from a table near the window. 'What are you drinking? Ale?'

'I've already ordered, thanks.' Luke joined the three men, which included his cousin Huw, at the table. 'I've just left the *Windrush*.'

Len Brown, the third man, raked the room with a swift glance before asking in a low voice. 'Is everything all right?'

'Yes.' Luke smiled grimly. 'I had to wait to dodge old Jack Nichols,' he said, referring to the Coastguard Officer in charge of the area. 'He was hanging around near the *Windrush*'s moorings. That's why I am late.'

'You think he suspects?'

'I am sure he does. He's watching to see who goes aboard. He wants to know who Captain Grace's visitors are.'

'Did he see you go on board?' Charles queried anxiously.

Luke grinned, shaking his head. 'No. I gave someone a shilling to create a disturbance and slipped aboard when he was preoccupied. I came off in shirtsleeves, carrying a cask on my shoulder,' he chuckled.

'Is there cause for concern, Luke? It could prove risky for you.' Charles asked.

Luke gave a nonchalant shrug. 'Won't be the first risk I've taken. Nor the last probably,' he drawled.

'Luke enjoys taking risks,' Huw said sourly. 'He thrives on it.'

'Nonsense! We don't want him ending up in prison,' Charles protested.

'And that would not be the first time either,' Luke said, with a crooked smile. 'Though it is an experience I would rather not repeat.'

'Perhaps we should postpone it?' Charles frowned uneasily. 'After all, if Jack Nichols suspects . . .'

'Can't postpone now! Perhaps if I had realised the situation earlier.' Luke nodded. 'But our liaison with the *West Indiaman* was set up well in advance. There's no possibility of cancelling at this stage. In any case, if we wait six weeks for *Windrush*'s next voyage, the days would be lengthening and it would be too light. We'd then have to leave it until the autumn before we could attempt another run.'

'Besides which, we need the money,' Huw said, watching Luke through half-lidded eyes.

Luke shot him a hard glance, his mouth tightening. 'I don't think our companions are interested in our business affairs.'

'When are you leaving?' Len asked, hastily changing the subject. The other two men realised only too well that there was no love lost between the cousins.

'First tide tomorrow, that's at two o'clock in the morning. She is scheduled to sail on the following tide, so as long as they are not prepared for the earlier start, we should not be bothered by the Coastguard at that hour.'

'Luke . . .' Charles said slowly, still concerned about his friend's safety. 'Couldn't the captain—'

'Definitely not,' Luke dismissed him abruptly. 'The Indiaman is my contact, I deal with him. But don't worry, Charles, I know what I'm about.' Luke grinned at his friend, punching him lightly on the shoulder.

'Well, at least let me order you another drink,' Charles replied, returning his grin, though worry still shadowed his eyes.

After a hearty repast of liver and bacon they rose to leave but Huw remained seated at the table, swirling the last of his ale in the bottom of his tankard.

'Luke! Could I have a word with you?' Huw called, as Luke reached the door. Motioning the others to go on, Luke turned back into the room and regarded Huw silently.

'Er . . . to tell the truth, old man, I find myself rather short of cash . . .' he hesitated, seeing anger flare in Luke's eyes, their intense blue turned now to steel. 'I wonder if you could possibly—?'

'Good God, Huw! What is it now? Not gambling again?' He rested one foot on a splintered wooden stool and leaned on his knee.

'Just a run of bad luck. You know how it is . . .?'

'I know exactly how it is . . . with you at least,' Luke retorted.

'Don't tell me you have never had the odd wager or two yourself?' Huw drawled, though his face was wary.

'I have never used other people's money to finance my weaknesses.' Luke ran his hand through his hair. 'I just don't understand you, Huw. You know the financial straits the firm is in. How can you do it?'

'It was pure bad luck, old man.' He took gulp of his ale. 'I was ahead, winning, and just about to leave . . .'

'Are you being threatened?'

Huw nodded, his expression lighting up hopefully.

Luke gestured irritably. 'You know, I've a good mind to let you take a beating this time. It might teach you a lesson. Who do you owe it to? Dickson?'

Huw reluctantly nodded again, not trusting himself to speak in case he antagonised Luke further.

'I'll call in and settle it before I return home,' Luke snapped, dropping his foot to the floor.

Huw banged his empty tankard down on the table and rose languidly to his feet. 'No need for that, I can save you the trouble if you—'

'I said I'll settle it.'

'Thanks, old man, I am in your debt.'

'Don't try the charm on me, Huw, it won't work,' Luke said wearily. 'Just remember this is the last time I get you out of trouble. Definitely the very last. Next time don't even bother to ask.' He pushed past Huw and stalked out, leaving Huw staring after him resentfully.

'Conceited braggart,' Huw snarled under his breath. He had been hoping to have the cash in his hand, so that he might pay half the debt and keep some to use. He kicked out viciously at a chair as he passed, sending it crashing to the flagstones.

Later, Luke strode down the street towards Dickson's office, still furious with Huw. The man is a complete idiot, Luke thought. However many times I bail him out he always ends up in the same penniless position. He doesn't care what happens to the firm; he has absolutely no sense of responsibility.

''Morning, Captain Llewelyn.' Dickson grinned knowingly, realising why Luke had called. 'Come to borrow some money, 'ave you?'

Luke pursed his lips, his expression savage. 'Dickson. I want to warn you not to lend my cousin any more money. This is positively the last time I will bail him out. Understand?'

'I understands full well, sir,' he said obsequiously. His eyes slid across Luke's face and dropped away hastily. 'Though 'e always seems to manage to pay it back . . . even before you joined Llewelyn's, like,' he added slyly.

Luke leaned across the table and grabbed the man's coat front in one big hand, and pulled him towards him, close to his face. 'No more!' Luke growled, recoiling slightly from the man's unsavoury breath.

Dickson's shifty eyes opened wide with terror. 'Mal!' he howled.

Two of his paid ruffians raced in from an inner room, pulling up warily as Luke released Dickson and with clenched fists, spun round to confront them, his face aflame with anger.

'Well?' he challenged, eyes blazing.

The two men hesitated, turning questioning faces to their master, who was pulling indignantly at his coat front. 'It's all right,' he whined to the men, adding hastily, 'but stay by here.'

'How much?' Luke snarled.

'Five guineas.'

Luke swore profanely in his best seaman's language and fumbled in his pocket for the coins before flinging them on the table. 'I want a note of redemption.'

White-faced, Dickson grabbed a quill, dipped it in the ink and scribbled a note. With a trembling hand, he poured sand over it and shook it, handing it silently to Luke.

Luke studied it. 'Where is the original?'

Dickson's eyebrows rose, and hastily he drew a pile of papers towards him, scattering some on the floor as he shuffled through them. He thrust one at Luke who scanned it swiftly, flashing Dickson and the other two men an intimidating glance before striding out into the street.

'We'll get 'im for you, won't we, Ben?' Mal leered at his employer. 'Just give us the word, sir.'

'Maybe. But it'll need more than two of you to teach 'im a lesson,' Dickson snarled. 'That man's a rough customer, been around some. Not your normal gentry, that one isn't.'

'Just leave it to me, sir. When you're ready give us the word, I'll arrange it for you.'

'Yeah. I might think about that. See if I can turn it to my advantage.'

Luke passed through the outer office of Llewelyn Shipping, nodding a greeting to the clerk who was seated at his high desk, busily scribbling in a thick ledger. Huw was already in the other room, feet up on the desk, reading the *Cambrian* newspaper.

'I see you are hard at work as usual, Huw,' Luke said, with heavy sarcasm.

Huw hastily crushed the paper together and shoved it under the desk, his eyes wary. 'Just catching up on the shipping,' he said mildly, unsure if Luke had paid his debt yet.

Luke shook his head, exasperated. He threw a heavy ledger on the desk in front of Huw. 'How about taking a look at the week's schedules then? Seeing I'm not going to be here for a week.'

'I was just about to do that.' Huw hurriedly picked up some papers. 'Eh . . . did you manage to . . .?' He paused expectantly.

'To what?' Luke said blankly, letting him squirm.

'You know? Call in to Dickson's?' He swallowed, letting the papers fall back to the desk.

'Can't it wait until I come back?' Luke said casually, strolling towards the door.

'God no!' Huw yelped, leaping to his feet. 'Luke, for the devil's sake you can't—'

'Can't what?'

'Well . . . you know! Do you want Dickson to . . .'

Luke regarded him coolly. 'Can you give me even one good reason why not?'

The colour drained from Huw's face. 'But you said—'

'I have already paid it,' Luke sighed, turning away.

'You bastard.' He sank back down, rubbing a distracted hand over his face. 'Why did you pretend?'

'It is all right to call me names now?' Luke smiled grimly. 'Well just let me tell you, I have warned Dickson not to lend you any more money.'

'You did what! How dare you interfere,' Huw snarled, thumping the desk with his fist. 'It is none of your business. Just because—'

'If I pay the bloody bills, it is very much my business.' Luke's voice was low and angry. 'So try and manage to do some work for a change when I am away.'

Huw's eyes glittered, for once unguarded, pouring hate at Luke. 'I'd like to . . .' He broke off, scowling.

'I know what you'd like, Huw,' Luke barked, adding the challenge: 'You are welcome to try . . . any time you like.'

'You would love that, wouldn't you, Luke? But I'm not one of your poor seamen, at mercy to your bullying.'

'God! Not that same tune again!' Luke grinned sourly, shaking his head, and turned his back on the younger man.

Fifteen

For the last fortnight in February a cold easterly wind had blown almost continuously across the promontory from the sea, bringing with it rough weather, gale force winds and tumultuous seas. Venturing out to ride, Miranda left the shelter of the path and emerged onto the cliffs, gasping as the full force of the icy wind caught her. The freezing air rushed into her lungs, searing and blistering. Tearing at her clothes, the wind suddenly flapped them behind her, snatching off her hat and sending it bowling along the cliffs to become entangled in the middle of a gorse bush. Exhilarated, she urged Star to a gallop.

Overhead, seagulls swooped and screamed, riding the wind, dipping and wheeling with effortless grace in the turbulent air. Breathing hard, Miranda reined in, her clouded breath billowing out in front of her to join Star's. Moving nearer to the edge but not getting too close, she stared down at the sea below. Grey and enraged, it peaked everywhere into white foam, churning into a bubbling cauldron. On the opposite side of Pentrebach Bay, thundering waves erupted onto the rocks, exploding in clouds of spray, before being sucked greedily back into the maelstrom. Star's ears flicked uneasily, and Miranda leaned forward to stroke the horse's glossy neck.

'Are you ready to go home, my beauty?' Conscious of the burning wind on her face and fearing for her complexion, she turned for home. 'Let's get you back to your nice warm stable,' she told the horse.

Although fires were generously banked up in most of the grates, coal seemingly the one commodity used generously in Bryncarog, Miranda still found the draughty house permanently too cold for comfort. She climbed the stairs, huddled in an extra layer of clothing, topped by a thick woollen shawl.

Shivering, she entered her bedroom, placing the candle on a table near the grate, where her nightdress was laid out to warm. Outside, the wind still howled, moaning as it swept around the exposed house; rain battered at the windowpane, rattling the glass. The repaired window, still a poor fit in its splintered frame, funnelled draughts into the room, and Miranda shot it a baleful glance as the curtains lifted in the current, billowing eerily into the room.

Teeth chattering, she clutched her shawl tighter around her, loath to face the ordeal of undressing. Unwillingly, she stripped off her clothes and pulled on her nightdress as quickly as possible. She grasped the handle of the brass warming-pan which was filled with hot coals and drew it out of her bed.

Hours later, Miranda woke cold and shivering. Lifting her head, she peeped over at the sulky fire which had burned low in the grate. She groaned, fearing it was going out. Deciding she needed an extra covering on the bed, she edged from beneath the blankets, tugging a shawl around her shoulders. Sinking to her knees in front of the fire, she stirred it with the poker and coaxed it into reluctant life. She was adding more fuel when she saw the curtains lift again in the draught. Muttering under her breath, Miranda crossed to the window and held up her hand, testing for the cold air sweeping in around the frame.

'This is ridiculous. It will have to be repaired properly,' she grumbled, wondering how best to seal off the icy gusts. She unlatched the window, intending to slam it back in more firmly but the wind wrenched it from her hand.

'Damnation!' Exasperated, she knelt on the window seat. The noise of the rain, hammering on the chippings below, was loud in her ears as she cowered behind the curtain for shelter. Reaching for the window, she stretched a tentative arm into the torrent and heard an additional sound somewhere below.

Turning her head to detect its source, she listened for it to be repeated. She peered into the darkness with eyes screwed against the rain. Even as she strained to listen, the rain began to lessen and stop. Apart from the distant crash of waves thundering onto the rocks, the black night seemed strangely silent after the rain.

I must have imagined it, she decided, reaching out again for the window. Then she distinctly heard the noise again, louder this time. A sort of metallic clink.

Whatever is it? Miranda realised it was a familiar sound, one she should recognise. But what? Suddenly it clicked into place, shooting a ripple of alarm through her. Of course! A horse's harness, that's what it was! She stared out but with no moon, all was inky blackness. Then came a suppressed cough. Miranda sucked in her breath and rising to her knees, leaned precariously over the sill, her hair whipping across her eyes as she strained to see the path below. Still she observed nothing, but with her head out of the window she could now detect muffled sounds from across the forecourt. Then quite clearly she heard the snort of a horse.

'Hey there! What are you about?' she yelled. The sounds stopped and there was a hush, as whoever it was held the horse quiet, obviously waiting for her to give up and return to bed. Miranda also waited.

What are they up to? she wondered. She took a sharp breath. Were they stealing the horses?

Running over to her closet, she flung open the door and began pulling on a house dress. Then, changing her mind, she scrabbled at the bottom of the closet, searching for her boys' riding clothes. Pulling them on haphazardly, she then tugged on her boots and ran onto the landing. She raced lightly down the stairs to the heavy front door, fighting to draw back the stiff bolts.

'Damn!' she swore softly as she caught her finger on the rusty metal, tearing the skin. Thrusting her finger into her mouth, she dashed along the corridor to the kitchen, easily managing the well-used back door bolts. She hesitated for an instant, wondering what to do and then sidled forward to peep out. Seeing no-one, she slipped into the night. For the sake of silence, she kept to the grass, her feet sinking into soft soil. Her boots were soon coated thickly in mud. She ran to the corner, pausing to peer round it. Nothing!

She had been slightly sheltered alongside the house but as soon as she left it the wind buffeted her, making her stagger. Hair lashing in wild tendrils across her face, Miranda dashed across the courtyard towards the stables, trying to prevent her feet scrunching on the gravel. She paused, crouched against the wall, just able to make out moving shapes in the darkness and hear subdued sounds.

Now what do I do? she thought, belatedly realising that if they were horse thieves, she could do little on her own to prevent them escaping with the horses. I should have called Luke . . . no, he's away. I'll get Huw then, she thought. No, by then, it would be too late! Perhaps, if I make a lot of noise with something, I can frighten them off? A metal pan from the kitchen and a big ladle should do the trick. She spun back and took one step, straight into a dark figure looming behind her. She gasped, turning to flee as two hard arms shot around her and when she opened her mouth to scream her aggressor released one arm and a calloused hand was clamped firmly over her mouth.

Attempting to bite the offending hand, Miranda struggled ferociously, kicking, fighting, clawing, trying to reach behind to her abductor's face. But she was firmly pinioned. Held tightly against a hard body, she was lifted effortlessly from the ground. Her heart thudded wildly as the man carried her back towards the house and into the kitchen and, kicking the door shut with one booted foot, he deposited her on the flagstones, still keeping his hand over her mouth.

'Miranda. It's Luke,' his deep voice whispered in her ear. 'You won't scream if I take my hand away, will you?'

She shook her head vehemently, her eyes round with terror, and he released his hand.

'How dare—' she began yelling, as she spun round to face him but, to her added fury, he clamped his hand back over her mouth. Reaching up with both hands, she grabbed handfuls of his wet hair, tugging down vigorously, as she kicked out fiercely at his legs, connecting hard on his shins with her leather boots. She had the satisfaction of hearing him give a muffled yelp and he tried to pull his head away from her onslaught.

Her eyes had become accustomed to the dark by this time, and with the aid of the fire embers in the grate, she was able to see him grinning wryly at her. 'Shall we try again?' he asked.

Cautiously, he removed his hand for the second time, and this time she said nothing but brought her hand back, putting all her strength into a stinging slap across his face. He gave a sharp intake of breath, then a low chuckle, catching her hand in mid-air as she would have repeated the action. Her chest heaving, Miranda stared at him with her eyes pouring venom. His hair, dripping with water, tumbled untidily over his face. He was dressed like a labourer, wearing a coarse homespun woollen shirt of some dark hue. Over this he wore a leather jerkin and rough canvas

257

breeches. His clothes were soaked through and clung wetly against his body.

'I'm sorry,' he whispered. 'I deserved that. I frightened you.'

'I thought you were a horse thief,' she whispered back, her voice shaking with anger. 'How dare you treat me like—'

'Listen, Miranda,' he interrupted, flicking the wet hair out of his eyes. 'I'm terribly sorry, but I'm afraid I have no time now for explanations. Please, go back to bed . . . and, please, don't make a noise.'

'Why? What are you doing? You are supposed to be—'

'Miranda, I must go. I have no time to argue with you. Please understand, many other people are depending on me. I promise I will explain.' He gripped her arm firmly, pulling her towards the hall door and thrust her through. 'I give you my word, I will explain fully.'

'But why . . .?'

'Later,' he repeated and closed the door.

Miranda took several shuddering breaths, trying to calm her jangling nerves. Reaction to her fright had now set in and suddenly she felt drained, shaking violently, her teeth chattering. Her knees were wobbly and she clung to the handrail as she climbed the stairs, leaving a trail of muddy footprints in her wake. Grateful to reach her bedroom, she dropped into a chair, tugging off her boots and wet clothes, scattering them on the floor. Listlessly, she rubbed at her numb limbs and soaking hair with a towel. Then she dropped the towel, struggled into her nightdress and then wrapped a thick shawl around herself. She pulled a few heavy cloaks from the closet, flung them on top of the bedclothes and crept under them, chilled to the bone.

Huddled up in her shawl, she lay shivering, listening for further noise outside, but all was quiet. What were they doing? She knew there were others with Luke, but what were they up to? And Luke is supposed to be in Bristol, had gone for a week, so Huw told her. Was he trying to cheat Huw? Miranda sat bolt upright as the thought struck her. Could Luke be stealing from Huw? But what was there to steal that wasn't Luke's as much as Huw's? For a minute she was tempted to get back out of bed and return outside, but the thought of facing the cold and wet again was daunting. Also Luke would be alerted and watching for her. She would tell Huw about it in the morning; he should know about this.

Luke sighed as he squelched back to the stables, mud oozing up round his boots as he crossed the soaking grass. Trust Miranda to wake up and how typical of her to dash out, heedless of any danger. She has plenty of pluck, he conceded. And now I'll be forced to explain to her about the smuggling, he realised resentfully. Luke did not want her involved, preferring to keep her from any knowledge of this illegal activity. Now it would be impossible!

'All right?' a low voice whispered.

'I think so. Time's getting on. Let's speed it up!'

Most of the horses, including Satan, were out of their stables. The straw in his stall was pushed to one side and a heavy flagstone had been lifted back, revealing an opening beneath. A subdued yellow light gleamed from it as Luke picked up a cask, heaving it easily onto his shoulder before descending the slimy steps into the yawning hole. The air in the cellar hung dank and musty, its damp walls dripping with water, as the men worked steadily and methodically, clearing the cargo from the stable.

'That's the lot here, Captain. Do you want me to get the straw back down and the horses in?' David asked.

'Please! If you can you manage on your own, you needn't come back to the beach. I'll get back there and take Nezer with me to bring back Satan.'

Luke leapt up onto Satan's back and accompanied by Nezer on Dancer rode out onto the cliffs, then down the treacherous path, greasy with mud, which led to Pentrebach beach. Once on the beach, both men rode the horses into the river, fording it to the opposite bank. They followed it inland towards the hamlet which crouched around a rocky outcrop where the river normally tumbled over in a waterfall.

Men, carts and animals milled around in the darkness. The feet of animals, men and the wheels of the carts were all bound in sacking to deaden any sound. In the river above the outcrop, rocks had been heaped up against a board to divert the water's flow to flood to either side, leaving only a thin stream still running over the edge. Sliding off Satan, Luke ducked down through the falling water, going almost on his knees as he entered the low entrance to the cavern behind the waterfall. Here two men were still stacking bundles and casks, aided only by the dubious light of a flickering candle.

'How are we doing?' Luke whispered, running a hand over his wet head to stop the water dripping in his eyes.

'Just finished, sir. We can douse the light now.'

Bending low again and followed by the two men, Luke crawled out into the river. The remaining stream poured down their necks from above as they emerged. Before joining the rest of the party, two of them manhandled a boulder across the low opening to the cave. Men already waiting aloft on the outcrop began heaving the rocks and board back out of the river to allow the water to return to its original path as a waterfall. The entrance was well hidden now, and even if anyone ventured to look behind the fall, a rock protruding downwards above the cave opening further camouflaged it, making it practically invisible.

As the last of the carts lumbered off into the night, a horseman came racing along the path from inland with reckless disregard for weather and darkness.

'Coastguard about,' he called in a hoarse whisper, as he dragged the horse to a slithering halt.

Luke gritted his teeth, his heart skipping a beat, as he flashed a speculative glance around. 'It's all right. We're all clear, Jon,' he called. 'Everyone disperse . . . and thanks for your help, men. I'll see you in a few weeks.' His eyes darted in a final scrutiny. 'All my men are back aboard? Right! Nezer, come with me, I'll get back to the ship. You can bring the horses back here then. Leave Dancer in Jon's stable and return to Bryncarog with Satan. You can collect Dancer in the morning.'

Leaping on Satan, Luke raised his arm in a salute to those remaining, then galloped back down to the shoreline, closely followed by Nezer on Dancer. Throwing himself off the horse, he flung the reins to Nezer and without hesitation, plunged straight into the violent sea. Fighting the waves breaking over him, he waded towards the rowing boat where the waiting sailors were struggling to keep the plunging craft afloat, to carry him to the *Windrush*.

Sixteen

'Whatever have you been doing, Miss Mirry?' Ellen exclaimed, when she saw the tumbled bedclothes piled on top of Miranda. 'How did they get all tangled up like that?' She stopped, wrinkling her nose in disdain when she saw the mud-caked boots, sodden riding clothes and towel kicked in a heap on the floor. 'You were never out riding last night, were you?'

'Do stop talking so loudly, Ellen,' Miranda groaned. 'I'm still half asleep.'

Ellen placed a jug of hot water on Miranda's washstand and pulled back the curtains, regarding with dismay the open window, wet curtains and soggy window seat. She returned to Miranda, who peered crossly at her from beneath the pile of clothes.

Pursing her lips, Ellen raised her brows, shaking her head in amazement. 'Do you want to stay in bed any longer, Miss Mirry? I'll come back later if . . .'

No,' Miranda said peevishly, sitting up with reluctance. Sighing loudly, she pushed back the clothes. 'I'm so uncomfortable.'

'I'm not surprised. Why ever did you wear that shawl to bed, Miss Mirry? Were you cold?'

Miranda frowned, looking down in surprise, then she gasped, recalling the events of the previous evening. Immediately she leapt out of bed and ran to look out of the window but everything appeared as normal.

'If I was not still wearing this shawl I should believe I'd been dreaming,' she mused.

'What happened then, Miss?' Ellen asked, her face curious.

'I heard a noise outside and went down to see . . .' Miranda paused, chewing her lip and gave another disbelieving look through the window, scanning both ways.

'You went down to see?' Ellen exclaimed with horror, joining her mistress at the window. 'What if someone had grabbed you?'

'They did!' Watching Ellen's face, she added mindfully. 'Have you seen Captain Llewelyn this morning?'

Ellen's eyes widened and she turned away. 'No, Miss. He's away in Bristol.'

'But he isn't! I saw him last night.'

Ellen shook her head. 'No, Miss, you really must have been dreaming. This morning I heard Mr Huw say the Captain would be back tomorrow.'

'Did he?' Miranda said thoughtfully. So she was right, Huw was unaware that Luke had been at

Bryncarog last night. 'I'll take my toilet later, thank you, Ellen. I want to hurry and catch Mr Huw before he leaves for the office.'

Miranda scrubbed at her face with a washcloth to freshen it, swiftly pulled on a dress and raced downstairs, arriving in the dining room just as Huw was about to leave. He regarded her with some surprise and Miranda suddenly realised how unkempt her appearance was. She dragged a hand through her tangled hair. 'Huw. Ellen tells me you are expecting Luke home tomorrow.'

'That is true. Are you well, Miranda?' He raised one eyebrow. 'You look rather . . . dishevelled this morning.'

'I could have slept better,' she retorted, pulling at the neck of her dress. 'But I hurried down because I wanted to catch you before you left. Luke was here last night,' she declared. 'I saw him!'

'Last night?' Huw darted a swift glance at his mother. 'You saw Luke last night?'

'Yes. I just told you. I thought I heard a noise and went out to see what it was . . .' Miranda broke off, taking a sharp breath and scowling, her face flushing angrily as she remembered Luke's behaviour.

'You went out to see?' Huw said with astonishment. 'That seems extremely unwise.'

'I told you! I thought someone was stealing the horses or something . . .' Miranda's voice trailed off as she saw the amusement on Huw's face. 'You think that amusing, cousin?' she snapped. 'I thought you should know. I believed you would appreciate my efforts. Obviously I was wrong.' She turned and flounced out of the room but Huw came after her before she could reach the stairs.

'Miranda. Of course I am grateful. I was rather surprised and more than a little worried to hear you were wandering around at night, that's all.' His face dimpled into its little boy smile, instantly calming her wrath. Miranda found herself smiling in return.

She grasped Huw's sleeve and dropping her voice whispered: 'I wondered if Luke might be trying to trick you in some way.'

Huw's brow furrowed. 'Trick me? What makes you think that?'

'Why would he pretend to be away? And why would he not want me to witness what he was doing?' She regarded him earnestly.

'Sit down and tell me exactly what happened,' he said, leading her to the table and pouring her a cup of tea.

'He put his hand over my mouth and manhandled me into the house.' Her voice rose in fury. 'He was most ungentlemanly.'

'Did he indeed?' Huw said sharply. 'I'll not have that! I must challenge Luke about this behaviour.' He placed the cup in front of her. 'Miranda . . . I'm afraid Luke is not quite the gentleman he appears on the surface . . . but I shouldn't be saying things like that to you,' he added hastily.

'Why not, if it is true?' Miranda was mollified by his concern.

'I would not turn you against your own brother.' He sat in the seat alongside her and began buttering another piece of toast.

'I think it needs no effort on your part, Huw.'

Restlessly she pushed away the tea, rising to her feet. 'I must change.'

Huw followed her into the hall. 'I hope the experience was not too terrifying,' he said, putting his arm around her shoulder. 'I hope you will always depend on me to care for you, Miranda.' His voice was low and tender.

Miranda looked up at his face and smiled tremulously, aware of her heart beating faster. 'Thank you, Huw,' she whispered.

He pressed her close to him. Comforted, she leaned against him, breathing in the fresh lemon tang of his cologne. 'You mean so much to me, Miranda,' he whispered into her hair. 'I . . . I wonder if you return my feelings?' She raised her eyes to find his heavy-lidded gaze fixed on her face.

'Yes, Huw. I believe I do,' she murmured.

'Then may I hope . . . but perhaps I speak too soon?' He paused, judging her reaction, then continued. 'I love you, Miranda. I would like you to become my wife.'

She stared at him for one moment, heart fluttering irregularly against her ribs. 'Thank you, Huw . . . but . . . I'd like time to consider before . . . before I give you an answer.'

His face lit up. 'Then you will consider it? Miranda, it is more than I had hoped for.' He bent his head towards hers, his face tantalising near. For a moment he brushed her cheeks with his lips, then when she didn't pull away, he gently kissed her. For a split second Miranda remained still and unresponsive in his arms then her mouth opened to his, returning his kiss briefly as he pulled her against him. Eyes wide, she pulled back, her face burning.

'I hope you don't feel I took a liberty? But your lips are so provoking.'

She pressed both hands to her face, her eyes not meeting his and shook her head.

'If you decide to accept my proposal I'd have to approach Luke about your hand. He will not be pleased,' he said bitterly.

Miranda lifted her chin. 'Why not? In any case, once I am twenty-one, it will no longer be his decision. Then he will have no further jurisdiction over me.'

'That is a long time to wait. I'd have to bide my time and find the best opportunity to ask his consent.'

'As long as we know our own minds it doesn't matter what Luke says. Now I must go and complete my toilet.' She flashed him a brilliant smile before flying up the stairs, her heart singing.

Miranda hurried back to her room, to find Ellen clearing up the mess of soggy clothes.

'What did Mr Huw say, Miss Mirry?' Ellen asked, observing her flushed cheeks.

'What do you mean?' Miranda looked at her sharply.

'About the intruders?' She dropped a wet towel onto the pile.

'Oh! I . . . eh . . . he will confront Luke about it.'

'Confront the Captain?' She yanked off another sheet. 'He'll need to be careful, Miss Mirry. The Captain's a powerful m—'

'And you think Mr Huw is not?' Miranda exclaimed, spinning to face her maid.

'No, Miss. I think Mr Huw is very strong too,' Ellen hastened to say, realising her mistake. 'And very handsome.'

Miranda leaned forward and whispered to her maid. 'I'll tell you a secret but you are not to tell a soul. He has asked me to marry him.'

'Marry him!' Ellen squealed. 'That is really exciting, Miss Mirry. Did you accept?'

'Not yet. But I think he has the impression I will.'

'I am so happy for you.' Ellen put both arms around Miranda and kissed her cheek. 'I won't tell anyone, I promise.'

When Miranda saw herself in the mirror she realised how dirty and muddy she still was. Her hair had been snarled into tangles by the wind the previous night, and wisps of straw and bracken could be seen among her curls.

'I think you need a bath, Miss Mirry,' Ellen declared, studying her with amazement. 'Just look at your hair! Whatever did you do last night to get in that awful state?'

As Ellen prepared her bath Miranda began to describe the previous night's events to her: ' . . . so I crept over to the stables . . .' She broke off abruptly in mid-sentence, suddenly having reservations about telling her maid everything.

'I am sure the Captain wouldn't be pleased to hear you were trailing about at night, Miss Mirry . . .'

'I am sure he was not,' she smirked.

'You mean you saw the Captain then? Last night?' Ellen's eyes grew round with astonishment and then narrowed, a thoughtful look creeping into them. 'You could have been hurt if they'd been horse thieves,' she scolded.

'How do you know they weren't?' Miranda snapped, stepping into the bathtub, growing cross again as she recalled the events.

'I . . . well . . . I would have heard about it by now.'

Miranda turned to observe her maid more closely. 'Do you know anything about what was going on, Ellen?'

'Me? I wasn't up last night,' she declared, turning away and picking up a jug of water.

'I didn't ask if you were up but whether you know anything about it. Ellen. Look at me!'

Ellen shook her head. 'How would I know what was happening, Miss Mirry?' she muttered without conviction.

Miranda pouted with frustration. 'I'm sure there is something you are not telling me.' She was silenced as Ellen poured water over her head.

'Morning, Miss Miranda,' David said, coming out of the stables.

Miranda scrutinised the area for signs of the previous night's activity but apart from the mud in the yard being more churned up than usual there were no visible changes.

'Has the Captain returned from Bristol yet?' She flashed David a searching look.

'Don't know, Miss,' he replied, his eyes not quite meeting hers.

'So you haven't seen him at all today?' She walked around the yard, searching for clues.

'Today? Not today, Miss.' He grabbed a bucket of feed and began walking away.

She held up a hand, palm facing him. 'Last night perhaps?'

'N . . . no. No Miss.' He stumbled over the words, his open face flushing slightly as he turned away from her.

He has seen him, Miranda decided, fuming that Luke had not put in his promised appearance. Luke has too honest an accomplice in David, she thought.

'And where is Nezer this morning?' she enquired, following him into the stables.

'Gone to fetch Dancer, Miss Miranda,' he said, emptying the contents of the bucket into the manger.

'Fetch her from where?'

'Eh . . . taken her, Miss,' he amended, finding her standing immediately behind him as he turned. 'Nezer's taken her to ask the smithy to come'n make a new shoe for Moonlight.'

'When did she manage to lose a shoe?' she asked as she was entering Star's stall. The horse turned his head, whinnying softly as she moved towards him. He reached his nose forward to nuzzle Miranda, brushing her face with his whiskers. 'You are pleased to see me, darling,' Miranda whispered, kissing his nose.

Satan, in the next stall, snickered when he heard her voice and Miranda brushed past Star, standing on tiptoe to peer over into Satan's stall to talk to him. 'It looks very messy in there,' she remarked with surprise, David was usually very meticulous in his care of the horses.

David muttered something inaudible, still looking

decidedly uneasy in Miranda's opinion. She turned to leave the stall as David took Star out and noticing mud powdering her skirt, brushed at it with her hand. 'What's this?' she exclaimed, staring at her hand. She followed David, bending down to examine Star more closely, observing the mud caking his legs.

'Star has been out. Who's taken him out?' she demanded, spinning round to face David, eyes flashing fire.

David stared at her mutely, licking his lips.

'I asked you a question. I insist on knowing!'

'Er . . . it was the storm last night, Miss. It upset the horses something awful. They was all terrified . . .' He dropped his head.

'And?' Miranda was tapping her side with her riding crop.

'I took 'em out, walked them round the yard like,' he said hoarsely.

'Rubbish! You don't really expect me to believe that?'

White-faced, David swallowed hard, at a loss for words.

'David, I know horses, I understand them . . .' Hands on hips, she heaved a huge sigh of exasperation. In spite of herself she felt sorry for the unhappy groom. 'I think I had better tell you I heard a commotion here last night.' She paused. 'Were you part of that?'

David remained stubbornly silent, his mouth turned down mutinously.

'I see I will get no satisfaction from you. I think I need to mention this to my brother.'

Relief flooded his face. 'Yes, Miss,' he agreed eagerly. 'You could do that, Miss.'

Miranda dusted her hands on a sack. 'I suppose it's no good for me to expect any of the horses to be ready for a good long ride?'

'Well, they're not too lively like. The storm . . .' he muttered defensively, studiously occupying himself with harnessing Star.

Miranda studied the rest of the stalls' occupants, but everything appeared normal.

Her temper running on a short fuse, Miranda needed some release, so once seated on Star she cantered the horse around the yard a few times before nudging him towards the gate, cleanly leaping it before continuing on towards the cliffs. Watching her departure with relief, David shook his head, his face filled with admiration.

How dare Luke not keep his promise to explain, she fumed, especially after the rough manner in which he treated me. At least I gave him something in return, she thought with satisfaction, recalling the severe slap she had applied to his face.

Miranda heard hooves thundering behind her just as she reached the open grassland. She turned to glance over her shoulder, expecting it to be Luke.

'Miss Miranda,' David called, waving his arm. 'Miss, I've got a message from the Captain.' Miranda reined in and waited. 'I got a message for you to meet Captain Llewelyn down in Pentrebach cove,' he said.

'On the beach?' Miranda exclaimed. 'What on earth for? He will be there himself?'

'I think so, Miss. At the village of Pentrebach, I expect.'

Miranda, feeling rebellious, was inclined to ignore Luke's command, but curiosity got the better of her. She was impatient to know more of this cloak-and-dagger intrigue. Recalling the flashing light she had seen last winter she was positive the bay held some mystery.

'You lead the way,' she commanded.

The narrow path wound its way down, clinging precariously to the cliff-side, with a sheer drop onto the rocks below on the right-hand side. Even though the surface of the path was muddied and churned, she perceived it to be in remarkably good order for such an obscure beach. Fresh horse-dung bore witness to recent use.

'Why is the path in such good repair?' Miranda called to David. 'Who uses it?'

David ignored her, either not hearing or pretending not to hear. They lost sight of the valley as they rounded the bend, coming across a fallen log obstructing the path ahead, obviously a casualty of the last night's storm. As David reined in his horse in front of her, Star laid his ears back, prancing nervously. David cast an anxious glance over his shoulder at Miranda as she fought to control Star on the precariously restricted path. All at once they both heard a rumbling noise above them.

'Watch out!' David yelled, peering up in alarm as a torrent of boulders poured down on them. Desperately he tried to back his frightened horse away from the fall but was unable to avoid a jagged lump of limestone which struck him squarely on the head. With a groan he slumped forward in the saddle as the terrified Cariad gave a whinny of alarm and reared up, legs flailing, and toppled David from the saddle with one foot still caught in a stirrup. The distressed horse surged forward, scrambling wildly through the debris and boulders still raining down to race headlong down the narrow path, dragging David suspended by one foot with his head jarring along the rough ground.

Miranda gasped, then without hesitation kicked her heels into Star's side, urging him forward to soar cleanly over the loose rocks and chase the other horse down the path. She was beginning to gain on them when to her horror she saw Cariad, in her headlong rush, miss her footing on the edge of the slippery path. Icy fingers squeezed Miranda's heart as, kicking and screaming in terror, the horse tumbled head over heels over the brink, pulling her rider along with her. Both horse and rider appeared to hang suspended for a brief instant in time before seeming to speed up, to plunge down to the savage rocks below.

For another instant all was still, sound seeming to cease: the horse's screams, the waves, the gulls, everything. All she heard was the blood pounding through her veins. Fighting back nausea, she leaned forward to peer gingerly over the edge; dread jangled through every nerve as she saw them sprawled on the jagged rocks below. David lay quite still, his head twisted at an ugly angle to his body, with Caraid, now silent but still struggling weakly, on top of him. Bile rose, burning her throat, and turning to place a hand against the cliff wall, she vomited violently.

Wiping a shaking hand across her mouth she forced herself to look over the cliff again and even as she watched, the horse gave one last pitiful whinny and lay still.

'Dear God! What can I do?' she screamed aloud, hysteria engulfing her. 'What can I do?' Star pranced apprehensively beneath her, his ears laid flat, and Miranda pulled herself up sharply, sucking in a ragged breath. Nothing if you panic! Think! Think! Luke is down there somewhere – he must have heard something.

Trembling uncontrollably, her heart thumping, she slowly made her way down the rest of the path. She emerged onto soft sand alongside the river, well above the high water mark clearly defined by the seaweed and flotsam left stranded by the storm. The tide was well out beyond the mouth of the bay with more storm clouds glowering, black and heavy on the horizon.

Hastily she followed the river inland. Not finding Luke, she forded it, searching on the opposite side but the beach was quite deserted. Catching a movement on the cliff above the path, she glanced up, scanning the skyline for the source of the rock fall but could see nothing. She nudged Star into a canter towards the little hamlet of cottages clustered near the waterfall and dropped off him alongside one of the whitewashed walls. Keeping hold of Star's reins she thumped on the door which was opened cautiously by an old woman, her worn face burnt and shrivelled by too many seasons. Her mouth dropped open as she saw Miranda.

'Who be 'ee?' she asked, her voice more Cornish than Welsh.

'I need help,' Miranda gasped. 'There's been an accident on the beach. Is there anyone else here?'

The woman shook her head. 'Be only me grandson. 'e be here. I'll send 'e for help.'

A boy of about eight with a runny nose pushed out behind the woman as Miranda explained what had happened.

'I'll go,' he agreed, rubbing his sleeve across his nose. 'I can take the donkey.'

'Thank you. They're over there near the path.' She pointed. 'I'll go back to them,' Miranda said, climbing up on a stone to remount.

She skirted the rocks on the path side of the beach, continuing towards the sea until she had reached the spot immediately below the accident. Flinging the reins over a spur of rock she hitched up her skirt, hastily stuffing the hem into her waistband out of her way and began clambering up the rocks.

'Stupid, impractical clothes,' she groaned, impatient with the hindrance of her trailing garments. When she reached the top she stared in horror at the carnage. Horse and rider lay unmoving and covered in blood. Cariad's eyes were already glazing over and David, his battered face almost unrecognisable through the lacerations, was firmly pinned to the rocks by the horse.

'Poor David. Poor Cariad,' she whimpered, tears flooding at last, pouring unchecked down her face. She sank to her knees and reached out a hand, hesitating before placing two fingers on David's throat. She felt for the throb of his pulse as her father had taught her many years earlier. There was nothing. Sobbing quietly, head drooping, she was oblivious to the figures approaching along the beach.

'Miranda! Miranda!' Her unfocused eyes turned blindly towards the voice, not recognising it. 'Thank God! You're alive.' She was unaware of Huw climbing up towards her.

'My God, Miranda! Where are you hurt?' Huw's voice shook as he gathered her trembling body into his arms, holding her close. 'Are you hurt?' he repeated.

Recognition seeping through her torpor, Miranda shook her head dumbly, feeling very sick and more than a little faint.

'Did you fall, Miranda?' Huw's voice was urgent. 'Tell me, my darling? Did you fall? Are you injured?'

'No! Only poor David . . . and Cariad.' She began to cry, deep racking sobs shuddering through her. 'David always looked after me . . . he . . . he was always looking after m . . . me,' she sobbed. Vaguely she became aware of Nezer tugging at the horse as he tried to release David. 'He's dead, isn't he? He's dead.' And she fainted in Huw's arms.

Seventeen

Miranda's first thought on waking was that she'd had a terrible nightmare. Her eyes flew open and she tried to sit up, only to slump back feebly, still affected by the laudanum she had been dosed with. Ellen's worried face hung over her.

'It's all right, Miss Mirry. Lie back down.' Gently, she smoothed her mistress's hair off her face.

Miranda tossed her head away, restlessly. 'Is he dead? Is David dead?'

Ellen bit her lip, not answering, her face crumpling and tears filling her eyes.

'Is he?' Miranda screamed, trying to sit up.

''fraid he is Miss. But the physician says you are not to fret . . .'

'Not to fret!' She closed her eyes weakly, tears squeezing out between her lids. 'Stupid man!' she groaned. Opening her eyes, she caught Ellen's arm. 'Where is my brother? Where was he?'

'The Captain was really furious when he heard, I've never seen anyone so angry . . .'

'I want to see him!'

'He's gone out again now; I'll fetch Mr Huw.' Ellen scurried out, her face anxious.

'Miranda, my love.' Huw hurried over to the bed and took her hand, his face tight with concern. 'Thank God you were not harmed, I was so afraid . . .'

'I'm all right,' she whispered. 'But not David. Not David . . . and poor Cariad.' She began to cry feebly again, her shoulders shaking, tears trickling down her cheeks onto the pillow.

'Who gave David that message, Miranda?' Huw's voice was tense. 'Did he tell you?'

'No. I don't know . . . Luke, I suppose . . . I thought . . . But Luke wasn't there . . .' She broke off, trying to gather her numbed thoughts. 'How did you know I'd had a message?'

'Nezer met David as he was leaving to follow you. David told him he'd received a message for you to meet Luke at Pentrebach cove. It was only after David had gone that Nezer remembered Luke had mentioned being on his way to Llanmor.'

'But why would Luke ask me to go down the bay to meet him if he wasn't there?' she said, her voice faint. 'Do you think it could be someone else?' Then she perceived his strained face. 'Huw, what is it?' she asked, alarmed by his fierce expression.

'If I thought it was—' He broke off, gritting his teeth angrily. He got up, pacing the room with quick, angry strides.

'You do believe the rock fall was an accident? Don't you? Don't you?' Her voice rose to a shriek. 'Tell me! Tell me!' When he didn't answer she said: 'You think someone pushed those rocks over the edge deliberately? Oh God!' Terror speared through her, leaving every nerve raw and jangling. 'Huw, I'm frightened.'

He put his arms around her, rocking her gently, rubbing his cheek in her hair. 'It's all right my love, try to calm down. You are still suffering from the shock of it all,' he whispered. 'The physician left another draught in case you needed it. I think you should take it. I'll call Ellen.'

'No! Please, Huw, don't leave me!'

'I'll stay here until you go to sleep,' he promised.

A pale, morning sunshine peeping through the muslin curtains woke Miranda the next day and her mind immediately flooded with the previous day's trauma.

Huw's manner had made it evident he believed someone had intended her harm, but she veered away from this notion, weakly refusing to consider the inference. She was glad when her thoughts were interrupted by Ellen.

'You're awake, Miss Mirry.' Ellen came fussing around her, plumping up her pillows. 'You just stay there, I'll bring you some breakfast. Just something light,' she said as Miranda protested.

But once Ellen left, Miranda struggled to pull herself out of bed, only to collapse shakily back down, surprised to find how helpless she still felt. Yesterday had been the first time in her life she had ever fainted. Always having had robust health, Miranda was unused to feeling weak, making it all the harder for her to handle. She had no appetite, the thought of food made her feel quite queasy but when Ellen returned she forced herself to eat a little.

Ellen bustled about and settled Miranda in a chair. She sat near the window with a shawl over her knees and a book lying idly on her lap when there was a tap on the door. At her bidding the door opened and Luke strode towards her.

Luke sent me there! She tensed with fear, as her stomach lurched sickeningly, leaving her cold and trembling. And what about the window?

'Miranda. I hope you are a little recovered.' His face was drawn into forbidding lines, his eyes steely. 'I came in to see you last night but . . .' He paused, noticing the pale skin stretched taut on her face. 'You poor girl, you look dreadful.' He reached a sympathetic hand towards her, only to snatch it back when she shrank away from him, eyes wide, her fear very apparent.

'My God, Miranda! You don't think I had anything to do with it?' he said hoarsely. His brow puckered and he regarded her uncertainly. 'I would never harm you.'

Hands clasped in tight fists against her body, Miranda studied her brother mutely. For once his confident manner had deserted him, his eyes dark, consumed with emotion. Can it be hurt I read in them? she wondered with surprise.

He opened his mouth as if to speak, then hesitated, clenching his jaw. 'I'd better leave,' he said bleakly.

Shoulders slumped he turned away from her.

He is wounded, she decided, a swift, unexpected relief surging though her. 'Luke, wait!'

He turned back, once more in full control, his eyes unreadable. He waited, his face hostile.

'Please, can we talk about this? Please.'

'As you wish,' he said indifferently.

'I . . . I'm afraid I had not given the matter true thought . . . I just reacted . . . I'm still feeling weak, unlike myself,' she admitted, twisting a handful of the shawl on her lap.

'That's understandable,' he acknowledged, his expression cold.

'Now that I consider it properly, I realise you could not be responsible, would . . . could never perpetrate such a thing.' She paused, biting her lip, studying his face for a glimmer of understanding. But his eyes glittered, cold as steel. 'Forgive me, Luke, but you must see how . . .' Her voice trailed off uncomfortably.

He continued for her: 'That I would be the one to benefit should you have been killed,' he supplied bitterly. He turned away abruptly, stalking stiffly over to stare blindly out of the window with his back to her. He ran a hand through his hair. 'And you really believe I could do that to you?' he asked harshly.

Her eyes filled with tears. 'No I don't! I have just said so. Please Luke, don't shut me out!' she whispered to his back. He turned and glanced sharply at her, his mouth set. 'I am truly sorry,' she repeated.

She saw his jaw clench again as he regarded her silently, his sapphire eyes narrowed with conjecture.

'Don't you believe me? Will you come back and

talk to me? I am not just saying it to pacify you, Luke. You know me better than that.'

He gave a humourless grin, but returned towards her.

'Please do sit down, Luke.'

He pulled up a chair, turned it and straddled it, leaning his arms on the back, the posture one of studied nonchalance. But his body was still rigid.

'Can you forgive me for doubting you?' Her voice wobbled slightly.

Again that flicker of uncertainty clouded his eyes, so alien to Luke, and he looked down at the floor. 'Of course.'

'I feel sure there must be a misunderstanding somewhere. Do you agree?' she said hesitantly.

Steel eyes contemplated her silently for a moment, his face preoccupied.

'Do you believe someone meant me harm?' she asked in a small voice.

'I will find out what happened,' he promised quietly, without answering her question.

'Thank you.'

'I would not . . . could never, do anything to harm you, ever. I give you my solemn word,' he vowed softly.

Tears flooded her eyes again. 'I accept that, Luke.'

Once again he reached to take her hand, only to stop, clenching his fingers in mid-air. She gave a twisted smile and grasped his hard hand, holding it tightly in both of hers. Relief flashed in his eyes like a light. 'And I will do my best to prevent anyone else harming you either,' he said brusquely.

'I know you will.' She reached both arms up to him

as he stood up and, with a quizzical smile, he hesitated before leaning down and to hug her.

'And please, you must take more care,' he said as he left.

On her own, Miranda felt more tranquil as though relieved of a heavy burden. How could it have ever crossed my mind that Luke could do such a thing? she wondered, flooded with shame. I know he will sort it out. Luke is so capable. He is invincible. . . though not entirely perhaps, she decided, recalling the hurt in those blue eyes, so dark and uncertain at her distrust. It was so completely unlike Luke that it brought it home all the more forcibly to her. He truly does care about me, she decided, a warmth flowing through her. Now I know why Papa entrusted me to his care.

Miranda grieved for David . . . and Cariad too, she admitted to herself. She felt responsible somehow for their deaths. She spent almost two weeks in her room, unwilling to face the world, now and then considering the concept of someone seeking her death . . . but who? No ordinary malice would inspire anyone to such a deed, and apart from Luke who else could benefit? It must have been an accident, she decided firmly, such musing does nothing but harm. And with her relentless strength of character, she firmly tried to eradicate it from her thoughts.

Miranda had been touched by Huw's concern; he had been loving and attentive and she could not fault him; but in some inexplicable way she found it irritating. And each time she saw Luke, instead of being his normal aloof self, he was so unusually solicitous she felt uncomfortable with him.

Eventually she dressed and went downstairs, determined to carry life on as usual. Luke still had offered no explanation for his ill manner the night before the accident and to her further exasperation, each time she approached him about it he made excuses, rushing off as if to avoid her.

Wrapping up well against the biting cold she ventured out to walk on the cliffs, accompanied by the ever-sympathetic Ellen. Frost had still not cleared by mid-morning but the universally grey sky held a promise of hidden brightness on the horizon. Ivy twining up the trunks of the few stark, leafless trees dressed them in a filigree of green. The gorse bushes were still dark and brown but even this early a few buds had appeared, the gold of one or two brave blossoms already trying to peep through.

Her face tingled from the wind as they returned, but Miranda was drawn almost unwillingly towards the stables. Though she had no urge yet to ride, she longed to see Star and also to take a regretful, cathartic look at David's territory. Nezer greeted them, his face compassionate.

'Are you wanting to ride, Miss Mirry?' His searching glance flashed over her face.

She shook her head sadly. 'I wanted to come . . . I just felt . . .' Her voice ended on a smothered sob and she blinked back tears.

Nezer nodded sagely.

'I know nothing about David's family,' she admitted hesitantly, looking at the gypsy.

'There is but his mother and a younger sister. The Captain has paid them a few visits. He's told them he'll make them an allowance. A fine man.'

In Star's stall, Miranda leaned against him, resting her head against his neck, tears soaking his shining coat as she talked to him. She had just composed herself to leave when her head rose in surprise as a party of horsemen clattered into the yard, dismounting into a milling, rowdy group, jostling and jeering at Ellen.

'Hey you! Gypsy! What are you about, you shifty bugger?' one called raucously. He swaggered towards Nezer, swinging round in surprise as Miranda came storming out to address him imperiously.

'What do you want here? What is your business?'

The man regarded her warily, realising she was a lady. He touched his whip to his forelock. 'Good morning, Mistress. Jack Nichols of his Majesty's Coastguard.' His thin lips pulled back in a tight smile.

Miranda gave a cursory nod. 'So? That does not mean you are at liberty to insult my staff! Your men are indisciplined, sir!'

'Your staff?' He eyed Nezer sourly. 'Are you of the Llewelyn family, Miss?'

'My brother is Captain Llewelyn,' she addressed him haughtily.

His eyes gleamed maliciously. 'I have reason to believe contraband has been concealed on these premises,' he said waspishly.

'Contraband? Do not be ridiculous!' She made to walk past him, halting when he spoke again.

'Then have I your permission to search, Mistress?'

'Of course you have not! You must obtain Captain Llewelyn's permission. He is not at home. Good day, sir.'

'I am afraid, Miss Llewelyn, that I do not need his permission. I have a writ, and the Constable from Swansea is present as required,' he sneered, indicating a bearded man alongside him.

'My name is Rushton, not Llewelyn,' Miranda informed him. She held out her hand for the writ, raising her brows at the second man.

'Idris Jones. Your servant, Mistress.' His voice was ingratiating, lips flashing pink and shiny through his full beard.

Her eyes scanned the writ briefly before returning to the Constable. 'Is this fully legal, Constable?'

'I'm afraid it is, Mistress.' He bobbed his head deferentially.

'Carry on!' Jack Nichols called harshly to his men.

The men who had all been watching this exchange with interest dispersed around the area. Jack Nichols turned to Nezer. 'What do you know about this then, gypsy?'

'You will not address my groom in such an ill-mannered way,' Miranda spat.

Nezer's dark face flushed slightly. 'And what would I be knowing about the goings-on at the big house?' he flashed, scowling.

'Maybe you were the informer?' the man asked slyly. 'That it? Your sort will do anything for money.'

Nezer turned his back on him and returned to the stables, followed by Miranda, Jack Nichols and the Constable and leaving a pale-faced Ellen staring after them, rigid with fear.

'If your men disturb the horses you will pay for it!' Miranda snapped, her temper rising as she watched them picking through the straw around the restive horses' feet. 'You will answer to the magistrates.' She gave the Constable an inquiring glance.

'They are to be respectful and polite, Mistress,' the Constable concurred.

'Except it might not be my men answering to the magistrates,' Jack Nichols said sourly.

With increasing fury Miranda watched as they pulled and pushed in every nook and cranny, emptying boxes, tipping out sacks of meal. She heard bangs up above as they threw things around in the loft.

'You will replace everything exactly as you found it!' Miranda shouted, her fists clenched tightly.

As one man started to enter Satan's stall the horse whipped out in fury with his hind feet, knocking him to the ground. White-faced, blood dripping from his head, the man scrambled out on his hands and knees, staring up at the whites of Satan's rolling eyes as the animal surveyed him over his shoulder.

The officer swore softly and made to enter himself, hesitating as Satan bucked again, baring his teeth menacingly. 'Get that horse out!' he roared at Nezer.

'Then to be sure it is the Captain himself you will have to wait for,' Nezer said mildly, a glint of triumph in his eyes. 'Himself is the only one who can handle that horse.'

'I think 'e's right, Sir. I've 'eard about that 'orse,' one of his men volunteered. ''alf wild 'e is.'

Jack Nichols grunted and rubbed his jaw thoughtfully, his eyes roaming around the chaotic stable. 'Get hold of a broom and see if there's anything there,' he said savagely.

Cautiously the man sidled towards Satan's stall and with a broom clutched in his sweating palms he poked at the straw beneath the horse. He gasped as Satan squealed, lashing out with his feet in several successive kicks of rage. 'Nothing there Sir,' he panted, watching the discarded broom splintering into pieces.

'Satisfied?' Miranda demanded scornfully.

'Seems I must be, Mistress.' Jack Nichols' humourless eyes were calculating. 'Until the next time!'

They got back to Bryncarog to find the house in turmoil. Charlotte fluttered up to greet Miranda, her hands nervously twisting her lace handkerchief into a tight little knot.

'The Coastguard have been here,' she wailed. 'They turned everything upside down. It was dreadful! Dreadful!' She dabbed at her eyes with the knotted scrap in her hand. 'I was terrified.'

'I am sure you were. Why on earth should they expect us to know anything about it?' Miranda said furiously. 'They were so rude. They came to the stables too; I was there.'

'The stables?' Charlotte said fearfully. 'Oh dear! Oh dear!'

'Never mind,' Miranda soothed her. 'Don't worry, it's all some awful mistake. I'm sure they will return full of remorse and apologies.'

Charlotte stopped dabbing her eyes, hand poised in mid-air. 'They're gone?' she whispered.

'Of course. Come along! I am going to pour both of us a glass of brandy . . .'

'Brandy!' Charlotte exclaimed with horror. 'Ladies do not drink brandy.'

'They will today,' Miranda insisted, leading her towards the dining room.

Taking charge, Miranda set about getting the servants organised to clear up and sent Nezer to Swansea to inform Luke and Huw what had happened. By the time the grim-faced men returned home order had been almost restored. Charlotte and Miranda took it in turns to communicate their displeasure with the Coastguard officers but when Miranda recounted Satan's part in the action both men began to chuckle and then laugh, their shoulders shaking.

'Seems he has some use as a guardian,' Huw said, slapping Luke's back to Miranda astonishment. She had never seen such camaraderie between the two men.

'I told you,' Luke spluttered, laughing again.

'I don't think it is funny,' Charlotte retorted, tossing her head. 'I was very frightened.'

'I am truly sorry, Mother.' Huw put a placating arm around her shoulder, squeezing it. 'Never mind, it's all over now.' He flashed his little-boy smile at them both, his chin dimpling. For once it failed to work its magic on Miranda.

She frowned. 'There is no need to patronise us, Huw. You may regard women as inferior beings but we are not children,' she snapped and stalked out of the room, leaving both men staring after her.

Miranda checked Luke just as he was about to leave the house again, taking a firm grip of his coat sleeve. 'A word. Now, if you please, Luke. I believe you promised me an explanation several weeks ago,' she said.

'I believe I did.' He smiled wryly, motioning her into the library and pulling out a chair for her. 'You look much improved. I trust you are feeling a little better?'

Miranda nodded. 'But I do miss David dreadfully. And I still feel responsible for his death.'

'You are in no way responsible,' he said firmly, perching on the edge of the desk.

Miranda gave a heavy sigh. 'I wish I could believe that . . . I must stop thinking about it.' She was silent a few minutes, then looked up at him expectantly. 'So?

He raised his eyebrows.

'About that night?'

'What do you want to know?' he hedged, picking up the paperweight from the desk.

'You were very rough,' she flashed challengingly, her chest heaving as she recalled the event.

'I agree. And I realise I frightened you badly. There was no other way,' he said frankly. 'Please accept my apology again, Miranda. But you really should not go wandering around in the—'

'I might not, if I knew the reason.' Her eyes flared fire at him.

He took a deep breath, exhaling slowly, tossing the paper weight from one hand to the other. 'Well. You now realise there is smuggling carried on in these parts.'

'Smugglers? You were out trying to catch the smugglers and afraid they would hear you? How exciting!' She clapped her hands, her face lighting in anticipation.

He blinked, his mouth dropping slightly. 'Well . . . not exactly.' He took another deep breath, adding reluctantly: 'I'm afraid we were the smugglers.'

'You? Smuggling . . .?' She stopped. 'So that is why the Coastguard were here,' she exclaimed. 'They knew!'

His gaze held hers. 'I am sorry you were upset.'

'I was absolutely furious with them, they really disturbed the horses . . .' Her eyes narrowed speculatively. 'The stables?' she said slowly. 'That is where you were that night?' It was a question.

His face remained impassive and he said nothing, but she thought there was laughter lurking in his eyes.

'But how could you? It is illegal.'

'It does come into that category,' he admitted, laughter rippling through him. 'It may be illegal but it is widely accepted as an extra source of income . . .'

'That doesn't make it right! And you being an ex-sea-captain makes it even worse.'

He pursed his lips, subjecting her to a scarching look. 'On the Indianamen we were allowed cargo space on board . . .'

'For smuggling? I can't believe it was intended for that!' Her tone was scornful.

'It was widely . . .'

'What if you had been caught the other night? Or today?' she exclaimed, the horror of that situation suddenly reaching her.

At loss for a reply, he said nothing, fiddling with the paperweight again.

'What if you were caught?' she repeated.

He rubbed his hand across his chin thoughtfully. 'Well . . . . It is not as if . . . I mean most of the people in the area are involved in some way, many of the magistrates, even the rec—' He drew a quick breath.

'The rector?' she guessed.

His face remained impassive.

'Don't tell me! You . . . you never hide it in the church?' Her voice rose incredulously.

His eyes widened, then he grinned wickedly. 'I think it is best you know nothing about—'

'What about Huw? Does he know? Well, does he?' she continued, when Luke made no reply.

'Why don't you ask him?' he said dryly, putting the paperweight back on the desk.

'But he said nothing when . . .?' Miranda leapt to her feet and began pacing around, as she always did when disturbed. 'He must know. Why didn't he tell me?'

Luke gaze followed her path. 'Probably he thinks it better for you to be innocent, as I would have preferred.'

'Did Huw take a part?'

Luke shook his head, his face dismissive.

'But what would happen if you were caught by the Coastguard? Could you go to prison? Well, could you?' she persisted, stopping in front of him.

'Perhaps,' he admitted reluctantly, rising to his feet. 'It would depend on who the magistrate—'

'But that's terrible. Imagine it? You, a gentleman! An ex-sea-captain! In prison with all those ruffians! It doesn't bear thinking about.'

Amusement flashed across his face, but another emotion she couldn't decipher lurked in the back of those enigmatic eyes. 'Would you care then? I thought you'd be pleased to be rid of me?'

She ignored that statement. 'What about the rector? Would he go to prison?'

He threw back his head, laughing aloud, his shoulders shaking with mirth. 'Miranda!' he chuckled. 'He would deny it. He could insist he knew nothing about any of it . . . Anyway, I didn't say the rector was involved,' he amended hastily.

Miranda regarded him with astonishment. 'But that's . . . It's . . .' She scratched her head. 'I can't really believe you are telling me this . . .' She directed a suspicious glance at him. 'You are not making it up?'

He shook his head, smiling ruefully. 'No!'

'Why do you do it?'

He shrugged indifferently, turning away, unwilling to admit to her how close the firm was to bankruptcy.

'That Coastguard officer mentioned an informer,' she said, suddenly remembering his words.

He spun back alertly, his eyes narrow slits of steel. 'Are you sure?'

'I'm certain. He was taunting Nezer, said perhaps he had done it. Ask Nezer.'

'I knew they were too close on our tails the other night,' Luke mused thoughtfully. 'I wonder—?'

'You mean you almost got caught?' she gasped.

'Let's say they were too close for comfort.' He took a deep breath, and began making for the door. 'If you will excuse me, Miranda—'

'Luke.' She caught his arm, aware once more of the

iron-hard muscles beneath the sleeve. 'I would care,' she said simply.

He turned, jaw clenched. His smouldering blue eyes searched her face for a few seconds but he said nothing.

Slumped loosely in the saddle, Luke rode Satan slowly along the headland above Pentrebach Bay, where the rockfall causing David's death had originated. He chewed his lip pensively, staring down at the recently disturbed rocks. It wasn't his first visit since the accident but he slid off Satan to bend down for another closer look. He rose shaking his head, still unable to make up his mind whether the rock fall had been accidental or had been levered off deliberately. The storm on that night had been violent, and heavy rain since had flushed away all traces of what had happened. There was no true way of knowing. He had a horrible suspicion about the whole affair but without evidence, that was all it could be. He would make sure his thoughts reached the ears of the one he suspected and in future he intended to be much more vigilant on Miranda's behalf. That way a similar incident was less likely to be attempted. His stomach tightened as he looked down at the rocks below. Miranda could so easily have been lying there!

Remounting Satan, he carried on towards the path and down to the little hamlet of Pentrebach. He tied Satan to the iron ring on the wall outside a cottage and ducked his head under the low doorway, entering directly into the main room. The cottage served as the local tavern and a group of men hunched around the table looked towards him as he entered. 'Afternoon, Cap'n,' one or two called.

Acknowledging the greetings, he joined them, accepting with a nod of appreciation the foaming tankard Griff placed in front of him.

'Somebody did tip off the Coastguard then?' Davo, one of the group grumbled. 'There's a bloody near thing, wasn't it?'

Luke gave a hollow laugh. 'You can say that again. If there had not been such a devilish storm they would have waylaid the *Windrush* with their cutter. Bloody near thing indeed.'

'They been up the big 'ouse, I 'eard, Cap'n.'

'Turned it over,' Luke affirmed, reaching for a hunk of bread and a slice of cheese from the board in the middle of the table.

'What do we do now about reaping the crop, Cap'n?' Dick, the fourth man, was referring to hauling in the casks which were sunk out in the bay, anchored to a recovery line.

'We'll do it as soon as possible,' Luke said, gulping his beer, 'otherwise I can see Jack Nichols creeping the bottom before we get a chance to recover our cargo.'

'Yeah! I saw them out with grappling 'ooks down near Llanmor yesterday,' Davo spluttered, through a mouth full of food.

'Did you? Then we've no time to waste!' Luke swallowed the rest of his ale.

'Tonight?'

Luke shook his head. 'No good. Almost a full moon. Give me a few minutes to think.' He scratched his head thoughtfully as the men all waited expectantly. 'I know what we'll do, create a diversion on Llanmor. Davo, you take a fishing boat and a couple of men along to the quarry end of the beach and hang around in that area. With a horse and cart nearby maybe? Late afternoon would be a good time, and try to look cunning, as if you are avoiding them. Hopefully Jack Nichols—'

'What if they wants to know what we're doin' there, Cap'n?' Davo asked anxiously.

Luke grinned. 'Fishing of course! You are a fisherman, aren't you?'

'But 'ell, Cap'n, that's not the right place for it.'

'You know that and I know that, but do they? They are not local men.'

'That's right! They knows bugger all,' Griff agreed. 'As long as we got our nets with us like.'

'And a couple of 'ooks,' Davo chuckled. 'To make them suspicious like.' They all sniggered.

'And while they are busy watching you, Dick and I will take his little boat and reap the crop,' Luke chuckled. 'The tide will be well up the mouth soon, so we can moor the boat just under the headland in readiness and wait.'

'Could we have someone to ride over and give you the word, sir?' Griff suggested.

'Good idea, Griff.'

'My lad will go, 'e's good with 'orses,' Davo interjected quickly. 'To tell the truth, I was wondering if you might be needing someone up the big 'ouse like? Now that . . .?' He left the sentence unfinished.

Luke flashed him a speculative glance. 'I do have

Nezer, but I will certainly think about it, Davo.'

Davo gave a grunt of satisfaction, nodding his head. 'I'd appreciate that, sir. 'e's a good lad.'

The plans were swiftly finalised and the group dispersed about their allocated duties.

Eighteen

The fresh April wind gusted, making the daffodils dance in the borders as Miranda made her way to the stables. The bright golden trumpets overflowed onto the lawns as if scattered by some giant's hand and Miranda stopped to admire them, realising spring was really here at last. It's a beautiful day for a ride, she decided, taking a deep breath, her spirits lifting.

Miranda had suggested she and Huw might ride together this morning, and although she saw neither Huw nor Luke at breakfast she arrived at the stables at ten o'clock as arranged. Nezer appeared as she pushed open the creaking stable door.

'Morning, Miss Miranda.' He was already backing Star out of his stall.

'Have both Satan and Dancer already gone?' Miranda said, surprised to see Dancer's empty stall.

'The Captain was off early as he's in the habit of

doing. It's to Swansea he's gone,' he said, throwing a blanket over the horse's back.

'What about Mr Huw? When did he leave?'

Nezer shook his head, lifting down a saddle. 'I've seen no sign of Mr Huw today. He must have gone off last night and has not been back since. To be sure he has spent the night somewhere.'

'All night?' Miranda exclaimed. 'But I understood we were to go riding this morning. He had dinner at home. Are you sure he has been out all night?'

Nezer eyed her thoughtfully. 'I'll not be knowing anything about that, Miss Miranda.' He had saddled Star and tightened his girth and now held a hand for Miranda to mount.

'Thank you, Nezer.' Disappointed that Huw was missing, she decided to have a good gallop and made for Llanmor beach. She thought she might repeat her visit to the village at its furthest end.

The sky was clear, a sprinkling of cotton-wool clouds being pushed briskly across it. The sea tinged blue rather than grey today and small white peaks whipped up all over its surface. Yes, spring is definitely here, she thought with a sense of exhilaration. Winter is over and the warm summer days lie ahead.

Once she reached the path skirting the edge of the beach, Miranda crossed onto the firm sand where Star could gallop. Reaching the village, they wandered down to the harbour where Star picked his way through nets and ropes spilled over the ground. Miranda saw heads turn her way in curious glances as she passed unaccompanied; men touched their forelocks. She wrinkled her nose as she caught the pungent fishy smell wafting up from the piles of rotting fish carcasses which were being fought over by shrieking, quarrelling gulls.

Large baskets were loaded to the top with the very last of the season's oysters and once again Miranda watched with amazement as the heavy baskets were hoisted up onto the women's heads, to be balanced and carried with apparent ease. She was making her way to the opposite end of the harbour when she noticed Huw's lanky frame lounging against a wall, deep in conversation with two local men.

He started, his eyebrows rising as he caught sight of her, and hastily straightened. 'Miranda!' He waved, and with a quick word to his companions, left them and hurried over. 'Miranda, what an unexpected pleasure.' His smile was warm and unguarded as he swept off his hat.

She regarded him coolly. 'I suppose it is unexpected,' she said frostily.

Huw frowned, catching Star's reins. 'I trust you did receive my message?'

'What message?' she snapped.

He looked concerned. 'Don't say you didn't receive it?' He took a breath, his expression baffled. 'I asked my mother to let you know I couldn't make our assignment.'

'She said nothing.' She gazed over his shoulder at the scene on the harbour.

'Really? She must have forgotten. My dear Miranda, please accept my humble apologies, you must think me an unmannered oaf. Do you forgive me?' His voice was contrite, disarmingly repentant, his expression that of a little boy about to be chastised.

'How could I refuse?' Miranda murmured, not entirely convinced. 'Nezer tells me you were out all night,' she said stiffly. 'I thought—'

'Did he indeed?' Huw's mouth tightened, his lazy eyes hardening. 'I must have a sharp word with Nezer. He has no business discussing my whereabouts.'

'He was not to blame,' she interjected. 'I asked if he had seen you this morning and it came out in that manner.'

'I see. Then he made a mistake,' he snapped. 'I left very early this morning; he was not even up. And I do not take kindly to gypsies discussing my business. He has no . . .' Noticing Miranda's disapproving face, he paused, allowing the subject to drop. Quickly recovering his good humour, his chin dimpled again in a smile.

'Where were you then?' she asked, with a searching glance.

'I had some unexpected business to attend to,' he said easily. His gaze studied her from under his heavy-lidded eyes. 'That is why I asked my mother to convey my apologies.'

'It must have been sudden. You didn't mention it at dinner.' Her eyes narrowed with speculation.

'Do you still wish to ride?' he asked, his voice contrite. 'I am free now.'

'You have no need to worry on my account. I am quite happy on my own,' she retorted caustically, freeing the reins from his hand.

He put a pleading hand on her arm, a scolded little

boy. 'Please, Miranda, don't be cross. I very much want to ride.'

'Is there an inn where we could take some refreshment?' she asked. 'I am uncommonly thirsty. A glass of cordial perhaps?'

'Well . . . not really. There is nowhere.'

'Isn't that a sign over there?' Miranda pointed with her whip. 'I can see something outside.' Miranda pressed with her knees, urging Star forward towards the sign. 'It is a tavern,' she remarked turning an accusing face to Huw. 'And Dancer is tied up outside.'

Huw had followed and shook his head reluctantly. 'It is not the sort of place you're used to, Miranda. I don't think—'

'Rubbish! I want to go in.' Huw's mouth turned down sulkily and he drew a frustrated breath as she waited for him to help her dismount. Instead of handing her down though, he lifted her, his hands lingering on her waist longer than was necessary. He bent his head towards hers, his breath warm on her face.

'My glorious Miranda,' he whispered.

She smiled, her ill humour ebbing. He really was sweet. 'Thank you, Huw,' she whispered softly.

They entered the low passage, Huw needing to duck his head to pass his tall frame under the doorway. A few splintered tables crowded the dingy room, all sticky with the ale slopped over their surfaces. Huw pulled out a chair, dusting it off with his handkerchief before offering it to Miranda.

As she took a seat a girl appeared, posing in front of them, hands on hips. Dark hair lay in wild untidy tendrils around her face and shoulders. Her eyes travelled boldly over Miranda before coming impudently back to her face. Deliberately she spoke in Welsh, looking straight at Miranda.

Miranda bristled, pursing her lips. 'Have the good manners not to stare, Miss,' she commanded. 'And to speak in the king's English . . . if you can?'

The girl's lip lifted contemptuously but before she could reply Huw broke in: 'Enough of that, Haelwen. You just behave yourself.' His voice held a warning and as she took a breath to answer he added: 'You understand me?'

Her stance challenged him for a few minutes, then she tossed her head sullenly, sending the curls dancing around her shoulders. 'What is it you're wanting?' she snapped insolently.

'Two measures of port.' He flashed his engaging smile at the girl and Miranda felt a sharp pang of jealousy as Haelwen's face melted into a wide smile. The girl was extremely pretty, in a bold, impertinent way, her figure voluptuous without running to fat.

'Do you come here often? You seem to know her well.' Miranda's tone was frosty.

'Often enough,' he said easily. 'I need to come to the village regularly to keep an eye on our boats.'

'I thought most of the boats here were owned by the villagers or came from Cornwall.' She lifted a disdainful hand as it encountered the sticky, unwiped table.

'That is true,' he agreed blandly, offering her his handkerchief. 'But the ones we have still need organising.' He threw his hair back from his face, regarding her lazily with eyes half closed.

'The girl is very insolent.'

'I did warn you before we came in, Miranda. We can go now if you wish.' He began to rise.

'What?' Miranda never stirred. 'Be driven out by a tavern maid?'

'Don't take any notice of her manner; Haelwen is all right.'

'She should still learn some manners and do her work properly,' she said, indicating the sticky table.

'I know, but try to understand. She is unused to contact with ladies, particularly sophisticated ones like yourself.'

Haelwen flounced back in with the drinks, almost flinging them onto the table. Then instead of leaving, stood there watching them sullenly, hands on hips again. Miranda gave her a scathing glance, her voice icy.

'Is there something you want?'

'No . . . Miss,' she added reluctantly, as Huw's eyebrows rose. She shot a sly glance at his face and grinned. 'I was just surprised to see Huw . . . Mr Huw back again so—'

'Haelwen!' Huw leapt to his feet, and grabbing hold of the girl's arm, thrust her roughly from the room. 'I've warned you already,' he hissed, his voice losing its warmth.

'About time you did that,' Miranda said with approval. 'The girl is far too familiar. She needs to learn her place.'

Huw smiled without amusement and tugged uncomfortably at his cravat, saying nothing. Reaching across the table he took a great gulp of his port.

'That's good.' He licked his lips appreciatively.

Two men entered, the first greeting Huw as he saw him at the table.

'Hello there, Huw boy.' He slapped him on the back, slopping Huw's wine into his lap, giving him an exaggerated wink. 'Back again already, are you? *Duw*, can't you leave the gi . . .' He stopped in confusion when he noticed Miranda sitting back in the shadows. 'Oh! Sorry, Mistress,' he exclaimed, touching his forelock. 'I didn't know Mr Huw 'ad company like.' He threw Huw a horrified glance, his face reddening, and backed out hurriedly with his companion in close pursuit.

'God!' Huw exclaimed. He sucked in a deep breath, letting it out between clenched teeth and banged the glass down on the table, brushing at the wine stain on his breeches.

'Huw!' Miranda chided. 'I am not used to blasphemy.'

'Forgive me, but the man is an idiot. Miranda, I really believe this is a most unsuitable hostelry for your presence. We must leave immediately.'

'But I am enjoying myself, Huw.' Miranda threw him an impish smile. 'What are you hiding here?'

'Nothing!' His voice was sharp, in a way that Miranda had never heard him speak before, and her mouth fell open a little in surprise.

She pouted, then lifted her chin challengingly. 'Nothing? Then why are you so defensive?'

'I am not defensive,' he barked. 'I did warn you not to come but you would have your own way.'

'For goodness sake, Huw, you are beginning to

sound just like Luke,' she snapped. Then still annoyed, added waspishly, 'I am beginning to wonder whether you know that girl better than you make out. She seems much too familiar with you.' Miranda spoke to annoy Huw, not even considering her words might be true.

Huw's eyes narrowed, his expression peevish. His tongue snaked briefly over his lips as he studied her warily through half-closed eyes. He swallowed hard. 'Don't talk nonsense. I want nothing from a tavern maid,' he growled. Recovering slightly, he forced a grin, which never reached his eyes: 'And I certainly hope I am never as overbearing as Luke.'

Miranda didn't reply for a moment, regarding him critically. 'At least I know where I am with Luke,' she snapped.

He reached over to touch her hand. 'Let's get out of here, shall we?'

They rode home in uncomfortable silence, Miranda's thoughts still with the girl in the tavern and far from happy about her. She was extremely pretty and had been very familiar with Huw. She knows him better than he has revealed. Why hide it? she wondered.

'Mother, you forgot to tell Miranda I was unable to meet her,' Huw chided Charlotte when they returned to Bryncarog. 'She waited at the stables for me,' he added swiftly, as Charlotte began to speak.

Her eyes met his, understanding dawning. 'My goodness! So I did! That really is thoughtless of me,' she said glibly. 'Can you forgive me, Miranda?'

Miranda's eyes, wide with suspicion, flashed to Charlotte's face.

'Of course, Charlotte,' Miranda said coolly. Charlotte flushed guiltily, aware of her doubt and Miranda wondered why they should both lie to her. She ran up the stairs and hurried along the corridor. leaving them both staring after her. She stopped halfway and tiptoed back to hear what they said.

'You are foolish, Huw. Why on earth do you risk . . .' Charlotte's voice faded away as they entered the drawing room.

So she was right! Huw was making excuses and had not asked his mother to pass on his message. Why? she wondered. And why risk what?

The months wore into summer and Miranda took to riding Satan sometimes when Luke was away. One day she trotted into the stable yard to find Luke waiting.

'Miranda. How long have you been riding Satan?'

Her eyes danced mischievously, a smile creeping over her face. 'So you have found out? Do you disapprove?'

Luke exhaled slowly, frowning. 'I don't disapprove, I am just concerned that you—'

'Fiddlesticks! You don't like the idea of your little sister, a mere woman, riding Satan,' she said scornfully.

'Don't be exasperating.' He assisted her down, his face grim. 'I have no illusions about the myth of women being weak.'

'But you still want to be the dominant male, the only one capable of riding Satan.' She gave a gurgling laugh. 'And now I have spoiled it!'

'You still believe I am trying to thwart you?' Luke snapped, his eyes cold.

'Frankly, yes.' Laughter rippled through her. 'You are often away. I thought you would be pleased for me to exercise him. He really is a wonderful horse,' she added sincerely.

'All right. You have my permission to ride Satan as long as someone is with you.' He gathered Satan's reins in his hand.

'Why? Do you think I might fall off?' she said scathingly.

'I don't want to risk anoth . . .' He broke off, unwilling to remind Miranda of the accident. He sighed and turned away. 'Just please make sure you do not go unaccompanied,' he repeated dismissively.

'Yes, Captain,' Miranda giggled, watching him stride away. But she was left feeling slightly disappointed; his discovery had not been as satisfying as she had expected. Luke had not appeared in the least upset to see her riding Satan; in fact he hadn't even seemed surprised.

At dinner a few days later they had words again.

'Huw warned me months ago you would think him a fortune hunter,' Miranda flashed, sawing viciously at her meat.

'How very astute of him,' Luke drawled, reaching for the salt.

'You believe the worst of everyone,' she fumed. 'Do you believe no-one likes me for myself? That every man is after my money? Or is it just Huw?' She gestured at Huw who was listening to this exchange with apparent enjoyment.

'You are the one making that remark,' Luke pointed out mildly. 'I didn't bring up the subject.'

'Not everyone thinks about money all the time.' Her voice rose.

'Some people do not need to,' Luke pointed out icily, piling his plate with vegetables.

'How dare you say that to me! To think I really thought I was growing to like you. I was wrong, you are obnoxious. I hate you!' Miranda threw down her napkin and stormed out of the dining room as Luke carried on eating, quite unperturbed. He really is unbearable, she fumed. His gentleness towards her and concern in the weeks immediately after the accident had soon worn thin. Now he was as overbearing as ever. Worse, if anything! How could I have begun to like him? she raged. Huw followed her out as she stamped into the garden, pulling his mouth down in a caustic grin.

'I believe Luke does not take kindly to the idea of us becoming close,' he chortled. 'The way he acts you would think he saw me as a rival.'

Miranda frowned at him. 'Don't be silly,' she snapped. 'You know Luke. He just likes to manipulate everyone. To be in total command at all times.'

Huw threw her a lazy glance, his eyes hidden beneath their hooded lids. 'That is completely true,' he agreed. 'But it is certain he will never control you. I think it's just as well he never had you as a crew member on board his ship.'

Miranda giggled, regaining her good humour. 'Actually running away to sea sounds like a good adventure. I sometimes wish I had been born a man instead of a frail . . .' She pulled a mocking, feeble face, then continued, '. . . woman. The trouble is I never feel feeble or frail.'

'Miranda, you are incorrigible. I have never met another woman to compare with you. Where on earth do you get these strange ideas? I am certainly pleased you were born a woman.' He took her hand, turning her to face him, placing his hands lightly around her waist. 'You are far too beautiful to be a man,' he whispered, his hands pressing harder, pulling her close to him. 'That would be such a waste. A few months ago you said you would give my proposal thought. Have you done so? May I ask Luke for your hand soon?'

'Yes,' she agreed eagerly. 'Yes, you may. As soon as you wish.' Her eyes sparkled. 'That should ann . . .' She broke off, realising what she was about to say. That Luke would be ill-pleased at the idea of her marrying Huw. She didn't want Huw thinking that was the reason she had accepted his proposal.

'Miranda. That is wonderful,' he breathed. 'I'll approach him as soon as possible.' She noted his delighted face with a pang of guilt and wriggled from his arms impatiently as he leaned down to kiss her. Twirling away she continued marching briskly along the path, wondering if she should have agreed just yet. Maybe she was still unsure. Perhaps she should have considered longer? Behind her, Huw's mouth turned down petulantly like a spoiled small boy and he gave a sigh of irritation, scowling after her.

Nineteen

Miranda gave a cursory tap on the library door and burst in as Luke's head shot up. He was seated behind the worn mahogany desk and rose as she rushed towards him, automatically reaching behind him for his jacket which was hanging over the back of the chair. It was so stiflingly hot this evening that he had been working in his shirt-sleeves with the neck of his shirt unbuttoned.

'Please.' Miranda held up her hand imperiously. 'Don't dress on my account, it's far too hot. I shall take but a few minutes of your time.'

He nodded formally, eyeing her warily, and remained standing until she was seated before slumping back into his chair. 'Can I help . . .?

'You most certainly can!' she interjected. 'Today, Huw came to ask you for my hand in marriage! How dare you refuse him!' Using her most haughty tones,

313

Miranda gestured impatiently with an arm and knocked over the inkwell, flooding the desk and papers with ink.

Luke cursed as he leapt to his feet and reached over to rescue the papers as Miranda also leapt to her feet and away from the extending black pool.

'I am truly sorry for the mishap,' she snapped insincerely. Lifting her chin, she moved a step closer again. 'But I also feel you should be aware that I am unused to such language.'

As he leaned across the desk, their faces were close and his glance wandered over her face before meeting and holding Miranda's own eyes. This close to him, Miranda was aware of his black side-whiskers curling down his cheeks and almost reaching his firm jawline. Dark hairs were visible against the tanned skin at the open neck of his white shirt. She stared at them, finding them stirringly, sensually attractive, before tearing her gaze away.

He emptied the dish of fine sand onto the spreading stain and pulling out his linen handkerchief, he began mopping the excess ink with it. Miranda noticed a jagged, heavy scar snaking a shining path up the knotted muscles of his forearm.

'I hope there is not too much damage?' she murmured, slightly flustered, her gaze held now by the scar.

'No.' Noticing her contemplating the scar, he pulled down his shirtsleeves and buttoned them. 'I apologise for my slip,' he said abruptly.

Miranda stared mutely at him, confused by the unfamiliar emotions coursing through her body. 'I . . .

I . . .' she began. Frowning, she sank back down on her seat.

He sat back also, dropping his gaze to his papers.

'Luke!'

When she said no more he glanced up again, a sardonic smile twisting his mouth. 'You were asking about Huw,' he supplied harshly.

'I . . . Yes! I want to marry him. I love him!'

He clenched his jaw, staring at her again, his eyes cold as steel. 'You love him?' His lip curled. 'Are you sure?'

She hesitated, suddenly uncertain. 'Yes,' she affirmed, her voice doubtful.

'I suggest you give yourself more time to consider. There is no going back.'

'What do you know?' she challenged him. 'Have you ever been in love?'

He took a deep breath before letting it out very slowly. 'I do not see that the question serves any purpose.' His voice was cold, clinical.

'You wouldn't! You are too controlled ever to fall in love!' Her voice had risen. He ignored her while methodically stacking his papers and placing the stained ones aside. 'What about Gwennie?' she shouted. 'What about her mother?'

His head shot up, his face amazed. 'Gwennie? You think Gwennie is my child?' His mouth remained slightly open in surprise.

Miranda felt her temper cool. 'Isn't she?'

He didn't answer, but she saw concern flicker, softening the stern lines of his face.

'Whose child is she then?' she whispered.

Luke bit his lip, rubbing a hand through his dark curls and rumpling them across his forehead. 'I do not see . . . ' He stopped, rose and walked over to look out the window. 'That information is not mine to divulge.'

Miranda stormed over to him, grabbing his arm, tugging at it. 'I don't believe you,' she cried. 'If she's not, why is she your ward? Why do you care so much for her welfare? Bring her presents?'

He turned back towards her, his face austere. 'Because I know the pain of being an unloved and unwanted child,' he said savagely. 'I would not see it repeated.'

Miranda gasped and she dropped her hand from his arm, so tense beneath her grasp. Her lip trembled; sucking in a shaking breath she tried to gain command of herself. 'Then it is for revenge against our father that you are treating me so harshly?' she whispered, her voice shaking.

'Revenge?' he roared. He gave a sharp bark of exasperation and grabbed her shoulders, shaking her slightly. 'Do you really believe I want to fight you all the time? It's because I care about you! I want you to . . .' He swallowed hard, leaving the sentence unfinished. His eyes wandered over her face once more as he tightened his grip to pull her closer. He lowered his head towards her and then stopped. Taking a taking a deep breath he almost pushed her away from him. He turned abruptly and stalked from the room, slamming the door behind him.

Miranda stared after him, rubbing her arms, a pulse throbbing rapidly in her throat.

Luke flew up the stairs, yanked open his bedroom door and slammed it viciously behind him. 'Damnation! That infuriating bloody woman!' he exploded, going on to release a stream of expletives. 'What the hell am I going to do?' He stormed across the floor with quick angry strides, kicking out at anything which got in his way.

She cannot marry Huw! The idea is impossible, he seethed. He is an indolent spendthrift. He would relish spending her money, aimlessly gambling it away without a second thought. He doesn't love her; he loves only himself. He doesn't even care enough about his own mother to consider her welfare. If I didn't see to it, he would leave Charlotte struggling while he gambles. And his child? What love does he spare his own child? He gave a sardonic laugh. And Miranda thought she was mine . . . I suppose everyone does, he realised bleakly.

Now I understand why Uncle George was so concerned about Llewelyn Shipping; he knew what would happen. If I hadn't taken over, the firm would have folded long ago, Luke raved. Damnation! Miranda is such as stubborn little madam, she would marry Huw just to see me in hell . . . He broke off his angry reverie, visualising her face up close to his as it had been in the library. Those challenging eyes, green and changeable as a cat's . . . her mutinous pulled down lips, full and luscious, aching to be properly kissed . . . that slender neck leading to those white breasts, heaving with temper . . . God, she's so lovely! In frustration he punched his fist hard against the bedpost, again and again. Nursing his split knuckles, he thrust them in his mouth and continued pacing. Why did I make any promises? I should have obeyed my instincts and refused; why did I ever have to get involved with Miranda?

Left in the library, Miranda stood gazing sightlessly at the closed door, confused and alarmed by her erratic thoughts. Luke is so virile, so essentially, unnervingly, male. She pushed the thought away, ashamed of her body's violent reactions. Her heart thudded against her ribs, a strange ache tightening her abdomen. How can I possibly find my own brother physically attractive? she anguished. My brother! It is wicked! It's because we were never together as children; that I never knew him as a brother, she reassured herself. I've known him only as a man. A man! A beautiful male animal! Stop it!

Now I realise why I fight with him all the time; it is because I haven't wanted to acknowledge this fascination. But his character equally attracts me. Huw pales alongside him. Luke is so sure of himself, so dependable, so . . . so manly . . . I must not think like this! He's my brother! She bit her lip. Wouldn't this amuse him . . . if he realised? She put a hand to her mouth, chewing her thumb. The situation is impossible!

The more consideration Miranda gave it, the more erratic her emotions became. I'll have to leave here . . . leave Luke. The idea was unbearable. I must marry Huw as soon as possible and move to Rushton Hall to put an end to all this. That is the only solution. But I won't see Luke then, she thought disconsolately.

Huw had been waiting in the drawing room and hurried out as Miranda left the library. 'I saw Luke go storming up the stairs. What did . . .'

'Not now, Huw!' Miranda turned a distracted face towards him, her eyes wide and unfocused. She shook her head. 'Not now!'

'Don't just fob me off, Miranda!' he said, his mouth tightening with annoyance. 'I have a right to know what his response—'

'I don't wish to talk about it. Not now. I . . . I have a headache.' She tried to push past him. 'Will you excuse me, I think I'll lie down.'

'Has that unmannerly brute upset you?' Huw growled. 'He really—'

'No! No. Just leave me alone!' Her voice rose angrily as she whirled round and raced up the stairs.

Huw scowled, and turned away, nearly bumping into his mother who was standing at his elbow. 'Is something wrong?' Her shrewd eyes studied him curiously.

'That brute has upset Miranda again,' he barked.

She followed him back into the drawing room. 'Upset her? In what way?'

'I wasn't going to tell you yet, mother, but I suppose you should know. Miranda has agreed to marry me,' he declared.

Charlotte's face lit up. Her lips pressed together in a tight little bow, her expression smug. 'She has agreed? That is wonderful news, Huw. I am so pleased for you.' A speculative look crept into her eyes. 'And you have approached Luke? Is that why he has upset Miranda?'

'Yes. It is. He actually had the audacity to tell me he would not give us his permission. Told me I could go to hell! But he won't get away with it! Once Miranda reaches her majority, he can do nothing to prevent it then. Nothing,' he added with a self-satisfied nod. 'If I haven't fixed the arrogant bastard before then,' he murmured under his breath. 'There must be a way.'

'I'd tread warily if I were you,' Charlotte said softly. 'It is not like you to go into things head-on.'

'You know me well, mother.' He gave a sardonic grin. 'I will do nothing to jeopardise this, I promise you.'

'In that case think well about Haelwen,' she slipped in slyly. 'I would not go—'

'Damnation, mother. Do you need to tell me my business?' He glowered, his face irritable and bad tempered.

'I'm just warning you, Huw,' she said mildly. 'You can be indiscreet.'

'Just leave it!' he snapped. 'I can't stand it when you keep on and on at me. I'm going out.'

Alarm flashed across Charlotte's face. 'Huw! Where are you going? Do be careful.' She bit her lip as her words fell on thin air as Huw barged out of the house.

Miranda kicked off her shoes and stretched out on her bed. If Gwennie is not Luke's child then whose child is she? A terrible niggle of doubt crept into her mind. Could it possibly be Huw? Just because Gwennie had Luke's colouring she had assumed . . .

but that wasn't the only reason. Luke so obviously cared for Gwennie . . . but he had just supplied the reason. The pain of being unloved and unwanted, he had said. An ache squeezed Miranda's heart. Poor unhappy little boy, forced to run away from home because of a father's harsh treatment. And if Gwennie really was Huw's daughter then who was her mother? Miranda sat up. Yes, who? She would ask Huw about it point-blank. Now was as good a time as any.

She found Charlotte alone in the drawing room.

'Where is Huw?' she asked, looking around.

'He went out for a ride, I believe.' She flicked a sharp look at Miranda. 'Huw told me you have agreed to marry him. I'm so pleased, Miranda, my dear. I shall welcome you as a daughter.'

'Thank you,' Miranda murmured, feeling slightly uncomfortable, knowing she was rapidly changing her mind about this marriage.

'It seems we will have two weddings to celebrate,' she chirped. 'Yours as well as Kate's. How exciting! Do sit down and tell me.'

Reluctantly Miranda took the chair Charlotte was patting.

'Has Kate decided on a date yet?' Charlotte enquired.

'Yes, next month. Depending on Will's availability of course. He is back on duty now, although his new ship has not yet taken to sea. It will be sailing from Bristol to the West Indies, Kate tells me. It is being refitted or something.'

'Will they live at Bristol then?' Charlotte asked, fluttering her fan.

'Yes. Will has been looking for a suitable residence. He intends to take Kate along to view them, once he has some choices to offer her,' Miranda explained.

'You will be able to visit them there. You and Huw,' she added with satisfaction.

'I wish to ask you a question, Charlotte. I would like a truthful answer, please.' Charlotte shot an apprehensive glance at her. 'Is Gwennie Huw's child?'

Charlotte's face turned bright pink, and she ruffled her shoulders indignantly. 'So that is what Luke said to upset you? He will do anything to deter you from marrying Huw,' she spluttered.

'No. He did not.' She directed a sharp glance at Charlotte. 'In fact he said the information was not his to divulge.'

'He should never have brought the child here in the first place,' she muttered indignantly. 'I was always against it.'

'You haven't answered my question, Charlotte.'

Charlotte's book dropped noisily to the floor and Miranda bent down to retrieve it for her.

'Charlotte. Is Huw Gwennie's father?'

Charlotte pressed her lips primly together. 'I want nothing to do with this conversation.' Shaking with outrage, she rose from her chair and bobbed furiously from the room with her cheeks flaming.

Miranda sat on her own, drumming her fingers impatiently on the table. It had to be Huw. Why else would Luke take on the responsibility? Though Luke seems to shoulder everybody's responsibilities, she realised, remembering Christmas and how he had increased Charlotte's allowance when Miranda had mentioned her problems. Even me, she thought bleakly. He's responsible for me.

Huw's eyes are not blue, they're hazel, Miranda thought, but Charlotte's are blue, if not as arresting as Bronwen's. Suddenly she had a vision of the girl in the tavern. Blue eyes and dark hair; yes, it could be her. She had been over-familiar with Huw and had annoyed him. Miranda sucked in a breath. And Huw had been out of the house all night on that occasion, so Nezer said. Miranda knew Huw was never a particularly early riser and would not be likely to go off to Llanmor at an unearthly hour of the morning on business. The men there all knew him and one even made a snide remark, until he saw me, Miranda remembered. Yes. That girl could be the child's mother.

Huw did not appear for dinner and Charlotte, obviously still cross with Miranda, said little. Luke turned up as they were about to start, pouring himself a big measure of brandy, which he downed in two gulps before taking his place at the table. Grim-faced and distant, he did not bother to talk, replying only in monosyllables if addressed; his eyes were steely when they considered Miranda.

Luke left immediately after dinner and from her bedroom window Miranda saw him ride off on Satan. She was still no nearer to solving her dilemma and she made up her mind to tackle Huw as soon as he came home. But he never returned that night.

Miranda had told Ellen she would like to buy them a cottage as a wedding present. As first Nezer had refused point-blank but Ellen was trying to talk him around.

'Miss Mirry said she wanted to get something really special for us and she decided that would be the best.' She beamed at him. 'It would be nice to have a place of our own instead of living over a stable.' Nezer looked unconvinced. 'Would you prefer to live over the stables?' she persisted, her heart sinking at the idea.

Nezer shrugged uneasily. 'To tell the truth 'tis unsure I am about living in any building of stones and mortar,' he admitted. 'But that is not the reason. I don't want to be beholden to any man . . . or woman.'

'But it's not charity, Nezer. Miss Mirry wants to give us a present that will please us. And I don't fancy living with the horrible smell of horses all the time.'

Nezer laughed. 'I can see that you wouldn't. But—'

'Please, Nezer. The Captain said we could even build one, if we've a mind. He said there's plenty of room near the house. Or near the stables, if you wanted?'

Nezer's eyes gleamed again, his resistance dissipating. 'Near the stables? Now that's an idea I like better. If I was to be building it myself I'd not feel it was all charity. A Romany is a proud man, Ellen.'

'I was hoping you might like that idea,' she said, with a sigh of relief. 'I do love you so, Nezer.' She put her arms around him and pressed a warm kiss on his mouth. 'And once it is ready we could be wed?' She looked expectantly at him with shining eyes.

Nezer hugged her tightly against his chest and returned her kiss with passion. Then he took a deep breath. 'If that is what you want, my sweet girl, then I'll agree.'

Nezer,' she shrieked. 'You really will? Build our own cottage?' Her face was radiant.

He nodded, grinning at her expression. 'I'd never go back on my word, Ellen. Shall we tell Miranda?'

'Right this minute,' she said, taking his rough hand in hers. 'Right this minute. The sooner we start the better.'

They hurried over to the manor and into the kitchen, where Ceridwen regarded Nezer sourly. Ellen left him to look for Miranda.

'I 'ope your feet are not dirty,' she grumbled. 'Don't want that 'orse mess over my kitchen.' She scowled at his feet and Nezer grinned good-naturedly.

'Perfectly clean, Ceridwen. That I promise.'

Ellen returned to take his hand. 'Miss Mirry wants to see us in the drawing room,' she said, beaming all over her face as she led the way.

'Nezer. I am delighted that you have agreed to Captain Llewelyn's idea to build the cottage,' her mistress said. 'Ellen is very dear to me. I don't know how I would have survived without her, but I expect you already know that.'

'That I do, Miss Miranda,' he agreed.

'I will provide all the materials you need and labourers to help, if you wish. And when it is completed Ellen and I will shop for furnishings together. We will enjoy doing that, won't we Ellen?'

Ellen was pink with excitement. 'I can hardly believe it yet, Miss Mirry.'

'We will have to all go to Rushton to see your family before then. I expect you will want to get married there?' Miranda asked.

'I would like that,' Ellen admitted a little wistfully. 'I'd love to see my mother again and for her to meet Nezer.' Her eyes went lovingly to his face. 'For her to know how happy I am with him.'

His eyes hung on her face as he smiled back at her. 'Whatever you are wanting,' he said simply.

'Well, that is settled,' Miranda said. 'I'll see Captain Llewelyn about arranging things as soon as possible.'

'Thank you, Miss Miranda,' Nezer murmured. 'I'll be getting back to my work.'

'Yes. Thank you, Miss Mirry,' Ellen repeated as they left together.

The library door was ajar when Miranda left the drawing room and hearing raised voices, she paused outside to listen.

'Do you think you can manage to put in an appearance at the office tomorrow?' Luke's irate voice demanded.

'Are you my keeper or something?' Huw's lazy tones drawled. 'I am not obligated to you, neither do I have to make excuses to you.'

'The devil take you! And I am not your bloody meal ticket,' Luke snarled. 'You do damned near nothing in the firm. You never take any part when we have a run. We could have done with an extra pair of hands last—'

'I don't agree with it, old man. I thought you knew that?'

'Damnation! The only thing you disagree with is putting your precious hide at risk. You are glad enough of the profits. I wouldn't mind that so much but you are hardly ever in the office.' She heard a chair scraping across the wooden floor.

'Well, isn't that just too bad! And there is nothing you can do about it.'

'I could keep you short by keeping a tighter fist on funds. I could make you toe the line.'

'You mean you'd keep my mother short too? Well?' There was a derisive laugh. 'As I thought, you have no answer to that one. Despite your tough exterior, Luke, you are surprisingly soft-cent . . . Keep away from me! Don't you threaten me!' His voice had risen in alarm.

Miranda heard footsteps rapidly approaching and hastily walked away from the door towards the stairs. Huw yanked open the door and barged out, his face red and his mouth twisted into a thin angry line.

'Huw. Can I have a word?'

He spun towards her, eyes still glittering angrily. 'Yes. Of course, my dear. I am afraid Luke has been bickering again.'

'In here, if you please.' She beckoned him towards the dining room. 'I require an honest answer. She looked him directly in the eyes as she continued: 'Is Gwennie your child?'

'What? Who has been saying . . .?' he began snarling.

'No-one has been saying anything, that's the whole point.' She threw him a penetrating stare. 'I want to know.'

'What makes you think she is mine?' he blustered,

rubbing his hand across his mouth.

'I want an honest answer.' Her hands were clenched tightly at her sides.

He looked crestfallen. 'Miranda. I don't know what to say.'

'Yes or no would be sufficient.'

'But it is not. You need an explanation.' He gave a self-depreciating shrug, putting on his little-boy expression. 'I was but a boy when it happened. You—'

'So the answer is yes,' she said quietly. 'Why didn't you tell me? Why didn't you tell me I would have a step-daughter?'

He gave an astonished laugh. 'Don't be ridiculous, Miranda. You don't think I would expect you to take Gwennie as our—'

'You would rather not acknowledge your own child?' Her voice rose with disbelief.

'It's not like that.' He waved a distracted arm in the air.

'What is it like, then? You never show her any consideration at all. She doesn't even know you are her father.'

'She should have stayed with her . . .' He broke off, slightly flustered.

'Her mother? I think I have guessed who she is! Haelwen? The girl in the tavern?'

Huw's mouth tightened and he flushed a dull red.

Miranda read the truth in his eyes. 'Why did Luke decide to become her guardian?'

'Because he can be maudlin.' He dismissed it with derision.

'Maudlin?' she said contemptuously. 'I really

misjudged you, Huw. You are a very good actor.'

'Miranda!' he yelped, his face full of consternation. 'Don't say that. I didn't tell you as I believed you would not want the responsibility of taking on—'

'I don't believe you, Huw. I begin to realise just how selfish you really are, not easy-going at all! I'm sorry Huw, but I am afraid I can never marry you.'

'Don't say that, Miranda! Please think about it! I love you very much, I will make you—'

'I have thought about it, Huw, and I have reached my decision.' She walked out, leaving him staring after her in complete horror.

Twenty

Hands in pockets, Huw sauntered into the grubby room which served Dickson as his office. Dickson looked up warily and his eyes slid towards his henchmen, before flicking warningly back to Huw. 'Good mornin', sir. What can I do for you, then?' he asked, his voice oily.

'The usual,' Huw said carelessly.

Dickson's face eased and Ben and Mal slightly relaxed their alert stance.

'Certainly, Mr Huw. You know there is never any problem seeing you all right. But I don't know what Captain Llewelyn would 'ave to say though? Last time 'e—'

'Damn my cousin, Dickson,' Huw snarled. 'I was a good customer of yours long before he arrived. I must have paid for many a gold necklace for your lady love.'

Dickson smiled sourly. 'The Captain's a difficult

man, sir. I'd not want to cross 'im like.'

'Cross him, be damned! I could see him cheerfully in hell,' Huw cursed.

'I takes your meaning, sir,' Dickson said carefully. He hesitated for a moment, eyes narrowing speculatively. Then he addressed Huw again, watching him cautiously as he spoke. 'Of course there's always ways of doing that . . . sir.' The last word added insolently.

'Doing what?' Huw looked at him sharply, frowning.

'Like you said, sir, seeing him in 'ell . . . or what feels like it.' His expression was sly.

'What do you . . .? Are you saying . . .?' He studied Dickson, understanding dawning, a smile sliding slowly across his face. 'Are there indeed?'

Dickson grinned evilly. 'Indeed there are, sir. Ben and Mal are very 'andy with their fists like . . . or anything else for that matter,' he added with a snigger.

Huw rubbed his finger under his collar thoughtfully, recalling his impotent fury with Luke earlier in the week. He was nothing but a bully, and had turned Miranda against him now.

Dickson went on. 'Any service for a good customer like you, sir. And I can't say I likes the man any more than you do. Arrogant 'e is. It would be a loan of course, all written down proper and lawful. Nothing else to show . . .?' His voice trailed off knowingly.

Huw grinned. 'God, wouldn't that be wonderful? Just to teach the conceited bastard a lesson . . .'

'One 'e won't forget in a 'urry,' Dickson agreed, his eyes gleaming banefully. He beckoned to his men.

'Come over by here, lads. Let Mr Huw get a better look at you.'

The two heavily-built men slouched over. Mal, the larger of the two, smirked at Huw, his piggy eyes gleaming malevolently from folds of red, unwashed flesh. His partner leered, lips drawn back to reveal large amounts of gum, sporting an assortment of broken or missing teeth. Huw drew back from his midden-smelling breath, eyeing the two roughnecks with distaste. He shuddered as he remembered how he had nearly been on the receiving end of their attentions a few months ago.

'What do you say then, sir?' Dickson prompted. 'A bargain?'

'You've got yourself a deal. But you'll need more than those two,' Huw warned with a grin. 'Luke is a hard bastard.'

'Yes, sir,' Dickson purred. 'I knows that already. I'll draw up the paper for this . . . loan as well as the other then, will I?' And they all chuckled.

Huw was strolling out jingling the gold coins in his pocket, a self-satisfied smile on his face, when he turned back. 'I know my cousin has business at the *Windrush* today,' he said casually. 'I believe he will be in the dock area about three o' clock. He usually comes along Severn passage.'

'A good thought, sir. It's nice and cosy there, and not overlooked, like. Thank you, sir. And thank you for your custom.'

Huw nodded cheerfully, turning his collar up against the drizzling rain. Even the overcast, wet day did nothing to dampen his spirits; in fact it made things all the easier. He chuckled maliciously. It would be good for Luke to get his comeuppance for once in his life. 'It should teach him he can't control everything in life,' he muttered under his breath. 'Yes. Well worth the money: I shall enjoy this!'

As soon as Huw left, Dickson winked at his cronies.

'Good work there, Mr Dickson,' Mal growled, rubbing his knuckles in anticipation.

'Getting paid for what I wants to do anyway. But I had a fright when 'e come in. I thought perhaps they'd found out about my tip-off to Jack Nichols,' Dickson admitted with a leer.

'But that's nothin' to do with 'im, is it? Mr 'uw I means?'

''course it is. He got shares in the *Windrush* too.'

'They never found nothing though, did they? I wonder where they puts it?'

'Try and find out for me by next time. Put some feelers out,' Dickson said. 'Now who else do you need to 'elp you with this job?'

The tavern was nearly empty as Luke leaned back in his chair. He pulled out his watch and flicked open its cover. 'I don't know where Will has got to but I'll have to be leaving,' he said. 'I have an appointment with Harry Grace. He'll be sailing on the next tide so I can't leave it.'

'What time was the Bristol coach due to arrive?' Charles asked.

'Supposed to be around two-thirty; it must have been held up. I'll have to catch him later.' He put his

Coral Leend

watch back in his vest pocket. 'Are you staying on, Charles?'

Charles hesitated. 'I hadn't intended to, I should be getting back. My father will not be pleased at an extended absence.'

'I'll stay a while,' Huw offered quickly. 'Half an hour will not make much difference,' he said glibly as Luke raised his eyebrows.

'All right. Do you mind asking him to follow me down to the *Windrush* before he goes on to Kate's?' Luke asked, rising to his feet. 'I shall see you at luncheon tomorrow, Charles.'

Huw licked his lips, his heart beating a little faster as he studied Luke's self-assured bearing from under sleepy, half-closed eyes. Hurry up, he thought. Go now, before Will arrives. Luke beckoned to the pot-boy and paid his bill, raising a hand in salute to his companions as he left.

'You need not wait,' Huw suggested to Charles hopefully. 'I'll be here to meet Will.'

'I can spare just a few minutes longer. After all it is my sister's fiancé I am meeting; that should ease Father's wrath a little.'

Huw smiled thinly, cursing mentally. He had not taken Will into consideration, when he'd told Dickson the time. But if Charles would only leave now, with a little luck he could delay Will long enough. If not, there was always tomorrow, he thought with anticipation.

Luke strode along Wind Street towards the docks, swaying slightly with the seaman's swagger he still retained after a life at sea. He passed around a corner into the shadow of Severn passage, a narrow windowless alley. A sixth sense, born of a life of danger, made his hackles rise. He spun around to find two men walking behind him, the blubbery red-faced man was vaguely familiar. Studying them both, he balanced lightly on the balls of his feet with knees flexed and his arms loosely in front of him. As his glance swivelled watchfully between them, he saw one man's eyes look past him and immediately Luke ducked, simultaneously whirling round and moving to one side.

He managed to dodge most of the blow from the club aimed at his head, feeling it jolt sickeningly onto his shoulder, jarring down his arm. He counteracted as the man was forward and off balance, bringing a hard fist thudding into the man's solar plexus, doubling him up with a groan. As his arms were grabbed from behind Luke flexed his knees, surprising his assailant and seized the man's wrists, leaning forward to fling him over his head. Luke had not lived all those years in the Orient without learning a few unorthodox methods of street fighting and before the man could rise, Luke aimed a vicious, sideways kick at his jaw which sent him reeling.

Luke grunted and staggered as a cudgel landed against the side of his head. He shook his head, reached forward to grasp the man by his coat front and butted him sharply with his head. Luke felt the crunch as the man's nose smashed, his teeth grating against the skin on Luke's forehead. The man retreated with a howl of anguish, holding his face with blood streaming through his fingers.

'Quick! Grab 'is arms, Mal!' Luke flailed his arms, resisting their attempts to hold him but the men hung on doggedly as he shook them to and fro. Held at their mercy, punches began slamming at his face and body. Luke gritted his teeth, concentrating on kicking out at the man in front of him whilst still battling to free his arms.

'God! 'e's bloody strong,' a voice gasped.

The attacker in front of him gave an agonised scream as another of Luke's kicks found its target. 'The bastard's broke me bloody leg,' he howled.

'Let me 'ave a go,' the fourth man growled from behind, having recovered from Luke's earlier blow. Luke felt a solid jolt against his skull and green and white spots flickered before his eyes. He sank to his knees fighting stubbornly to remain conscious. Agonising kicks rained onto his body and limbs and then suddenly ceased. He blinked open dazed eyes and looked up to see Will Owens, aggressively on the offensive against the three of his attackers still left standing. He was using both his hands and feet, oriental style, as Luke had been doing. Shaking his head to clear it, Luke struggled to his feet and returned into the fray, standing back to back with Will. The roughnecks, realising they were in trouble, turned tail, unwilling to face these two devastating opponents who were veterans of many dark alley attacks. As one attacker lumbered off bloodied and bruised, Will caught one of the others and flung him headfirst into the muddy dock. One still rolled on the floor, moaning and clutching his injured leg. Mal was sprawled unconscious on the ground.

Will fingered his jaw tenderly while studying Luke with a concern he hid behind a grin and a jocular: 'I'd have thought you could wait for me to arrive before picking a fight? You never could manage on your own.'

Luke returned his grin weakly, wincing as his cut lip split further. He cast a savage look at the men on the ground and the one nursing his leg licked his lips nervously.

'It was nothin' personal like. Honest, sir,' he whined. 'I was just picking up a shillin'. I haven't worked since the war.'

'The war, be damned! You're a bit young for that excuse,' Will snarled. 'You must have been only a child then. Get up! I want to hear more about this.'

'I can't. My leg's broke,' he snivelled, eyeing Luke apprehensively. 'He did it. He kicked me, he did,' adding in a puzzled voice, 'and he looked like bloody gentry too.'

Luke and Will both let out a guffaw of laughter, Luke flinching and clutching his side.

'That's a good one,' Will chuckled, his shoulders shaking.

'Teach you never to go by appearances,' Luke growled, beginning to regain his poise. He had been on the receiving end of too many beatings to let this one conquer him. 'We'll let the Constable deal with you roughnecks. A spell behind bars might set you right,' Luke dismissed them carelessly.

Will looked down dubiously at them. 'I'd like to find out more first. The truth now, fellow. You said you wanted to earn a few shillings? A likely story. You were after his purse, weren't you?' He shoved the man with his boot and he screamed.

'No, sir. We wasn't robbin' him, that's the truth. Someone paid to have him roughed up, they did.'

Puzzled, Luke frowned down at him, still very dazed.

'Who?' Will barked.

'I dunno. I don't know nothin' about that.' He was nursing his injured leg.

Will turned the unconscious man over with his foot and he moaned. 'Do you know either of them?' he asked Luke.

Luke shook his head, then wished he hadn't as hammers thudded painfully inside his skull. 'No! . . . Wait a minute, I don't know. That one looks familiar. Maybe it will come to me.'

An audience had gathered by this time. The Constable appeared on the scene and took charge of the injured men. He considered Luke and Will with consternation, taking in their battered appearance. 'Are you gentlemen all right? Did these men do this?'

'These men and two others set upon Captain Llewelyn. One of them is crawling around in the mud over there,' Will said pointing. 'I just happened to come along in time. Not that he needed much help.' He grinned at Luke.

The Constable regarded Luke with new respect. 'Looks as if they picked on the wrong one, Captain?'

Luke grinned wryly. 'This time they did!'

'Was it a gambling debt, sir?' he probed.

'Gambling debt!' Luke growled. 'Good God, no, man! Not me . . . wait a minute!' He stared thoughtfully into space for a moment, then looked down at the unconscious man. 'But that is one of Dickson's men,' he said. 'I knew I'd seen him somewhere before.'

'So you do frequent Dick—'

'I said I do not,' Luke declared, his voice rising angrily. 'I was there a few months ago paying a bill for . . . ' He paused reflectively again, a bitter expression creeping over his face. He pursed his lips grimly.

'For who, sir?'

'For . . . a friend,' he supplied quietly.

'And can you tell me any more, Captain?' the Constable persisted.

'Nothing,' Luke said in a tired voice.

The Constable turned to Will. 'May I have your name, sir?'

'Captain William Owen of the East India Company.'

'Captain!' The Constable gave a little bow. 'I am Idris Jones, at your service, sir. You gentlemen knew one another previously?'

'That is correct. Now if you will excuse us, Mr Jones, we will be on our way. If you need to contact me in the next week I will be staying at Westfield Manor.'

'The Dart residence,' Jones acknowledged. He turned with concern to Luke. Blood was trickling down Luke's face from the cut on his head. His lip was swollen, one eye was puffed and already going purple and a deep cut split his cheek under the other eye. 'You will wish to press charges against these . . .'

'No!' Luke declared.

'But, sir—'

'I said no!' Luke snapped, aware of Will raising his eyebrows.

'As you wish, sir,' the Constable said with disapproval. 'But I shall take them along and see if I can find out what is behind it.'

Luke said nothing.

'Can I call a cab for you, sirs?'

Luke pulled himself erect, smothering a wince, his face pale. 'No need,' he growled. He nodded to the Constable and managed to walk away, though he felt as if he had been kicked by a horse. From past experience he realised a few of his ribs were cracked again.

'Just like the old days,' Will chuckled.

'Yes.' Luke shot him a lopsided grin, not quite able to conceal the affection behind it. 'I only hope your bruises are not still visible for the wedding,' he said with a sardonic expression. 'Kate will not be very pleased with me if her bridegroom has a black eye!'

Will's eyes widened in horror, then he grinned wickedly. 'If I'd thought of that earlier I'd have left you to it.'

'Then you'd have to have found yourself another groomsman,' Luke quipped.

'Rubbish! Are you saying they would have got the better of you?'

Luke gave a crooked grin. 'They were having a bloody good try. I'm glad you were around.'

'Since when? You've been ashore too long; you must be getting soft,' Will scoffed.

Luke snorted derisively but Will avoided looking at him. 'You have an idea who's behind this, haven't you?' he said carefully.

Luke continued walking, staring ahead saying nothing.

'I can see you're not going to tell me; as stubborn as ever. Shall we make for your office to clean—'

'No!' Luke said sharply.

Will looked at him with bewilderment, his brow furrowing. He studied Luke for a few moments then ventured. 'Perhaps we should see a physician?'

'What for?' Luke's voice was nonchalant.

'Luke, I know you too well for this nonsense. You've cracked those ribs again for a start.'

'You never worried about me before.' Luke grinned.

'You're getting to be an old man now, Luke. Not like me! I'm young and virile . . .' He staggered sideways theatrically as Luke punched him on the arm, laughing as Luke winced. 'Serves you right! Well, if not to the office . . . where? Home? Kate's?'

'How about the *Windrush*? I think they are well able to attend a few cuts and bruises.'

'And well experienced to stitch a bit of catgut in those cuts,' Will observed cynically. 'I'd still like to know why you don't want to return to the office?'

'I don't know who may be there,' Luke said defensively. It sounded like an excuse even to his own ears.

Yes, who? Will wondered.

'There you are, Luke, that's your broken head mended,' Harry Grace chuckled as he sliced off the end of the catgut. Harry Grace, thick-set and grizzled, was near to retiring age; a man who had seen service in the navy during the war. Twinkling button eyes gleamed from a weather-beaten face, his teeth like yellow fangs through his beard. He was fond of Luke and wished he had had a son like him. 'I think this calls for a tot of rum all round.' He poured three fingers of the golden liquid into tankards. 'And this needs a stitch too,' he said, examining the cut under Luke's eye.

'How about those ribs?' Will prompted when the stitching was completed. 'How many did they kick in?'

'Let's take a look at them,' Harry said. 'I've got some strips of linen here somewhere.' He rummaged in a wooden chest.

Luke winced, sucking his breath in between his teeth as he pulled off his shirt. Harry pulled a face as he saw the dark bruises, weals and lacerations staining Luke's chest, arms and shoulders. 'If any of these ribs have punctured your lungs, you need to see a physician,' he said, probing the ribs with a stubby finger.

Luke gritted his teeth. 'Just cracked,' he gasped. 'I've had a puncture before. I'd know!'

'If you're sure.' Harry bound the ribs firmly with the linen strips, tearing the last one into narrower strips to make ties, which he knotted securely. 'Now I shall send someone for a cab.'

'I don't need a cab,' Luke interjected. 'I've got Satan up at the Mackworth.'

Meeting Will's eye, Harry raised his eyebrows. 'As you wish, but I don't think you are fit enough to be riding home on horseback.'

'Rubbish! But I would be obliged if you will lend

me a shirt, Harry.' Luke pulled a face at the grubby, bloodstained one in his hand. 'I don't fancy walking into the Mackworth in that.'

'Of course. And I'll call one of my lads to clean up your jacket whilst we down another tot.'

Luke would not be dissuaded, and as Will reluctantly watched him stiffly mount Satan he observed his drawn face as he forced a grin.

'I'll call to see you tomorrow,' Will called after him, as he cantered away. Just what is Luke concealing? he wondered. Who is he shielding?

Twenty-One

The cantering motion sent waves of agony coursing through Luke and he half closed his eyes against the explosions of pain bursting inside his skull. He swallowed hard, bile rising in his throat. Grimly he considered the facts. The roughneck had claimed someone had wanted him 'roughed up' and the more Luke thought about it the more certain he became that Huw was the culprit. Who else could it be? Not many people bore such a grudge against him. Dickson himself . . . maybe? Luke was aware his cousin resented him but was disturbed to think he would go to such lengths. He knew Huw was infuriated when he had refused his permission for him to marry Miranda and was further enraged when Luke had suggested he might pull his weight in work.

Well, if it was Huw indeed who had arranged this attack, his cousin would not have the satisfaction of seeing him brought home in a cab; Luke was only sorry that he bore such visible signs on his face that he could hardly pretend nothing had taken place. Huw would not see him cowed. But he could never press charges and have it all come out in the magistrates' court. He pulled a wry face . . . his own cousin!

Grateful to reach the stables, Luke slid gingerly off Satan and turning, was dismayed to find Miranda staring out of the stable door at him.

'Luke! What have you done?' She rushed out to him, putting a hand to her mouth in horror as she saw his battered face. Reaching up, she gently touched his split mouth. 'What happened?'

He smiled ruefully. 'Footpads,' he said laconically.

'Luke! You poor thing!' His heart rose at the concern on her face. She put her arms out as if to put them around him and he instinctively took a step backwards, unconsciously protecting his injured ribs. She immediately dropped her arms, clenching her fists into tight balls. 'Are you badly hurt?' she whispered.

'No! Just a few bruises,' he dismissed it.

'Nezer has taken Star to the blacksmith, I'll take Satan and—'

'There's no need, thank you,' he said gruffly, wishing she would leave. 'I'm fine.' Acutely aware of her watching him he unsaddled Satan, gritting his teeth against the agony of his ribs as he moved. Waves of dizziness engulfed him once more, his head pounding. Meeting her worried eyes he hurriedly dropped his away, afraid that she might in some way be able to read his pain.

With Miranda trailing him, Luke made sure he

stood up straight and walked normally, entering the hall to meet Huw coming from the drawing room. Luke carefully studied his reaction and saw a gleam of gratification alight in Huw's eyes.

'Good God! What happened to you?' His voice had a false ring to it.

'Nothing much,' Luke drawled. 'Footpads.' He forced a laugh. 'It would need more than those puny scoundrels to take my purse. Idris Jones has them now,' he added deliberately. He had the satisfaction of seeing alarm cross Huw's face.

'The Constable? He caught them? Did . . . did he happen along at the right time then?'

'If you mean did he arrive to take them from me into custody? Yes,' Luke said blandly.

Huw studied him from under half-closed lids. 'How many of them?'

'Four, though one ran away,' Luke said nonchalantly.

Huw's mouth turned down petulantly. 'Was anyone else there?' he asked casually.

'Such as?' Luke's eyes met Huw's.

'I just wondered—'

'If Will came along in time?' Luke's eyes were cold as steel.

'No . . . I . . . do you intend to press charges?' His voice was studiously unconcerned.

'What do you think?' Luke's eyes blazed and Huw's eyes lost their hooded expression, widening with alarm. Luke grinned sardonically, keeping his gaze fixed on his cousin to let Huw know he knew now for sure!

Huw licked his lips nervously and turned away as Charlotte came fussing out to see what was happening.

'What is it?' she chirped.

'Nothing!' Huw said savagely, pushing her aside.

Miranda watched Luke walk up the stairs, not taking them two at a time as he normally did. She was sure he was more badly hurt than he'd shown. She had seen his drawn face when he arrived at the stables and noticed him wince as he dismounted, not realising she was watching him. She had seen the tell-tale beads of perspiration on his forehead as he had unsaddled Satan. She wanted to hold him, comfort him . . . Heaven forbid! She was doing it again! She bit her lip, tears filling her eyes. What ever she did, she couldn't stop thinking like this about him. Her own brother!

She turned abruptly, hurrying into the drawing room.

'How dreadful!' she exclaimed. 'Footpads in the middle of Swansea.' Huw turned, a drink in his hand, his eyes hooded again. 'Let's hope the Constable—' she began.

'For heaven's sake, Miranda, does it matter?' he snapped irritably.

'Aren't you concerned?' She studied his face.

'Why should I be? And I'd have thought you'd have very little feeling to spare for that braggart.' He poured himself another drink, overflowing the glass.

'But he . . .' Miranda's voice trailed off. She had been about to explain how hurt Luke had appeared on arriving home, when it struck her that Luke would not wish Huw to know. Luke kept his feelings hidden and did not wish others to share them.

'Serves him right,' Huw muttered. 'He probably brought it on himself; he's always too conceited for his own good.'

He was pleased! Miranda's blood turned to ice as she stared at him, seeing him as he truly was. Not easy-going and good-natured at all, but uncaring, selfish and self-centred. Thank God she had found out before she had married him. How could she ever have imagined she loved him?

She ran from the room, running blindly up the stairs and along the corridor. Outside Luke's door she hesitated, her hand on the knob, a pulse fluttering in her throat. Making up her mind she gave a brief knock and opened the door. Luke had stripped off to his waist and turned stiffly in surprise as she entered, his mouth dropping slightly. She pushed the door shut behind her and went over to him as he stared silently at her.

She studied the bandages around his chest, the black and purple weals and bruises covering him and the lacerations where his skin had been broken with the cudgel. She could also see blood seeping from his hair, coming from the stitched cut on his head.

'I thought you said it was nothing?'

He gave a rueful grin.

'Luke.' Her eyes filled with tears. 'You wouldn't show it, but I knew you were badly hurt.' She looked up at his face to find his eyes on her, swirling with that same dark emotion as before. 'I didn't tell Huw that.'

He gave a bitter barking laugh. 'Huw! He would have been delighted. I think he arranged it.' As the words left his mouth he could have cut out his tongue. He was still not completely in control, he realised.

Now she would think he was trying to turn her against Huw, again.

'What makes you think that?' she gasped.

'You believe me?' he asked, amazed.

'I'm not sure if I agree, but I realise you wouldn't make up an accusation like that. I think you should know, I have already told Huw I wouldn't marry him.'

'You have?' His eyes locked on hers.

'I realised he was not truly the person I believed him to be,' she whispered, her voice trembling slightly.

'I'm glad you realised,' he said with relief. 'I was hoping you would.'

'What makes you suspect Huw?'

'I've no proof Huw was involved,' he admitted. 'It's just a feeling I have. One man admitted someone wanted me 'roughed up', as he put it.'

'That's barbarous!' Again her eyes travelled hungrily over his muscular shoulders and arms and the parts of his torso still visible without bandages. Above his waistband, two lines of clearly defined muscles rippled downwards. 'Knowing you, I'm surprised they managed it.'

'Not easily,' Luke asserted, with grim satisfaction.

'Why would Huw do it?' Fury welled up in her, fury that anyone would deliberately do this to Luke. 'I could happily kill him!' she spat.

Miranda saw delight flare through those blue eyes as they fully revealed his emotions for the first time; then that shutter came down again, cutting them off.

'Perhaps the Constable will be able to prove it?' Miranda said.

'I told them I'd not press charges . . . but don't tell Huw that; I'd like him to sweat on it. I can hardly see my own cousin in the courts,' he said bitterly. 'If only for the memory of Uncle George.'

'I suppose not, but it's disgraceful for him to get away with it. Perhaps my decision not to marry him was the goad which made him arrange it?'

Luke made no reply to that suggestion, thinking she was probably right. He steered her away from it. 'I'm afraid he does have a weak character but I wanted you to find out on your own.'

'I did. I kept comparing him with you.'

His eyes flew back to her face, but he said nothing.

'I also found out who Gwennie's parents are . . . but you knew already?'

'Of course.' He shrugged without thinking, then smothered a wince. 'And I suppose if you know that, you should now understand my other fears for you . . . Wyn and Ceridwen are her grandparents.'

'Grandparents? You mean Haelwen is their daughter?' she gasped. 'Yes. I remember you telling me Wyn was fond of Gwennie.'

'I suspected them in regard to that accident at Pentrebach. When David went over the cliff and was killed.' His face was savage.

'You think Wyn . . .?' Miranda's eyes widened with horror.

'Not Wyn, his two sons.' Gingerly, he picked up his shirt from the bed and untangled it. 'They keep the tavern at Llanmor.'

'But why would they do it?' she asked, distraught. 'What have I ever done to them?'

He gave a sardonic chuckle. 'I believe they were hoping Huw would marry Haelwen. You are interfering with their plans.'

'That's why they have been so hostile to me from the beginning? And . . . and the window? You think Wyn did that?'

Luke nodded, half-closing his eyes as his head pounded excruciatingly. 'I'll admit that could have been accidental, the man's a moron. The thing is, I can't get rid of the pair of them just on a suspicion. I have no proof; quite apart from them being Charlotte's servants anyway. But I told Wyn I suspected his sons and that if they tried anything again I'd kill them!' he added savagely.

Alarm crossed her face. 'You sound as though you mean that!'

'I mean it!' he said harshly, his eyes glittering steel slits.

'Then you really would go to prison. And I would be left on my own!' she said quietly. She walked towards the door, turned with her hand on the knob. 'Are you sure you don't wish me to call a physi—'

'Definitely not! It really is nothing, honestly. I am perfectly all right. I've had many worse injuries than this, I assure you.'

'I am glad I wasn't around then,' she said quietly. 'I couldn't have borne it.'

Luke's face softened and he just grinned at her.

For several weeks Huw's normal nonchalant air deserted him, a slightly hunted manner taking its place as each day he wondered if he was going to be charged with assault. He was infuriated with Luke's apparent lack of injuries, seeing him carry on as though nothing had taken place. How had Luke found out? he wondered, quite certain that Luke knew the part he had played. Although Luke ignored him completely, not even bothering to talk to him at work, Huw was still apprehensive and afraid he might decide to undertake his own physical revenge on him. As the weeks went by and nothing seemed to happen he began to relax again, realising that Luke would not wish it to go through the courts. He decided to tackle Dickson however.

'I hope you don't intend asking me for repayment of that second loan,' he snarled at Dickson.

'What d'you mean? The job was done—'

'Was it hell!' Huw thumped the table furiously. 'One of your men ran off and he handed the others over to the Constable.'

'That's not my fault,' Dickson whined. 'Anyway, I 'ad to pay them apothecary's bills as well as gettin' my men out. Lucky to, at that.'

'He wasn't very badly hurt,' Huw accused.

'Oh yes 'e was, take my word. 'e may 'ave put up a fight, but my boys assured me they gave 'im a good roughin' up. They 'urt 'im all right. 'e definitely 'ad a few ribs kicked in.' He nodded with satisfaction.

'He didn't act like it.'

'You can't go by that. The Cap'n's a tough man. 'e's been around some.'

'I did warn you,' Huw said petulantly, though slightly mollified.

'Anyway. If you needs money there's other ways to pay off that loan. Ways we can all benefit,' he added slyly.

'Such as?' Huw said suspiciously.

'Is the *Windrush* insured?' He pulled up a chair for Huw, who took it warily.

'Of course it . . .' Huw broke off frowning, eyes narrowed. 'Why?'

'Well insured?' Dickson leaned forward, his expression furtive.

'I don't know. I leave all that to Luke.' He pulled out a cigar from the case in his pocket and smelled it before cutting off the end.

Dickson leaned over and lit it for him. 'Maybe you shouldn't. Maybe you should think of taking out some insurance of your own.'

'What on earth for?' He gave a few puffs at his cigar, blowing rings in the air.

'What if it should founder? Would you benefit?' He leaned back in his chair, watching Huw closely.

'You mean shipwrecked?' Huw tapped his cigar on the filthy floor. 'What makes you think it's going to be wrecked?'

Dickson shuffled through his papers. Pulling out the one for Huw's loan, he placed it in front of him. 'Once September is out we're goin' to get bad weather again. There's ways of giving it a 'elping 'and, like.' He smirked. 'You should know that, you have friends in Llanmor, I've 'eard?'

Huw gasped, astounded at the very idea. 'I don't know what you are talking about,' he hedged.

'I thinks you do. Sleep on it.' He pushed the paper closer to Huw, tapping it with a grimy finger.

'I want nothing to do with—'

'You wouldn't need to, any more than with your

last . . . loan,' he sniggered. 'Information would be enough. Just think about it, we can all benefit.'

Miranda was in her room gazing out at the gusty rain falling from a darkening sky when Ellen came to her.

'Miss Mirry.' Ellen's face was grim, her voice hesitant.

'What is it, Ellen? You look very worried.'

'I am, Miss. I'm troubled about something Nezer told me . . .' she hesitated again. 'It is something he overheard in the village . . . he doesn't know what to do about it . . . and he doesn't want to show people he . . .' Her voice trailed off uncertainly.

'I understand what you mean, Ellen. Do you want to tell me about it?'

Ellen nodded, dropping her head and still reluctant to speak. 'It's plans . . . Nezer overheard plans . . . for wrecking.'

'Wrecking? Isn't that when boats are deliberately lured onto the rocks to be shipwrecked?'

'Yes.'

'It seems unbelievable.' A shiver of apprehension went through Miranda.

Ellen raised her head to face Miranda. 'Nezer has heard lots of tales about wrecking round the Gower coast before now, Miss. That wreck at Rhossili was supposed to have been caused by the wreckers. Well anyway, he overheard these men talking in the village this afternoon. Llanmor village. A couple of scoundrels, Nezer said they were. They were laughing, saying they should be lucky with salvage tonight with this storm blowing up. He pricked up his ears at that, to see if he could learn more. Then . . .' her voice trailed away.

'Then?'

'He . . . he heard Mr Huw's name mentioned.'

'Huw? Are you trying to tell me Huw is involved? Is that what you are saying?'

'I don't know exactly, Miss. Nezer wasn't sure about that. All he knows is he definitely heard his name mentioned . . .' She twisted her hands together, her eyes filling with tears.

'What? Ellen. Tell me!' she demanded.

'He said . . . ' Her voice was low. 'He heard them say that Mr Huw had sent word that the *Windrush* was expected back on this evening's tide. With this storm blowing they were planning to . . . '

'The *Windrush*? Luke's on board that now!' Miranda voice rose. 'Dear heaven! They plan to wreck it?' White-hot terror shot through her.

Ellen's face crumpled and her tears overflowed; she nodded her head. 'I had to tell you, Miss. I know it's not as if you and Mr Huw were going to be wed now, but in any case we couldn't let the Captain and all those poor sailors be drowned.'

Miranda stared at her maid in horror. 'Tonight? What can we do?' she whispered.

Ellen looked at her mutely.

'Does Nezer know how they carry it out? The wrecking I mean?' She shook Ellen's arm.

'I don't know, Miss.'

'I'm going around to the stables right now. I must talk to him immediately. There must be something we can do. It's all right, Ellen, I'll make sure we are not overheard,' she assured her as she saw fear shadow Ellen's face. 'I understand what Nezer means to you.'

'Thank you, Miss. You know what some people are like about gypsies. I wouldn't want . . .'

Miranda gripped her shoulders. 'Ellen, I will do nothing to jeopardise Nezer and will not mention where I have received my information.'

Miranda and Ellen pulled on their warm cloaks, clutched them tightly against the raging wind and left by the front door instead of going through the kitchen. As they hurried around to the stables, Miranda's heart dropped as she realised it was already dark. What help could she possibly get in such a short time?

Nezer was leading Moonlight out of the stables as they arrived.

'Is anyone else here?' Miranda asked, surprised to see him with the horse.

Nezer shook his head, not offering an explanation.

'Mr Huw is not back?' She peered past him.

'He's not returned from Llanmor.' He stroked the horse's wet neck, his expression wary.

'Come inside, we can't talk out here.' Out of the rain, it was easier to hear. 'Ellen has just told me what you overheard . . . Tell me! Was the *Windrush* to be concerned with any smuggling activities tonight?' she asked without any preamble.

'No, Miss,' he said, sighing with relief that she knew. 'There was no smuggling arranged for tonight.'

'How do the wreckers work, Nezer?

'They will be lighting a big fire out on the point That one yonder.' He pointed through the door towards the cliffs at the end of the promontory. 'I am just about to make my way up there to see if I can find it before they put a torch to it,' he said.

'What does that do?'

'When the sailors see the beacon they will think it is the Mumbles lighthouse. They'll turn into Llanmor Bay, thinking they are round Mumbles Point, and they'll be caught on all those rocks this end of the beach. They stretch way out under the water.'

Miranda swallowed hard, imagining those jagged crags tearing into the ship. 'I'll come with you.'

'No, Miss! I don't think you should,' he said, his face anxious. 'These are dangerous men. Killers. It would be better for me to go on my—'

'It's no good arguing, I'm coming with you. Two of us are better than one, we can keep a look out for each other. And we can get away more easily if we have fast horses.' She picked up a saddle. 'Don't bother with Moonlight, we'll take Star and Satan, they're the fastest.'

Nezer opened his mouth as if to argue, then changed his mind, shrugging. 'As you wish. To be sure I will never win an argument with yourself.'

'Do you know when high tide is?' Miranda asked, thinking it must be relevant.

'In a few hours. The flood tide is running now, the current at its fastest until the ebb,' Nezer said with surprising knowledge. 'I've learned much about the tides this year,' he admitted, 'from David and the Captain.'

Ellen stood biting her lip, watching them ride off into the storm. Miranda sat astride Star, crouching down over his neck and gripping with her knees, wishing she'd stopped to put on her boys' riding clothes. The howling wind attacked them as they left the shelter of the house, tearing at them as though it would throw them into the sea. As the path ascended they clearly saw an orange glow lighting the sky ahead.

'It's already alight,' Miranda groaned. 'What can we do now?'

Nezer didn't answer and they urged on the horses, whose flattened ears showed they were unhappy with the storm. Miranda glanced to her right towards Pentrebach Bay and made out the outline of a sailing ship, well into the bay. She reined in for a better look, gesturing to Nezer who also peered into the night, shielding his eyes with his hand against the driving rain.

Miranda rode up close to him, shouting so her voice could carry above the storm. 'Does that look like a ship to you?'

'It does,' he agreed, shouting back.

'You don't think they are already wrecked?'

'I can't see much but it appears to be anchored. Let's go on and see if we can put out that beacon.'

They fought their way to the cliff-top, guided by the luminous flames now leaping and reaching high into the sky. Two men were feeding the fire from a prepared heap, throwing armfuls of bracken and gorse bushes on top of the tarry logs already ablaze. The wind fanned the flames, carrying sparks crackling up into the darkness like a million fireflies.

Nezer made signs to Miranda, indicating she

should stay back out of sight and he would take a closer look. She nodded to show she understood, and he tied Satan to the bush alongside her and crept off. Miranda dismounted, impatiently trying to peer around the bushes, anxious to be doing something positive. The rain was coming down in sheets now and her cloak was soaked through, clinging damply against her. She shivered as water ran down her face, trickling uncomfortably down her neck and inside her collar. She had nearly made up her mind to follow Nezer when she heard raised voices, followed by a pistol shot.

Miranda gasped, her heart freezing. Oh God! Had they shot Nezer? Unable to see what was happening, she dropped to her hands and knees and crept forward cautiously in the shadow of the bushes. Here the wind was quieter and she stopped for a moment to listen. She put another hand forward only to find it was on top of a lean, hard leg. She gave a smothered yelp of alarm, trying to retreat, but a hard hand grasped her wrist, and dragged her forward as she struggled ineffectively. She found herself looking into Luke's astonished face.

'Luke!' She flung her arms around his neck in a strangling grip, her relief overwhelming. 'Thank God!' she gasped. He wrapped both his arms around her, enfolding her against his chest as she burst into tears.

'It's all right,' he murmured softly. Her hood had fallen back and he was smoothing her soaking hair gently. 'It's all right, my love.' Her eyes roamed his face, so close to her own, and she stroked his wet cheek, feeling a rough stubble of whiskers scratching her hand.

'God, Miranda,' he groaned. Crushing her body against his, he bent his head, pressing a cool, salty, demanding mouth to hers as she eagerly responded. His tongue probed gently at her lips and she opened them to his caress, aware of his heart pounding steadily in his chest. They drew apart reluctantly and she heard the short ragged gasp of his indrawn breath. He dragged her back towards him, gathering her into his arms to kiss her again. His lips crushed hers with the force of his passion, his hand wandering inside her cloak to envelop her breast.

Miranda shuddered, giving a little groan of ecstasy. He pulled away again, still breathing hard. 'Miranda. My precious love, I . . .' He broke off as they heard shouting. 'I'll have to go,' Luke exclaimed, scrambling to his feet. 'I have to see what's happening out there. Someone could get killed.'

She nodded mutely. 'Nezer's there,' she said. 'He went to see if he could put the fire out.'

'Stay here! Don't move,' he commanded.

She grabbed his sleeve. 'Luke! Please be careful!' He nodded briefly and vanished around the bush, leaving Miranda staring after him with her heart beating an erratic tattoo against her ribs. Then realisation struck.

'Dear God! What have we done?' she whispered. She put a hand to her lips, still smarting with the passion of his kiss, her skin scratched and burned by his unshaven face. Her breast tingled where he had caressed it. Indescribable surges of desire coursed through her body as she trembled uncontrollably. Luke had betrayed their father's trust. This was incestuous; Papa had trusted him! She began weeping quietly with despair.

Another shot rang out and she heard more raised voices. Brushing away her tears she crept forward until she could see. Luke had two men covered with a pistol. A group of four men were around the brazier, dragging off the blazing fuel with long staves, scattering it widely on the ground. Once removed from the fire it spattered damply, the rain dousing it, leaving an acrid smell hanging in the sea air as the men stamped on the embers.

'Right, my fine fellows,' Luke said grimly. 'It seems we've foiled your cowardly intentions for tonight.' He gestured with the pistol. 'Come on! My men are already gathering in the rest of your brave lads from Llanmor beach, then we're going to give you all a trip on the *Windrush*. You will no doubt enjoy that,' he said with menace. 'Seamen love people like you.'

The two men began protesting, struggling with the men who were manhandling them roughly.

'Maybe you'd like to tell me who is behind this?' Luke snarled.

'I will, sir! Keep them off me and I'll tell you,' one of them howled, clearly terrified. 'It was Dickson and . . . and . . .'

'And?' Luke thundered.

'Mr Huw, sir.'

Miranda could not see Luke's face but she heard the other men give a collective gasp.

'I don't believe you,' Luke growled.

361

'It's the truth. He told us when you would be arriving home,' he gabbled.

'You are making it up. He has part shares in the *Windrush*. He wouldn't—'

'Yes, sir. He did. For the insurance,' he stuttered, eager to explain. 'Dickson paid for more insurance. We was all goin' to get a cut, as well as the cargo.' He gave a howl as one of the sailors punched him. 'I've told you! Don't let 'em hit me!' But the other sailors joined in, mercilessly pummelling the two captives. Luke made no move to stop them for a while, letting the men release their fury.

'Right. That's enough,' Luke said with reluctance. 'We'll hand them over to the Constable in Swansea tomorrow. Get them aboard.'

'Aye, aye, sir.' They dragged the reeling men away, supporting them to prevent them from collapsing as they made towards the path leading to Pentrebach Bay.

Once they had left, Luke picked up the spluttering lantern from the ground and held it aloft. 'Nezer,' he called. 'Are you there, man?'

Miranda stood up, walking out into the clearing. 'Can you see him?' she asked anxiously.

A slight figure materialised out of the darkness. 'I'm here, Captain,' Nezer said faintly.

'He's hurt,' she exclaimed.

Luke strode towards him, grabbing him as he swayed and nearly fell. 'You're shot?'

Nezer nodded. 'Aye. 'tis only my arm. They'll not be burning my wagon just yet.'

'Good man! I appreciate your help. I'll not forget it. Can you make it home? I have to return to the ship immediately, otherwise we won't make harbour in time.'

'To be sure I can. Miranda is with the horses. As long as I am able to mount.'

'Let's get you up.' Keeping a grip on Nezer, Luke hastily followed Miranda to the horses.

'Put him on Star, I'll ride Satan,' she said briefly.

Luke threw her a wry grin and helped Nezer mount Star. Miranda avoided his eyes, her face blushing hotly in the darkness as he assisted her to mount. Her damp skirts clung around her, hindering her movements. Luke squeezed her arm but she jerked it away without looking at him and urged Satan forward.

Ellen rushed out as they arrived at the stables, gasping as she caught sight of Nezer swaying in the saddle.

'Is he hurt?' She reached out to help him down.

''tis all right, Ellen. Nothing to worry your sweet head about.' He almost fell from the saddle.

'He was shot.'

'Shot!' Ellen exclaimed in horror. 'What happened? I saw the glow on the headland. What happened?'

'I am not really sure,' Miranda admitted. 'The *Windrush* was anchored in Pentrebach Bay and Luke and some of his men caught two wreckers on the cliff. They have taken them on board; others from Llanmor beach as well, I think. We'll have to wait until they get back to know the full facts.'

'Let me take a look at your arm,' Ellen began, tugging at Nezer's jerkin.

Miranda began making for the door. 'I'll send for a physician right away.'

'No! Thank you, Miss Miranda, but I will not be needing him,' Nezer interjected. 'The bullet went clean through and if Ellen will just bathe off the dirt I have some herbs that will do as well as any physician.'

Miranda began to protest but Nezer insisted. 'I would prefer it, if you don't mind.'

'Are you certain? We can get him over in—'

''tis certain I am. I will be telling Ellen where to find the herbs, if you've no objection to her attending me?'

'Nezer? After what you did? I shall be pleased to have her attend you. If you don't need my help I'll return to the house and get out of these wet clothes. I suggest you do the same.' She turned back as she reached the door. 'Stay here with Nezer, Ellen. He needs you more than I do tonight.'

Back in her room, Miranda poked at the fire trying to stir some life into it before she stripped off her saturated clothes. After drying herself and rubbing her hair briskly with a towel, she pulled a thick shawl around her and sat hunched in front of the fire, trying to get warm. Her cheeks burned again as she thought of Luke's caresses. She touched her lips, imagining his salty lips against hers. She hugged her arms around her, rocking to and fro. How could I ever have thought he was unfeeling? she wondered. 'If only he were not my brother,' she groaned aloud. 'He is all I could ever want in a man.' Now the situation is impossible, I can live in the same house as him no longer. I will have to write to William Langdon tomorrow.

Twenty-Two

Miranda had difficulty going to sleep, tossing and turning as she kept reliving what had happened between her and Luke. My God, he kissed me, she groaned . . . and I returned it. And his hands . . . God, his hands! Her stomach churned at the thought but she was even more ashamed to realise her body ached for more. When at last she dozed off Gwennie woke her, shaking her and sobbing wildly.

'What's wrong, little one?' Miranda asked, only half awake. 'Have you—'

'Mirry. Wyn and Ceridwen tried to take me away,' Her voice was almost incoherent. 'Olwen saved me.'

'You've had a bad dream,' Miranda soothed her. 'Come into bed with me.'

Shivering, Gwennie climbed in with Miranda. 'Not a dream, Mirry,' she said, shivering in Miranda's arms. 'They tried to take me.'

'There, there. Go to sleep,' she murmured.

Miranda rose early, leaving Gwennie still asleep in her bed. She was determined to write to William Langdon immediately but once seated at her desk she was too restless to compose a letter. What on earth can I say? she wondered.

There was a tap on the door and Ellen came in, her face anxious.

'Miss Mirry. Wyn and Ceridwen went off during the night. They tried to take Gwennie with them but Olwen prevented them. She told Gwennie to run to you.'

'It was true,' Miranda gasped. 'I thought she'd been dreaming. Let me talk to Olwen.'

Miranda was told a wagon had arrived for Wyn and Ceridwen in the early hours of the morning. They had piled it with their belongings and many other things which did not belong to them and then they had tried to take Gwennie with them. Her screams woke Olwen, who pulled the child away from Ceridwen. The couple had fled in the wagon before Olwen could do anything to stop them.

'Thank you, Olwen,' Miranda said gratefully to the shy girl. 'We will not forget your loyalty. We owe you a great deal.'

'I wonder what can have upset them?' Charlotte twittered, when she was told they had left. 'How ever will we manage now?'

'Far better, I would think,' Miranda said with satisfaction. 'At least we can get reliable people.'

Though I won't be here, she remembered with a pang.

'And where can Huw be?' Charlotte began fussing. 'I'm really worried about him. He never stays away this long.'

Miranda wondered if he had also been picked up by the sailors, as his name had been mentioned as an accomplice. She said nothing about any of the previous night's incidents to Charlotte, deciding to see what developed. At twelve midday the Swansea Constable, Idris Jones, arrived at the house, his face grim.

'I have come to see Mrs Charlotte Cain,' he said quietly. 'I am afraid I have bad news for her.'

Charlotte's face paled and her hands fluttered to her throat. She gazed at him fearfully. 'What is it?' she whispered, eyes wide with fear. 'It's not . . .? Is it my son?'

'Yes, Mrs Cain, I'm afraid it is. There was an accident last night and—'

'Oh no! Please no!' Her face crumpled, her eyes filling with tears. She stared appealingly at him. 'He's hurt?' she whispered, clasping her hands tightly together.

His expression was compassionate as he nodded. 'Yes. I'm afraid he sustained a serious injury. I am sorry to have to inform you, Mrs Cain, that your son died as a result of that injury.'

'No! No!' she screamed. 'Not Huw! Not my Huw.' She collapsed in a trembling heap on the settee weeping hysterically, quite inconsolable as Miranda tried to comfort her.

'Would you mind waiting in the hall, please?'

Miranda asked the Constable as she tugged the bell cord. She poured a small glass of brandy, explaining briefly to the maid, Nia, what had happened. 'Bring Ellen, please. And try to get Mrs Cain to take a little of this,' she said, handing Nia the glass.

In the hall, Idris Jones turned to her, his expression uncomfortable.

'What happened?' she demanded.

'I'm afraid there was a drunken brawl at a tavern, Miss. Mr Huw was fatally stabbed,' he explained.

'Stabbed! God! I can't believe it!' Miranda's hands flew to her cheeks. 'Poor Huw! Poor Charlotte.'

'Yes, mistress. Very sad.' He nodded piously.

'Who . . . who was to blame? Do you know?'

The Constable pulled a face. 'No-one really knows, Mistress. They're always having fights in the Nag's Head.'

'The Nag's Head? Isn't that the one in Llanmor?' Miranda cried, remembering the sign outside the tavern where she had seen Haelwen.

'That's right, Miss Rushton. A rough place. The two brothers who own it are always in trouble with the Law,' he agreed ponderously. 'We have them in prison. They were involved in an attempt at wrecking last night.'

'Wrecking!' Her mouth went dry as she recalled her fear.

'Indeed, Miss Rushton. The captain handed a party of would-be wreckers over to us this morning. We have already ascertained some details of the plot.' He nodded with satisfaction. 'We have also taken Dickson the moneylender into custody. He was involved.

We've been waiting for something definite on him for quite some time.'

'The crew of the *Windrush* are unhurt though?'

'They are, Miss. But if it is Captain Llewelyn you are worried about I'd say you have little to fear on his behalf,' he chuckled.

'I am well aware of that,' Miranda said, returning his smile.

As soon as he left, she returned to Charlotte, who was prostrate on the settee with a damp cloth on her head and her eyes puffed and swollen. Miranda knelt alongside her, putting her arms around the dumpy little body.

'Charlotte, my dear. I am so sorry. I think we should get you to bed for a few hours.' She looked up at Ellen. 'Do we have some laudanum?' she asked.

'Yes, Miss. I've brought it down already,' she said, pointing to the dark glass bottle on the table. 'Shall I pour out a draught?'

'Please.' Miranda said, grateful for Ellen's insight.

They supported Charlotte as she swallowed the medicine and then guided her up to her room. Miranda drew the curtains as Ellen helped Charlotte to remove her frock. Then Miranda sat with her, holding her hand until she drifted off to sleep.

As she waited for Luke's return, Miranda alternated between wishing he would come and dreading what she had to say to him. It was already dark when she heard his deep voice in the hall. She flew to the doorway but then stopped, although she ached to run to him and snuggle up against that hard body.

'Did you hear about Huw?'

'Yes. I'm sorry,' he said with regret. He moved to put his arms around her but she held up her hand, lifting her chin.

'No, Luke!' she said firmly, her stance rigid.

'You have no need to worry,' he murmured. 'I'll speak to you later. But I must see Charlotte. Is she in here?'

'Yes. We got her to bed for a few hours but she insisted on coming down again.'

Luke entered the drawing room and began talking gently to Charlotte. Miranda was touched by the compassion he showed his aunt. In a gentle manner he reported details of Huw's death, glossing over the unsavoury details and making out that Huw had been trying to help someone.

'So he was a hero, then?' Charlotte looked up at him, almost pleadingly.

Luke sucked in a breath, then nodded silently. He turned away and walked across the room for some glasses and the brandy decanter.

'Brandy?' he enquired of them both.

'Yes, please,' Miranda said.

'Charlotte?' He poured a measure and put the glass on the small table alongside her. But Charlotte seemed not to hear; her eyes were unfocused, staring into space.

'Luke. Wyn and Ceridwen tried to kidnap Gwennie,' Miranda told him in a low voice. She went on to explain and detailed the part Olwen had played.

'My God! Poor little girl. Thank God Olwen stopped them.'

'What is the situation legally?' Miranda asked, worried about Gwennie.

'Her mother signed her over to me, it is all official . . . Huw was quite indifferent. I am legally her guardian. I'll reassure her as soon as I can.' He looked thoughtful. 'Perhaps it would be a good idea if I adopted her.'

'You would legally be her father then,' Miranda agreed. 'So what happened last night?' Miranda asked quietly, sipping her brandy.

'What happened last night?' he repeated, his double meaning obvious by his intense expression and the glint in his eyes.

Miranda gulped the brandy, which made her cough slightly and ignored his remark. 'The wreckers?'

He half-grinned at her. 'Oh? You're asking about the wreckers?' His lip curled scornfully. 'Their plan was ill-chosen when they picked on me. I saw the beacon on the headland but I'm too familiar with the coastline to be caught. I immediately realised what was involved. We could easily have ignored it and gone straight past but I knew another ship was following us making for Swansea. She was due to leave port an hour after us. They would have seen the beacon and been snared.' Anger flared in his eyes. 'I decided to anchor in Pentrebach Bay and see off the filthy . . . to see them off,' he amended.

'Wasn't that extremely dangerous?' she asked, thinking they could easily have been caught on those rocks.

'No more than on any other occasion.' Luke shrugged. 'I've done it too often.'

'Does nothing frighten you?' she snapped, angry with his indifference.

He smiled wryly. 'Certainly. But I learned years ago that once you submit to fear you're lost.' He gave a snort of derisive laughter. 'And you should be the last one to ask such a question.'

'It is just as well you were not smuggling then?'

He pulled a face. 'Just as well,' he agreed. He glanced at Charlotte, who seemed to be in a daze and gestured towards the door with his head. Miranda shook her head vigorously, her heart thudding again.

'I need to talk to you,' he said quietly. 'Please!'

Miranda gazed into his eyes which were dark with smouldering passion, not masking his feelings this time.

'I must see to Charlotte first,' she muttered shakily, turning away from him. 'Charlotte, my dear. Could you manage a little food now? Or would you rather to go back to bed?'

Charlotte looked up, her face grey and pinched, her body sagging. 'Yes please.' Her voice was barely audible. 'I'm not hungry.' She stood up unsteadily and would have fallen but Luke caught her, sweeping her up into his strong arms.

Without effort he carried her up the stairs to her room while Miranda summoned Nia to sit with her. When Miranda came back to the hallway Luke was standing at the bottom of the stairs, waiting for her. She swallowed hard, feeling as though a hand gripped her throat tightly to prevent her from breathing. She began to tremble as he motioned her into the library.

'Luke,' she began, as he closed the door. 'In the

violence of the storm, we . . . we had a moment's . . . indiscretion. It cannot be repeated. Our father entrusted me in your care. We have both betrayed that trust.'

Luke shook his head, his face beaming. 'No! My very special woman. At long last I can give you some explanations. The most important being . . . I am not your brother.'

Miranda heard only those words. 'You're not?' She reached out her arms, her heart dancing wildly in her breast . . . then she froze. 'How can that be?' she queried, doubtfully.

'It's true, my love. I promise I can explain it all. So may I put my arms around you now?' His voice was husky as he looked at her, his unguarded eyes swirling pools of emotion. 'I'm so in love with you, my darling, that sometimes I feel a little unhinged.'

She flew towards him. 'Luke! I've longed for it to be possible. You know I love you.' She slid her arms around him as she had ached to do so often, aware of his swollen male hardness as he dragged her towards him. He pressed her tightly against the length of his body, his hungry mouth on hers. He lifted her up in his arms and sank down in an armchair with her on his lap, his hungry lips still seeking hers. His hands sent desire coursing through her as they explored her body. When he lifted his head she pulled it back, raining feather-light kisses all over his face as he laughingly tried to catch her lips with his own.

'Please! Wait!' Miranda gasped when they paused for breath.

'No! I never want to stop,' he groaned, pressing his

mouth back on hers. This time his kiss was lingering and sensual with his tongue probing her mouth gently.

'I want you to explain,' she whispered as they drew slowly apart.

'All right. If I must.' He pulled back with reluctance. 'Where shall I begin? For a start, I've always known you were not my sister. When I was a child, Stanton was so furious with me that, in a fit of temper, he told me I was not his son . . .'

'That must have hurt you terribly! My poor Luke,' she whispered, smoothing his face. 'How old were you then?

'Twelve. And I was pretty shocked, I'll admit.' His smile was bitter. 'Being told you are a bastard is not something anyone likes to hear. That's why I ran away, not because of the whipping. He didn't want me, and I didn't want to be indebted to him in any way. He told me in latter years he'd never intended telling me and had always meant to keep it secret. But he was so angry . . .'

'But how did you became reacquainted?'

'Purely by chance the first time. I was still serving at sea then. My Uncle George was taking the waters at Bath and I'd arranged to meet him there for a few days when I was on leave. When I arrived your father was with George. Of course they were brothers-in-law.' Luke chuckled. 'It was a strange reunion. We recognised one another immediately. He said I was the image of Bronwen and seemed quite upset. I'll admit I was short with him at first but then I could see he felt genuine remorse for the way he had treated me as a child.'

'Was he terribly harsh with you?' Miranda whispered.

Luke gave a laconic grin. 'I probably made him ten times worse. I was an insolent little . . .' He broke off with a shrug. 'Anyway, we got to know one another and he was anxious we should meet when I came home next. We did meet several times after that and reached a . . . mutual respect, I suppose you would call it.'

'But were you already born when he married your mother?' she exclaimed, suddenly worried. 'Otherwise we would still be considered—'

'Oh yes.' He nodded. 'I was born in Scotland. When I heard the details I realised he did love my mother very much. He was completely devastated when she died, leaving him with me! It seems he'd followed her to Scotland . . . my grandfather had taken her there to hide her pregnancy until I was born . . . Stanton promised to pass me off as his son. They were married there and returned to Rushton Hall with me.'

'But Luke? Doesn't that make you legally my brother?' she gasped, pulling back from him with horror.

'No. Luckily for us, he never adopted me as he'd intended. Before he died he gave me a true, witnessed copy of my birth, from the Parish records in Scotland. It doesn't bear his name. He also gave me a similar copy of his marriage record which bears a later date. But he'd promised my mother I would inherit an equal portion of his money with any children he might father in the future. To be fair to him, he only cut me out of his will after I ran away. And quite some time before he died he offered to honour his promise to my mother and share his fortune equally between the two of us.'

'Really?' she exclaimed with amazement. 'What did you say?'

'I turned it down, as I had done originally by leaving home. I wanted nothing from him then or since. Except you.' Luke shrugged. 'You know the rest.'

Shocked by this admission Miranda stared at him. 'But you haven't told me why you pretended to be my brother,' she protested. 'And why you carried on the pretence; with me I mean.'

Luke heaved a sigh, running a hand through his hair. 'Why indeed? It would have saved me a lot of problems if I hadn't. It was your father's idea. By then Uncle George had died, so I had already resigned my commission and was living here at Bryncarog. I was free to act as your guardian. He was very worried about what would become of you after his death—'

'I knew he was ill,' she muttered, snuggling up against his chest.

'He decided this was an ideal way of protecting you from fortune hunters and being your brother made me a much more suitable guardian . . .'

He broke off as she began opening his buttons and slid her hand inside his shirt, playing with the dark hairs on his chest. 'I always wanted to do this,' she whispered as he swallowed hard, his expression intense.

'I've wanted to do a lot more to you,' he groaned, squeezing her against him.

'But surely you could have told me we were not related?' she said.

'That's just it! I couldn't!' he said hoarsely. He held her hand, trying to push it further down his body. Miranda snatched it away and sat up.

'Why not?' she demanded.

'Your father believed it would work better if you accepted me as your brother. He asked me to promise not to tell you until you came of age. He was very persuasive. And I rather thought I was going to be guardian of another sweet young girl,' he said sardonically. 'Instead I got you.'

'But your promise? I'm not yet twenty-one.' She tugged gently at the hairs on his chest again, twisting them around her finger.

'I really tried hard to keep it up but I was beginning to fail miserably. I was so desperately in love with you.' He lifted her chin, turning her face up to his, their mouths lingering in another passionate kiss. She closed her eyes as his hand wandered over her body.

'When did you fall in love with me?' she whispered.

'Almost in the beginning.' He grinned. 'Once I recognised you were not the pampered, self-centred girl I took you for originally,'

'You mean you've changed your mind?' She raised her brows in mock surprise.

'Changed it? Well, you were pampered,' he teased. 'But never spoiled or self-centred. I discovered you were like no other woman in the world. Courageous, spirited and loving . . . but you absolutely hated me!'

'Don't say that.' Miranda put her hand over his mouth.

He pressed his lips against it and then pulled her close again, kissing her with long, passionate desperation. He pulled his head back, breathing hard, leaving one hand cupping her breast. 'God! I've never wanted anything so much in my life,' he groaned.

For a minute Miranda stared mutely at him, her own breath equally ragged. 'Then take me,' she whispered. 'Now.'

He took a shuddering breath, his eyes dark and wild, jaw clenched. 'Not like this,' he said hoarsely. 'I've waited this long. I don't want anyone to think I've taken advantage of you, sullied your name.'

She nodded, getting up from his lap. 'So what can we do? It is a peculiar situation.'

He rubbed his hand over his face. 'It will be all right. A few weeks before I last sailed I wrote to William Langdon, telling him I could no longer continue as your guardian and asked to be released from my promise. I received a reply just as I was about to leave port. He was amazed because it seems your father had tried to think of everything and left a letter for Langdon to open in such an eventuality. This clearly stated the true information about our situation and a proclamation to be read out in a magistrate's court should it ever become necessary.' She leaned over him and he pulled her back, kissing her tenderly. 'I think he must also have realised this could happen because he gave us his blessing should we wish to get married!'

Miranda flung her arms back around his neck, hugging him tightly again with tears of joy streaming down her face. 'That is just wonderful.' Her tongue flicked out, exploring his lips. 'You said you fell in love with me in the beginning?' she said, dodging as he tried to kiss her again.

'I did. And I was so sure you despised me.'

'I did!' she laughed. 'You were, still are, an arrogant, pig-headed, stubborn . . .' she paused, then continued, 'invincible, thoughtful, wonderful man. I know I am always safe with you.' She pressed her lips gently to his again. 'And you are all mine.'

'That is certainly true,' he said with deep satisfaction. 'And I warn you, I'm never going to let you escape.'

'And I warn you. You will have difficulty in escaping out of my sight,' she whispered, nuzzling up to him again.

'Does that mean you consent to marry me?' Luke chuckled.

'You haven't asked me yet,' she protested. 'Properly, on your knees.'

He raised his eyebrows.

'No! I didn't mean it,' she exclaimed, laughing.

'Miranda, will you marry me?' he said seriously.

'Would you have?' she asked wickedly. 'Gone on your knees?'

He gave a lopsided grin. 'If that was the only way,' he admitted. 'But I don't believe you really want a submissive husband.'

'How did you guess?'

'You still haven't given me an answer.'

'Yes please,' she whispered.

A slow smile crept over his face, his eyes glowing with satisfaction. 'But I'm afraid for the time being we will have to be circumspect and behave as usual,' he said. 'We cannot mention us until everything settles with Huw.' He ruffled a hand through his curls. 'It may sound hard but in some ways his death is almost a blessing. Imagine what would have become of him and Charlotte if all this wrecking and insurance business had got into the courts? And there is no way it could have been avoided. I couldn't see Huw taking easily to prison.'

'He would have let you go without a qualm.' Miranda's voice was bitter. 'Even seen you shipwrecked.' She shuddered, suddenly cold. 'I'm afraid my grief cannot be deep, other than for poor Charlotte,' she admitted.

Luke said nothing, just held her close.

'Wait until I tell Ellen. She'll be so surprised,' she chuckled gleefully. 'And at least you will no longer have to risk your neck smuggling,' she laughed. 'Llewelyn Shipp—'

'No!' Luke bristled. 'Llewelyn Shipping is still my—'

She put her hand over his mouth. 'Stop it! I assumed we were going to share everything,' she said plaintively. 'I thought you would want to share Llewelyn Shipping with me?' Her expression was deceptively innocent but her eyes were dancing.

Luke stared at her, pursing his lips which began turning up at the corners. He sucked in a breath. 'You little schemer,' he grinned. He began to laugh, his shoulders shaking, and Miranda joined in. 'Trust you to think of a way around my objections. I'll have to think about that,' he admitted, still chuckling.

Miranda smirked. 'I don't think there is an answer . . . not if we really mean to share everything,' she pointed out.

'I don't want to share your fortune,' Luke objected.

'That will be difficult if we are married,' she giggled. 'Anyway, I don't want you smuggling. What if you got caught? Or killed? Would you like me to be left on my own?'

He regarded her thoughtfully. 'I see your point. Changing the subject, what about Rushton Hall? Where will we live?'

Miranda pulled back from him, her face thoughtful. 'I don't know,' she admitted. 'I love my own home . . . but I must admit, I have fallen in love with the sea. I associate it so much with you. We could do this place up? Extend it? It could be beautiful again.'

'That is a marvellous idea,' he said enthusiastically. 'And we could spend time at Rushton as well . . .'

'There's enough money to keep both places going,' Miranda exclaimed, excited. Her eyes roamed around the room. 'I can hardly wait to start work on this place.'

'Would you be happy for Charlotte to continue living with us?' he asked.

'Of course I would,' she said, 'and to adopt Gwennie.'

'I don't know why I asked, knowing you,' he sighed, shaking his head.

'Even if we can't tell anyone yet, I can start planning my wedding in secret,' she said gleefully. 'Will it give us enough time to sort things out with William Langdon if we plan for a Christmas wedding?'

'If I can wait that long,' he sighed. 'Christmas it will be.' And he confirmed it with a kiss.